A CAGE OF KINGDOMS

A CAGE OF KINGDOMS

USA TODAY BESTSELLING AUTHOR

K.F. BREENE

ALSO BY K.F. BREENE

Demigods of San Francisco

Sin & Chocolate

Sin & Magic

Sin & Salvation

Sin & Spirit

Sin & Lightning

Sin & Surrender

Leveling Up

Magical Midlife Madness

Magical Midlife Dating

Magical Midlife Invasion

Magical Midlife Love

Magical Midlife Meeting

Magical Midlife Challenge

Magical Midlife Alliance

Magical Midlife Flowers

Magical Midlife Battle

Magical Midlife Awakening

Finding Paradise

Fate of Perfection

Fate of Devotion

Deliciously Dark Fairytales

A Ruin of Roses

A Throne of Ruin

A Kingdom of Ruin

A Queen of Ruin

A Cage of Crimson

A Cage of Kingdoms

Demon Days, Vampire Nights

Born in Fire

Raised in Fire

Fused in Fire

Natural Witch

Natural Mage

Natural Dual-Mage

Warrior Fae Trapped

Warrior Fae Princess

Revealed in Fire

Mentored in Fire

Battle with Fire

ACKNOWLEDGMENTS

This book was like getting reacquainted with old friends. It felt more like living in the world than writing a story.

Thank you to everyone who returned to this world with me and went on this journey. May you get your own fairytale, or even just a crass, mediocre butler to keep you out of trouble.

"Healing doesn't mean the
damage never existed."

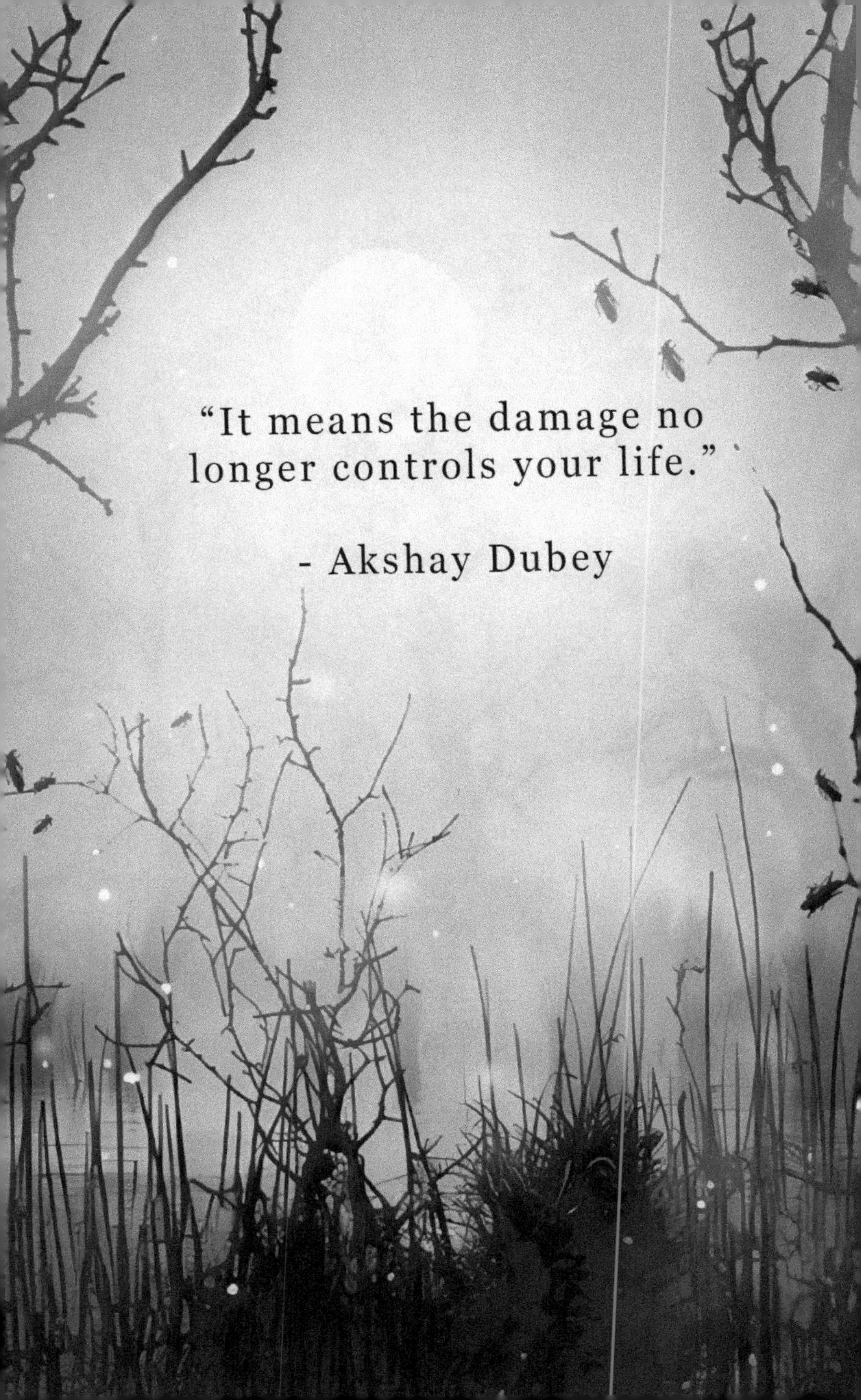
"It means the damage no
longer controls your life."
- Akshay Dubey

1

WESTON

"When someone asks you for a ball peen hammer, do you then take out a steel mace and repeatedly hit them over the head with it?" my wolf asked as I walked away from Aurelia.

She stood on the deck of the ship, watching the distance grow between herself and the only member of family she thought she possessed. Granny was alive and had made contact before I could get Aurelia out of this kingdom and away from her greedy grasp. Things just got a whole lot more . . . delicate.

Saying I felt sick to my stomach was an understatement.

"I wasn't lying," I replied. *"I did betray her. At first I did it on purpose, when I didn't really care about her emotions. Then I did it out of fear. She should know the truth."*

"She's open-minded. She would've listened to the truth, not your self-loathing summary of it, you moron. Turn around and go back to her. Explain everything to her. She has been very patient with you so far. That won't last forever."

"It shouldn't. I don't deserve it."

I could feel my wolf seething within me. *"Turn around and go back, you miserable prick, or I will assume this body and do it for you. Be there for her. She's a smart woman who has been ruthlessly manipulated and abused from a very young age by someone she trusted. Someone she thought of as family. She's probably damn confused right now. Granny twisted that woman's head all up with lies, torture, and then gifts. Whatever was in that note probably is an extension of the abuse. It'll be hard for her to steer her way out of that by herself. She needs support."*

Yes, she did, but the support she needed right now wasn't mine. I'd damned myself in her eyes. In my own eyes, as well. I'd betrayed my true mate—someone I should be protecting at all costs. It killed me, searing my insides with regret and remorse. No, from me, she needed the truth. Her support right now would come from her budding friendships, people I would also use to help me steer the situation in a way that would hurt Aurelia as little as possible.

Hadriel stood at the bow, leaning over the edge, moaning. He was not great on the water.

"Already?" I asked, stopping beside him. "We've barely left the docks."

The captain of the ship walked up and motioned at me, needing a word. I nodded but didn't move. This had to be seen to before I checked in on the pack and crew.

"Why the fuck haven't they invented a boat that doesn't rock?" Hadriel asked, groaning again. "I should've taken Finley's elixir a half-hour earlier. It hasn't kicked in yet. Fucking boats. Fucking waves. Fucking fuck!"

He groaned again and leaned farther over the side.

"I need you to pull it together. Granny made an appearance."

"What?" He straightened up, wobbled, and gripped the

handrail. His knuckles turned white. "What do you mean, 'she made an appearance'? Did she try to board?"

"No. She made a show of waving goodbye. She threw on a red cloak at the end of the docks. She must've seen Aurelia looking out, obviously looking for her, but waited to catch her attention. Then she waved."

"A red cloak?" He put a hand to his stomach and turned toward the water for a moment. After a deep breath, he turned back. "Like that one Aurelia was captured in? Tanix had to take it off her when he was tying her up because it was getting in the way."

I thought back, only vaguely remembering what he talked about. I hadn't paid much attention to her clothes.

Hadriel nodded. "Granny's good, I'll give her that. That was obviously a well-received gift with an emotional connection. She clearly used it to remind Aurelia of their ties. What was in the note?"

"I don't know. I didn't ask."

"You were too busy making a shitshow of the whole situation," my wolf grumbled.

"I'll have a look at it. What do you plan to do?" Hadriel asked.

"I want you and Dante and Nova to give her your time and attention. She might not ask for help, but she'll need it. You need to provide it. After I've checked on everything, I'll tell her the truth and stand in my own judgment. I'll also pull out her wolf so she can heal and get acquainted."

Hadriel turned, groaned again for a moment. "What truths do you plan to tell her?"

The captain cleared his throat, his hands behind his back. I needed to see to my duties.

"What do you mean? I need to tell her everything I've been keeping from her. Why I didn't tell her about Granny, why she feels this connection—"

"No." Hadriel put up his hand. "Fuck, throw up or don't, you know? This is bullshit." He spat over the side. "All due respect, Alpha, but don't tell her about the true mate thing just yet. She doesn't know what that means. She has zero frame of reference for it and will just view it as more betrayal. She won't realize you were in the same position she was, and she certainly won't realize what absolute hell it was treating a true mate like you did, readying to take her to her death. It's not anything like the Granny thing, which, yes, was definitely pretty shitty and all on you. A true mate bond is special. Don't tie it into you hiding the fact that you faked both the cold-blooded murder of her quasi family member and that you didn't care how she felt."

I stared at him intently, half wanting to throw him overboard. The truth was not a pleasant thing to hear.

My wolf said, *"He has a very good point. Not to mention, I want to meet her wolf and establish a bond before the human is told. The wolf will make better sense of it than the human. Then I want all four of us to walk through that situation together, helping the human through her past as a cohesive unit."*

He was making a very large assumption that the human would want anything to do with me after this, and that her wolf wouldn't take her side over ours.

Despite the desire to just be done with all the secrets, I found myself nodding. They both made good points. Besides, Aurelia needed to physically heal and deal with her separation from Granny before she took on anything more. She needed a vacation from her life; too bad that was the exact opposite of what would come next.

"Fine. Take care of it," I told Hadriel, knowing he'd do whatever he wanted anyway. Fortunately, he had experience in these matters. I was damn lucky he'd wanted a break from castle life to visit his home kingdom. It felt fated, somehow.

Hadriel

Once Finley's seasickness elixir started to work, I pushed away from the railing and wobbled my way down the gangplank or whatever the fucking side of the ship was called and tried to find Aurelia. I hated ships and boats and large spans of water. It made me question why I'd come on this rotten trip, with all its bugs and trees and sticks poking my balls.

Aurelia wasn't at the back of the ship, nor the front. *Fuck.*

Taking a deep breath, I went toward her room. Seasickness was always worse on the inside of this stupid vessel.

The door to her and the alpha's chambers was closed. I knocked lightly.

"Pretty bold," my wolf said, *"putting her in his quarters when she probably hates the sight of him."*

"Hate or anger or desire, they've always been in the same space. She craves the proximity as much as he does. I'm wondering what's going to happen when they get to the castle and she gets put in the dungeon."

"They wouldn't."

"How do I fucking know what they'll do? Finley is pissed about the drugs, and she gets crazy when she's pissed. We might all have to ride it out until she can be talked around."

My wolf did the equivalent of rolling his eyes. He didn't believe me.

Truthfully, I doubted the royalty would shove Aurelia into the dungeon once they learned she was Alpha's true mate. Not only would that be cruel to their prized commander, but there were plenty of us who would speak on her behalf. Finley might be unpredictable when pissed, but she listened to reason.

Still, I hated being sick, I was in a shit mood, and if I wanted to talk about horrible fates involving dungeons, I fucking would.

No answer came from within the room.

"I am not the alpha," I called through the door, "and I am still feeling sick and fucking terrible. Can I come in without you hurting me in some way?"

"I'm not going to get up," I heard.

That didn't trouble me.

The quarters were as fine as they ever were: fit for a king and queen. Which on a ship meant all of fucking nothing. The quarters were no better than a decent inn.

"Hello, my darling. How are you faring?" I closed the door behind me and crossed to the table and chairs at the end of the room.

Aurelia lay on the bed, over the covers, limbs straight, staring at the ceiling. Her expression was devoid of feeling, but I knew it was a survival mechanism. She was trying to shut down the gut punch of emotional pain, probably confusion, and certainly the sting of betrayal.

"Are we doing okay?" I hazarded.

"Did you know?" she asked softly. She still held the note in her hand.

"I heard that first night, yes. I was told to be on my guard—that Granny and her chief bruiser had escaped." I wanted to talk about the body they'd found but felt that could come after she acclimated to this. Granny's shenanigans left a lot to unpack, and Aurelia would need to take it a bit at a time.

"Why didn't you tell me? Did Weston ask you not to?"

"He didn't mention it, but I heard from the others why the decision was made not to tell you. He'll explain all that to you. I think what we really need to focus on is the fact that she lives, yes? Your found family member still lives. Aren't you thrilled?"

A tear leaked out of her eye. "I should be. I mean, I am . . ." She continued to stare at the ceiling.

Curious response.

"May I?" I stood and reached my hand out so she would see it with her peripheral vision.

She held out her hand so I could easily grab the note.

I stalled in the middle of my walk back to the table and instead headed to the small, ineffective window. Fuck this elixir. It wasn't half as good as Finley's other medicinal stuff was. This was a joke of some sort, and I was certainly the punch line.

"What's wrong?" she asked.

"Seasick." I burped and thought about visiting the toilet.

"They have medicine for that."

"Oh really? I live in a hole, I hadn't known," I said sarcastically. It was possible I might not be the best one to support her in her time of need.

Thankfully, she chuckled, not at all offended. "I think you mean that you live in a cave. Or maybe a small village cut off from larger society and the world as a whole, with no new ideas and no real way to get out."

When I glanced back, another tear was falling.

I steeled myself against reading on a moving ship and scanned the page, reading as quickly as possible. I didn't know if the resulting nausea was because of the moving ship or the fucking letter.

A hard knot formed in my chest. What a fucking message. Only a miserable dickhole would write something like that.

I toiled in finding your strengths and, once I did, built an empire around the only thing you were good at.

The only thing she was good at? That was rich. Had that fuckstain never tasted Aurelia's cooking? Or realized the intelligence it took for her to reverse-engineer those drugs already being sold? She *could* have done that with medicine, or any other fucking thing. But no, Granny chose drugs—because there was a big profit without any real risk of blowback. Someone dies or gets sick from drugs they got at the shadow market? Big deal, they shouldn't have been in those markets in the first place, because everyone knows that stuff is sketchy.

And why did Aurelia have to be good at anything, anyway? She'd been a child. Protecting her and making a home for her wasn't supposed to be dependent on what that child could bring to the table. Not in a real, loving situation, at least.

"I'm actually a little pissed," I said in an even tone, continuing to read. I didn't think the alpha would want me to yell and curse when trying to be supportive. "Oh, look. Fabulous, she's blaming a bunch of shit on you. Fantastic."

I'd be a sobbing mess if I got a note like this from Finley or Leala or Vemar back at the castle. Like with Aurelia and Granny, they were my family, though none of them were my blood. But none of those people had ever been a parent figure, either. None had ever had this sort of control over me.

"Why wouldn't she blame me?" Another tear fell down the side of Aurelia's face. "She's right. We worked to find something I could do within the village, and once we did, I labored to excel at it so that she wouldn't be able to get rid of me. I had no reservations about my work. I didn't care that they were drugs. I stood by my product."

"I know. We agreed to disagree about it in the beginning, remember? But that product isn't what is hurting people. Didn't you discover that yourself?"

"She applied the coating to keep the business thriving, which in turn kept me with a safe home. I didn't create it, but I am the motivation behind it. It's in the letter."

I huffed. "Bullshit! Aurelia, that is utter bullshit and you know—" I hesitated. "No, maybe you don't know it. All you saw was her tiny cottage. You didn't see her massive, sprawling estate near the castle and all her servants and the vast network she is bribing to sell *her* product, including the king and queen. If you were the motivation, she would be pouring gold into your pockets. She'd be setting you up for life. Instead, she's deprived you of almost everything, and given you small gifts to keep you happy and on the hook while she spends the bulk of the fortune on herself. With just your product and no coating, it's true she would make less. But it's only been in the last three years that the product has become so addictive and dangerous. In those three years, the business has soared. Have you seen any extra?"

She hesitated, turning her head to look at me, her gaze troubled. "A lot of extra work. Nothing extra for the village."

"Exactly," I said softly. "She—and you, and the rest of the village—were kept just fine with the nonlethal product you were making. It wasn't because of you that she took it to the next level. If you want to blame yourself for your product as you made it, fine. But do *not* blame yourself for the coating that almost killed you. Okay? It's fucking ridiculous. She stole your design because it's eye-catching and artistic and she clearly lacks the talent—look, there's another thing you're good at! Art. She changed that design because you can't have a fairy on it and have it sold by a wolf. She used your situation to get cheap labor. That's it. Romanticize her gifts, but do not romanticize the organization."

I'd tried so hard to keep the whole thing level, but I felt like shit, and this note and her situation was fucking garbage.

"Fancy a walk outside?" I asked hopefully.

"I could. I'm sore, though. I'd really rather not."

"You and your busted face and ribs. You're worse off than me. Fuck. Fine." I rolled my eyes at her laughter. "It's more fun when you're on the shit end of the jokes."

"Isn't it just."

I smiled despite myself and pointed at part of the letter. "She's blaming you for getting taken captive, huh? Wow. That's . . . charming."

"He did tell me to run and hide, but where was I going to go? No one in that village would hide me, I knew you'd search my house, and outside . . . you'd sniff me out. There was nowhere pre-planned."

"Pre-planning wouldn't have meant dick. We had that place locked down, and, as you now know, the alpha is excellent at his job. He would've found you. This way, though, you at least got to stick a few people with an axe. I call that a win."

"Silver lining."

"Sparkly silver lining, yes. What else have we got here . . .?" I scanned the note. "Evasive measures," I murmured with a hush. That was a nice term for killing an innocent in your stead to buy a little more time.

The pack had found where that innocent had been kept. Not pretty.

Aurelia could hear about that another day.

"Bring you in safely, sure," I said, finally starting to feel just a bit better. "Trap you again, more like. And I'll guarantee you Alexander didn't get punished for beating the shit out of you. He got punished for not getting you out. This woman is very good with honeyed words. No, I think she trained him exactly as she intended to. He is her number one in that organization. She trusts him above all others."

"Yeah," she said softly.

My heart cracked a little at the broken tone in her voice, and I lowered the note, turning for my chair.

"Tell me what's on your mind," I said, sitting back down.

"A lot, actually."

"I've got nothing but time and an inclination to never travel by boat again. Hit me with it."

She sighed, still staring at that ceiling. "She's always spoken to me the way she did in that letter. My usual response is 'I'll do better.' And I always have."

She paused for a moment.

"It's the last line that is tormenting me. I've wanted to hear her tell me she loves me for . . . forever. The only person who has ever said it before was my mom. And to do it after blaming me for getting captured, and the product, and for not knowing she was trying to rescue me . . .? How the fuck could I have known any of that, you know? Yet she makes me feel responsible for all the horror I didn't know was happening. The letter makes me feel like I'm in her debt, and then she finally slams home the one thing I've always craved. It feels . . . cheap." The tears that had been building finally spilled down her face. "Not real. Like she knew it would be the carrot in front of the donkey. It hurts."

"And the red riding cloak she wore," I said. "Sending Alexander to pick you up in that town instead of coming herself . . ."

"I hadn't thought about the last, but yeah. I don't feel . . ." She began to cry a little harder, wincing and resting a hand on her side. "I don't feel like she means it, and it's killing me. Was my life a lie, Hadriel? Was it all one big lie?"

Seeing her so sad was killing *me*. "No, love. It wasn't. It was the life you needed to live at the time, waiting for us to come and find you." I managed to offer a weak smile. "Sometimes we must travel through the darkness to appreciate the dawn—or some fucking inspirational quote like that. A smart person once said something similar, and I've probably dick-slapped it sideways."

She took a deep breath, and I knew it hurt her to do so. "I've asked myself if I would have said no to that coating."

I crossed an ankle over my knee, watching her quietly.

"She would've explained it in a way that sounded great. She might've even told me there would be a little sickness, but that it would help our business. Would I have put my foot down?"

I could hear the guilt in her voice, the helpless ache of being in a situation she had no control over. She worried she would've. She had locked down in her mind that she was responsible for the drugs, whether because of motivation, because she didn't know about it when she thought she should have, or because she assumed she would've been okay with it if Granny said they should do it.

I knew the answer, though, and I knew deep down that she did, too.

"No," I said firmly. "If you had been told a *real* account of what that coating did or heard about how dangerous it turned out to be, you would have stopped it. I know that without a doubt. I *know* it because I saw it when you woke up from nearly dying and tried it again. I know it because you are hellbent on fixing it. I *know* it because you may have done some questionable things in your life—which are much less questionable than many of mine, might I add —but you've always tried to help those less fortunate or those who were vulnerable. You are not the villain, Aurelia. Not in this story. Not yet."

"Not yet?"

I grinned at her even though she was still staring at the ceiling in misery.

"No, love, not yet. Soon, though. The second you get over the heartache and grow into your personal power, you're going to own your world, you're going to tear that organization down, and I'm going to laugh with glee while you do it."

She turned her head to look at me. "But . . . I don't want to hurt her. I don't want to hurt Granny. I want to ask her some questions, a whole lot of *whys*, and maybe I want to go my own way, but I don't want to hurt her."

"You don't have to hurt her, love, but you do have to burn that harmful organization to the ground."

She paused for a beat. "I know."

I'd never been prouder of her.

Before I changed the topic to less doom-worthy things, she said in a small voice, "She said she'd come for me. She said she has people everywhere. I . . . I want to talk with her, and maybe I will want to go if she agrees to reconcile and change, but I don't want to be forced into a life I don't want to lead. But in my gut, I know that her first inclination will be to try to do just that." More tears rolled down her cheeks.

The last lines of that letter had given me goosebumps. It was a threat if I'd ever read one.

"Don't worry about that, my darling," I said in all seriousness. "If you don't want to go, she won't be able to force you."

"How do you figure?"

"Because the alpha will turn villain and burn her world to the ground if she tries."

2

WESTON

"She's fucked," Hadriel reported as the sun was starting to set.

"Come again?" I stopped on the deck, my work for the voyage finished with very little that would need my attention in the days to come. It was the captain's ship now. He called the shots. It would be a welcome reprieve.

Hadriel grinned. His face was still pale, but he looked in better spirits than usual. "I haven't come yet today, actually. Was that an invita—" His grin faltered and he bent his head downward. "Sorry, habit."

I knew well. The crew that had endured the curse of the dragon court were all very colorful. It was a standing royal order to give them a little slack. Very little, sometimes. Like now . . .

He cleared his throat and told me about the contents of the letter.

Rage simmered in my gut, and I looked away. That woman was scum and clearly had no conscience. Poor Aurelia. She was probably the only one who didn't know.

Well, who *hadn't* known was more accurate. She'd told

Hadriel we'd cracked her world open and shown her what was inside. That was certainly true. Now she had to come to grips with the reality of the person she'd looked up to, the one she'd idolized and thought was family. It would be a hard reality to face.

"The good news is that I don't think the situation is unsalvageable for you," Hadriel finished. "I think she could use your company, actually. For the bond, if nothing else. She might be pissed for a while, but what's new, right? You two have gotten through worse."

"I'm headed that way now," I said, not daring to hope. What a mess this whole thing with Aurelia had been—what a terrible start to a true mate bond.

She didn't respond when I knocked lightly on the door. It wasn't locked, though, so I slowly pushed into the darkening room.

She lay on the bed, staring at the ceiling. Tear tracks cut lines down the sides of her cheeks, the slight sheen visible though no new tears fell. My stomach knotted from the pain she was in, that I had helped cause.

"Hey," I said, closing the door behind me and flipping the lock.

She didn't respond—not that I expected her to. It was time to eat crow.

"I'm sorry I kept that information from you," I started, crossing to the open side of the bed and sitting down. "I'm sorry I hurt you, and I'm sorry your journey has taken this sharp left turn."

Her lips curled, her expression turning sardonic. "Nice lingo. It's perfect for softening the description of the terrible things that happen when taking one of my drugs. It fits here, too." Her smile eroded and her gaze sharpened. "Why did you do it?"

I took off my shoes and turned to lie on the bed, though

I was careful not to touch her. "At first, because I hoped you would be less loyal if she had perished."

"Perished. Another nice term."

"Without someone to remain loyal to, I'd hoped you'd be more open to telling me about the organization and your role in it. I didn't care, then, about your pain." Not initially, at any rate. Learning I was hurting my true mate had created other issues. "I needed results, and that seemed like the best way to get them. When you isolate a person, they are easier to control."

She flinched a little. That was what Granny had done to her.

"And when it was clear I was being open about what I knew?" she asked.

I entwined my fingers, looking down at them. "Honestly? I was afraid you'd leave. I was afraid of your reaction —this reaction. I was locked in guilt, as well. I'd held back the information for so long. I didn't know how to tell you the truth."

"But you let me go."

"Yes, knowing you intended to hide yourself from Alexander. I hoped, in turn, you'd stay hidden from Granny. I-I hadn't really been thinking." About anything but losing her, that was. "I knew you were going to force your way out, I knew ultimately you weren't the guilty party, and I knew I couldn't stomach your being punished by the dragons. Letting you go seemed like the best course of action. Shortsighted, probably, because the bottom line was—and still is—that my duty forbids me to allow you to return to her. I can't have you making product for her. The kingdoms can't risk it. Hell, your life would be at stake if you made that decision. There is so much at risk, and it all comes to a head if you go back to working for Granny."

She was quiet for a long time in the wake of my jumbled explanation.

"Hadriel left some time ago," she finally said, "and all I've been doing is thinking. Thinking about the present, about the way you've treated me, about the past . . ."

I wanted to reach out to her, to touch her and offer her some physical comfort. Or to pull her close to me and soothe her. Maybe even brush the strands of hair away from her wet cheeks. She'd reject it, though. Reject me.

My heart filled with pain. "What about the way I've treated you?"

"I'll get to that. I never really processed Granny's death —well, what I thought was Granny's death. I felt the pain when it was fresh, but I pushed it away to deal with it another time. Then all that stuff came up about my situation, and the journals shed some light on my past, and I pushed that down as well. I've been too busy surviving to reflect."

"Understandable."

"I'll get to that, too. It isn't totally a relief that she is alive because I didn't fully process her death. Her not being in the picture, though, meant I didn't have to fully process my own situation. I have been moving forward, taking each step as it came, dealing with one thing at a time. I've been trying to carve out a new life because there was nothing left of the old one. Now I find out that there *is* something left of the old life. Knowing Granny is still in the picture makes me feel like I'm doing something gravely wrong. I'm betraying her in the worst possible way, and I know I'd have a serious punishment to go home to. It . . . scares me. Yes, the punishment itself scares me, but the thought of going back to that life, working intensely long hours in a place where everyone hates me, with no one to talk to . . ."

She reached up to smooth her hair away from her face before she went on, taking a moment to collect herself.

"What about the organization?" Her voice was faint. "Without Granny in the picture, it would be tearing down a harmful legacy. It would be fixing the wrongs and then mourning her loss. But now?"

She stared at the ceiling.

"Now . . . it feels like an act of war." She swallowed. "It is ripping her livelihood, however crooked, away from her. It is dismantling what she built in my name."

"She didn't build it in your name."

"She built it with my product and with my packaging design. She built it in my image. My signature is written all over an organization that creates pain and suffering. It can't be allowed to remain, but to go against her is to go against someone I have viewed as a parent. Someone I have loved. Someone I can't help but still love, regardless of how she treated me . . ." She shook her head. "It can't be helped, and I won't deny it. It is what it is, as Hadriel would say."

I nodded slowly. "The dragon king knows something of pushing back on parents. I can ask him to speak with you. He can probably help with your state of mind."

She huffed and then put her hand to her ribs. "Don't be absurd. I'm a captive and a criminal. A commoner. The dragon king isn't going to speak with me." She shook her head. "I am glad Granny is alive. I know you wish it wasn't true, but I am, and despite all she has done to hurt me, I will do everything in my power to keep it that way. But I can't shake the terrible feeling that I am doing something fundamentally wrong, that a violent punishment is coming, and when I figure out a way to stop that coating, it will be considered a declaration of war. I don't want to do this. I don't want to . . . travel this journey." Tears leaked out of her eyes. "I wanted her to truly love me and treat me as such. To realize that she probably never did . . ." She blew out a breath, clearly trying to calm her shaking body. "It's a lot, all of this. Being willing to stand in judgment—to decide to go with you when she is still around—will be seen as a betrayal she will want to kill me for. She does not suffer those who are disloyal."

"When you were on the pier, it was my call to keep you moving. You had no choice at that moment, and you have no choice at this. You will go to stand in judgment. It is beyond your control."

"I could have left."

"You tried. You were . . . rescued by them and retaken by us. Or you would've died. Either way, they wouldn't have gotten you. This wasn't your fault. It was me and my people."

She turned her head, focusing her gaze on me. "Yes. You and your people."

I braced. *Here we go.*

"Your people hated everything I stood for, hated me, and yet they treated me with respect. Mostly. I stuck an axe in some of them and they forgave me for it."

"Truthfully, Dante hit you over the head and nearly killed you for that. Then I forced you to share my bed. I hardly think we treated you with the utmost respect."

"I was part of the reason I had to share your bed."

"You're quick to take blame."

Her smile was slight. "A lot of practice, I guess. You were the enemy and you never punished me. You never lifted a finger to your people or had to threaten them to do your bidding. You don't control them with violence."

"That is because I am an alpha."

"I'd thought Granny was an alpha."

"She is. A pretty strong one, actually. She and your product gave me some trouble near that port city. Not all alphas are the same. I lead by example. She's chosen to lead a different way."

"She doesn't have a unified pack like you do."

"She does, it just didn't extend to your village. Her guard and her protection, the people on the perimeter of the village—they were a pack. Not as unified or as connected, no, but they *were* connected."

"Ah." She looked back to the ceiling and nodded, more tears falling.

I knew what she was thinking—she wasn't privy to that connection because she hadn't thought she'd had magic, something else Granny had been keeping from her.

Unable to help myself, I slid next to her, needing to be closer. Needing to feel the heat of her proximity.

She looked my way, and I drank her in: her beautiful sunburst eyes, glassy with emotion, the black and blue on her cheek, that luscious, heart-shaped mouth, the delicate curve to her neck.

"Do you want me to release your animal?" I asked softly. "I can do it right now. It'll help you heal. It'll make sure you are never alone again."

"Hadriel has told me he will make sure I am never alone again—at least until the dragons kill me. He thought that was a great joke."

I couldn't help but stiffen. I didn't comment. That would never happen. I'd stand against the dragon king if he ever sought to harm her, a battle that would undoubtedly begin as soon as the ship docked.

"It's why I trust him." Her tone was subdued. "He might joke, but he's always been upfront about the situation. You're certain I have magic? An animal?"

"Absolutely certain. I can prove it right now."

She hesitated. "As much as I want that—and I have, my whole life—I want to ask someone with the same magic level as Granny or less. I want them to pull my animal out, or at least tell me I have one."

"Dante, Tanix, Sixten, Nova—they can all do it. They are all strong enough. If you want an alpha, the captain of the ship counts. He is the leader of the ship crew. He has not met you before."

"No," she whispered. "I want to partially travel in my mother's footsteps. I want to walk up to a stranger, like she would have. I'll ask if I am suppressed. I want to look them in the face like I looked at Granny and hope they say yes. And then, finally, assuming they do, I want to experience a dream come true."

She fell silent after that. I could tell she was done talking. She needed time to reflect.

I asked if I could see the note, and she handed it over wordlessly.

Some fucking note.

The last lines sent a rush of rage through me. Granny planned to snatch Aurelia back.

Over my dead fucking body. Literally. That was the only way Granny would get her hands on my true mate again.

I'd make Aurelia want to stay in my kingdom. I'd show her what love could really feel like, what non-blood family could mean. I'd give her unlimited reasons to stay, and end Granny if she didn't leave Aurelia alone.

I just hoped my efforts, the efforts of a man who had never bothered with romance or wooing, could accomplish what I needed to. With my pedigree, I'd never needed romance. Now I'd need to overcome Granny's conditioning while tangoing with the dragons to prevent Aurelia from being thrown in the dungeon.

Easy as pie.

. . .

Come morning, I wasn't sure if Aurelia had slept. She'd been awake when I roused in the middle of the night. She hadn't uttered a peep. It killed me to watch her go through this, but she wouldn't accept comfort.

"I want all my journals," she said after breakfast. "Every single one."

I complied, telling Nova to bring them, and then raiding the infirmary for a healing elixir. It would help Aurelia speed up her recovery.

After taking the elixir, she got right into her journals.

For the next three days, she stood along the railing on the deck or sat in our room, a chair pulled up to a little table, not speaking to anyone. Sometimes when I walked by to check on her, she was staring out at the ocean, letting the salty sea air dry wet streaks on her cheeks. Other times, there was anger in her expression.

On the fourth day, after her face had cleared of bruising and her ribs no longer hurt—that elixir was pretty incredible—she stopped me as I passed. The clouds sat heavy above us, gray and forbidding, threatening a storm.

"May I please have something to write with, and something to write on?" she asked, and it was almost as if she was addressing a stranger.

My stomach clenched in unease. "Of course," I said, not showing it.

That and "I need more paper, please" comprised the sum total of her interactions with me. Hadriel and the others didn't fare much better, everyone on the ship cut off as she internalized her situation.

At night she crawled into the sheets, but always with a

layer of clothing. She never curled up close to me. She was distancing herself, creating an island of emotion.

The unease within me grew, but her resolve hadn't changed. She would stand in front of the dragon royalty. I had time to bring her around. To crack whatever shell she was erecting around herself.

Fucking Granny. She was the unrelentless bane in so many people's existence.

On the fifth—and what I thought was the last—day, I stood on the deck and looked over the bow. I'd thought we'd have time to connect on the ship, for our wolves to form a bond, and to deepen our knowledge of each other without my duties interrupting. That had not come to pass. I knew as we headed into the kingdom that things would only get more complicated.

3

AURELIA

The pages of my journal fluttered before a burst of wind flapped the pages against my hand. My hair whipped around my head. I slapped my palm onto my notes before they could blow away and looked up from the little table at which I sat. Dark clouds boiled overhead, having gathered in the distance and raced closer. The first smattering of rain splatted against the wooden tabletop through the window of my room and pelted my forehead. The sounds of metal dinging and sails snapping overhead, billowing and straining against the rigging, filtered in alongside the rain.

Nervous flutters danced within my belly at the natural but turbulent violence quickly escalating around me. I'd never been on a ship before. I'd never seen limitless azure ocean stretching for as far as the eye could see, the land drifting away and leaving the vessel an isolated floating island. If something went wrong, no help could reach us in time to save us from a watery demise. We couldn't seek shelter or hide from the elements around us. At no time was that so evident as when the storm bore down on us.

Unable to concentrate, I shut the window and made my way to the deck. Crew members ran in all directions as they made ready for the storm. Someone groaned, and I twisted to see behind me. Hadriel clung to the railing, head hung over it, fingers white. There probably wasn't enough elixir in the world to keep him from feeling the roll and surge of the ship.

A streak of lightning cut across the sky, a flash of incandescent white-blue against the tempestuous shades of gray. I stood as a white-crested wave swelled in front of the ship. As the bow lifted and then plunged down, my nervousness turned into a tingling of fear. I braced my hand on the railing to keep from falling as a deck hand stopped near me.

"We're going to need you to go below deck," he yelled over the growing howl of the winds. "Let's get you secured."

I didn't respond to him verbally, still locked inside of myself as I processed my life and the feelings of betrayal against the woman who'd sheltered me.

Who'd used me.

The ship heaved as I turned and passed him, now using the railing to steady myself but unable to keep from looking at the surging, swirling waters. If I fell overboard, I'd be a goner. I knew how to swim, but not well. I wouldn't be strong enough to keep my head above those rolling waters.

Fear starting to churn now, I veered left as the ship pitched, stumbled right when it crashed down the other way, and worked my way back to my cabin. Weston wasn't there—he was probably checking in with the captain or making sure his pack was secured against the growing aggression of the storm.

I'd shut him out the past few days—I'd shut everyone

out—because I needed time to figure things out. In this moment, though, I really wished he'd been waiting in here for me. I needed his confidence that we'd make it through this. That we weren't about to be taken by the waves and quickly sink into the depths.

I moved to organize the things I'd left on the table as the wooden world around me shuddered. In the next moment, the boat pitched forward and I nearly cried out. Lightning flashed beyond the windows and thunder growled in the air.

Terror bled through the numb fog of the last few days, gripping me.

I couldn't stay in here. I couldn't just sit and wonder if we were about to go down. I'd need to see it. I wanted to watch the wave that crested the sides of the ship and washed us all overboard.

Walking in zigzagging lines, I pushed out of the cabin and headed back for the bow of the ship. Spray slapped my face and a gust of wind buffeted against me.

My mother had made a voyage like this. She'd just been rejected by her lover and thrown out of her home. With little coin and a baby on the way, she'd crossed the ocean to a new and uncertain future. She'd braved just such a situation, but she hadn't had a powerful alpha who would protect her. She hadn't had a pack to talk to, or the promise of an animal. She'd been utterly alone. Magicless. Friendless.

She'd been courageous.

Her voice echoed in my mind.

Remember me.

Memories rose like the waves around us—her smiling face, her comforting voice. Reading to me, pretending and playing games with me, trying to give me the best life she could manage under such horrible conditions. She'd sacrificed for me, told me she loved me every day, tried to make me happy.

Granny had done none of those things. She hadn't done anything a parent would or should do. She'd performed the duties of an employer only.

Tears blending with the rain on my face, I edged closer to the bow of the dramatically pitching ship. Lightning spiderwebbed across the sky. Thunder boomed, making my heart sprint. Monstrous waves rose all around the ship, and men and women shouted and screamed as the captain barked orders. Hadriel was gone, probably seeking shelter.

What shelter? How could one secure themselves amid the power of the raging storm?

How could one secure themselves from the devastation I'd wrought at Granny's behest?

I felt just as powerless in this storm as I did in my life: I had no choice but to watch it bear down on me, to ride the waves and hope I made it through.

"Aurelia!" Weston's voice barely cut through the ripping wind and thrashing rain. The ship shuddered before pitching again just as I felt his strong arms wrap around me and pull me close to him. "Baby, what are you doing out here? It's not safe. Gods, you're soaked. C'mon."

I didn't hear a single quiver of worry in his voice regarding our surroundings, toward the boiling sea or the lightning striking ever closer. He gently but firmly turned me. His strong arm wrapped around my shoulders, grounding me.

"Are all storms at sea this bad?" I asked in a small voice as he helped me along the deck, stopping to brace as the boat pitched.

Somehow, he heard me above the crashing waves. "Some, but not all," he said, and I welcomed his unflinching truthfulness. "The captain has been through worse, as have I. He's going to steer us around it. It'll add a little more time to the journey, but it'll be safer. We'll be okay."

I bathed in his unyielding confidence as we made it to our cabin. He ushered me inside. He closed the door behind us before grabbing a large cloth and tossing it on the bed.

"We need to get you out of those clothes before you catch your death of cold," he said, wasting no time in stripping off my shirt. It wasn't even remotely sexual. He wasn't turned on; he was taking care of me.

Heat warmed my heart even as my teeth chattered in the chill of the room.

"What about you?" I asked as he pushed down my pants, and I noticed his wet clothes plastered to his delicious display of muscle.

He wrapped the large towel around my nude body, rubbing away the moisture.

"Don't worry about me. Here, hold this and I'll grab more towels."

I did as he said, drying the damp ends of my hair as I watched him hang up my wet clothes along the pegboard and grab more towels from the chest before returning to me. I shivered as he worked at my legs, blotting between my thighs and around to my butt without lingering. I found myself wishing he would.

"How do you feel?" he asked, peeling the towel away from my upper body just enough to see the continued bruising on my ribs. I closed my eyes as his fingertips gently glanced against my flesh.

"Much better," I murmured. "The elixir really helped."

He pulled his hand away and headed to the closet to grab some nightclothes.

"What if we need to swim for it, though?" I asked as he

made ready to help me into them. I didn't mention that I had no idea where we'd swim *to*.

"We won't." There was zero concern in his voice. "We'll need to brave the rocking of the ship, that's all. It'll be a rough afternoon, but if we can hold on to our stomachs, we'll get through."

Gods, that confidence was so sexy. Fear still pinged along my nerves with each crashing wave, with each drop of the angry, pelting rain against our small windows.

He tucked me into my soft nightclothes, and I found myself wanting to say I was sorry. Or maybe just cry? Maybe scream. It felt like the storm was shaking something loose, as did the way he so selflessly cared for me right now. It was stripping away the numbness I'd wrapped myself in.

"Thank you," I said instead, slipping under the covers for a little warmth.

"My pleasure," he said, and meant it.

He pulled off his shirt and quickly slipped out of his pants. I could see the raised bumps along his skin, showing his chill. He dried himself quickly and shrugged into dry clothes before hanging up his wet items.

"The rest of the pack has already been seen to," he said. "Now all I have to do is wait it out like everyone else."

He approached the side of the bed, all business, before slipping in. He didn't scoot close, respectful of the distance I'd implemented these past few nights. And while I might need it again as I worked through the part he had played in all of this, right now, as my world tilted around me both literally and figuratively, I needed a strong body to hold on to.

Specifically, *his* strong body.

"My mom crossed an ocean," I said, reaching for him. I scooted a little closer.

He closed the distance quickly, pulling me onto his chest and breathing me in. His arms wrapped around me tightly, and I issued a sigh of relief, melting against him. Fuck, this felt so good. *He* felt so good. I hated that we had a muddy history between us. I hated that my mind and body always seemed to be at odds where he was concerned.

"That's right, I remember you saying that." His deep voice rumbled in his chest. Even though the ship tilted ever more to the right, the room now at an angle and my heart crawling into my throat, his heartbeat was strong and sure. He, somehow, was not worried. It made me feel a little better.

"She never mentioned a storm, though." I laid my hand against his warm neck. "She didn't say much about it at all. I think if I were to tell someone about my crossing, this would be the first thing I mentioned."

I tilted my face up, grazing my lips against his skin.

His breath hitched and his heart sped up.

My belly flipped. A vicious storm at sea didn't affect him, but a little kiss from me had this big alpha's body reacting. Something about that fact tightened my insides in all the right ways.

I sucked on his skin and ran my palm down his chest and to his stomach, heading lower still. Before I could reach his cock—I was now salivating to taste it—he flipped me, spooning me from behind and holding me there with his strong embrace.

"If you do that, my little wolf, I'll lose control and lock you up."

"Why is that bad?" I asked, my stomach flipping again as the ship tilted further still. I closed my eyes, but could still feel the angle. "I could definitely use a distraction. I do not like how far this boat is leaning."

"I think, instead, you could use some sleep."

"I will never be able to fall asleep in this storm."

"You will." His large hand drifted up my outer thigh before ducking under the hem of my nightdress. "I'll get you good and relaxed, and then I'll hold you tightly. You will trust me when I promise that nothing will happen to you."

His touch lightened, only a tease, drawing my focus. His lips skimmed the shell of my ear before dipping to my neck, taking little nips.

"Do you know how I'll get you good and relaxed?" he murmured, his fingers reaching my hips and then angling in and down, slipping beneath my panties. "I'm going to stroke this pretty pussy until you explode."

I could feel his hardness against my butt, and I tried to reach back for him.

"Ah-ah-ah," he chided, capturing my wrist with the hand that wasn't busy. He pulled it away and secured it alongside the other; both my wrists were now gripped in one of his hands. "You're being a naughty girl, Little Wolf. I'm going to make you beg."

He ran his fingers between my thighs, and I spread wider to give him more access.

"Mmm, you're so wet for me," he growled, dipping one of his fingers into me before circling my clit. "Do you like that?" He nipped my neck.

"I want to feel you inside me," I panted.

"I am inside you." He dipped two fingers into me roughly, stroking while the heel of his hand ground against my clit. "I can make you scream just like this."

His other hand tightened against my wrists and his strong arms created a tighter cage around me, dominating me with both his strength and size. I groaned as his fingers plunged inside me again, hitting the perfect spot.

"Move your hips, baby," he said, scraping his teeth against the sensitive skin on my neck. "Fuck my fingers with that wet pussy."

I whimpered at his dirty talk, eager to comply. I rocked my hips into him and was rewarded with that exquisite rubbing, the heel of his hand creating the most delicious friction.

"Good girl," he purred, and I lost all control.

I cried his name as I thrashed against him. I'd spent too many days in close proximity while denying myself the feel of his body and the sweet surrender of release. I chased it now, my pussy tightening around those thick fingers as he pumped them into me.

"Mark me," I begged, pushing back against his throbbing hardness.

He cupped his hand against me, rough and punishing and so fucking good.

"Please, Alpha, mark your Little Wolf."

He growled against the shell of my ear as he quickened his pace, finger-fucking me with abandon. He thrust his hard cock against my ass, dry-humping as though he couldn't help but chase his own pleasure.

"Yes, Weston," I said, stretching my neck to give him access, my world reduced down to this moment, to the feel of his body, the hard plunge of his fingers, the pulse of his hips. *"Please . . ."*

He bit into my neck, very near to my shoulder but just outside of a permanent claiming mark. I gasped as raw hunger lit me up and my whole being exploded. Pleasure tore me apart in the most glorious of ways; it felt as though pieces were scattered all throughout the universe for him to collect and puzzle back together. Waves of ecstasy shook my body as he shuddered, finding his release against me.

He kissed up my neck softly, breathing deeply. I settled against him, my eyes closed. All I knew was the feel of him, his arms around me, his face close to mine. Nothing mattered save his proximity.

"Sleep, baby," he murmured, relaxing against me, his heart still beating quickly. "I've got you. I won't let anything happen to you."

Defying all odds, I slipped into a comforting, dreamless sleep with the alpha's strength coiled around me.

4

AURELIA

"Hello, hello." Dante sidled up to where I stood at the railing on the deck of the ship, up in the bow, where I was once again mostly out of the way.

Weston had been correct—the captain had directed us around the storm. The sky this morning had dawned fresh and bright, the buttery sun sparkling against the sapphire waters and the forbidding clouds now in the distance. I almost couldn't believe it. Part of me had truly thought the storm would take us down.

Until I'd fallen asleep in the alpha's arms, that was. I'd only awoken near dawn as he slipped away, needing to check on his people. I'd relished his kiss on my forehead, and then hated the turbulent emotions rising a moment later.

That storm had shaken something loose inside of me, though. The time for internal reflection, for numb detachment, was over. It was time to regain some form of control over my life.

Dante held up a book as he leaned against the railing,

nodding at the journal I held in my hand. "It's time to read something that isn't so depressing."

"No, honestly, it's fine." I hugged the journal closer to my body. "I need to get through these."

"Didn't anyone tell you? You're a captive. You'll have all the time in the world to get through those before the dragons kill you in a spectacular fashion. It's time for a break and a little adventure." He showed me the cover of a book featuring a large ship, not unlike the one we were in but much less fine. "This is about pirates and a shipwreck and love. Hopefully there is also banging, am I right? Now, put your things away. We don't want them falling overboard and have you losing memories you clearly did not originally struggle to hold on to."

He had me there. Half the stuff in these journals I'd entirely forgotten about: snippets of conversation I'd overheard, things Granny had said, and especially the beginning years—the horrible, dark beginning years. At least, that was how I'd portrayed them. Honestly, I hadn't been treated much differently as time went on. I'd just gotten used to it, I think. I'd acclimated. That, or everyone else was just as miserable, and therefore my life seemed equal in comparison. I'd kept my head down and my hands and brain busy. I'd gotten my gifts, I'd had my illusions, and I'd been avoided by all. On and on had continued the daily grind of life.

That life had been a lie.

All of it had been a fucking lie.

I knew that now.

The patterns were so clear once I went back and looked for them. I'd get in trouble for something, and after a punishment and a stint of good behavior, I'd get a gift. If I did something great, like creating a new product that did well, I got a gift. I'd been trained like a pet. A favorite pet, held on a pedestal above all the others, but a pet nonetheless. I had not been a family member, not a friend; I realized during the storm that I'd been nothing more than an employee.

My delusions had made me think there was more to it.

The whole thing made me sick.

The truth made me sick.

I'd helped her build her fucking empire and didn't once press about the specifics. I hadn't cared about the specifics. I had rarely asked questions, and when I did, I'd let her shut me down. I could've gotten to the bottom of what the product had become but I didn't want to; that would've upset my equilibrium. Without magic, I was stuck—and I knew it.

One thing had become incredibly apparent: in the beginning, I had been good at a great deal else.

I'd cured animal hides, learning quickly enough that, despite not liking me, Old Gus had seen my skill and agreed to take me on as an apprentice. The blacksmith had, too, though the work was too demanding. I hadn't had the strength to keep up. Baking? That had been my favorite.

All of it had been shut down. Instead, Granny brought in the goods we needed and shepherded me back to developing the product. I hadn't even been good at plants in the beginning. Even now, I could barely garden. I could turn the natural elements into chemicals, though. I could use their properties and bend them to my will.

I'd also been good at art, of course, probably allowed to keep it solely because it had inspired the designs Granny used for business, and I was good at cooking. One skill she needed, and the other I needed to survive. Everything else I had done without. We had all done without.

Put your head down, stay blind, keep busy. She'd created a production village, just as Weston had said. I was the pet that churned out the product. We were all kept on a tight leash, in a solid cage.

My anger couldn't be measured. It could barely be contained. With the exception of last night, I'd been unable to sleep because of it. I didn't want to eat. I had a million questions for Granny, but if I had to choose only one to ask, it would be this: why did you take me in?

Knowing more about the organization and the world outside, I could see how her motives made a sick sort of sense. Our placidity did, too. What could our village do against her trained and bloodthirsty patrol? Valuable as I was to her operation, even I'd been punished severely when I wandered too close to the perimeter. We stood no chance against them.

But in the beginning, I'd had nothing. I'd been nothing. I'd been too young for my animal to have budded, and I had zero skills to bring with me. I knew why she'd kept me, but why had she brought me in? If Hadriel and Weston and others could be believed—if my own journals could be believed—she wasn't overly fond of charity.

At this point, I just wanted to know why.

I kind of wanted to cry, too.

And burn things.

And present myself to the dragons so they could end this miserable, aching, physically and emotionally pain-filled existence. That was probably the scariest thing of all: the desire to give up and stop surviving.

For now, I stared placidly at Dante, my hands stilled, my mind whirling. This was why it was important to keep busy—no thinking required.

"Everyone loves the *death by dragon* joke, it seems," I said, making no move to do as he said. I was kind of done doing as people told me.

"Of course they do—it's funny. Come on, put your

things away. This book promises to be good." He waved it at me. "The alpha passed it on to Nova, who passed it on to Burt, who tried to keep it all to himself but whom I stole it from because it wasn't his to begin with, and he needs to learn to share. Let's get into it." He paused, staring at me. His eyebrows lifted slowly. "Listen, I am your friend, remember? You made a big fucking deal about that fact, so now it's a big fucking deal to me. Friends force other friends to try books they're unsure of. It's sacrosanct. Now, there is only one copy, and I read slowly, which means you'll be able to understand everything. I can't have you read it because I've noticed how fast you whiz through those journals. You'll talk too fast, and I won't have a clue about what you're saying. Here we go. Let's get cracking. We have, like, a day. We'll need to do this round the clock if we are to finish in time."

I sighed but couldn't hide the smile. "Fine."

"There we go."

"You call him Burt too, now?" I started to gather up my stuff.

"Yeah. I did it by mistake and he got all huffy about it, which was strangely hilarious, so I did it again and acted like it was a mistake just to see what he'd do. He threw something at my head. So now I do it because I want to see if he'll ever hit me."

I smiled even wider. "That's probably why Hadriel does it, too."

"I'm sure. Do you want me to run that back to your room?"

I turned, slid down to sit on the deck, and placed the journal beside me as I leaned against the side. "No, it's fine. Go for it."

"Cool. Okay . . ." He sat next to me and leaned back as he opened the first pages. "There's a map." He turned the book to show me a black-and-white image. "Fantastic. Moving along." He licked his pointer finger and pushed a page out of the way. "I'd like to thank, yada-yada. You wrote a book, we get it . . ."

I blurted out a laugh.

"Now, here we go." He groaned. "Once upon a time, really? They might as well have started with 'it was a dark and stormy night.' So clichéd. Are we sure this book is any good?" He arched an eyebrow at me.

The laughter kept coming. "You're the one who brought it to me! I've never heard of it. It's in poor taste, though, I will say that."

"What?" He looked at the cover, then the back. "Why?"

"Oh, I don't know, because there's pirates and a shipwreck and *we're on a ship.*"

"Bah." He waved that away. "What are the odds?"

"After yesterday? Higher than I originally thought. Do you even like this genre?"

"No idea. I don't usually read fiction. I'm more into nonfiction. Now, if we were reading nonfiction about pirates and a shipwreck, well then *that* would be cause for alarm. Some dude's imagination? Nah. It's very rarely inspired by real events."

I really hoped he was wrong.

"You like this genre, though." He turned his gaze back to the book. "And so we will read this genre. Here we go, stop interrupting."

I laughed again as my heart warmed and tears of gratitude filled my eyes. I could allow myself a few more tears on this ship. Maybe I'd just cry my fill later tonight and let Weston hold me again. I could tell he was unhappy with the distance between us. It didn't matter, though. It couldn't. He'd broken me down under duress. I would not allow him to shape me anew, not like Granny had. I would not put my head down, stay blind, and keep busy. Not this time. I barely knew him. If he wanted to use me, he'd need to put in more effort than simply forcing us to share a bed. Until then, he'd just have to find someone else to meet his needs, a task I was sure would be fairly easy for him once he returned to his element.

I gritted my teeth against the intense wave of jealousy at that thought. It was unwelcome.

Once we docked, I'd start carving a new me out of the hard stuff that now seemed lodged within. I needed to find that personal, inner power Hadriel spoke of.

I needed to keep surviving until I could pay for my crimes.

5

AURELIA

"Fuck, am I glad to get off this boat," Hadriel said later that day as he shoved past me.

"It's a ship, dingle-dick," Nova told him.

"I don't give a shit what it is as long as it lets me off." He waded through more people to get to the gangplank as fast as possible.

"Dante, when you gonna finish that book?" Tanix called back from near the front of the line.

"I would've already finished it if you hadn't kept asking questions," Dante responded from his location back near me.

Tanix, Sixten and Niven—one of the guys I'd stuck an axe in when they invaded the village—had joined the read-through, with Hadriel occasionally sitting in, too. We'd had to start over, and then Tanix had asked questions about every plot hole he found and those he made up. We would never have been able to finish by the time we arrived, but Tanix made sure we'd only gotten halfway.

"Things need to make sense," Tanix said.

"They do make sense, you're just too dense to see that," Sixten replied.

Weston emerged near the front of the line, in the space people were leaving for the captain to make ready to depart. Everyone quieted down; they were so much more reserved when he was around. I got now why he removed himself from their company during meals and why he didn't take his leisure around them. It truly was a lonely life as a good alpha, one that respected the needs of his pack.

Weston looked everyone over, his gaze landing on me for a moment before he turned around and waited for the captain. Once everything was set, Weston disembarked like he owned the world. The sun shone on his dirty blond hair, highlighting it like a crown. His broad shoulders were pushed back, his bearing straight with measured, purposeful steps.

"He's really good at looking like he's in charge," I murmured as we followed along like a herd of cattle.

"He's had his whole life to learn." Dante grabbed my upper arm to maintain our proximity in the bustling crowd. It was clear the pack wanted to be off the ship and headed for home as fast as possible. "Here's how this is going to go. You're going to put your hands in front of you like they are bound. You're going to walk with me, keeping your hands like that, until we stop in the first village. We'll be treating you like a captive, because of both Granny's threat and because the people here won't like you very much. We need to keep up appearances until you can stand in front of the dragon royalty. Okay?"

"Weston explained this at breakfast."

"Yes, but you've been very obtuse toward him lately, and we all just want to make sure everything goes smoothly. Your life is literally on the line."

"*Obtuse?*" I turned to him with raised eyebrows. "That's what he said?"

Dante's grin made me huff and turn to the front.

"No," he replied. "He said 'distant.' I just wanted to see if that axe wielder was still in there."

"Now more than ever."

"Atta girl."

The horses and supplies were already waiting, the disembarkation having been planned remarkably well. Those who were riding mounted up, and the rest of us filed in to walk near the carts. Dante would serve as my guard, so his horse was being led by Hadriel, who wouldn't let the stable hand near it.

As we waited to move, I got my first look at the dragon kingdom. Docks stretched out from the land and fine ships bobbed across the sprawling harbor, the wharf buzzing with life as people went about their day. The market lay beyond, not unlike the one I'd passed in the last port city, but the establishments and even the stalls here seemed so much . . . newer. Nicer. Fresh paint adorned walls; new roofs lay atop buildings. The footpaths were swept clean, no litter in sight. People wore attire ranging from decent to nice to fine, with none of the evidence of poverty I'd seen dotting the way in the last kingdom, or even in my village. It was almost as though this place was built recently.

"The first village is the farthest away from the castle in the kingdom," Dante explained as we walked. Shapes ghosted through the trees alongside us, utterly silent and only noticed because of the feeling of danger that tingled across my skin. "It's the smallest and used to be the poorest. Now it does a decent amount of trade. The queen was originally from there, so it has special significance because of her and her brother. Their family no longer lives there, of course."

"Are you my tour guide?"

"Yes. I can't walk and read or I'll trip and fall on my head. Then you'll make fun of me, so this is a safe alternate."

I laughed.

"Don't laugh," he hissed, looking around. "You're supposed to be a captive! Which means we're enemies."

"Sorry," I whispered, trying desperately to wrestle away my smile.

"We've landed later than originally planned," Dante went on, staring straight ahead. "Skirting around that storm put us behind. Factoring in the stop, it means we might not get to the castle until just after dark." He leaned in a little closer and dropped his voice. "Not to worry—this kingdom is very safe. We have patrols on the regular. If you are to be re-abducted, it won't happen now."

"Fantastic," I said in a dry tone, still wrestling that smile.

He straightened and resumed his tour guidance. "Yes. Now, if you'll turn your attention to the right, this whole area used to be called the Royal Wood. Back in the days of the Mad King, it was for use by royals and the court only. Peasants called it the Forbidden Wood. To enter for any reason would be punishable by death."

I paused and turned my head to look at him. "Are you serious?"

"Very, though I wasn't here then, or for the curse that followed the Mad King's death, so this is all secondhand." He huffed. "Stop interrupting or I'll kick you off the tour. Anyway, now the wood is open to all, but with strict requirements regarding hunting. You need to apply for licenses and whatnot so that we don't kill off all the game."

"Who owns the land on the left?"

"It's also part of the Royal Wood, but I thought it would be more dramatic if I gave you a direction in which to look." He stuck out his hand, gesturing toward a field through the trees on the left. "Ah, here we have the famous Everlass plant." The plants stood in rows, green and leafy and tended to with much more care than our gardens in the village. "It is the pride and joy of the dragons, growing wherever they live and carrying all sorts of amazing healing properties."

The name was familiar. "That's what they gave me on the ship, right? Everlass?"

"The elixir was made with Everlass, yes."

"And the one that saved me after the run-in with my drugs?"

"Your product mixed with Granny's drugs, you mean? Yes, that had Everlass, but the plant that elixir was made with was blessed by the phoenix."

"Blessed? Is the phoenix their god or something?"

Dante looked over at me in confusion. "The phoenix is the queen's brother."

Hadriel had talked about that with me. While I had been blown away, I wasn't sure I'd fully processed it, because it still didn't seem real. Phoenixes were a myth. They were in books. They didn't walk on mortal lands.

But just like Hadriel had said, apparently there was one. A real one—a walking, breathing phoenix whose magic had already saved my life not once but twice.

"Wow," I said, blown away all over again. "I honestly thought Hadriel was being overly dramatic. That's . . . insane."

"Yeah, right? The guy can't ever die. Isn't that wild?" He shrugged. "Moving on—well, now we've passed the Everlass field."

I let out a low whistle. "I need time to adjust to a myth coming to life anyway. You didn't even need to capture me. If you'd just told me I'd get to meet a phoenix, I would've come willingly. Holy crap. Is he hot?"

He held up a hand in exasperation. "For the love of the gods, don't ever ask that again." He dropped his hand. "Come on, let's talk about the history of the kingdom as it was told to me until we get to the village and can get your wolf pulled out. That'll give me a lot fewer headaches."

Before I could protest, he launched into specifics about the Mad King and the curse. I lost track of the miles through the woods while listening. Hadriel had been over much of this, but his accounts were told from his personal point of view, which were often crazy, colorful tales that kept my attention for different reasons. The history told to me by a nonfiction lover gave me a whole new perspective, and I was completely engrossed in his tales.

We passed another Everlass field, this one much closer to our path. Unlike the other field, people wandered through this one. Some picked leaves and placed them on the trays they carried—probably to harvest for medicine, I surmised—and others just threw the leaves onto the ground.

I asked about the latter, and Dante shrugged.

"That's how they take care of the plant. Dead leaves or something. I've never asked, mostly because I don't really care."

I blurted out a laugh as Weston took a right, looking over his shoulder at me. His eyes were still hard, no expression on his face, and I figured it was probably his "I'm the alpha and I'm very important" mode, something he hadn't often done when we were traveling. It was like looking at an entirely different person.

"Beasts used to roam this wood," Dante went on. "They were created by harvesting pain and suffering from the people in the demon dungeons. I had personal experience with that. This one time . . ."

6

AURELIA

I didn't need to be told to keep my hands together now. I twisted my fingers in nervousness as I spied a village along the edge of the wood. Dante had been doing a great job of keeping my mind off what I was about to do, but now the reality of the situation was sinking in. It was just about time to prove whether Granny had been lying to me all my life, keeping me separate and alone as a means to control me.

I couldn't imagine anyone heinous enough to do something like that. Try as I might, I simply could not believe anyone could be so cruel.

The moment of truth was upon me.

Weston stopped just outside the tree line, and everyone else with him. Wolves emerged from the shadows around us, one shifting into a robust lady with nipple piercings and buzzed, dyed-red hair.

Weston pulled his long leg from across his horse and jumped down.

"Beta, welcome home," she said, offering a bow.

I furrowed my brow at the title she used.

"The king and queen are the alphas within the kingdom," Dante whispered to me, having noticed. "Weston and Micah, the dragon commander, use the title of beta."

I understood the logic, but still thought it was a little confusing.

"Captain." Weston glanced at Dante, who walked me up the line, before turning to speak to the woman who'd greeted him. "We'll need a quick stop here before we head to the castle. Send word to the king and queen. I would like to request an audience with them as soon as I arrive."

"Yes, sir." She bowed again, sparing a glance at me before stepping away.

No emotion played across her face, her expression a stone mask, but her eyes didn't lie. She clearly knew who I was and had a strong distaste for the very air I breathed.

A cold shiver washed through me at the thought of standing in front of the dragon royalty. Animal or no, nothing would be able to save me from their judgment. So much of my life had been spent surviving, and now it could all end tomorrow.

My legs felt wooden, and I scarcely dared to breathe as we neared Weston.

"Hadriel," he called out as he watched me approach. His expression was as closed down as his captain's, his eyes hard. He gave nothing away.

I took a steadying breath as Hadriel hurried to my side. Dante stepped back.

It was to me Weston spoke. "Hadriel will ensure you are seen by the village head, who is basically the village alpha. His power level is about three-quarters of Granny's. The village head will not know why you're being seen, just that he has to comply with the court. You will need to give him directions. After he answers your questions—"

Weston gritted his teeth, his expression turning frustrated. Something moved behind his eyes, and a heat like lava burned down my sternum. Something must've been happening with his wolf.

"He may pull out your wolf, if you'd like," he finally gritted out. I could tell it cost him dearly to do so.

His eyes zipped back and forth between mine. Electricity crackled between us.

My stomach dropped out, and it suddenly felt like I was free-falling. The lava burned down a little faster, the heat starting to spread through me. Weston's wolf clearly wanted to be the one to end my suppression. He—or they—didn't want to leave it in the hands of another.

But I needed a stranger, someone with the same amount of magic as Granny or less, to give me the answers I needed. I needed to put this to bed, and Weston was too powerful for this need.

I nodded, stepped back, and straightened my spine.

"I'm ready," I said, the wobble in my voice barely contained.

Weston's burning gaze shifted to Hadriel, whose back bowed immediately under the alpha's command.

"Watch her," Weston said. "Straight in, and straight back out."

"Yes, sir."

My body shook as we crossed the tree line, walking slowly but still faster than I would've liked. This felt like my death march, my doom waiting just up ahead. It occurred to me that I might experience a few of these such walks in the next day or two, waiting for one slice of bad news after the other.

"Having an animal will be a dream come true," I remembered, licking my lips.

Dried grasses hugged the lane toward a village up ahead. A lone tree grew off to the right, the trunk slightly curved and the branches reaching out over a little tuft of green. It would be a nice place to draw, or just pass the time.

"Of course it will," Hadriel said, patting my arm. "Just remember, no shifting. You need instruction and guidance for that. It's very dangerous the first time. I bet you can't wait to heal quickly, though. I'd forgotten how long non-suppression healing takes. Ugh, *ages*. What a fucking nuisance, huh? Soon that'll be behind you."

Fast healing wouldn't matter if the dragons sentenced me to death.

I swallowed down my trepidation. One thing at a time.

A shape above us caught my attention. I glanced up only to stop dead, my mouth dropping open.

A huge, winged creature cut across the sky. Glimmering purple scales covered most of its body, except for a light blue belly. Its great wings beat solidly, the feet curved under its body tipped with long, glistening black claws.

A dragon.

"Holy fuck," I said softly, staring as it glided through the air. "It's gorgeous. And *huge*."

"He's average. Wait until you see the king."

Weston's assertions that he would protect me from the dragons was even more laughable after having seen one. What would he do, bite their ankles?

"Listen, Aurelia . . . What's up with you?" Hadriel took my arm to get me moving. "What's going on? I mean, besides your life being turned upside down and finding out your past was a pile of garbage that was just set on fire and being dragged to a new kingdom to face the possibility of death. What *else* is troubling you?"

I watched the dragon soar for a moment longer, taking jerking steps to keep up with Hadriel.

"They're beautiful," I gushed. "Is it too much to hope

that I have a dragon in me instead of a wolf? I'd love to be able to fly."

"They're a bunch of mean fuckers with rage problems and no regard for boundaries. Fuck them. Listen, I want to help you. I'm on your side. But you can't shut everyone out. You're creating an internal world not unlike the one you just left."

I could hear the worry in his voice. It poked that soft spot he'd created within me by being friendly. By caring.

"I'm . . . hardening up." I refocused on the lane leading into the village. "I'm now in another place where I will not be welcome, but this time it isn't because of what I am, it's because of what I've done. This time it is valid. I need to stay strong."

"What we think makes us strong can sometimes make us brittle. It isn't the same thing as locking yourself inside. It's okay to grieve."

I let out a shaky laugh I didn't feel. "If I start grieving, I might never stop."

"It might seem that way, but the dawn is just around the corner, I know it. Just . . . do me a favor. Give this place a chance. Endure the accusations of your murdering their villagers, tell your story, and yes, take the judgment. But until then, give it a chance. I know you'll love it."

I sighed softly. It was hard to deny him after all he'd done for me in staying by my side and helping me escape when I'd needed to.

I nodded. "Okay."

He gave me a tight smile and a nod in return. "Good. Here we are—we're entering the village."

Homes dotted the way, roads and lanes meandering over the natural rise and fall of the earth to reach them all. The main strip held small shops and cute little eateries leading to a central square where traders had set up their tables and tents. In the far corner, some sort of traveling show was rolling out an awning.

"This is the village where the shadow market dealers lurk the most," he murmured, walking close in at my side. "The stalls are torn down as soon as they're discovered, but they pop up again in a blink. It drives Finley mad."

"Granny never mentioned the shadow markets being torn down." I scoffed at my own statement. "I guess we now know she didn't mention a lot of things."

He patted my arm. "Your filthy kingdom probably never bothered," he said as we heard, "Hah!"

Hadriel flinched and slowed, stepping just in front of me. "What in the gods' assholes?"

"You won't take me alive!" a man shouted. "Go ahead, try it! Try to get me. I will take every last one of you."

In an alleyway, a nude, skinny man with a bony chest and thinning brown hair slashed a knife through the air. Three wolves stood around him, their fur bristling, having backed him against a wall around the corner from a small shop. Their lips were pulled back, revealing their teeth, as they inched closer. They were clearly trying to subdue him without getting a knife in the ribs for their efforts. The problem was they were doing it all wrong.

I sighed and wanted to cry. It was probably my product he had taken; he'd been on a journey and was obviously angry at the interruption. Nothing like an example of my crimes to push the dragons toward action.

I looked away for a moment, wanting for all the world to go back in time and do my life over. To make different decisions, push Granny down a different path. Or maybe just claim ignorance about drugs and hope she pointed me in a less damaging direction.

"Obviously, there was a shadow market here recently," Hadriel muttered.

"Fuck," I ground out, altering course and heading toward the man.

"No, love, let them handle it." He hurried after me. "No, no. Aurelia, they'll get him, don't worry."

"They aren't doing it right. It's likely I created this situation. I have an obligation to fix it. It won't take more than a moment."

Reaching the wolves gathered around the man, I stuck out my hand to keep them put.

"Back off," I barked. One of them snarled, making my stomach clench in unease. I didn't slow, though, wedging myself between the various parties.

"Foul toadstool!" The man slashed, his knife cutting through the air straight for me.

I twisted out of the way easily; he was a bit slower than Raz, and much slower than some of the people I'd fought on the way here. Child's play.

"He's in a nightmare," I told the wolves. "It's fine. Get me a big, dark tarp or a thick blanket or something else that will fit over him. It needs to cut out the light."

"You vicious shroom!" The man flared his arms, which were bent at the elbows, and dropped his head while bending over—a very strange sort of pose. "You harbinger of fungus!"

I noticed Hadriel walking closer, stopping at the corner of the alley. He wore a grin. He did love odd things.

One of the wolves pushed forward, its growl rising.

"Back off," I said again, looking off to my side so I could stare down the obvious leader. He stood just in front of the others, and they took their cues off his movements. After being around Weston, I knew the signs.

"Give me some room," I commanded, needing them to just fuck off so I could get this done quickly. They were a distraction no one needed. "Send someone to get that blanket. *Now!*"

The lead wolf hesitated for a moment before sending one of the other wolves. The man swiped again, stepping forward this time, hellbent on cutting me.

I turned at the last moment, just out of reach, letting the knife harmlessly glide by. Hadriel's eyes widened, and I wasn't sure why. This was a walk in the park.

Now to get the man's attention so that I could talk him down.

"Hello." I swung my hands up over my head and clapped them together.

The man's eyes narrowed in my direction. "Don't you dare *hello* me. Hah!"

He thrust, and I sidestepped, twisting again. I brought my hands up into another clap. "Hello?"

"No!" the man said, flaring his arms and moving like some sort of bird. "No *hello* for you."

If I wasn't worried it might set him off, I would've laughed. Raz was always so filled with hate around me. He was never this playful.

I clapped once to the side and then did a little jig, my eyes never leaving his. "If the fungus grows, we stomp. We shove it down! Hello?"

He slowed, watching me, taking my cues to gradually shift in his journey. He looked at my feet, unsure what to make of my movements. That was perfect. It meant he was malleable.

"We must stomp it down. Hello!" I did the jig again.

"*Yassssss.*" He didn't stomp. His motor skills weren't totally in line with his eyesight, it seemed. He just kinda shimmied back and forth a bit. "Hello, toadstools."

"Hello, toadstools," I mimicked, actually having a bit of fun. "Goodbye." Another jig, then a clap. "Goodbye!"

"Goodbye!" the man roared, shaking his limbs against the sky. "Begone, fungus of the fire. Spore of eternal stink."

"Oh look." I lifted my hands like he had, drawing back his attention. I pulled them down, elbows first, bending my knees at the same time, making myself into a sort of square. "Look."

"Look," the man said in wonder, watching me. I started to sway. He followed suit as though mesmerized.

"Lo-ok," I drew out, swaying with my whole body. "Look!" I pointed skyward. "We are the sun. Oh my! We are the bringers of the light. Or are we a cave?"

I bent and tilted my head at him.

"Or . . . are we . . . a cave . . ." he said hesitantly, again not quite sure.

"The sky collapses into a cave." I made a popping sound and started to shrink.

He, utterly transfixed, followed, getting smaller, then smaller still. It occurred to me that he didn't have the drooling, strange, sightless quality that the man in the city I was captured in did. He certainly didn't have the same level of malnourishment. I wondered if that meant he was new to the product. Maybe he could still be salvaged if they could keep those shadow markets out of the area.

I splayed my fingers wide, and he followed, the knife dropping and clattering away. He didn't notice.

A man—probably the wolf from a moment ago—jogged up with a large woolen blanket. He slowed as he neared, his face a mask of confusion at the scene. He clearly had no sense of humor.

"The cave is deep, the roots are long," I said softly, reaching back as he repeated the phrase. When the blanket wasn't immediately offered, I shook my hand to get him moving.

"The blanket, man, give her the gods-fucked blanket," Hadriel groused.

The man did, stepping back again.

"The cave is . . ." I let the words trail away.

"Deep," the man supplied, on his knees now.

"The roots are . . ."

"Long," the man breathed.

"Where are the roots?" I asked in a haunting voice. "Where are they?"

He looked at the ground, and I stepped forward and laid the blanket over his body, fully covering him. As I watched, the blanket shivered, and then settled as he eased into the darkness.

"Right." I turned toward the others, kicking the knife away as I did so. "He should be fine. I'd check on him in half an hour. Just lift up the tail end of that blanket to give him some air. It's not a hot day, but that's a heavy blanket. The drug will go dormant, and he will go with it. It'll slowly erode away. Toward the end, he'll likely get sick—that's the coating. He won't die—that would've already happened—but he might throw up. If he stays in the current position, just leave him be. It'll make the drug less appealing. If he lies down and you fear he might choke, help him." I paused in the sudden silence, the man in his human form blinking at me and the wolves staring. "Okay?"

The silence stretched.

"Just move on, love," Hadriel said. "They heard you. They're either dumb or confused. They'll figure it out."

There was nothing more I could do right now to help the man, so I did as Hadriel said.

"In the future, if it is one of Granny's drugs, all you need to do is talk the person around and get or throw him into a small, dark space. A cupboard will do, or a closet." I shrugged. "Doesn't matter. If the person is like this, with a weapon, usually they'll yell and then they'll strike. Wait, dodge, bat the weapon away, then force them into that small, dark space. But be careful, because they often bite. Close the door, maybe lock it, and wait. Okay?" I took a deep breath. "But please, whatever you do, stop making it worse by threatening to assault these people."

I paused a beat, looking between them, hoping my lecture sank in. When they still didn't respond, I headed back toward Hadriel.

The man who'd brought the blanket cleared out of the way. "Who are you?" he asked in a wispy voice.

"Didn't you hear?" I didn't look back and recited what the man had said. "I'm the harbinger of fungus."

7

AURELIA

"I thought you said the dragons eradicated Granny's product from this kingdom?" I asked Hadriel as we continued through the center of the cute little village. Bright and cheerful homes were nestled close to each other with little pops of color from blooming flower boxes. The cobblestone lane at our feet was so clean it almost looked scrubbed. The area had a lovely, welcoming feel, like a community that stuck together. It was so different than the place I'd lived, the contrast stark.

"What can I say? People keep bringing it in. That trick with the blanket—how'd you know that would work?"

"I made the stuff, remember? I baked in fail-safes. I told you that. I had to, or Raz would've driven me mad."

"So you've had a lot of experience talking people around?"

"A lot, yes. I tended to cause the nightmares with Raz and many of those who routinely sampled the batches to make sure they were okay. Others just lost their way. It's a lot easier and faster if a closet is close by, or the person hasn't been incensed by wolves foaming at the mouth."

He raised an eyebrow and pursed his lips. "Harsh."

I shrugged as he slowed near a little building with a large window at the front. Hadriel knocked, then opened the door and motioned me in before following behind me. The natural light shone across his sparkly, colorful jacket; he was allowed to dress how he preferred now that he was back in his home kingdom.

A man sat at the desk, paused in putting a piece of paper into a file.

He looked up as Hadriel approached. "Yes, how can I—" His eyes rounded and he stood quickly. "Hello. What can I do for the royal court?"

Hadriel stepped aside and motioned me forward. "This woman needs a quick moment with the village head. Beta's orders."

"Oh! Yes, of course. The beta is back, then? Was he successful?"

"Yes and no." Hadriel put his hand to my back, guiding me.

"When did you return? I hadn't heard."

"Just now. We're stopping in on the way to the castle."

Butterflies swarmed my middle as the man opened a door and stuck his head in, repeating what Hadriel had said.

"Yes, of course," I heard from inside the room. The butterflies in my stomach started to speed up their flight.

The man pushed the door wide and waited for us to enter. Hadriel didn't move.

"I'll be right out here," he told me, rubbing my back. "Do you want the door opened or closed?"

I shrugged one shoulder as I took my first step. "I don't care." I swallowed as I entered. Fear had bile burning up the back of my throat.

I'd always wanted this. I'd wanted magic, an animal, a

way to fit in. Now that I faced the possibility, I was terrified of what the man would say. I was terrified my dream wouldn't come true, knowing I'd be devastated. But I was just as afraid, if not more, that it would. Because of what it would mean about my past.

The village head was a short, squat man with graying hair and brown eyes. He sat at a messy desk in a room lined with books.

"Yes, how can I help?" he asked, leaning back in his chair.

"I've come to ask if I have magic," I said in a firm tone. "An animal, I mean."

The man's brows knitted together as he stood. "Of course, yes. But didn't I hear that you had come under orders from the court and the beta? Surely you didn't have to stop to see me if you've traveled with him . . ."

"It's complicated. I preferred to speak with someone who didn't know me."

He stepped around his desk. "Well, sure, but I'm not one of the more powerful alphas. I'm in this position because I know how to run a budding town, not a pack."

"That's fine. I just need you to check and see."

He shrugged and approached. "Well okay, if—"

His eyes turned sharp, and he stopped, glancing at the door.

"Is this a joke?" he demanded. "Is that Hadriel out there? Am I the punch line?"

Hadriel stepped through the doorway. "Like she said, it's complicated. She just needs a stranger to tell her, without a doubt, if she has an animal or not. Then yank it out and we'll be on our way. My jokes are never this simple."

The man's brow pinched together in a frown at Hadriel's explanation. "I don't believe you. Look, I've always been very upfront about my lack of power. I said it just a moment ago, didn't I? I'm good at my job. I don't need—"

"I've been told my whole adult life that I don't have any magic," I interrupted, tingles of unease making my nerves dance. "My mother didn't have magic. I believed the person who told me that I didn't either. I'm not convinced I can believe the alpha—"

"Beta," Hadriel corrected me.

"Beta, whatever, when he tells me that I do. I just need a second opinion from someone who has no vested interest in the situation and who doesn't know my past. Please, can you tell me—do I have an animal in there?"

The man's expression cleared of doubt, kindness taking its place. He stepped a little closer.

"Sweetie, you have a very powerful animal in there, yes. Trust the beta—he would know." My heart started thumping. "I don't have a lot of power myself, which is why I thought Hadriel was making fun of me, but I can certainly feel it, my dear. Who is this person who told you that you didn't? They must not have had much power."

I started to sweat. "My guardian. She is quite powerful, hence my uncertainty. Can you tell what kind of animal it is?"

His confusion was evident, but he didn't ask questions. Instead, he shook his head. "No, that can't be known until you shift, and you shouldn't shift without guidance. The first time can be very dangerous. Don't worry, though, you've come to the right kingdom. The queen herself has only been shifting since the curse fell a year and a half ago. Many people here are new to their animals." He smiled at me warmly. "You aren't so far behind. The beta was smart to bring you here. Would you like me to end your suppression?"

A rush of sweet adrenaline ran through me. Tears crowded my vision. My mom would be so proud, so relieved. She'd always wanted this for me—for me to have magic, to belong. She'd be singing and dancing if she were here right now, hugging me endlessly.

Granny had kept this joy from me. I'd been treated like shit all my life, spat on, avoided, kept from having friends . . . She'd watched me endure the censure from the village, isolated because of their prejudices, picked on as a teen, taunted by her own employee. That whole time, she had said nothing.

No, that wasn't true.

She hadn't said nothing.

She'd looked me right in the eye . . . and lied.

That wasn't love; it was cruelty. If I'd needed any more evidence, this was it.

Tears overflowed as the enormity of this news threatened to pull me under.

I blew out a breath. "Yes, please."

It was time to get on with my life.

He nodded, and I felt his power reaching into me, taking hold. A flash of panic froze me up. This felt wrong, unnatural. It almost felt intimate, but in a violating way, slithering through me. I was used to Weston's power, not this. I wanted his delicious feel, not a stranger's.

"What the—"

The man windmilled his arms as he fell backward. It was only then that I realized I'd shoved him.

"Oh my—I'm sorry!" I stepped forward, reaching out to catch him. He'd hit his desk, though, then toppled over it.

Hadriel bent over in a fit of hysterical laughter.

"It's not funny," I told him, hurrying to the desk. "Gods, I'm so sorry. I panicked. I've only ever felt the alpha—beta, I mean—Weston! I've only ever felt Weston's power like that, and feeling yours tripped me up. I'm so sorry! I think I'll just have him grab my animal, if that's okay. I'm sure he'll do it."

"Oh yes, he'll do it. Let's go." Hadriel reached for me, still laughing.

The village head picked himself off the ground slowly. His eyes were wide. "You'll have a bright future ahead of you, young lady. A real bright future. I've never seen someone without their animal move so fast."

"Uh, thank you. And again, I'm sorry." I offered an awkward wave as we left his office.

"At least he wasn't mad," I muttered, looking over my shoulder as Hadriel guided me out. The man was straightening his desk while watching us leave.

"He's probably wondering who you are, given you use the beta's first name so casually and know his power so intimately."

"He'd probably be shocked to find out."

"He definitely will," Hadriel said, and for some reason I couldn't put my finger on, I didn't get the impression he meant because of my affiliation with Granny.

We walked in relative silence back through the center of town to rejoin the group. We passed the spot where the wolves had cornered the intoxicated man from earlier. The man remained under his blanket. It didn't look like he'd moved at all, which was what I'd expect if he was left alone. An aging woman sat on the ground by his head, her back bowed, sightlessly looking at her feet. It was so sad to see her waiting for him, worrying as he lay stuffed under a blanket after a display of wild behavior from unlawful drug use for all to see. I hated being responsible for that. I hated my part in tarnishing the people of this lovely little village with the kind village head.

I crossed her way without thinking, stopping beside her and putting a hand on her shoulder.

"I'll fix this," I said, the enormity of my situation still churning within me. This moment felt monumentally important. Helping her, everyone Granny had affected, felt more important than anything else in my broken, tattered life. If I had to beg the dragons to postpone my punishment, possibly my death, I would more than grovel. "I will fix this, I promise."

Tears leaked out of the woman's eyes. She didn't ask who I was or what I'd fix, just nodded gratefully.

My head was in a fog as we walked out of the village, my thoughts swirling as I ruminated over the product, about the coating. I'd need to learn how to create it so I could develop something to dissolve it. I needed to render it ineffective, both as a poison and as an addictive agent. The dragons already had an idea about the latter, but it needed to be better, work faster. It needed to be cheaper—free, if possible.

Weston stood at the tree line, leaning against a trunk, watching as we approached. His gray eyes were laser focused on me, and suddenly I couldn't help but feel everything crashing down around me. The emotion churning inside me bubbled up, and before I even realized it, I was running at him, hitting his chest with my fists, crying angry tears. I was behaving like one of those women I'd read about and always thought was ridiculous, but I got it now. I wanted to hit him but not do any damage. I wanted to be incredibly dramatic, to flail around as I wailed, forcing him to crush me to his chest. I needed him to make me be still, to calm me, to contain me. I couldn't handle it on my own, not this. I didn't want to.

"It's okay," he said softly, his strong arms around me, his cheek on the top of my head as he rocked me gently back and forth. "It's okay. *Shh, shh, shh,*" he cooed, as if trying to comfort a child. And maybe he was. The part of me that hurt worst of all was my inner child, the one who'd mistakenly loved the caretaker who had been hurting me all along.

"It's okay," he whispered.

I stilled against his now-wet shirt, sinking into him as he continued to rock me.

"Why didn't he pull out your animal?" he murmured.

"His power felt gross. I didn't want him to do it. He . . . he wasn't you."

He kissed my head. "It's time for you to meet your animal, Little Wolf."

I blinked away my tears and looked up at him. "How do you know it's a wolf?"

His answering gaze was open all the way down to his soul. "I just know, baby. We'll work on actually shifting after we get your situation at the castle sorted out. You're not going to wait any longer to feel your magic, though."

His power reached down into me, familiar and tantalizing. I closed my eyes as the lava seeped into my middle. I sucked in a breath as power coursed through my veins. I blinked at the feeling of another being stretching into my skin.

My senses were immediately overloaded, his scent going from mouthwatering to utterly devastating, making me salivate. My vision crystalized, the image of his face clearer than I could have imagined as I noticed little flecks of green dotted within his slate-gray eyes. His touch felt so natural, so necessary, so primal, like there was no one else in the world that could feel this perfect under my palms.

"Mate," a voice within me said, its recognition evident. The lava within me throbbed in time with the word.

I clutched him, dragging his head down so that I could

connect my lips to his. His tongue swiped through my mouth as a pounding need to mate with him stole my breath. It was stronger than the chemistry we'd always felt between us, stronger than the previous pull, stronger than any drug that existed in the world. He was life, and I needed to taste it, to feel it, to bond with it.

"I need him," the voice within me said even as I said, "Hurry!" I ripped at his belt. "I need you inside me. Gods, hurry!"

His pack was still behind him, sitting on their horses or standing in line, watching the display. I'd never so much as been nude in front of them, having always been bashful and covered up.

I didn't fucking care right now.

I didn't care that he was stripping me out of my pants and feeling along my wet pussy. I widened my legs, dragging him with me so I could lean against a tree trunk, moaning when he plunged those fingers into my depths.

"I need you, Weston," I groaned, sliding my hand along his hard length. "Fuck me. Fuck me hard."

I was so wet his fingers squelched; I was dripping for him. His thumb made circles around my clit, and then he shoved me down to my knees, quickly feeding me his cock. I sucked it in greedily, running my tongue over the crown and taking it all down deep until his balls slapped against my chin. I hollowed my cheeks with suction as I pulled off before sucking him deep again, over and over.

"I need this done quick so that I can go slow," he labored out, holding my hair with one big fist as he looked down on me.

I didn't need a reason. He tasted like fucking candy and felt like delicious sin.

I watched that handsome face as my head bobbed on his cock. His gaze was heavy and wicked, his pupils blown wide with raw need. I felt up into his shirt with one hand, running my fingers over his rippled muscles.

He let go of me and yanked his shirt off, exposing that perfectly cut torso dappled in sunshine.

I moaned on his cock as he fucked my face, his movements ever faster.

"I'm going to come," he warned. Then he tensed, grunting through his release.

I sucked it all down. I'd never be able to suffer giving anyone else head, not when he tasted and felt so damn good.

He pulled me up to standing, peeling me out of the rest of my clothes as I rose.

"Mine," he growled as he picked me up, wrapping my legs around his waist. The creature within me writhed in glory hearing him say that. He leaned me back against the tree, rubbed his cock head against my opening, and then stilled. He looked into my eyes and growled, *"Mine,"* then thrust his hips, filling me in one motion.

His animal moved within him. I felt it, like it was rising to the surface. My animal was right there, too; I could feel her continuing to stretch within me, as natural as breathing air.

"I feel her," I said in excitement. "I feel her, Weston. I have magic!"

"You have a lot of magic, baby," he murmured, seated within me, holding himself there. "I hate that I had to keep it from you for so long."

"They will pay for that," the voice inside of me said ominously, and I knew she was talking about him and his wolf. *"But later. Right now, I need to connect with my mate."*

I grimaced inwardly at her use of the term *mate*. That was . . . awkward. She'd clearly gotten the wrong idea about things.

We could deal with that later, too.

I fell into his kiss as the two animals prowled within us. They felt like two halves of a whole. He pulled out and then thrust again, his body fitting so perfectly, so erotically against mine.

"Touch yourself," he murmured against my lips. "Play with your clit while I fuck you."

I reached between us, letting my head fall back and closing my eyes.

"You should send on your people," I said, breathless from his next thrust. "This has to be awkward for them."

"I want them to watch me fuck what is *mine*." His tone was possessive and fierce, and delicious goosebumps broke out across my flesh as my animal basked in delight.

I went with it, circling my hips in time to his movements, working my clit so that I built quickly.

"Mmm, yes, Weston," I said as I felt his knot butting against me. We didn't have time for him to lock me, and I'd probably be incredibly embarrassed when I thought back on this, but I wanted it. My animal needed it. His animal was desperate to give it—I could feel it. "Yes, give it to me. Give me that big knot, Alpha."

He did, slamming me against the tree, shoving his cock deep into my slick pussy. His wolf stretched out toward me, and my animal reciprocated, the feeling almost like they were reaching through our chests toward each other.

"Can't . . . stop . . . them," he said, panting with effort.

I didn't know why he'd want to. It felt amazing.

He pushed against me. The rough bark scratched my back.

I worked with his rhythm, was consumed by his kiss. I had just enough sense to wonder why he felt so fucking natural, like his body was built specifically for mine. Somehow, this time was different than before. It felt better, more decadent. It just felt so . . . *right.*

"Tell me how bad you want it," Weston commanded, holding himself deep. "Tell me how badly you want your alpha's thick cock."

"Please, Weston. Alpha," I groaned, bucking on him while massaging my clit. "Please, fuck me. Mark me."

He reached between us, taking over for me and massaging while twisting just right. His lips grazed my shoulder, and I shivered in delight as he worked them up to my neck. His bite made me groan and clutch him even tighter. The animals surged toward each other, pulling us with them, swirling together as he filled me with his size. Power flowed from him into me, like a pathway had suddenly opened between us, connecting us. The power then flowed back into him, a give and take. A union.

"What's . . .?" My mouth dropped open, unable to finish the question as the incredible sensations washed back and forth between him and me, between his animal and mine, between all of us.

He held me tightly to him, locking us together, on full display in front of his pack. My animal preened, and his was full of smug pride.

His finger moved faster. I rocked and twisted, pinned against the tree, just on the verge—

The explosion ripped a scream from my lips. He was right behind me, groaning, his ecstasy flowing through that pathway and making my high ten times better.

I shook against his delicious body. "What happened? What is that feeling?"

"A four-way bond," my animal answered. It was like she was circling his wolf. *"I need to shift. I need to feel that wolf."*

"Gross. No. We can't anyway. We have to have help. It's dangerous."

"It's instinctive. I'm not afraid."

"His dick is literally still locked within me. Even if we knew how and wanted to, we couldn't shift right now. Can we just . . . take a moment? What is a four-way bond?"

I could feel my animal's growl, which was kind of a trip. I could also feel her annoyance. Having magic was going to take a little getting used to.

"We are connected to our mate," she answered, and I was suddenly unsure if she really *knew* the answer. It was clear her thoughts were primal, innate. It seemed I was to be the logical one in our pairing.

Weston was still holding me against the tree, but he'd leaned back a little so that he could look down upon my face.

"What's a four-way bond?" I asked him.

"It's a connection between your wolf and mine, and you and me. The wolves initiated it. I wasn't able to stop it. Our wolves are powerful, and we were swept up in their moment."

"Wait." I tried to lean back, but the tree prevented me. I put a hand to his chest, pushing him away a little. He took a step back, and his cock yanked against me before throbbing within.

I groaned in pleasure. I couldn't help it.

"Wait," I said, breathing heavily as he sat down with me now on his lap. "Wait, wait."

I rubbed my hand across my slick forehead as the throbbing intensified. I gyrated against it without meaning to, another orgasm already building. They were never far away when Weston and I ended up like this.

"This thing that I'm feeling . . ." I motioned between his chest and mine. Wariness leaked in through that pathway we'd just created. "Wait, am I feeling your actual emotions?"

"Yes."

"And you're feeling mine?"

"Yes. And our animals are feeling each other's."

I shook my head in confusion. "When does it go away? When you release me?"

The wariness intensified. "It doesn't. A four-way bond is permanent."

8

AURELIA

I laughed. "No, no." I shook my head. "Wait, wait. *What?*"

"This type of bond is permanent. It's nearly impossible to deny it if the wolves want it."

"We don't even know if I'm a wolf."

"In order to have a bond like this, a four-way bond, you'd have to be a wolf."

"Well, that's . . . just fucking crazy." I looked at his expression for some hint that this was a joke. "Weston, that's nuts. We can't have a permanent bond. I—"

It was really bad fucking timing for an orgasm to tear through me, but I was powerless against it. "Mmm, Weston," I said, shaking against him. His fingers dug into my hips as I writhed. It took me a few seconds after the high abated to gather my thoughts.

"Damn it. No, hold on—this has to be some kind of a joke. You don't want this. I definitely do not want this. I'm a criminal, for crapssakes! I'm headed for the prison."

He stilled and growled out, "You will not go to the dungeon."

"Wherever I go, we can't . . ." I moved my finger between our chests. "We can't do this. I'm right in the middle of a very dark time in my life, and that is saying something because—well, you know my history. You'll be miserable!"

"I can help you through it. It's my duty as . . ." His jaw tightened. "As your bond member."

"But . . ." I shook my head again and forced out a laugh, hoping someone would start laughing with me and share in this ridiculous joke. "Weston . . ." I put my hands on his shoulders. "I have no words for how crazy this is. You can't shackle yourself to me forever. You're a powerful alpha. I mean, what happens when we meet other people? How will this work?"

He ground deep inside me, and I gasped. "You won't be meeting anyone else. No one else will touch you. Ever. You're mine." His vicious growl was back, making me shiver in annoyed ecstasy. I moaned, and he pulled me in close. He nuzzled my ear and asked, "How do you want to get back, awkwardly on a horse or in the back of a cart? I doubt I'll be releasing you anytime soon. Our wolves want the connection."

"Our wolves can fuck off, that's what our wolves can do. What the fuck—" I stared hard at him. "This is really fucking awkward, being stuck with you right now when all I want is to kick you and your damn wolf in the balls. I'll tell you what, I'm not yours, someone else *will* be touching me, I won't be trapped in this bond, and I have my own duties to tend to. I need to render Granny's coating ineffective."

"They are ours and we are theirs," my wolf said. *"They are our mate. Can't you feel it?"*

"You are brand new in this world and you've already created

a mess. No, I cannot feel it, and more importantly, him being our mate is impossible. I'll explain another time."

"Cart it is." Weston tightened my legs around his waist before he stood. "Hadriel, gather up our clothes. For anything that's ripped, go to the supply cart and get a replacement. We'll be riding near the back. Clear people out. Aurelia is going to have some angry orgasms, and she's already getting a little bashful."

"Don't worry, my darling." Hadriel winked at me as he hurried past to grab our clothes. "We've all been there."

"I don't think I have ever been laid that well, actually," Nova said thoughtfully.

"Oh, definitely not. That was clearly something amazing," Hadriel replied. "I just meant fucking in front of people."

"Speak for yourself," someone said.

"I was."

"Do any of them have a four-way bond?" I asked as Weston carried me away.

"No. It's a rare bond. And before you ask, yes, I knew of the possibility our animals would push for a bond, but I thought I could thwart it. No way did I think they could be this strong. I wasn't prepared. I've known of the possibility since I met you, but because of our situation, and because you wouldn't have understood given your past, I didn't mention it. I'll go over it more tomorrow, after I speak with the royals, and hopefully things will make more sense."

Hadriel opened the cart for us and spread out a blanket. Weston sat with me on his lap, his arms wrapped around me, keeping me put. Even now, as annoyed and frustrated as I was, his strength wrapped around me felt so fucking good. My wolf and his continued to flow power back and forth, and it felt like a piece of them was sent and received in each interaction.

"Enjoy." Hadriel closed the back and walked away, leaving us to ourselves.

"How is this going to work for you?" I asked as our caravan got underway.

Weston traced the line of my jaw with his knuckles and then dropped his hand to run his thumb over my nipple.

I batted his hand away, feeling a spark of passion when I did. His grin said he felt it.

My inability to hide things from him was going to get old really fast.

He dropped his hand further still, his eyes searching my face as he brushed his thumb against my clit.

"This thing between us has always been hell for me. It still is," he murmured, sliding his other hand across my hip and pulling. The movement shifted his cock inside me. His thumb stroked, and pleasure coursed through my body. I could barely focus on his words through the exquisite sensations. "It won't get easier for a while, either. The royals aren't going to give me much leeway, even with the bond. I intend to figure it out. I *will* keep other males from touching you. Your wolf has made her choice. You're mine now."

The shiver of raw lust that coursed through me at his words, at his possessive growl, made me gasp.

Damn it, why did I like hearing those things so much?

"I'm no one's," I said defiantly.

His grin was smug. "We'll see."

His thumb kept stroking. The cart bounced, jostling us, creating a delicious friction. I basked in the pleasure and leaned harder against him. Some things couldn't be resisted.

"I'm really angry that my first day with magic has me in this position," I grumbled.

"In this position?" he asked, leaning me back so that he could lick my nipple before sucking it in. "You mean properly fucked?"

I rolled my eyes . . . but didn't push him away. He'd be able to feel how damn good that felt.

"What's going to happen when they sentence me to death?" I asked quietly as I rolled my hips.

He stilled and then caressed my neck, sliding his hand around to the back and holding me in place. He leaned forward, running his lips along my skin.

"I won't let anyone harm you, Little Wolf. If it comes to that, I'll secret you away and suffer the consequences. Handling the pain myself will be a blessing if it means you won't have to endure it."

Even though I could never allow him to take the fall for something I'd done, it was hard to be angry when he said things like that.

I closed my eyes so I wouldn't see people along the lane or working in the Everlass fields while I gyrated on top of him and just took the orgasms as they came. There wasn't much else I could do for the time being. I'd deal with my future, my reception at the castle, when it came.

"I really could've walked," I said with my arms wrapped around Weston's middle and my cheek resting against his shoulder, fully dressed and sitting behind him on his horse.

"You probably should've walked. Or at least stayed in the cart." He looked out to the side, paying no mind to the traffic on the road as we meandered through the wood. People watched him pass with fondness and respect; it showed in the smiles on their faces or stars in their eyes. It was clear he was important here.

This road must've been some sort of thoroughfare. It was wide enough for two carts to pass, and there were enough people moving along it to suggest travel between towns or cities, none of which I could see from this point. We passed various other roads or lanes leading from this one, some with signs and some just single dirt lanes.

"It's going to muddy the waters with your being taken in like this," Weston murmured.

I didn't ask why he allowed it. I knew the answer: our animals craved the closeness, and it was almost physically painful to deny them. I should've been the stronger one and forced the distance for the sake of my situation, but in all honesty, I didn't want to. So, here we were.

"How do you feel?" he asked as my vision slowly altered, going from kind of normal, if a lot more detailed and vivid than pre-magic, to a strange sort of lightness—I was able to see in the dark, but in shades of blues with tinges of greens.

I shrugged because I really didn't know how to answer that. I felt . . . fine. Normal. I had power and I knew it. I was almost certainly faster and likely stronger than before, but I didn't have any proof. I felt my animal pulsing inside of me, a comforting kind of hum as she basked in Weston's wolf's proximity, but otherwise I just . . . felt like me.

"How is it going with your wolf?" he asked, and I found myself wishing I knew more about this four-way bond that made him so sure she was a wolf.

"She seems sort of headstrong."

"The more powerful animals tend to be. Once a wolf settles into a pack, he or she usually calms down."

"And I'll be able to do that? Settle into a pack? At least for a little while, maybe, until the dragons decide my fate."

His power pulsed and his wolf did the equivalent of pacing. It was such a trip that I could feel that! That I knew what it meant!

"Please stop mentioning that," he ground out.

"Sorry," I whispered, watching the people we passed. Most of them wore well-made clothes in fine fabrics. Nobility, maybe? That, or this kingdom had money at its disposal and the people prospered because of it. Even the small, out-of-the-way village had seemed well taken care of: well fed, well dressed, everyone groomed. My village must have seemed poor and shabby when they invaded. We certainly hadn't had any of this finery.

"In answer to your question, I don't know." He glanced at a woman on the road, a pretty lady with a gorgeous dress and long, flowing hair. She waved at him, her face lit up in delight. It was clear she knew him. Intimately, if I had to guess.

An uncomfortable tightness squeezed my chest. My wolf coiled within me, teeth bared.

I looked away. *Maintain logic, maintain logic,* I said inwardly. His personal life had nothing to do with me. He was home now; he had to resume his life regardless of what our animals were doing.

He dropped his hand to my thigh, rubbing supportively. He'd felt my jealousy through the bond and was offering comfort. My heart swelled, and I tightened my arms around him a little more. It was a small gesture, but until I could figure out all these primal urges, it was welcomed.

"What are the complications of my joining a pack?" I asked, seeing another woman light up. This one looked more hopeful. My guess was she didn't know him well but wanted to. I put my forehead against the center of his back and closed my eyes. It was probably time to go ride with Hadriel.

"Your power and our bond. I can easily dominate most wolves. They fall in line. Yours . . ."

"You can easily dominate me."

"Physically, yes." A rush of desire surged through the bond from all four of us. Weston took my hand and slipped it under his shirt, my palm on his warm skin. I started tracing his muscles absently, eyes still closed so that I didn't see anyone else look at him like their next meal. "Magically, likely not. I've never heard of an alpha pair who were—" He swallowed. "Who shared a four-way bond. I don't honestly know how it works, and I can't have you jeopardizing the safety of the pack."

"I would never do that," I said in a rush of anger. "I would never put other people's safety at risk for my own benefit." I paused. "Aside from that issue with the drugs, obviously." I sighed and turned my head so my cheek rested against his back. "Kind of a black mark on my character, that."

"Granny's addition is hurting people, not your product."

I scoffed. "Agree to disagree."

"We can't afford to agree to disagree on that, Aurelia. You can't own the story that you're hurting people, not if you want an escape from the dragons' wrath."

"All due respect, Alpha, but this isn't your life. I know it'll affect you now, but you and your animal really should've thought of that before you pushed all of us into a bond. You should've thought of your pack, too. I will travel my journey, come what may. I will not make light of what—"

I'd opened my eyes to stare at the back of his neck in frustration when, out of the corner of my vision, a throb of pink glowed. Not a lighter blue, not a heavier green, but pink!

"Oh gods!" I swung my focus right, ignoring the people on the road looking at me in confusion at my outburst. The swell of pink increased, localized to a little area beyond the trees and nestled within taller plants I couldn't really make out in the strange blue of my new nighttime vision. "Oh my—"

I scrambled off the back of the horse, easily dodging Weston's attempt to twist and grab me. The horse grunted and kicked, its hoof nearly clipping my side. I ducked around it, in between people, in front of a donkey pulling a cart, and practically dove into the bushes. The pink glow continued to swell, growing in both size and strength as I got closer to it.

My heart thundered, and I knew my grin was crazed, but I couldn't help it. I trampled through the plants—fuck, Everlass grew everywhere—and then slowed as I came up on the flower in question. Its swell of light hit a crescendo, the pink so beautiful within the hues of blue in my vision, the image soft and serene.

Weston stepped in behind me, trying to be careful where he placed his feet, and reached for my arm. I evaded his grasp easily, moving around the Moonfire Lily.

"You can't be walking through here," he told me, trying to follow. "You'll ruin the plants."

"Seriously, the Everlass is like a weed. It's commonplace here. It'll choke the whole forest at this rate. This flower, though. Do you know what this is?" I pointed down at it. "This enhanced my product like nothing else ever has. Just one petal boosted the effectiveness. Just *one*! It must be useful in other ways, but it's always been so hard to find." My mind was racing. "I wonder if that's why it is called the Moonfire Lily—it keeps the pink in our vision even when everything else is blues and greens." I just about squealed with excitement. "It'll be *so* much easier to find this way."

"You need to stop trampling the Everlass. The dragons do not take kindly to people mucking up their plants."

"No, what we need to do is . . ." I grimaced as I looked around. "We really should take it with us. By the roots, I mean. I want to rehome it. I don't want to leave it here and have the dragons come through and squash it or pick it thinking it is invading their weeds."

I bent down to look more closely as it went dark. It didn't have anything over the top of it and grew in what looked like a pathway between the Everlass. It was easy to get to.

"I just need a shovel. I can hold it in the cart if we don't have a bucket." I glanced up at Weston and saw that he was watching me with a blank expression. Warmth slid through the bond, though. Humor. "What?"

He shook his head. "You do remember that you're a captive, right?"

"Yes, but seriously, your queen is going to want this plant. There is hardly anything written in books about it. It's a ghost, this flower. And look, here it is, growing right among the dragon weed!"

Now his expression was bewildered. "Who cares about Granny's drugs? You're going to get yourself killed with that mouth. You cannot keep calling it that." He shook his head, turning to his pack and calling out, "Bring a shovel and a bucket. We're taking a plant as a prize."

We waited for Dante to climb down from his horse and bring us the items found by the pack member digging through the carts.

"I took the petals from your work shed," Weston told me, carefully removing me to a "safe area" just outside of the Everlass. "You'll have those, if they're still good."

I gasped. "You did? Why? To analyze?"

"Mostly, yes, but also because they were pretty. I'm not sure if they're still good at this point."

I shrugged. "I don't know. I've never let it sit this long. But this way we'll have an actual plant. Assuming the rehoming goes okay and I can get it to grow."

"If anyone can, it will be the palace garden keepers. I've seen your flowers. You should turn it over to them."

It didn't show on his face, but I could feel his humor. I narrowed my eyes at him and laughed when he hooked his hand on my hip to drag me closer.

"Okay, it's true, I'm not very good at growing things. This one doesn't like growing in the open, either. I half wonder if other plants should be put around it so that it's happy."

"I have no idea. All that stuff is over my head. You can mention it to the queen."

"I'm a captive, remember? I doubt she'll want to talk about plants with me."

"On the contrary. That'll be one of the main things she'll want to talk about."

9

AURELIA

We rolled down the road through the trees and toward the palace entrance after full night had fallen. Dante and Sixten were able to get the Moonfire Lily carefully loaded into a bucket, staring at it in amazement for a long moment before tucking it away. They'd never seen anything like it, even though they had to have come across it once or twice in their lives. They probably just hadn't noticed. It was easy to ignore.

A large and imposing castle came into view as Weston's horse exited the wood and entered the palace grounds. It was lit up from the inside and stretched an impossible distance to either side. Wrapped around it were lawns so well maintained that their lushness was evident even at night. Spires reached into the sky and huge dragons circled, one opening its maw and spitting fire into the darkness. Arches curved over a great entrance with wide stairs leading down.

Granted, it was the first castle I'd ever seen, but it was still extraordinary, grand and noble.

Nervousness dried up the words in my mouth, the

looming structure intimidating, the circling dragons even more so. Suddenly, I wasn't at all sure this was the right place for me, especially as a prisoner.

Weston directed his people every which way; some to take in the supplies, some to take the horses, some to follow him into the castle. He let me down first, and his horse bent his head around to glare at me. It was probably happy to be done with me.

Weston hopped off next and stood beside me, watching everyone follow his commands. He reached to hook a hand on my hip like he had near the Everlass but paused halfway, his body tensing, his emotions in turmoil.

"It's okay. I'm a captive, remember?" I said softly, taking a step away. My wolf grumbled at the distance. "Starting now, we're not traveling anymore. You need to settle back into your life, and I need to find a new normal. Time to get to work."

He stepped with me, facing me, bending down into my space to look me in the eye. "You are a captive *at present.* Your new normal will be settling into my life just as soon as I can arrange it. You are mine—don't forget that."

Despite the shivers of desire, I couldn't help thinking that his wolf was riding him a little too hard. The humans were clearly supposed to be the logical ones in the pair, and he was failing. Still, I didn't comment. It wouldn't have done any good, not with the way his wolf was pacing in growly frustration.

"You are to be on your best behavior," he went on. "Do not give the dragons any cause to punish you, do you understand? Mind your business and answer only direct questions. They are a prickly sort of shifter, prone to challenging. Don't engage."

"Okay."

He held my gaze for a long moment, the raw intensity prickling my skin.

"Okay," I repeated. This was overkill. Did he forget the village I'd come from? We were all very good at keeping our head down to avoid punishment. There, I hadn't deserved it. Here, I did. I knew the difference. Not to mention, it was so much easier going with the flow.

"If you need help, you contact me. You tell someone to get me, is that clear? If you are challenged *by anyone*, you submit quickly and find someone to get me. Do *not* engage."

"I said okay," I replied as my wolf said, *"Fat fucking chance."*

"We don't know how to fight," I told her.

"You know that I have access to all your memories, right? What you know, I know. What you've clearly forgotten, I haven't. You took a knife to Alexander's wolf when you hadn't yet been trained in knife work. Now you'll be faster, stronger, and better. If someone challenges, we'll stab them with whatever is handy and we'll make it permanent. We do not *submit. That ends now."*

Weston's brow knitted, and I could feel his wolf buzzing with pride.

"I'm really gonna try," I said with an apologetic shrug.

Weston's sigh was barely perceptible. "I need to speak to the royals, and I'm sure they will want to question you. The questioning will almost certainly happen tomorrow. After that, and before . . . whatever comes next, I will walk you through shifting. Please, for your own safety, wait until then."

I lifted my eyebrows, waiting for the voice inside my head to respond.

"Promise me," Weston growled, and I knew it wasn't me he was speaking to.

"Fine," my wolf murmured. I nodded.

He reciprocated my nod and then stepped away. "Hadriel, put her . . ." He stalled.

"How about the lovely little oasis known as the tower?" Hadriel was at my side in a moment, and I could feel a strange sort of warmth emanating from him. "We can lock her in, to prove she is a captive, but it'll at least be comfortable. After we get all this straightened out, we can find something less . . . serious."

Weston's nod was stiff. He about-faced and walked into the castle as everyone else departed along a sort of lane, probably toward the stables.

"What about my flower?" I asked, not yet having taken a step.

"I'll . . . " Hadriel looked around. "I'll check in and make sure it goes out to the gardens. I'll tell them to wait for you before they plant it, how's that? We can get you some lovely books and other boring shit, and you can learn all about what environment is best for them."

I nodded. It was probably my best bet.

"Okay, then." Hadriel winked at me before hooking his arm through mine and guiding me toward the entrance. "This is great. The last time I had to look after someone in that tower, I worried she'd stab me or hurt me in some way. You're much more civilized."

"I don't think my wolf would agree."

"Oh, she's fine. The animals we turn into all come out super primal. It takes a second for the wolf to acclimate to the human world and for the human to acclimate to a more primal set of feelings and emotions. Usually, we have to battle this as we go through puberty, with all the hormones and insanity rolling around. You'll probably have a much easier time of it. Here we are."

He motioned for two men to open the grand front door

and I couldn't help the small *"Whoa"* that escaped as I took in the interior. The grand foyer had huge ceilings that went up into the heavens and a wide, sweeping stairway descended to the center of the main floor. Stone and crystal glimmered and shone everywhere. It was gorgeous and decadent, and there was no way I belonged here.

I tried to scoot back out the door. "Is there a servants' entrance or something I should be taking?"

He slapped my hands away from plucking at my drab brown clothes. "Don't be absurd. Not that long ago, people were running around with big purple dicks strapped to their person. Cocks and vadge everywhere. No one is going to bat an eye with your drab *chic* attire. Come on, up this way."

"I don't think there is anything *chic* about it."

"It's fun to pretend. Come on."

The servants all wore a similar sort of attire, a regal red-and-gold shirt with a high collar and black slacks with black shoes. They didn't hurry but they didn't dally, most of them walking straight and tall like they were the most important people in the world.

"Hadriel, you're back," someone said as they made their way down the hall toward the stairs. He was a weaselly character with a wispy combover. "We missed your little prick around here. We had no one to laugh at."

"I've heard what you've been saying about me, Liron." Hadriel waggled his finger at the other man. "Not wise for a guy who doesn't know which hole he should stick his dick into. People don't laugh at you because they are too busy groaning you showed up at all. You ruin every party you attend."

"Eat lint."

"Lick a mushroom."

I could feel my eyes widening at the exchange, loud and

public and clearly antagonistic but not in an overly threatening way. This sort of behavior lined up exceptionally well with the sorts of stories Hadriel was always telling.

Liron stalled when he noticed me, stopping to stare. "Who's this?"

I recoiled, not wanting to be sucked into whatever was going on with them. I was definitely not on this level. I would listen and laugh at the stories, but I was not even remotely comfortable enough to engage.

"Don't you worry about it," Hadriel replied. "And don't think for one second she'll appreciate your advances. She's taken."

"By whom? You?"

"By Nonya."

"Who's Nonya?"

"Nonya fucking business, jackass. Be on your way. There's got to be a set of stone balls for you to dust around here." Hadriel guided me up the first few stairs.

"Hello, lovely lady," Liron called after us. "You just let us know if you want an actual good time, not what that idiot calls fun."

"Says the king of cornholing women," Hadriel shot back. "Do us all a favor and fall down the stairs."

"You first," Liron said.

I barked out a laugh before quickly covering my mouth.

"Don't mind him." We reached the second-floor landing and continued up the next set of stairs. "He's left over from the curse days. He is an *ab*-solute disaster. He kicked me out of an art class because I did watercolors of dicks. The literal worst. If we ever get an orgy together in the woods, we have to be very careful not to let him know, or he shows up with dick in hand and no idea what to do with it. It's no wonder the dipshit hasn't procreated."

"His stories didn't do that exchange justice," my wolf said, and I was a little too bewildered to agree.

"Speaking of group activities, on a scale of one to ten, how embarrassed are you that you banged the beta in front of an audience?" Hadriel asked as we walked up the next flight of stairs.

I grimaced. "I hadn't actually thought about it."

"Good. Don't. It was insanely hot. So you have a four-way bond now, huh? That happened?"

I clutched his arm, intensely curious about it and hoping he'd give me answers. "Yes. Why is it so rare?"

"He didn't tell you?"

"He said I wouldn't understand. Is this yet another thing he's keeping from me?"

Hadriel trudged up the last of the stairs and started down a long hall. "It's true you wouldn't understand. This affects him more so than you, I think, so maybe cut him a little slack. Now that your wolf is out—or not suppressed, at least—it'll probably be easier to explain."

I furrowed my brow as a middle-aged woman came toward us. Her hair was cut into a short gray bob, and, upon seeing me, she veered in my direction until she stopped in front of me.

"Hadriel, welcome back. Any news?" She lifted her eyebrows, clearly asking about me.

"Lena, meet Aurelia. She's who we captured regarding Granny's drug ring, but isn't actually the person we needed to have captured."

I curled my lips inward to keep from arguing. It wouldn't do any good right now.

"It's complicated," he said. "Anyway, she's a special sort of prisoner. The beta's people can better explain. She won't be staying in the dungeons. For now, I will take her to the tower and get her locked in. She'll need food and a bath. I can organize both."

Lena lifted a single eyebrow. "Reprising your role of butler?"

"No, the role of taking care of the captive. The situation is very similar to the queen's when she was in that room, but with a much more willing partner." He looked around for a moment and then leaned toward her, speaking out of the side of his mouth. "And lady, that man can hold his knot. Holy shit!" He leaned back, fanning his face. "We timed this last one. Four-way bond, two hours after climax."

Her eyes widened a little before she took me in, noticing my (suddenly crimson) face first and then my clothes. I tried to shrink away from her assessment.

"You create the drugs?" she finally asked me.

Hadriel put his hand on her shoulder. "It's complicated, trust me. It's a whole big thing. I'll explain later. I'm tired and I'm hungry, and I need to deal with a very pretty glowing flower. Oh, and you'll never believe how she refers to the Everlass! I about died."

He patted her arm and then guided me around her, even though it had been clear she wasn't finished.

"She's the head housemaid," he told me. "She was the one always walking around with that big purple dildo I talked about, strapped to her person. She loves pegging."

I had no idea what that was, and I didn't plan to ask. I was having a hard time not being intensely uncomfortable with such loose exchanges. The pack on the road hadn't been nearly this . . . outgoing.

"Here we go." He led me up a narrow set of stairs. "Oh, the memories. I'm sober this time, though. There's a big change. Maybe I'll rectify that tonight."

He reached a lonely door at the top, the only room on this level. It was a genuine tower.

"I don't have hair long enough to turn this into a fairytale," I murmured as he opened the door and walked into the room.

"Fairytales are for losers." Hadriel crossed to the windows at the far side and shoved open the curtains. "It's a lovely view, actually. The queen mother's garden is right below us. That's the mother of the king. I helped restore it. It's gorgeous. You can see the grounds and the wood—it's great. Tomorrow morning we'll take a trip to the library. Now, in here—" He paused in a doorway at the back. "What's the matter?"

I still stood in the entrance to the room, my jaw slack as I took in all the very large and extravagant furniture. The space was three times as big as the front room in my cottage, and held a huge, plush bed, a giant armoire, and a few chests.

"Who needs so much stuff?" I asked, not wanting to touch anything. "I'm too dirty for this nice place."

"Sweetie." Hadriel clasped his hands and tilted his head. "I know you loved your cottage, but it sounds like a shithole. We're in a literal tower where you are being imprisoned. This furniture was put in here when the king was young. It's old as fuck. The washroom hasn't even been updated. Do not worry about dirtying anything. Now, we need to get you a bath. I can smell the beta leaking out of you. That wolf is a power shooter, gods help you. He could probably flood a valley with all that cum."

I felt my face heat again. He was right: our combined climaxes were running down my inner thigh, the sensation a reminder of how much Weston had put into me and held there as I rocked against him in that cart.

"We do at least have taps now, so that's something,"

Hadriel muttered as a woman came up the stairs behind me. I still hadn't entered the room.

She had curly blond hair and bright blue eyes, and looked to be somewhere in her late twenties, maybe early thirties. She wore a burgundy top and black slacks in the same style as the rest of the house. I wondered what the different colors denoted.

I stepped out of the way, and she hesitated, slowly unhooking what looked like a whip from a belt wrapped around her waist.

"Hadriel," I called out, staying against the wall. "There is a woman with a whip out here. She seems like she spooks easily. I'm not supposed to get in any altercations."

The woman stopped and held up her free hand. "I'd rather not use the whip."

"That makes two of us. I don't much like them."

"Oh no?" She hesitated in continuing to unhook it. "Not into pain, huh?"

I frowned at her. "Not . . . really, no."

"Hmm." She nodded. "Pity. You're very pretty. Petite and delicate. You'd be a sexy sub. How about randomly attacking strangers? I see you've been left out here on your own. Are you not a flight risk, or is Hadriel drunk?"

I blinked at her for a long moment. She was yet another one with a very sexually open way of speaking. I'd gotten used to Hadriel—it was easier because he was so over-the-top about everything—but the calm, collected way the others spoke such bold things . . . I suddenly felt very prudish.

"I'm not a flight risk, no," I finally said. "To start, I've chosen to be here, but also . . . Well, honestly, I have nowhere else to go."

I stopped there. I wasn't going to tell her about the reward for my capture or what would befall me if Granny recovered me. If this woman needed the information, Hadriel or someone else would give it to her. Otherwise, I assumed Weston would want to navigate who knew what and when.

"That whip wouldn't even faze her, Leala." Hadriel appeared at the doorway with his arms crossed. He'd clearly been listening. "I bet you wouldn't even hit her, actually. You have no idea how fast she is now that she has access to her wolf. She went to pick some flowers, and she moved so fast she almost blurred."

"Just so we're all speaking the same language," I interjected, unsure if this woman was at all like that Liron character who had hole confusion, "I'd really prefer you didn't whip me."

The woman, Leala, hooked the whip back onto her belt. "The beta requested someone attend to *his* captive, and since no other lady's maids are readily equipped to handle violence, I volunteered."

"What about the queen?" Hadriel gave me an sidelong look. "She's the queen's head lady's maid. Very prestigious role. She was assigned to the queen in this very room—before she was queen, obviously. We've had a lot of very experienced people travel to the kingdom to take the position, and none of them have been able to. My girl here is fire."

Leala rolled her eyes as she ushered me into the washroom. "The queen is loyal. There are others better at the job than I am."

"Those others wouldn't march into a demon dungeon for their employer."

"Which is why the queen is loyal. Come on now, miss, let's get you a bath. My goodness, the beta has left his scent all over you."

"As well he should." My wolf preened.

I ignored her.

"I'm not a miss," I said as I let Leala manhandle me into a corner and get the bath ready for me. She seemed very nice and lovely but also had a very firm way about her. "Honestly, I can do it."

"She is as calm and balanced as the beta." Hadriel picked some dirt out of his nails. "It's been an absolute dream. I don't know what I'm going to do with the dragons."

"Annoy them and get picked on, probably." Leala wasted no time in stripping me and settling me into the bath. Resisting would've been futile, though I was sure my face was flaming with Hadriel still in the room. I might've lost my senses and fucked Weston in front of everyone, but I still wasn't comfortable stripping down with an audience. Leala turned to Hadriel and asked, "What are we doing for clothes?"

"We have some of her drab *chic* attire, or she can wear some of my clothes until we figure out what to do with her. She thinks the dick jackets are funny. We bonded over them."

She smiled. "I love that."

I lifted my eyebrows, opening my mouth to interject again. Those dick jackets were definitely funny, but I wasn't sure I was the right one to pull one off. What if someone like Liron thought it was an invite for more crass language? Or if the head maid thought I might want to try on a purple dick for size? But before I could mention that my drab attire might help me disappear a little better, the conversation had rolled on without me.

"You're going to love her," Hadriel said. "Hopefully she won't be put to death, or we'll all be very sad."

Leala tsked. "Don't be a dick. That isn't going to happen. The royals feel bad about the beta's predicament."

"Aurelia doesn't. She keeps doubling down about how

terrible she is and how many people she's hurt and how she single-handedly created Granny's empire."

"I'm not quite that—"

Leala cut me off. "Well, if that comes to pass, we'll get drunk and reminisce about the good old times, of which we'll hopefully have many by then." She gave me an encouraging smile.

"Hear, hear." Hadriel raised his hand before looking at it. "Damn it, that would've been better if I'd had a drink. Aurelia, my darling, Leala will take great care of you. Tomorrow morning I'll pick you up early and we'll head to the library, okay? I'm going to go order you dinner and find myself a big bottle of wine." He sighed contentedly. "It's good to be home."

Later that night, after I was cleaned and fed and lay in the most comfortable bed I'd ever felt, I stared out the window and thought of my mom. She would never have imagined I'd be in a room so fine. She would be ecstatic that a queen's maid—a dragon queen's maid, no less—had attended me. She'd also be thrilled that I was trapped in a tower in a big castle. Her imagination would be running wild.

My mind didn't, though. I didn't conjure up any stories of princes fighting the dragons and climbing up to save me. The man on my mind had ripped me from my home and put me here. He was the hero in his story, but the villain in mine.

And yet my bed felt empty without him. My body craved his touch. I needed to break this hold he had on me before he broke *me*. His duty was done. Mine had just begun.

10

WESTON

As I entered the throne room, Nyfain, the king—a dragon with an intense aura and golden-eyed stare—said, "Good to have you back. I hear you brought us Granny's prized drugmaker."

Finley, the queen and his mate, sat in the throne next to him on a dais at the head of a long, grand room, smiling in welcome. "How was the journey? Did you have any trouble?"

Where to start . . .

"Hello, Your Highnesses. We were met with a few complications," I said before telling them about the clues we were able to follow, the break we'd gotten from Hadriel sussing out intel via gossip, and the village we had found.

"Wow." Finley sat back, her long brown hair draped around her face, and crossed an ankle over her knee. "The village was way out in the middle of nowhere, huh? Smart. It's not like someone would just wander into it."

I gritted my teeth at how blasé she was in speaking about that horror village. What did I expect, though? They hadn't seen the beating Granny had given her gardener or walked through that hopeless and run-down place. They hadn't looked into the haunted eyes of those villagers and been confused about why no one had bothered to protect their home. They hadn't heard firsthand accounts from Aurelia's life or read about the hard times in her journals.

Fighting off the need to tell them about my status with Aurelia, wanting to wait until they understood the situation a little more, I painted a picture of what I'd seen and what we'd learned. Detail by gritty detail, I made them feel the environment Aurelia and the villagers had survived.

"They weren't just a production village, they were trapped there. They were forced to make the product or risk severe punishments."

"So . . . wait." Finley leaned forward, confusion knitting her brow. "First, sit down, will you? You've got to be tired, and I can see how tense it's made you."

The tension wasn't from fatigue, but yes, I was fucking exhausted. I had hardly slept last night, instead passing the hours holding my mate, listening to her breathe. I'd worried about this meeting, about what would happen when we arrived here.

About what I'd be forced to do to this kingdom to protect her.

I pulled a chair over and sat in front of their thrones, just the three of us in this great room. I'd asked for that specifically and they hadn't questioned it, having always trusted my judgment. I hoped, after this, they still would.

"So . . ." Finley scratched her nose. "I don't understand this. You're saying *one* person made all the product coming out of that . . . production village, you called it? That's what you said, right? Just one person, not several?"

Nervousness rippled through me at how she focused solely on the drugs and seemed to discount the environment Aurelia and the others had lived in. They needed to be viewed hand in hand, or Aurelia would be regarded as an accomplice and not a victim.

"One person made the base of the drugs, yes."

I explained the difference between the villagers versus Granny's workers and patrol. I also mentioned about the village not getting paid, instead getting just enough food and goods brought in. Nyfain leaned back in his throne when I told them how Granny kept them from leaving by essentially holding a child hostage to ensure the parents returned.

"They were more captives than workers," Nyfain said, finally—and thankfully—getting the picture. "That's why you didn't bring us back more than one?"

"It's why I left everyone, save one, in the village, yes," I responded. "I did initially capture some of their patrol, but they were able to escape. I'll get to how in a minute, but they're all dead now. They attacked us farther along the road, and we took them down. It wasn't worth keeping them."

Nyfain dipped his head once, accepting that. Their death was punishment enough.

"Okay, but . . ." Finley held up her hand. "*One* person is making *all* of those drugs? What did you mean about the root? I'm still not understanding this."

"There are two parts to Granny's drugs." I explained the details and what each village did.

"So the person you brought back is the one who'd been making the non-addictive element of this drug," Finley surmised. "The main element of the drug, really."

"Non-addictive and not dangerous. But yes, the main element of the drug."

"And a single person is making all of that?"

"Correct. Granny's people then mash it into a different shape, apply the colorful coating, package it, and send it out for distribution. We found the production village, but not the packaging center."

She shook her head. "You must be mistaken. I'm not questioning the job you've done, Weston. I know you are thorough, but there is simply no way that one person is responsible for the amount of product Granny is pumping into the market. The other place must make a portion of it."

"I brought all the product with me. They're unloading the carts now. It's not pretty, but the quantity checks out. It was kept in a supply shed in the market square. Without a lock."

Nyfain sat forward. "What do you mean, without a lock?"

I explained what we'd found. What I'd seen with my own two eyes.

Nyfain steepled his fingers, and a wave of nerves washed through me. He was excellent at reading people, amazing at guessing motives. He knew there was something I was holding back.

"I was not able to capture Granny or her beta, Alexander. I learned about the second location, the packaging center, after I had the drugmaker, but by then we were trying to rush her out of the kingdom. They were trying to reacquire their prize. We'd nearly lost people as it was. We'll need to go back for the others. Or, more likely, we need to wait until they come for her. I'm confident they will."

I explained about the letter, fighting the rising rage at Granny telling Aurelia that she'd come for her. That had been a direct challenge to me.

"Granny is cunning," I said. "We heard that when we were searching for information near the castle, but seeing it in action . . . We had a well-organized plan of attack that was executed perfectly. Granny had been our main target, but even so, she was able to evade capture and escape. I still don't know how. She got her dog out as well, and later released her captured patrol, all disappearing without a trace. Without a *scent*. She's not as good during face-to-face confrontations—I exceed her there—but when working in the shadows, she is exceptional. She can't be underestimated."

I knew her plans would be complex. Masterful, even. I'd need to overhaul our defenses and ensure there were no holes in coverage. No lapses in our patrol. Our people would need to be operating at optimum levels at all times, not lax, the way we'd allowed them to be in peacetime.

"Why should we bother going back for the others, or even holding Granny's bait?" Finley asked. Nyfain continued to study me silently. "If you're to be believed, and I'm still questioning that, then we have the supply maker. You said yourself we have the root of the problem. If we kill her, we kill the organization. Problem solved."

My rage throbbed, a black weight in my middle. My wolf paced, snarling. Nyfain watched me without expression.

"There are two problems with that," I said evenly, trying to maintain my composure. "The first is that, given the coating is what makes it dangerous, Granny can replace the drugmaker and resume all activities. Anything she makes will be just as addictive. The second . . ." Nyfain's eyes gleamed. He clearly knew the shoe was about to drop. "She's my true mate, and our animals have established a four-way bond. If you kill her, it'll destroy me. If you try, I'll annihilate your pack and cripple your kingdom while I take her out of here."

The last was said on a growl, and the rage got away from me, flooding the area with a burst of my power.

Finley froze. Her eyes kindled fire; dragons were always on the brink of a challenge, and this was more than enough to set them off. Nyfain didn't react, though, watching me closely, studying me. Thank the fucking gods. Going up against them would be brutal at best.

"Did you know right away?" he asked, his voice subdued. I could see Finley fighting with her dragon to keep from jumping off her throne and attacking me. It was probably her and Nyfain's four-way bond that helped her keep her head. They, too, were true mates, and I imagined his bond was likely feeding her soothing emotions.

"Yes, even from a distance. I lost my head the first night I saw her and fucked her in the middle of a path in the woods behind enemy lines. Obviously, that was a problem. The next night, we captured her as intended, and I tried to maintain my composure throughout the rest of our journey. It . . . mostly worked. Sometimes. We fought, but I didn't do a great job of keeping my hands off her. It's been a rocky journey."

"Even fighting a true mate is a turn-on," Nyfain said, and I released a breath.

"Yeah," I replied, thankful he'd been through it and understood. "Honestly, I was doing my duty despite the sex with her. It wasn't until things stopped adding up that my opinion started to change. I had her journals. I had the truth, a truth that she hadn't realized herself." I paused. "I know, based on my bond with Aurelia, that my judgment in this situation is compromised, but I ask that you keep an open mind. The rest of the sub-pack that went can attest to all of this. It wasn't just me that started to question things. I wasn't even the first, not even close."

I worried for a moment I sounded like I was pleading with them to give her a chance, and honestly, maybe I was. I didn't want to go to war with these dragons. It wasn't because of their power, which was substantial, but because I respected them and what they'd done for this kingdom. I admired them as leaders and trusted them. I didn't want to push against them. I certainly didn't want to destroy the pack that I'd painstakingly put together. This place was just as much a labor of my love as it was theirs.

But for my true mate, I'd do anything. It wasn't even a question. I would protect her at all costs.

"Basically," I said, getting back on track, "she creates the fun, someone else creates the danger, and Granny controls the operations. Aurelia didn't know what had become of her product. She didn't know about the coating. She nearly died when she saw it in the market, and took it to see what changes Granny had made. If we hadn't had the phoenix healing elixir, she would have died. Aurelia—that's her name—still doesn't know she is my true mate. She only met her wolf earlier today—"

"Wait." Finley screwed up her face, holding up her hand again. "*What?* She just met her wolf?"

"She was suppressed."

"But if she's your true mate, she is powerful. If Granny is as strong as people say—"

"Granny kept her suppressed on purpose and lied to her about it."

I explained why Aurelia had believed she lacked magic and how she'd come to make the drugs at a young age.

Nyfain's fingers were still steepled as he studied my every move. "You certainly did seem to encounter a *few* complications, yes," he finally said, humor laced through his tone. I wished it had eased the tension somewhat, but there was too much on the line here.

"I'll say," Finley mumbled.

"You said the pack learned about Aurelia as you did?" Nyfain asked.

"Yes. You can ask them about it. Any one of them. I can release their bond if you want to question them without my influence."

"Releasing the pack bond won't be necessary," he said. "But yes, we'll need to question them. Her as well."

The idea of them questioning her, of making her stand in judgment and punishing her for a shitty life that was forced on her, made rage blister through me again. More power pumped into the room. I closed my eyes and tried to regain control.

"Oh gods, his rage is setting off my rage, and this is getting dicey." Finley blew out a breath and bent, nearly putting her head between her legs. "How are you so fucking calm, Nyfain?"

"Because I know what he's going through. Weston, I hear you—I want you to know that. But you have to realize that yes, your judgment has been compromised. You can't help that. It's primal. I promise you that we will be thorough, and when we know the truth, we'll be fair. We'll figure this out. Can you accept that?"

"Yes," I said, not knowing if that was true. We would all be walking a very fine line.

"Where is she now?" he asked, usually the easiest to set off and this time the calmest of us.

"Hadriel recommended putting her in the tower. She'll be locked in. I could not suffer her being placed in the dun—"

Nyfain held up his hand. "Is she dangerous?"

"Not at all. After she saw what her product had become—how Granny altered it—she requested to stand in judgment. She is not prone to random fits of violence unless attacked."

"Makes sense if she's your true mate," Finley murmured. "You're *usually* as calm as they come."

"She did just meet her animal, though," I continued, "and that animal is an alpha. I have no idea how that is going to work out."

Nyfain nodded. "It's been a long journey with some . . . *surprising* revelations. Why don't we end here for today, and we can pick this up tomorrow morning in our private chambers. We can go over the details more thoroughly and talk to some of the other pack before we need to question her directly. I do have to warn you, Weston, that her questioning needs to be formal. That can't be helped. But we'll get as much information as we can before that time. In the meantime, get some sleep. You need it."

"Just bring Hadriel in tomorrow," Finley said, sagging back in her throne. "He can yay or nay whatever Weston says. He won't lie to me, and he *won't* leave out any details. He doesn't know how."

Nyfain nodded and excused me. My mind whirled as I replayed how that had gone. Badly, if I looked at it from a surface level.

When talking them through it, I'd worried it seemed like I was coming up with excuses why Aurelia was ultimately innocent—excuses to get my true mate out of trouble. That they had not seen that village in person, and had not seen Aurelia break down with each realization regarding Granny's treatment of her, lessened the story's impact. My inability to properly articulate Aurelia's situation made it easier for Finley to look at it in black and white: Aurelia made the drugs, and so she was guilty. What should the *why* matter?

At least the fact she was my true mate would make them more careful. At least Nyfain sympathized with me. If he hadn't, telling him I'd rip apart his kingdom's pack would've definitely incited violence.

This was all so fucked up. Worse, I couldn't go to Aurelia. I couldn't hold her and feel the comfort only she could provide. I missed her already and craved her in my bed. I was adrift in a way I'd never been before, terrified for what tomorrow would bring—terrified they'd sentence her to death, and me with her. Because one thing was for certain —I would not stand by if they tried to hurt her. I would make good on my threat and tear this kingdom apart.

11

AURELIA

The early morning light filtered through the windows, the sun just cresting the surrounding mountains. Time to get up and get going.

I was halfway out of bed before I remembered my situation. This wasn't my village and I didn't have a job to get to. Granny no longer dictated my time.

Then again, I did have a duty, and I wasn't in the habit of lazing around.

The lock on the door was a standard, double-way affair that wouldn't take much effort to crack—if I had the right tools. I'd had a similar one on the work shed and on my house before Raz went through a spell of stealing my keys and locking me inside.

Luckily, the tower had a plethora of items that could work: a bunch of hairpins, a screwdriver set, cotton swabs with easily removable ends—the options were endless. Why did they bother even locking the thing? Did it actually keep anyone in?

I chose the hairpins, spent a few scant minutes fashioning them into the shapes I needed and picking the lock, then stashed my makeshift tools at the bottom of one of the trunks full of clothes.

Since the room didn't afford me any better options, I'd dressed in my clothes from yesterday. I slipped out the door and headed down the stairs like I was supposed to be there. Sometimes, being left alone required only confidence. At the bottom of the staircase, I waffled for a moment about which direction to turn but then headed down a hall with paintings I thought I remembered passing on the way to the tower. A few servants walked past, most going the same direction as me and all of them giving me double takes. No one commented, though, nor spent too long looking me over.

Near the end of the hall, a very tall, dark-skinned man sauntered in my direction. His face was strikingly handsome, his frame enormous, and his demeanor loose and easy, like he hadn't a care in the world. A sparkly jacket adorned his torso, not unlike something Hadriel would wear, and matching yellow trousers led down to black velvet shoes, the fabric the same as the jacket's lapels.

He noticed me immediately, and I felt like a mouse trapped in a serpent's gaze. Nothing changed about his bearing or his easy stride, but I could tell he was suddenly on point, ready to handle a potential problem. With his size, he'd handle it in no time flat. I stood no chance.

He didn't veer into my path and I didn't veer into his, but we watched each other as we closed the distance. Neither of us pretended we didn't know what was happening here: I was out of my cage, and he would not stand for it.

Within five feet, outside of his arm's reach, I slowed to a stop. He did as well, a partner in this dangerous dance.

"Hello, Captive Lady," he said pleasantly, flashing me a wide, beautiful smile.

"Hi."

"What brings you out and about?"

"The sun came up and I figured, rather than lying in bed, I should be up and about my duties."

"Is that so?" He took a half step and leaned against the wall. Only a fool would think he was letting down his guard.

Tendrils of unease wound through me, and I wondered how fast he could run in those fancy shoes.

"And precisely what duty are you about this early in the morning?" he asked.

"It's dawn, and that's when I usually get up to go to work, but . . . well, I'm here now."

He nodded. "Right you are. No work for you."

"Well . . ." I huffed out a deep breath. "I created Granny's empire, and now I need to tear it down. I need to figure out how. And I can't do that if I'm sitting idle."

He quirked an eyebrow. "I heard something about that. I'll be honest, I didn't believe it. A person that makes drugs unlawfully doesn't usually up and change their tune, becoming a model citizen."

"You can take him," my wolf said, obviously delusional. I shushed her.

"I'm not interested in becoming a model citizen. I'm just trying to right some wrongs. Simple as that."

"Simple as that," he repeated, and looked at me for a very long moment, right in my eyes. I could tell he was assessing me, and the scrutiny made me want to babble nonsense just to scare him away.

"Simple. As. That." He pushed off the wall. "Where did you envision going first during your jaunt around the castle?"

"Are you mocking me?"

"I'm not sure yet."

Fair.

"I thought I'd find the library and see if it contains any books on Moonfire Lilies. I unearthed one yesterday. It should have been sent to the gardeners? I wanted to make sure they rehomed it properly. They are rare flowers—very hard to find. I want to make sure I know how to grow it."

"You don't trust the gardeners?"

I grimaced, worried I'd just been offensive. "I've heard they're skilled, but I don't know them. So I don't know if I should trust their skills just yet."

His lips stretched into a smile. "Fair point, Captive Lady. But I have bad news, I'm afraid. It's too early to use the library. The royals are very protective of it. There are posted hours for non-approved persons."

I pointed at my chest. "I'm not approved, I take it."

He mimicked my movement. "No, you are not."

I braced my hands on my hips, thinking. He went back to leaning on the wall patiently. Servants came and went around us, giving us a wide berth. He was the protection, I was the enemy, and they were just trying to do their jobs.

"How about the gardens, then?" I thought out loud, then bit my lip. "No, there really is no point unless I have something intelligent to offer. How about my stuff? If I can have my appliances and access to a few plants— Oh! My journals. That's a better use of my time. I need to finish up going through those and gathering information. That's something I can do in the tower. That way everyone can rest easy. Can I have my journals?"

He was back to watching me, but I could tell he was paying attention to my body language. I had no idea what he was reading.

"I can't get your journals," he said. "All of your things have been taken to the royals to look over."

"You can definitely take him. Lure him to a dark corner,

knock him out, tie him up, and go find the library. This is doable. He's in the way."

I looked off to the side with one raised eyebrow and a deadpan stare and hoped she could feel it. That ridiculous plan didn't even warrant a vocal response. Tie him up? I didn't have any rope, and I doubted the servants would search out any for me, especially when they realized this man was nowhere in sight.

"What'd I miss?" the man asked, clearly seeing my expression.

I shook my head. "My wolf has delusions of grandeur. I haven't known her for long."

She growled within me.

"I heard. Let me save your wolf some trouble—a wolf can't take a dragon in animal form. It'll never happen. A wolf's strength is in pack unity—"

I blinked up at him with wide, wonder-filled eyes and a smile. "You're a dragon?"

He paused with his mouth open. "Yes."

"That's so cool! What color are you? Do you glitter? Is your stomach a different color than your body? I just saw one like that and had never known that was a thing. Do you know the phoenix? What's he like?"

"You finally got to the babbling, I see," my wolf said dryly. *"Much better than my plan, yes. Not at all embarrassing."*

I snapped my mouth closed and was thankful to see him grinning.

"Come on, Captive Lady." He jerked his head in the opposite direction of the tower. "I know what we can do to pass the time."

I followed him like a little lamb, a habit from the village I couldn't seem to shake. Then again, it was better than being chased by him.

"My dragon is blue, and in the sun, yes, he glitters," the

man said. "His stomach is a little lighter. He's preening to hear how excited you are about him."

"Do people ride on dragons?" I asked softly.

"Typically, no. For you, though, I feel like my dragon would find a way to make that happen."

I crossed my fingers. I really wanted to fly.

"Yesterday was my first time seeing a dragon," I said. "They are really fucking cool. I mean, you are, I guess. And big. I half hoped to be one, but I've been told I am a wolf."

"It would not be easy for a male wolf to fuck a dragon, so be happy you are a wolf like our mate," my animal said.

"You are definitely not a dragon, no," the man said. "Much too . . . calm, we'll say. You have this way about you —you make me feel very comfortable just now, even though you're obviously dangerous."

I chuckled. "I'm flattered, but I'm not dangerous. To you, I mean. Well . . . probably to anyone." I shrugged. "I've never had any training."

He looked down at me as he stuck out his arm, nearly the same length as my damn leg. I'd thought Weston was big, but this guy was fucking enormous.

Up ahead someone crested the flight of stairs onto the landing. Once they were out of the way, the man retracted his arm so we could pass the landing within the hallway.

"I think you lack confidence," he finally said. "As I said, in a solo match, a wolf will not beat a dragon. But we are humans. Maybe you don't know it yet, Captive Lady, but you are dangerous. It's in the way you walk, in your fearlessness. Let Weston guide you. He's the best non-dragon I have ever known. He'll bring out the ferocity that I saw furled within you as you approached me a moment ago. It made me nervous."

My middle warmed and I smiled, but my eyes got

watery, and it made me frustrated because I had told myself the crying was over.

The man stopped at a closed door, his hand on the handle. "Are you laughing or crying? I can't tell."

"Nothing. Both? Neither. I don't know. It's just . . . Everyone in your pack has been so nice. That's not normally the case for me. It makes me a little sappy."

His eyes softened and he pulled his hand from the door, sticking it out for me to shake. "I'm Vemar. Nice to meet you."

"Nice to meet you too. I'm Aurelia."

"Yes, I heard. Come on, Hadriel said you liked his jackets. Let's get you one so that you and he match. It will drive him crazy. It's endless fun."

"Oh . . ." I blew out a breath but followed him anyway, unsure about the whole jacket situation. This guy wasn't immediately bold and crass with the sexual talk, so that was something.

The room was an explosion of color with fabric everywhere, piled on chairs and heaping on tables. Some slid off into a bright puddle onto the ground, the early light catching the sequins and shooting flares of colored reflections across the ceiling.

"What are you doing?" A middle-aged man with a rounded belly stepped back from a human-shaped dress form half draped in a red sash. He had an accent, but I didn't know enough about the world to know where it might've come from. "Oh, it's you. Did we have an appointment? Who is this with you? You don't want your night to end? I don't care. She is much too small for you. Your peen would split her in two."

I froze on the spot. Vemar bumped into the back of me.

"It's fine." He patted my shoulder. "He says outlandish things all the time. Don't worry about it."

The man scoffed in indignation. "That is not outlandish. Look at you! You're twice her size!"

"Honestly, it's a lot nicer when Hadriel comes and distracts him," Vemar murmured, stepping around me and gesturing toward the man. "Aurelia, this is Cecil, the seamster. Cecil, she's our captive. Haven't you heard? She's the beta's true mate."

It took me a moment to process what he'd said, the words replaying in my mind as I tried to make sense of them.

My belly whooshed. "What did you say?" I put out my hand, catching his sequined sleeve. "I'm his *what?*"

Cecil's eyes rounded. "Oh yes, I heard." He grinned. "I also heard that I wasn't supposed to tell her that she was his true mate. What did you hear? Something different?"

"What's a . . . a *true* mate?" I asked as tingles danced along my spine.

"What we are," my wolf told me. *"You feel it. That is a mate."*

I replayed her words: you feel it.

Feel it.

My mind replayed that night on the path, the very first time I touched him. I'd felt the pull of him. Thought he could never be real, not with how good everything felt. How perfect.

Even when we argued, fought, I couldn't help but close the distance to him. I couldn't help the desire to wrap my body around his and lose myself in the moment until its climax. I'd hated him in the beginning, *hated* him, and yet I'd still craved him in an unnatural way.

A primal way.

"What is a true *mate?"* I said more urgently, the butterflies in my belly turning ravenous. *"I've never heard that term."*

"Something humans make up to explain a mate."

My wolf had known Weston's wolf was her mate right away. She'd felt the pull, like I had. They—we—seemed like two halves of a whole, fitting together seamlessly. Perfectly.

Weston's growling declaration flashed through my memories.

You are mine.

"Can someone have more than one true mate?" I asked in a shaky voice, the enormity of this revelation seeping in.

"Just the one, Captive Lady," Vemar said, watching me closely. "Finding one's true mate is really quite rare."

The room started to spin as my world was tipped on its axis yet again.

Why hadn't Weston told me this from the beginning?

Then again, what would've been the point? I wouldn't have understood what it meant. I might've even held it against him, been angry at the pull I felt no control over. I would've blamed him when it wasn't his fault. I wouldn't have understood that it was fate, especially since I'd been so sure I hadn't had magic.

But why hadn't he told me after I got my animal?

I thought I knew the answer to that, too, though. He hadn't had the time. I'd climbed him like a tree the moment my wolf came roaring out, and then sulked about the four-way bond. I wouldn't have wanted to tell me then, either.

I let out a shaky breath.

I wasn't sure what to think. How to react. This sounded, well, special. Rare. I should feel privileged to have a true mate, not confused. Not kind of . . . let down.

Because a big part of me realized I hardly knew him. Certainly not well enough to consciously choose him. Part of me wanted to date for the first time. Wanted to meet new people and fall in love.

Being handed a mate—nature essentially assigning me one—felt like a cop-out, especially in our fucked-up situation. It felt disingenuous. I felt like I was being robbed of a choice, yet again.

I needed to think about this. I needed more details.

I needed all these revelations to just stop for a fucking second so I could catch my breath.

Vemar was still studying me. When my eyes met his, I knew he could tell how rattled I was. He nodded once in response.

"I just wanted to know if you were genuine, Captive Lady. I hope you understand. Given all we've learned in the last few years, nothing about you made any sense. I heard the head of the organization was cunning and cutthroat, with a *way* about her. That her people were good at lying, stealing, and cheating for her. You seem kind and genuine. Too naïve to be a renowned drugmaker. The feelings I get when I'm around you don't make sense, either. I was in the demon dungeons. I know a mind-fuck when I feel it, and you, Captive Lady, are mind-fucking me."

Cecil's mouth clicked shut and mine dropped open. The people in this fucking kingdom! If they weren't accusing me of one thing, they were accusing me of another. The Granny thing—fine. Eventually, I got the picture. Now it was mind-fucking? Was this guy serious?

"Get him," my wolf growled. The accompanying surge of power was so potent that it blotted out all reason.

I ducked around him, registering his slow turn in response. From my bubble of adrenaline and anger, I registered he didn't put up his hands to defend himself, an action I found odd. I scooped up a pair of old-looking scissors, noting the hint of rust meant they were probably dull, and figured that would be good enough. I dipped back the way I'd come, rolled, stood up at his back . . . and wondered what in the holy fuck I was actually doing. Was I going to stab a guy for saying words I didn't like? Kill a guy who wasn't attacking me or putting me in any harm?

"What in the crap is wrong with you?" I yelled at my animal.

It took me a moment to realize my voice was reverberating against the walls, not an inward yell at all—and that I'd thrown the scissors in frustration.

"Oh my gods, I am so sorry!" The scissors were lodged in the back of Vemar's thigh. He'd frozen, his hands held high, not engaging. I'd stabbed an innocent guy for no fucking reason. "Fuck! Gods . . . Help! *Help!* Don't . . . move, probably? Don't move. I'm so sorry, I meant to throw them, but I wasn't aiming. I just— Don't—let's— Cecil, what do we do?"

"Enjoy the show, that is what I am doing," Cecil said, very unhelpfully.

"What? No! No, Vemar, don't move!" I pointed at Vemar because I didn't know what else to do. "Don't move. You have scissors stuck in your leg."

"Yes. And you put them there. Who are you hoping will help you, Captive Lady? Someone to take me down or bind me up?" He turned with a manic smile and started laughing. "That was refreshing. You're fierce when you lose track of yourself."

Hadriel was right. Dragons were crazy.

"I don't . . ." I was breathing heavily. I swiped my hair away. "It's fine. You're a shifter. You'll heal, right? So we need to pull them out."

He reached around, took hold of the scissors, and yanked.

I swayed and fanned my face. I suddenly felt a little faint.

"Whoops, here we go." Cecil directed me to sit in a

chair. His smiling face filled my vision. "New animal, yes? Fun. Do not worry, he is the mad dragon. He don't care about a scissors. Dicks on a jacket, scissors . . . He don't care."

The door ripped open and Weston rushed in wearing boxer briefs and a glistening, sweaty chest, probably from the run here. His eyes were wild, sighting in on Vemar immediately.

Vemar put up his hands again. "I didn't touch her, boss. *She* stabbed *me*. I did not engage."

"It was my fault." I stood, swayed again, felt stupid for my reaction because this was all my fault, and then took a deep breath to try to steady myself. "It's fine. Sorry. I—" It all came out in a torrent of words. "I was okay but then my wolf threw power at me and then I was fighting her over scissors and I realized that was dumb so I threw them in a huff and . . ."

"I'm only bleeding a little," Vemar said, such a good sport.

"A little? He's bleeding all over my floor," Cecil grumbled, not as good a sport.

"Why are you out of your tower?" Weston stalked toward me, reaching me and cupping my face in his large, gentle hands. I swayed now for a different reason, soaking in the deliciousness of his proximity, drunk on his scent. His gaze slid over me and he stroked his thumb softly along my cheek, assessing for damage. I closed my eyes and basked in the exquisite hum of him.

True mate, the feeling whispered.

"Why are you fighting, Little Wolf?" His deep voice rumbled through his chest.

I struggled against the tide of his heat, the magnitude of my want.

I took a deep breath, wrapped my hands around his

wrists, and fought the urge to run them up to his shoulders and down his chest, pushing him away instead. I was the logical one in my human/wolf pair. I owed it to both of us to learn more about this situation before allowing her to push us to act on it. I owed it to myself, maybe my future. I was just so confused about it all. About my wolf, about that burst of power—hell, I was still a captive, possibly facing a death sentence. How the fuck would a true mate situation even work?

"What happened?" Weston asked. "Why are you out of the tower?" he repeated.

"It was dawn," I said, sitting again. "I wanted to get to work. I picked the lock and Vemar found me in the hall. He said it wasn't okay for me to wander but decided it would be okay to run errands, so he brought me here. And was rewarded with scissors in his leg."

"Why did you stick scissors in his leg?" Weston demanded, delicately curling a lock of hair behind my ear. I shivered, wanting to stand up and work my way into his arms. But was that me, or just the bond?

Did it matter?

I took a deep breath, miserable with this confusion.

"Stop thinking so much. This is the way things should be," my wolf said.

"What do you know? You've been in the world for less than a day."

"I stuck scissors in his leg because I think my animal is unhinged. Maybe I *should* just get a jacket covered in winged dicks so that I'll fit in with this crazy place—I don't know. Everyone seems a little off-kilter. If you can't beat 'em . . ."

"Let your mate destroy him," my wolf said. I nearly lost my shit again.

"She's on my last fucking nerve," I said to the room. "I'm

about to shift just so Vemar's dragon can temper her a little."

"Hey." Weston's palm smoothed across my cheek. "We'll deal with this soon, okay? I promise. We'll get you shifting, and my wolf can help temper these primal surges. It's not uncommon—you have a lot of power and no idea what to do with it. Mistakes happen."

I nodded, unable to stop myself from leaning into his palm.

"Do you have time for her?" Weston asked Cecil, and his tone was much, much different. It was clear he wasn't being an alpha with me a moment ago.

"Yes, I do. I have the big dragon and now the little wolf. Dick jackets with wings for all." Cecil moved around, gathering fabric.

"Do you really have fabric with dicks with wings on it?" I asked in bewilderment.

"I have all the dick and a little vagine."

Weston kissed my forehead. "You don't need to keep Granny's hours," he murmured. "You're not under her influence anymore."

"I am, though. It's a race. I need to unravel her company before the dragons kill me or she captures me again. This is not a vacation, Weston. I have no excuse to rest. I will win this battle between us, even though it will crush me to do so. She will not keep this enterprise alive."

His plush lips thinned a little, but he didn't respond. His thumb glided down my cheek before he pulled away.

"Stay out of trouble," he told me seriously. "You were lucky it was Vemar. Any other dragon would've lost their head and reciprocated."

"Other dragon would not have put up hands, and would now be dead," Cecil said. "Lucky he only got it in leg, I think."

Weston didn't spare Cecil a glance, instead turning and sticking out his hand for Vemar. "Sorry about that. She's learning."

Vemar took it but shook his head. "She's beyond learning. She's starting to live. I'm here for it."

Confusion filtered through the bond, but then Weston was gone, closing the door with a last look at me before he did.

I turned and noticed Vemar staring at me. "You didn't tell him I told you he was your true mate."

"I figured that might've gotten you in trouble. I'm not interested in causing more problems. Besides, I want to get some more information before . . ."

Before what? He told Weston I knew? Gave in to it? Rejected it?

I didn't know.

"I just want to keep my head down and get my job done —" I cut off as Cecil tried to strip me. "Whoa, no." I pushed him away. "Really? You don't have a slip or something?"

Cecil stared at me. "I have slip. I have lots of slips. I have no idea where they are. You shifter, yes? You get nude a lot. I've seen all the boobs. Too many boobs. I don't care about boobs. Vagines, peens, I don't care. I just need measurements."

"Do you need some scissors?" Vemar asked me, his eyes sparkling again.

Cecil put up a finger. "I find slip."

12

AURELIA

This library was glorious. I'd never imagined one so big and so perfectly laid out. Upon walking in, I stopped dead in my tracks in wide-eyed amazement at the sheer size of the space. With two stories and a domed ceiling arched over it, it had to be bigger than the square in my village. Little niches within the beams were covered in hand-painted murals. Shelves lined the walls on each floor, and wood columns were dotted between the stacks. Each section had its own rolling ladder, and the second-floor balcony, constructed of the same polished wood as the beams, ran around the perimeter of the room.

Plush rugs covered the polished wood floor, and several seating areas were placed around the room, each holding large and fluffy pillows. Various little nooks offered more privacy, many of them cleverly positioned between the stacks and outfitted with blankets and cushions for a cozy feel.

It was . . . sensational. Better than anything I could ever imagine. The sheer amount of knowledge contained in this one room.

Not only that, but it was organized perfectly. I was in heaven. It was all categorized, labeled . . . Everything made sense here.

Everything except the hidden romance room. That space was a nightmare. Nothing was labeled, and all the subgenres were grouped randomly. I wanted to peruse the titles, but the haphazard way they were shoved on shelves gave me hives.

I scoured the library for gardening books while I contemplated the true mate conundrum.

I put back the book I'd been looking at as footsteps sounded down below. Various village librarians wandered the stacks, it being still early and within their perusal hours. None of them were up in the nonfiction area.

The next book had the same problem as the last few: no information on Moonfire Lilies. I found it fascinating how elusive the flower was. It was a challenge, protecting its secrets from those that were unworthy. I was determined to unlock its properties.

I gently pushed the book back, my mind drifting to what Vemar had explained to me while Cecil took my measurements.

Apparently, no one knew for certain if there was only one true mate for each person, but it was the common belief this was the case. Just the one. Regardless, they were so rare that most people never found theirs. The four-way bond was supposed to be proof we were true mates. Further proof would be if Weston could claim me twice, one mark on each shoulder, made permanent by magic. No one person would be able to cover a true mate's scent. The connection was wholly primal.

What I kept getting hung up on was the logic—or lack thereof—of it all. Shouldn't a bond like that be more than just blind lust? Shouldn't it be more than touching and fucking? Where was the love I craved? The *human* connection. I couldn't deny that I liked Weston for many reasons, but I didn't know enough about him to call it love. I didn't even know if we were compatible. We'd spent half the time we knew each other fighting.

If I accepted a claim, I wanted it to be for emotional reasons. Being handed a mate, like it had been assigned, felt like it was robbing me of choice. Robbing us both. After Granny, that idea terrified me. What if I ended up in a worse situation, a permanent one?

My wolf was not pleased about my stubbornness. Her vocabulary could be quite colorful. She'd learned a thing or two from Hadriel.

I grabbed the next book, opening to the back to check the glossary.

My thoughts were interrupted by a strange crawling sensation stealing over my skin and tingling between my shoulder blades. My movements slowed as I focused on it, pricks of unease warning me that danger was near.

I glanced at the bottom floor again, but the scene had not changed. People stood at the stacks or looked through books. None of their bodies had tensed; no one looked around. Whatever was setting off this feeling didn't disturb them.

Furrowing my brow, I returned to the book in hand, running my finger down the *'M'*s. Finding the flower, I grinned with a surge of joy.

The sense of danger intensified, though, wiping away my smile. It slithered over me, sinking down into my flesh. The warning pulsed now. The weight of eyes pressed between my shoulder blades. Someone was watching me.

"You need to pay attention to this feeling. Take another look around," my wolf said.

I did, taking a step closer to the railing and peering

over. The new people I was able to see, though, weren't any different than those I'd seen before. No one moved with a sense of urgency; no tension tightened their shoulders. Everything was the same as when I'd walked in.

Unwilling to give up, I flipped the book open to the page I wanted, turning more and getting right near the railing now, at the edge of the balcony. My gaze swept over the entire room.

A gigantic man had been somewhat hidden by a curtain a moment ago, but my change in position now made him totally visible. He was Vemar's height but much broader, with popping muscles filling out his frame. Scars ran across his face and his neck; they were not terribly pronounced but hinted at a very hard, pain-filled life. His well-cut shirt held the sheen of some sort of fine fabric but did not detract from the sheer viciousness in his golden eyes, in his bearing. His handsome face did not hide or minimize the ruthless power emanating from within him.

He looked at me, his countenance unflinchingly hostile, as though he'd love nothing more than to make me hurt, to peel off my skin and make a doll out of it, or something else as horribly gruesome.

My wolf had wanted to assault Vemar for no real reason. I waited to see if she thought we should attack, but all she said was: *"Run."*

Terror gripped me.

"No! Fuck you!" I shouted for reasons unknown, chucking the book at him on impulse and running like fucking mad. I hit the end of the balcony, swung up onto the banister, and slid down to the bottom so fast the wood burned.

I did not fucking care.

There was no way I was facing that behemoth of a man

with the crazy eyes. All the confidence in the world would not save me from that creature. My wolf was not arguing.

I sprinted out of the library, much faster now that I had magic. I didn't hear footsteps behind me, but I hadn't heard him enter the library, either. I'd just felt him, felt his dangerous aura and then his vicious intent.

"Let me out. I can go faster," my wolf screamed in panic, and I almost tried.

Down the hall I saw Hadriel, who had just finished descending a small set of stairs. He took one look at me and his eyes widened.

"Fuck!" he shouted, turning in the direction I was going and putting on a burst of speed.

Fear gave me a gush of adrenaline. I caught up to him in no time.

"Fuck me, you're fast. Do not leave me behind to get killed," he said, struggling to go faster. "I will fucking trip you and leave you for dead if you don't slow down."

Someone ahead saw us and stopped walking. The older woman with tight curls and wire-rimmed glasses held a book in her hand. Without a word, she dropped the book, turned, and started to run.

"What's happening?" someone else asked, sprinting out of a door we were passing. "Ghosts?"

"Worse," I said, noticing I was barely out of breath. Despite my fear in the moment, I couldn't help but think having magic was great. "Way fucking worse."

"Quick, this way!" Hadriel pointed right, down a corridor, picking up two people as we passed. No one asked questions, just saw us running and took the fuck off. This place had obviously seen some shit.

After another two turns and picking up two more people, we burst through a back door out into the bright sunshine. I glanced over my shoulder as we hurried across a patio and down three stairs to spongy grass. I almost expected the door to burst open behind us and for that monster to come barreling out.

"What was it?" Hadriel asked, hands braced on his knees as he panted. "Fuck, I'm winded. I hate running. What was it, Aurelia? The king? Was he pissed?"

Everyone else stood around us, on edge, glancing nervously at the door.

"Ghosts? I knew it," one of the women said, peering at corners of the building. "This place is riddled with them."

"It's not fucking ghosts, Andrelle," Hadriel said, rolling his eyes. Then to me: "Is it?"

"Not ghosts." I watched that door, seeing a shadow on the other side of the paned glass and bracing. The door pushed open. "Fuck!"

Everyone scattered in different directions. Even Hadriel took off running, yelling, "Come on, I have a hiding place!"

Before I could move, Dante stuck his head out the door. "What is going on?" He stepped all the way out, looking around at the others, at one running across the grass to the trees beyond. "Where's everyone going?"

My heart was still beating quickly from the terror and then the sprint. I had felt like I was twelve years old again, being chased out of town, prey to people larger and stronger.

I pointed over his shoulder. "Is that monster behind you?"

He turned and looked. "There's no one behind me. The beta said you're freaked out about something and to check on you. He's busy taking care of some pack business. What's up?"

I heaved a relieved sigh. "Nothing. I got spooked, that's

all. There was a huge guy glaring at me in the library. He looked ready to kill me."

"Oh." He nodded, then grimaced. "Yeah, you aren't a favorite around here. Not yet. You'll meet with the royals this afternoon. You'll get to straighten everything out then. Maybe just . . . go play with the plants or something? Lie low for a while. Was that Hadriel I saw taking off?"

"Yeah. He was spooked about the guy following us."

Dante looked behind him again. "That's weird. It's not like him to run off. Don't worry, though, no one is allowed to touch you—king and queen's orders. You're safe. Just stay away from the woods, and don't leave the palace grounds."

"Okay."

"I need to scout the woods and make sure everyone is doing their job, but how about we read the rest of that book after that? I have some rest time owed to me, since I just got back. We'll keep each other company."

I smiled. "Sure."

He winked at me, frowned in the direction Hadriel had taken off, and disappeared back into the castle.

"Wait, which way are the plants . . ." I let my words die away, looking around.

Shrugging, I randomly chose left and started walking. The grounds were beautiful and well maintained, with large expanses of plush green grass and various manicured shrubs dotting the way. Little benches were set here and there amid potted plants and pops of colorful flowers. I passed several little birdbaths, active with life.

Numerous people tended the grounds, all of them looking up as I walked by. Most of them straightened up, watching me, but no one stopped me from continuing on. It didn't bode well for my safety; Granny's people would be able to roam around easily.

That in mind, I kept plenty of room between me and anything someone could hide behind. If someone wanted to grab me, they'd need to cross some highly visible space to do it, and I'd have a head start toward safety.

I should've brought something sharp . . .

Around the back of the castle, I found a large field of Everlass. I saw two people amongst the plants, picking leaves and dropping them to the ground. I reasoned it must keep the plants healthy or something. Seemed like a shitload of work.

A huge, sprawling garden was set beyond the Everlass field. Several people worked within, picking things or weeding or doing whatever else gardeners did. Raz had usually dealt with all that stuff. I never had to bother. He hadn't had this kind of help, though. I imagined he would've been happier if he had.

Five large work sheds stood along the far side of the garden, smoke rising from each. The area buzzed with activity. Gods help me, this operation was swarmed with people. How'd they stay out of each other's way?

A dragon flew overhead. A dazzling green, this one was smaller than the one yesterday. It tilted its wings lazily, performing a half-circle overhead, its great head looking down at me. I watched it for a moment, loving the way it cut through the sky, before heading toward the gardens. I figured I could ask about the Moonfire Lily. Hopefully someone would know something.

Each grouping of plants was labeled with a little sign, the name written in the middle and a little flower symbol at the bottom corner. Some had a few of the same plant in each group, and some had as many as ten. After reading a few, I realized it was not just a flower symbol—the symbols changed from card to card. It must denote the type of plant. That was quite helpful. I gathered the flowers were right behind me, this group ahead had vegetables, and, as I continued, I found one with a sign for poison.

That was interesting. Did they just let anyone wander through this area, allowing free access to dangerous plants?

A stern voice called out, "May I help you?" indicating clearly, they did not.

I turned to find a late-middle-aged woman with perfectly styled graying hair, chestnut-colored eyes, and a regal air. She wore fancy flowered pants and a plain white top. She held sheers in her glove-adorned hands.

"Maybe," I said as she walked over, full of authority. "There should've been a Moonfire Lily delivered here last night for potting. I wanted to check on it. It's a little flower that glows pink and would have arrived in a bucket."

She studied me silently for a moment, showing no reaction to my presence or words. I could tell she was wary. She looked at me like most people tended to, though I knew it wasn't because she thought me magicless, but because I was a potentially dangerous stranger.

"Of course. Please, follow me." She carefully stepped out of the way and motioned for me to go first.

"Sure, yeah, thank you. Um . . ." I headed out of the garden area. "Which way are we going?"

"Just that workstation over there." She pointed at the far work shed, dingier than the rest. The structure looked much older than the others. "None of us knew the name of it, and only one of us has ever seen it before. It grows in the wild, right?"

"Yes. They like to hide. It's hard to spot, even though it glows. I always keep an eye out for it. It's easier to see with access to my wolf. At night, I mean. It's nearly impossible to find during the day."

She stepped sideways through the doorway, her eyes

never leaving me. "Hannon, will you come out here, please?"

A man about Weston's height with wide shoulders and trim hips walked through the door. A halo of red hair swirled around his head, and thick arms hung at his sides. The sun highlighted a bit of stubble along his strong jaw on an otherwise handsome face.

"Hannon, this is our guest from the Red Lupine kingdom," the woman said. "She makes Granny's drugs." She turned to me. "Is that correct?"

"Yes." I offered a light bow. "I'm Aurelia."

"Hello," Hannon said pleasantly, offering me a smile.

"Would you mind escorting her back to the castle?" the woman said. "She shouldn't be wandering around the grounds on her own."

My heart sank. "Could I at least see the flower? If you plan to let it die, you should at least pick the petals first."

Hannon tilted his head as he looked at me, but didn't comment.

"We do not plan to let it die," the woman said. "It is pretty. We'll plant it and examine its properties. Hannon, if you please?"

I pouted as he stepped closer, motioning for me to walk with him. At least Dante had promised to read with me. That would ease the boredom of just sitting in the tower.

"Are you a dragon, too?" I asked as we walked back the way I'd come.

"No, I'm a phoenix. It's why I am charged with getting you back. It's safer because I can't die. You don't mean any harm, though, do you."

It wasn't a question, though I couldn't really focus on that now. I'd turned and grabbed his arm in excitement, beaming up at him.

"You're the phoenix!" I half shouted at him. "And you have red hair!"

"Guilty as charged."

"Until Hadriel told me about you, I'd thought phoenixes were just myths. It blows my mind that they are real—you are real, I mean." I was brimming with excitement. "Tell me truly, is it super cool being you? I bet it is. Are people just always delighted to be near you?"

He laughed. "No, definitely not. They don't love that I can read their emotions, especially when that emotion is sadness or fear. Warriors don't like to admit their vulnerabilities."

"That's right! You gain power through consuming other people's emotions, right?"

"Correct." His eyes sparkled as he looked down at me, his focus acute. My belly wiggled at the notice, unused to the interest. "Something tells me it won't bother you."

"Why is that? I mean, no it won't. I don't really care if you can read me. How did you know, though?"

His head tilted again. "You advertise your emotional state. What are you?"

"A wolf, I guess," I replied, but something prevented me from telling him how I knew. Maybe it was his confident, relaxed manner and easy smile, or his attractiveness, or how comfortable he made me feel—light and carefree. Hell, maybe I was just awestruck. Whatever the reason, I just wanted to keep my business to myself. Maybe hide my baggage a little.

He shook his head a little at that. "Not just a wolf, though, surely."

"I didn't know I had magic until recently. My . . . guardian, I guess—Granny. You know of Granny?"

"I do. She and her organization are not well liked here."

"Right. Well, she should've been able to feel my animal,

and yet she told me all this time that she couldn't feel any magic."

"I feel your pain. Why did you believe it, if you don't mind my asking?"

I told him about my mom and my upbringing, noticing how he veered away from the castle doors and took me across the grounds instead. He asked how I'd ended up with Granny, and I tried to give him a summary. He stopped me, though, with a gentle hand to my forearm, and asked for the full account.

He listened with a patient ear and then reciprocated with his own experiences. He'd grown up dirt poor, barely able to put food on the table. His grandma and mom had been lost to the sickness that plagued the kingdom, and his dad had barely made it. His sister had been the hunter of the family and he the caretaker, a role he greatly enjoyed.

Something about that last fact sent butterflies through my belly. I loved a strong man who enjoyed taking care of his own.

Memories of Weston's attention to his pack surfaced, as did the constant small things he always did for me, even when he and I were at odds with each other.

"Shall we sit?" Hannon said, cutting through my reverie.

He stopped in front of a bench placed before a bed of flowers.

"I'm not keeping you from anything?" I asked, hesitating.

His gaze was unwavering. "No."

I grinned like a dummy. A mythical phoenix was taking a moment with me.

A *phoenix!*

"Okay," I said. "I don't really have anything to do, especially since the royals have all my stuff."

"About that . . . What brought on the change from making the product to wanting to stop it? Other than how Granny has treated you?" he asked.

My smile dwindled. "Oh. Is this step one of my interrogation?"

"No—well, yes." His vivid blue eyes sparkled. "I'm sure the royals will want to know a lot of this information and, coming from me—with my type of magic—they'll know it is genuine. But I'm asking because I *am* curious. I enjoy talking with you. You're so fresh and honest, so forthcoming with your emotions. I'm interested."

My face heated, and I had no idea why his words would cause a tingle of both embarrassment and delight. "I like talking with you, too."

13

WESTON

I could barely focus with the feelings seeping through the bond. Delight, intrigue, *attraction.* I didn't know whom she was with, but I wanted to find that person and snap off his or her limbs.

"Dismissed," I growled when the meeting had come to an end. The various shifters gave me cagey looks, knowing something was wrong but not really wanting to find out what it was.

"What's up?" Micah asked as I stood and gathered my things. He was the dragon commander—the same rank as me. Together we oversaw the armies and guard.

"Nothing. I gotta go. My—the captive has a meeting with the royals."

He and I were constantly on shaky ground. The old and mostly untrue adage that wolves didn't get along with dragons was accurate in our case, but even still, his look held commiseration and pity. "Heard about the true mate. Tough break."

He had no idea—especially since she was out right now with someone who had clearly interested her.

A list of who it might be scrolled through my head as I handed off my stuff to a palace assistant and stalked down the hall. I could feel the pull of her throbbing in my core, her location somewhere to the northeast. Stationary.

"Beta, there you are." Hadriel jogged up to me, then kept jogging to keep pace.

"Why aren't you with Aurelia?" I growled.

"Yes, about that. Don't worry, she is in great hands. She went out to the flowers to check on her moon lily thing and Arleth sent her back with Hannon."

Hannon.

The fucking phoenix.

Trust Aurelia to find the one being I could not kill.

"They're out— Well, I can tell you know where they are," Hadriel said. "Fuck this running. I'm doing way too much of it today. Anyway, sir, they're just talking."

That feeling of attraction rattled my nerves. Hannon was handsome. Anyone with eyes could see that.

"They're about to be fucking done talking."

"Yes, well, if I may." He cleared his throat nervously. "You do not have a claim on her, sir. She is newly out of an abusive relationship. It doesn't matter that it wasn't romantic. She needs to find her feet. She needs to figure out who she is. Your crowding her isn't going to make her come around. She's stubborn, remember? She needs to find an attachment to you on her own, outside of the push from the true mate bond."

"She found an attachment to me on our way here. She's denying it, instead of deepening it."

"You can't blame her for being wary of an attachment formed after you took her against her will. You're the only male she's known outside of her village. She doesn't even know her wolf. You need to give her time."

"So that she can find an attachment with someone else?"

"So that she can realize she doesn't want an attachment with someone else. And come to trust that nature chose wisely."

I reached the back door and, instead of pushing it open, punched it. Glass shattered. Wood tore away from one of the hinges.

The feeling of her finding someone else attractive caused rage to run through my middle. Everything in me screamed, *Mine! End the threat to my claim!*

But Hadriel was right. I'd burned her life down and propped myself up as the only safe space she had to run to. It wasn't fair. Aurelia was in a new place with a new animal. An alpha animal, too, one pushing and pulling at her. She needed a little freedom to meet new people and figure things out. She didn't understand how to work with her primal side, and she'd need time to learn her wolf and merge everything together. My role right now should be supportive, guiding her through this time. It was what an alpha did. What a mate did. I had to trust that Aurelia would see, in time, that we fit together. That it wasn't just an attraction, an urge; not with us.

I took a deep breath to calm the rage. If it wasn't for the years of high-level training and constantly working on my control, this would've been beyond me. As it was, it took every ounce of effort I possessed to turn around slowly, unclench my fists and jaw, and stay inside the castle.

"Make sure she is dressed. We have an appointment with the royals." I pushed forward.

"Oh, and sir?" Hadriel huffed. "Fucking jogging. Why do people do this for fun?" He caught up to me again. "Just so you know, it was accidentally mentioned to her that you two are true mates. She didn't know what that was, so then it was explained."

I slowed. "And?" I looked over at him. "Was she mad?"

"No. She seemed kind of dazed. I don't think she really knew how to take the news. It didn't have the same impact on her as it would on . . . well, normal people. The hazard of not growing up as a shifter, I guess. Or with any friends. Or people who even wanted to talk to her."

Just my fucking luck. My true mate—a legendary thing, a gift from the gods—didn't realize the significance. The hits just kept coming.

"Go get her ready," I said, picking up the pace again. I needed a cold shower, or maybe to fight. I doubted the king would be pleased if I threatened him, so a shower it was.

Five minutes before our appointment, Hadriel brought Aurelia to meet me outside the throne room. Her new clothes wouldn't be ready from the seamster for several days, so she wore one of Hadriel's outfits, the jacket sleeves rolled at the wrist and the pants rolled at the bottom—basically swimming in his clothes. Hadriel and Vemar walked behind her wearing similar outfits. The only things obviously different were their shoes—Aurelia wore her boots while the men wore their velvet shoes.

Despite her odd attire, she was simply radiant, her smile infectious and her glow mesmerizing. Her long black hair, cut through with slices of white, fell around her beautiful face, her skin sun-kissed from her time outside. Her agile steps were more like a glide, her walk purposeful and effortless. I couldn't wait to see her wolf run.

"Aurelia," I said as she approached, my ill humor evaporating immediately in her proximity.

She spotted me, and her step faltered. Her gaze intensified as it lingered on my eyes and then roamed my face, pausing on my lips. Her eyes dropped, scanning my shoulders and turning hungry as she surveyed my chest. When she met my eyes again, I could see the heat burning within her. I could feel it within our bond, reacting to me the same way I was to her.

Flashbacks from yesterday played through my mind: ripping off her clothes and pinning her against the tree with my body; my cock plunging into her, as deep as I could go, locking her to me; the pack watching us establish a four-way bond, knowing who she belonged to.

She must've had similar thoughts, because her answering desire fanned my flame higher. I hadn't realized either of us had moved until we stopped just inches from each other—her looking up at me, chest heaving, my hands dusting her hips.

"Hi," she said breathily.

"She was just reminded that a pretty face or even a mythical creature will never compare to her mate," my wolf said.

He was absolutely correct.

My wolf's smugness worked into a grin on my lips.

"Hey, baby," I replied, confident she would come around.

"Gu-guess—" She closed her eyes while clearing her throat, and I knew she was trying to wedge in a little distance between her primal desire and her logical, unemotional brain.

All I needed to do was prove to her logical side that what she felt for me was genuine. She fit with me perfectly, as did her wolf with mine. I'd questioned it when I first met her—I hadn't understood how I could have been mated to a criminal—but getting to know her had brought me around. I couldn't wait to watch her feelings for me blossom and grow.

Besides, I loved a good chase.

I could feel my wolf's anticipation at the prospect.

She tried again. "Guess how many combined dicks we have between us."

She gestured at Vemar and Hadriel, who waited patiently behind her. Hadriel had a little smirk, and I wondered if it matched mine. He'd clearly picked up on all the same things.

I shook my head slowly, falling into those sunburst eyes. "Give me a hint?"

"At least two, but those aren't on the jackets." Her smile intensified as Vemar guffawed.

"I heard you met Hannon," I said lightly.

She radiated joy. "Yes. An actual phoenix! How cool is that? He seems really nice. Do you know him well?"

"Fairly well. I speak with him often. He's kind, and he's a gentleman."

Hadriel inclined his head in approval as Aurelia nodded. I felt no desire coming through the bond. The last bit of tension within me eased.

"Yeah, he seemed it," she said. "I spoke to the dragon queen's brother . . . who is a phoenix. While dragons flew overhead. While standing in a beautiful garden on the grounds of an actual castle. This does not seem like real life."

I answered her with a smile, while still standing within inches of her.

"He'll be in here." I gestured toward the door. "He can read emotions—he's essentially a human lie detector. They are also going to give you a type of elixir that pushes someone to tell the truth."

Time to start truly earning her trust.

"I thought about using it when I captured you from your village, but read your journals instead." She frowned at me, but no anger came through the bond. She no longer held resentment. That was probably the most promising thing of all. "You should know they have your journals, have looked at them, and have both your and my notes regarding them. I'm sorry about the invasion of privacy."

I meant it. I felt sick knowing that other people were reading her private thoughts. That I'd had to do it. I imagined it was a vulnerable feeling, especially with all she'd gone through, and it wasn't fair to keep dragging her through it. We didn't have much of a choice, though. They needed to see what the reality of her situation had been, how Aurelia had been pushed into her trade, and that I was telling the truth when I said she'd had literally no way to escape. Nothing proved her innocence better than the emotional accounts of the events.

She nodded mutely and took a deep breath. "Shall we?"

"I'm proud of you," I murmured. "I'm proud of you for being willing to put yourself through this. For being so strong."

Her eyes opened up all the way down to her soul and then filled with tears. "Thank you," she whispered.

I wanted to wrap her in my arms but refrained, instead turning to open the door.

The royals sat on the dais upon their thrones, equally representing the law of the land. To the side of the queen, a step down and in a smaller chair, sat her brother. Surprisingly, the seat to the side of the king was occupied by Calia, a fairy in the high court of the fairy kingdom who'd come to visit the royals for a few months. I'd known she had arrived in the kingdom, but hadn't been told she'd be sitting in on this interrogation. Arleth, the king's mother, sat off to the side with several elixir makers I didn't know very well. The crates of Aurelia's product sat in the center of the room, and a smattering of Granny's drugs lined a table beside them.

A shock of fear swept through Aurelia and she froze, her wide eyes staring at the king.

"It's the monster from the library," she mumbled, so low I could barely hear her. She started backing up. "I've changed my mind. Fuck this. I decline my invitation!"

"He's going to listen." Hadriel caught her by her shoulders and started pushing forward again. "He's not going to judge you yet."

"He looks like he's going to tear my arms off and play the drums with them."

"He always looks like that. He almost never rips arms off, though. It'll be fine." Hadriel pushed her harder, grunting with the effort. "Why the fuck can't I move you? You weigh all of a hundred pounds."

Vemar reached out to help, and I stepped in his way. The warning look I sent had him backing off.

"I won't let him hurt you," I murmured to her. The king would be able to hear me, but he might as well know where I stood before we got any further into this. "They are just going to ask you questions, and then let you go."

She stopped and looked at me then. I ducked my head so our faces were level, allowing her to search my eyes for the truth. Through our bond, I could feel her trust in me overshadow her wariness, and she nodded once. I nodded once in return. Aurelia took a deep breath and allowed me to guide her forward, even as her whole body shook. A solitary chair waited for her in front of the dais. Her seat didn't look overly comfortable, but neither was the vibe of the room.

She had no choice but to endure it.

Aurelia

Hadriel and Vemar stood behind me as my self-appointed support system. I hadn't known it, but the two of them were a sort of pair, working together after the fall of the curse to keep the castle running smoothly.

They couldn't be more different—the large, imposing dragon was utterly laid-back, while the much smaller wolf was loud and crass and blindingly colorful. Even if the worst possible outcome came to pass, it meant more than I could ever say that they stood behind me now.

Weston positioned himself at my side, his power and confidence soothing my nerves and relaxing my muscles one by one. This wasn't primal. My reaction to him now was built on the sort of unwavering trust one could only garner through repeated, intense danger. He'd already seen me safe through the dangerous situation with Alexander and gotten me through to this point. He remained by my side now, even as I faced one of the worst set of circumstances I'd ever been in.

"Hello," said a beautiful woman who sat on the dais in one of the matching thrones. She was the dragon queen, obviously. Her blue eyes shone with authority and power, her stare so much more intense than that of her brother. The effect nearly turned my spine to water. "You may state your name."

I took a moment to collect my courage against her stare, ignoring the king's golden-eyed menace altogether. "Aurelia Silverwood."

"Has Weston explained how this is going to work?" she asked.

"You're going to give me an elixir, Hannon is going to catch any lies, and you're going to ask me questions."

"That's the gist of it, yes." The queen motioned toward the table. "Weston?"

Weston crossed to where she pointed, picking up a little vial and turning toward me with a shuttered expression. I could feel his anger and wariness through the bond. He hesitated in pulling out the cork, fire kindling in his slate-gray eyes.

"It won't hurt her," said the queen softly.

Weston approached me, looking frustrated and apologetic.

"It's okay," I told him, reaching out my hand with a comforting smile. My heart swelled with the knowledge that he was so worried about me, primal need to protect me or not. This wasn't his wolf; this was the man. That meant something. "I'll be okay."

My fingers brushed his as I took the vial, electricity sparking in the touch. I gave him a wink as I pulled out the stopper and drank it down. Then winced. I couldn't place the taste, but it wasn't great.

"We've heard and read several accounts of why you started making drugs," the queen said. "Based on your earlier conversations with him, Hannon has authenticated those accounts. I'd like to hear it in your own words."

"I won't be as reliable as they are," I told her honestly. "I've read over some of my journals, and I've remembered some things, but until Weston took me from my village recently, I'd sort of glossed over the trauma from those years. Hidden it in my memory. I can't tell you why. Survival, maybe? Acclimating to the life as I knew it? Trying to protect myself? I'm not sure, though I am more than willing to tell you what I remember."

Then I did just that.

The timelines were easy to recall, but some of the details were still fogged over with age. When I started to explain the process I'd used to figure out how to make the actual drugs, though, my mind started to float, the sharpness of my thoughts turning fuzzy.

"I think this elixir is starting to work." I touched the back of my hand to my warm cheek. "It's making thought more difficult. Does that clear? Because it's going to get in the way."

"That's the point. It'll make it hard for you to fabricate stories," the queen said. So far, no one else in the throne room had uttered a sound.

I furrowed my brow. "That's faulty logic. It'll make it impossible for rational, coherent thoughts, and harder to remember my past. Forget about explaining what I know about the coating Granny placed on my product."

"Your drugs, you mean?"

I sighed. "Sure, my drugs." Frustrated that she was intentionally missing my point, I shook my head. "I'll go with this for a bit to see how badly it'll mess with me, but if it gets much worse, I'm going to stop the effect."

"Stop the effect?" asked the woman from the garden with poise and gray hair. She must've been of high standing to be in this room. I found it odd no one had told me who everyone was, not that it really mattered. Her gaze swung to Weston. "Did you allow her to bring in some other chemical or drug?"

I tensed, not liking that they might try to implicate Weston.

It was Hadriel who spoke up. "She's got nothing but her knickers. She can render her products ineffective. I've seen her do it."

"You, too, with 'the product'?" the queen asked Hadriel, her professional and authoritative tone smoothing into longstanding friendliness. It was clear they knew each other well. Hadriel hadn't been lying.

Hadriel shrugged. "I told you, love, it's complicated."

The queen shook her head and refocused on me, her tone hard now as she said, "I want to see you brush off that elixir."

"Okay, but it'll stop working, not that it is working very well now. My name is Dermia Foothold, the harbinger of fungus. I am the princess of a distant land with a mermaid for an assistant. I never see the bitch. She's always in the water. My—"

"Enough." The queen put up a hand as Hadriel and Vemar both spat out laughs.

"See? She is very creative," Hadriel said. "It is an absolute treat watching her take her hallucinogens, I'm telling you."

"Hadriel, quiet!" the king barked, and a wave of fear washed over me. Hadriel shivered, feeling the power, before hunching down.

Ordinarily, that might make me defiant, make me want to stick up for him. When that monster looked at me, though, I just wanted to hunch down with Hadriel and make myself as small as possible.

"Have you seen this before?" the queen asked the poised gardener.

The woman shook her head. "It's powerful. It should be working."

Didn't these people ever sample their products? They should know the effects intimately.

"It's trying to goad me into telling the truth," I relayed, "but if I apply a little resistance, it just breaks apart. Meanwhile, my mind is fuzzy and I'm annoyed. I'm going to brush it off. I hadn't planned on lying, anyway."

I closed my eyes and shook the effects from my system,

much more easily than with my product. When I blinked my eyes back open, the dragons wore scowls and Hadriel was saying, "That's normal for her. It scared the shit out of us the first time she did it."

I lifted my eyebrows. "So. Where were we?"

The queen scratched her nose, clearly perplexed. Unlike the wolves, the dragons seemed very expressive. "Right, well . . ." She cleared her throat. "Let's start with the basics."

We went through a typical day in the village. I answered questions about making the product and how I'd learned to improve it. I had to pause, feeling my face heat as I tried to think of how best to word my response.

"Um . . ." I said slowly, really wishing I hadn't promised to be completely honest and upfront. "Granny was able to procure a journal from this kingdom. From the court, actually. It helped immensely."

"One of *my* journals?" the queen said, her eyes darkening with anger. Power surged through the room.

Fuck, dragons were scary.

I impressed myself with my steady tone. "Not yours, per se. Someone who was learning di-directly from y-you." Well, almost.

"She stole one of our journals to help you make drugs?" the queen said.

"Yes. It worked."

She shook her head, mystified. "Do you feel bad about any of this? For the part you played in killing people?"

I felt my spine straighten of its own accord. Weston and Hadriel both stiffened.

"*My* product does not kill people," I replied. "It is habit forming for some, but it is not chemically addictive. You can see the differences in my product and what ends up in the markets. Granny's coating—apparently added to make it look like candy—is what's harmful. The only purpose I can imagine it serves has to be the addictive quality, but it's not a good business plan to make people sick. The actual journey—the high—is the part I make."

"How do you know what the coating does if you didn't have a hand in making it?"

"Because, apparently unlike you with that truth-telling elixir, I sampled the product to know what it does and how the body reacts. I took several of Granny's products, enough to addict me and to kill me if it wasn't for Weston. I made note of every effect. I am now intimately acquainted with how it works."

"How and where did you get several of them if they weren't created in your village?"

My stomach clenched. I knew my escape that one night from camp was a dereliction of Weston's duty. He'd done it to help me. I wouldn't repay that kindness by tattling on him.

I lifted my chin defiantly. "I don't want to say where or how or why. It's enough to know that I took them to figure out how they were altered from what I routinely turn in, which is what is in those crates."

The king leaned forward, his voice a rough growl. "I can make you say where and how and why."

Weston stiffened. This time I didn't, nor did I hunch. Fuck that guy. Pain wouldn't make me bend, and they probably planned on killing me, anyway. The queen, at least, didn't seem overly interested in pardoning me because of my upbringing. Fine, so be it. But I would not allow Weston to go down with me. I drew the line at making others suffer for my sins.

I met that menacing golden gaze and said, "All due respect, dragon, no you cannot. I do not break under torture, and I no longer fear death. Do your worst."

Out of the corner of my eye, I saw Vemar puff out his

chest, nodding in what seemed like approval. It seemed I had something in common with the mad dragon. I liked him more for it.

"She's protecting someone," Hannon said, watching me closely.

Weston's head jerked my way, and I realized belatedly he'd been staring at the king, his body tense. Now his gaze probed mine before realization dawned. The tender warmth coming through the bond momentarily stole my breath.

"It's me," he told the royals, his tone concealing his emotions. "She's trying to protect me." Now it softened as he spoke to me. "I already told them I knew you planned to drug me and that I let you do it." He turned back to the royals. "She bought Granny's product with the gold I gave her."

I clenched my jaw, unhappy that he was putting himself into harm's way on my behalf, but I didn't say anything. If things got worse, I'd find a way to excuse him of any wrongdoing. I assumed the dragons would be all too happy to take their grievances out on Granny's drugmaker rather than their prized commander.

"How did you know which product was Granny's?" the queen asked me.

I huffed, running my fingers through my hair. I explained about the design, unable to keep my anger in check.

"She didn't even change the fucking wings! It looks utterly absurd. Fairy wings on a butterfly? Ridiculous. It would've been a simple fix, not to mention I did that drawing when I was a kid. I can draw one so much better now."

The woman off to the side of the king--the one with beautiful blond-white hair so light it nearly matched my streaks, and flawless, radiant skin—spoke for the first time.

"The middle was originally a fairy?" Her voice was clear and pleasant even though she was visibly annoyed. "Why?"

I felt my face redden. I suddenly found myself really hating this interrogation. I hadn't realized parts would be so embarrassing.

"I've always been fascinated with the fairies. They seem so mystical and magical. I never knew I had magic, so that greatly appealed to me."

The queen looked over at the woman, I assumed to make sure she was satisfied, before continuing. We went over what I'd seen in the city where I bought Granny's products and how I reacted to the alterations. I described the people I'd spoken to, including those in the alleyway, before Hadriel gave his account of the tavern where he'd heard about my capture. He also described how badly I'd been beaten when Alexander tried to forcibly remove me from the camp, though I had no idea why.

"Let me get this straight." The queen adjusted herself in her seat to get comfortable. "You had the chance to go back to Granny, but you chose instead to come here and face punishment for the part you played in her organization?"

"I had the chance to go with Alexander," I answered. "I hadn't yet learned Granny was still alive. I'd rather die at the hands of your petrifying king than end up with Alexander."

"And now?"

"And now I just want enough time to derail Granny's organization, dismantle her product, and say goodbye to my new friends. After that, I'll accept my punishment with grace, whatever it may be. As I always have."

"You always have what?" the queen asked.

"Accepted my punishments with grace."

The queen studied me for a long moment as a line formed between her brows.

"And this?" She pointed at the crates before stepping off her throne.

"Crap, you're tall," I blurted with a release of breath. "Is everyone in this kingdom fucking enormous?"

"They're dragons, love. That's how it goes," Hadriel murmured.

"This is not dangerous?" the queen asked. "It's not addictive? I can pick out any of these things at random, from any of the crates, and you'll eat it?"

"Yes," I said.

Hadriel raised his hand. "So will I."

The queen looked at him before shaking her head. "It wasn't smart taking this stuff, Hadriel. What were you thinking?"

"In my defense, she did it first. But seriously, look at it. That stuff is a mess. It's way different than the finished product Granny sells." He pointed at the table. "Have her crack it open and show you."

I lifted my hand. "I would like to point out that taking just one is not an ideal test of my integrity. Granny's coating needs to build up in the bloodstream before it kills. Three, I believe, will be plenty. I'd happily take three of any of my products, either all the same or all different, whatever you prefer."

All movement in the room ground to a halt as several pairs of eyes widened, the gaze of each person in the room sticking to me.

I raised my eyebrows and shrugged. "If you're going to test something, you need to be thorough," I explained. "Taking just one of Granny's final products makes you sick, but it doesn't kill you. Not until it builds up."

Vemar barked out a laugh, and I had no idea what was

so funny. It was starting to worry me that these people made medicinal elixirs that they didn't thoroughly test or maybe even understand. How'd they ever get so good at it?

The queen looked at Hadriel for a moment before turning and taking one of Granny's products from the table. She handed it to me. "Show me how much of that is yours."

I did as she said, peeling off the coating and pointing to the crate holding the sleeping agent.

"This is what I gave to Weston. My product, I mean, not Granny's. It's that one, there. You can see the likeness." I read the name from the wrapper. "Huh. Dream Time is actually a good name for it. Clever."

"And this?" She handed me another.

"Ah, the relaxant, yes. In human form, this just settles the nerves. It's fairly mild."

"Too mild," Hadriel said. "I was bored."

"The fail-safe on this one is shifting into your animal form. It'll negate the effects. Now we are learning, however, that when this is taken in wolf form, it loosens the pack bond. Or something to that effect. Weston will have to explain it."

"I did," he replied. I nodded.

"Fail-safe?" the queen muttered, looking at Weston, then Hadriel, before shaking her head again. It was clear none of this lined up with what she'd been expecting. "Your explanation this morning, Weston, was the first I've ever heard about that. I don't understand how something like that could be . . . baked into a recipe, and I don't know how I've never heard about it before now. I've investigated Granny's product extensively. I, quite simply, don't believe it. I can't. Given all I've learned, it doesn't make sense."

"Let her show you." Hadriel pointed at me. "She can show you. I saw her do it in your old village."

The queen stared at him for a long moment.

"Be that as it may, Aurelia, you are still the foundation of this company." She moved the crates around to get at the right product. "You're the backbone. Without you, it doesn't exist."

"Of course it does," I said in annoyance. "That coating can be applied to anything similar."

"It takes three to five uses for the addiction to kick in." The queen bent to grab the product. "We thought it was two at one time, but it doesn't happen quite that fast. People would conceivably be fine if they just did it once or twice."

"Unless they did it within a twenty-four- to forty-eight-hour window, depending on the person," I replied. "Then that coating, which I think has some sort of poisonous element, builds up like I said. It took me three doses for a fatal attack, but I hadn't had anything in my system already."

The queen stopped in front of me with her hand out, offering the product. She was looking at Weston, though. "I'm going to have her take this. You're okay with that?"

"That? Yes. Granny's? No."

The queen shook her head yet again with a small, disbelieving smile and finished handing it off. I popped it into my mouth.

"My point being," the queen said, "that they don't get addicted right away. They keep taking it because it is, by far, the best on the market. It's the best high, the most fun, the best . . . stress reliever. It's the product you make that keeps people coming back until the hook."

"I take full responsibility for that." I clasped my hands in my lap, part of me having known it would come down to this.

"She doesn't feel remorse," Hannon said.

Surprise evident in her tone, the queen asked me, "You don't feel bad that you were making drugs?"

"No." I felt Weston's frustration come through the bond. "My life is not a fairytale. I was making products that were less dangerous than some of the medicines you sell. If people want a vacation of the mind, I'll make it for them, no problem. If they want to relax, or need something to chase away sorrow, I've got it. The only thing I feel bad about is that coating. That and the stupid fucking butterfly."

The queen braced her hands on her hips, shaking her head as she looked down at me. She was not as scary as that golden-eyed monster, but still plenty intimidating. My wolf was on edge in her proximity. "I really don't know what to say. I find it difficult to believe you had no idea about any of this. I can't fathom it. The maker of the drugs didn't know it was hurting people?"

"All due respect, love, but if you saw that village, you'd get it," Hadriel said.

"Yes, I intend to further question the group that went." The queen narrowed her eyes at me. "Weston, I don't know what to say. I understand this is complicated, but she made the drugs. She *made* them. She kept people coming back, they got hooked, and some of them died. There must be consequences."

"I accept that," I said.

"She means it," Hannon replied, looking hard at me.

Anger and something akin to violence kindled through the bond, but it didn't show on Weston's face. I tried to send calming feelings back at him. I'd already told him I'd accept what came, and Hannon was right—I meant it.

"I will, however, give you time," the queen told me. "I expect you to show us how you make that product, and let you try to figure how out Granny makes hers. I will be watching you, but I will allow you to try to do what is right. Is that fair?"

"Very," I said. It was all I'd been hoping for, actually.

"How do you feel?" The queen couldn't hide her curiosity about my product.

"Can I have one, and I'll tell you how *I* feel?" Hadriel raised his hand.

"It hasn't kicked in yet. It's a slow-release product. It seems more natural when the stress melts away incrementally, like soaking in a hot bath." I summoned my courage and stood. "It is time for me to demand some answers of my own. There are things you need to atone for, as well."

The queen towered over me. She didn't back up or seem threatened in any way. One of her eyebrows arched. "Things *I* need to atone for?" A little smile played across her lips. "How so?"

"You have been profiting off Granny's drugs. I highly doubt it costs that much to make, yet you sell the elixir needed to stave off the addiction at a cost only the rich can afford. And multiple doses are needed for it to work. You judge me for making drugs, yet you have your hand out, just like Granny. Additionally, you broke the laws of *my* kingdom. Her product is now legal there. Your people unlawfully crossed the shores under false pretenses, abducted one of their citizens, and kidnapped her from her home shores. You are not innocent. None of your people have clean hands. How do you plan to atone for all of this?"

"Fuckstains on wooden shoes, don't challenge that dragon," Hadriel murmured out the side of his mouth.

The queen's eyes sparked fire. Weston took a step closer to me. The king leaned forward, and suddenly I wondered if I'd made a huge mistake.

14

AURELIA

The dragon had a vicious gleam in her eyes, but I didn't back down. I'd heal faster now.

"We sell that elixir at cost. In all kingdoms but yours, it is offered at that price. Yours, however, has a heavy tax applied to it that we have no control over. *Your* royals are price gouging, not us. As for the rest of your accusations?" She shrugged. "I'll just have to make sure you aren't able to tell on us. But know I have no qualms about breaking the rules of your kingdom to stop people from dying. If they weren't so greedy, no one would be in this mess. Now it's gone way too far."

Learning about the cost took the wind out of me. They'd been trying to do the right thing, and were clearly the only people who had.

I sagged, not really caring about the rest. I'd thrown it in there to add weight to my claim, but it was clear their primary goal was to stop Granny's drug trade. They were taking desperate measures, something I understood.

"I understand." I felt defeated, but it served no purpose

to challenge the dragon queen further. Doing so would certainly end with me thrown in a dungeon.

I sat back down.

The queen tilted her head, her confusion evident. "That's it?" She looked at Weston, and then back to me. "No follow-up? No rage?"

"She's not a dragon, love," Hadriel said, still behind me. "She's as balanced and easy as Weston usually is."

"Not always," Vemar offered.

"I'm almost disappointed," the queen muttered, turning for her throne. "I wanted to see how fast she is."

"Lightning," Vemar said. "That little thing ran around me so fast I didn't even know what was happening."

"Calia," the queen said.

The woman with the beautiful indigo eyes and white-blond hair reached beside her and came back up with my lantern. I frowned at it in confusion. I had no idea why this would be involved in the questioning. The product I took kicked in at that moment, though, making it almost hard to care.

"Where did you get this?" Calia asked, holding up the lantern.

"It was a gift."

"From whom?"

"Granny. Like I told you, she knew I liked fairies. She brought me a fairy lantern."

"Why did you travel with it?"

I frowned at her as I leaned back farther into my chair, getting more comfortable. I took a deep breath and closed my eyes, enjoying the pleasant sensation.

"I said, why did you travel with it?"

I opened my eyes. "Why does anyone travel with a lantern? To see by. I didn't have access to my animal until recently, remember? I had it with me when I was captured . . . *in the dark*."

The queen's eyebrows slowly lifted. The golden-eyed king continued to stare menacingly. Thankfully, the product made it much less terrifying.

"Yes, but why did you have a lantern that didn't work?" Calia pushed, and I squinted an eye at her.

"It works if you know how to turn it on. It is magical. Like the fairies. Here, give it to me and I can show—"

She ran her finger along the top then the bottom in a practiced motion. The lantern flared to life, the color within perfectly matching her eyes.

I furrowed my brow. "Well, if you knew how to turn it on, why did you say it didn't work?"

She turned it off before walking over to me and holding it out. "You do it."

"She is really, really confused," Hannon said, grinning. "And very relaxed. The latter must be the drugs."

"Yes, Hannon, we could tell by her really, really confused expression and really, really laid-back posture," the queen replied, and I grinned. It was like two siblings talking instead of a queen and her advisor. Surreal.

I took the lantern, repeated the process, and watched it flare to life.

I held it out to her, shrugging one shoulder. "I've dropped it a couple times, but it's really resilient. I guess I won't need it now, though. Too bad, kinda. I really enjoyed it. It's so pretty."

"I wasn't able to turn it on," Weston said.

Calia's frown down at me was pronounced. "This lantern was a gift from the fairy kingdom court to the royals of the Red Lupine kingdom."

"Oh," I said on a release of breath, realizing what she was getting at. "It was stolen?"

"It appears so . . . unless their royals gave the lantern to Granny. Which, in all honesty, they might have. With the gift was a note telling the Red Lupine Kingdom that when they were worthy, they could make this lantern glow."

She continued to stare down at me.

"She is still really, really confused," Hannon supplied.

"*I* am also really, really confused," Vemar said. "What's the point that she and I are clearly missing, Kind Lady?"

"The point is," Calia said, "those royals will never be worthy, and therefore never able to use this lantern. In order to make this lantern glow, you have to be of fairy blood."

"Before you say it, Hannon," the queen said, "we can all tell that she is still very, very confused."

I laughed incredulously, pressing two fingers to the center of my forehead. If this kingdom didn't accuse me of one thing, it was another. It shouldn't surprise me at this point. I still hadn't worked out what the mind-fucking was all about.

I folded my hands in my lap. "Both my parents were shifters," I said patiently. I would not be randomly stabbing anyone with scissors this time. "I didn't know my father, but he worked in a shifter-run court. Both of my mother's parents were shifters. My mom would've said if they weren't. No one she knew had ever visited the fairy kingdom. She hoped I might get to see it one day. There is simply no way, not even a slight chance, I have fairy blood."

"Let me see that lantern, Calia," the queen said. Calia handed it off. "How do I get it to work again?"

Calia showed her. Just as when Weston had tried it, nothing happened. The king was next, then Hannon. None of them could get it to light.

"You may recall from Aurelia's journals that her father

was from the Flamma kingdom," Weston said. He briefly recounted my mom's history.

The queen looked at the king, then over at the gardener from that morning. "Ring any bells, Nyfain? Arleth?"

"I've already got it on my list of things to look into it," Hadriel said. "I heard that on the road. I'm burning with curiosity."

"And so her story becomes more complicated . . ." Nyfain said.

The others in the room tried the lantern, even Weston, who had tried it before. Through my haze of relaxation, I watched their fingers move over the surface in the right ways and in the right order. Nothing happened. As I watched, my apprehension grew, slowly burning away the influence of my product as my stomach started to tighten.

"No." I chuckled in disbelief and shook my head, my mind spinning. "This is ridiculous."

"Incredulity, fear, discomfort," Hannon said. "She definitely didn't know that."

I really liked Hannon, but he was starting to annoy me.

Sorry, he mouthed, and I wasn't sure if that made it better or worse.

"Did Granny know about that lantern, do you think?" Weston asked softly.

"Pain," Hannon said.

"I don't have fairy blood," I said with certainty, unwilling—or maybe unable—to believe there might be one more thing about me that I hadn't known, one more life-altering revelation hidden from me. "I don't. That's ridiculous. My mom didn't even have magic."

"She didn't have an animal," Hadriel murmured. "You said she had an effect on people, right? That they might have hated her in one moment but wanted to take her out in the next. Didn't you say that? She might've had a different magic."

I shook my head harder as pain broke through the lingering haze of my product. My mom had always had an effect on people—I'd noticed that, yes. They would be staring at her in hate-filled animosity one moment, then have moony stars in their eyes the next. Having magic, even a different, non-shifter magic, would've saved her life. It would've changed the whole trajectory of her future. And mine.

Then again, if she'd had magic like that, wouldn't she have used it to keep those men from breaking her body and setting fire to our home?

"But who would she have gotten it from?" I said logically, flames dancing in my memory. "My grandparents were wolves."

"A recessive gene, maybe?" Vemar tried. "A skeleton in the closet? Are they alive to ask?"

"No, they died when I was little." The tears building threatened to break free. "I can't have fairy blood. And if by some chance I did, which would be mind-blowing even without their magic, Granny couldn't have known about that lantern."

"Why is that?" Calia asked, setting it on the table. Her tone had softened noticeably, her expression full of compassion.

My emotions wobbled a little harder.

"Because if she knew about that lantern, then it would mean she'd kept another colossal secret from me, and I don't think I could handle that." It seemed I hadn't really known Granny at all. I'd created the illusion of a mother figure, and she'd happily let me believe it was reality. "I'm tired of being hurt. I'm tired of finding out things—" I wiped a tear away angrily. "I want to go now. I'm done with all this. I'm guilty, I'll be hanged at dawn, whatever. I don't want to do this anymore."

"Let her go," Hannon said quietly, a tear trailing down his cheek as well. "She's had enough."

Weston was beside me in a moment, helping me out of the chair and walking with me toward the door, his arm wrapped around me protectively. I breathed in his scent as I fell into his comforting embrace. Vemar followed as Hadriel took a little detour toward the crates.

"Boop," he said, taking one of the products.

"Are you serious right now?" the queen asked him just as he caught up to us. Weston opened the door.

Hadriel turned and called out over his shoulder, "I'm telling you, it's a good time."

Vemar went back for one as well. "Boop."

"Unprofessional," the queen hollered as we all exited into the hallway.

"Don't worry about any of that," Hadriel offered assuredly. I let Weston guide me. I didn't care where we went, as long as it was away from that room and those people. "We have time, Aurelia. We can do anything given enough time, even change their minds."

"Was she a fairy?" I asked a moment later, thinking back to the woman with the white-blond hair.

"Yes," Weston answered. "She's a member of the high court. She was in the demon dungeons with me, and also with Hadriel and the queen."

"At least I finally got to meet a fairy," I murmured, my lip wobbling at the magnitude of that. Of what my mom would say to hear that, how happy she'd be. "Or at least be grilled by one. Though if that lantern was intended to be a slight by the fairy court, why would they care if it was stolen?"

"A pile-on for these proceedings, maybe? Who knows," Hadriel said. "Don't let it worry you, love. I can get you a better one, I'm sure of it. She might even give that one back, since you can use it."

I didn't want that one back. I didn't want any of the gifts I'd gotten from Granny over the years. They all felt cheap now, dirty. Tainted. I wanted to put all this behind me and try to heal my tattered heart.

"What do you say we head to my quarters? It's only fair I let you poke around my things for a while," Weston offered. "Then we can run you a hot bath and maybe read for a bit. Or would you rather head back to the tower? Or . . . somewhere else?"

I could hear in his voice and feel through the bond his desire to help me. He worried over my wellbeing. He even offered me the space I'd thought I needed, giving me time to reflect on my own if I wanted.

I didn't want those things right now. I wanted *him*. Needed him, maybe. Craved him, definitely. I didn't give a shit if it was a true mates thing. I wanted to relish in his support and his body.

I leaned a little harder into him. "I guess I do owe you a snoop."

"Hadriel, tell Leala to bring her some things," Weston said, slowing at a corner. "I'll place an order for dinner." He looked down at me. "Or would you rather cook?"

I smiled, reaching out for his hand. "Tomorrow, maybe. Not tonight."

"Tomorrow, then." He threaded his fingers into mine. "We'll get you a room that can be set up for cooking, how's that?"

"Goodbye, Captive Lady," Vemar said, giving me a thumbs-up as he and Hadriel continued down the hall. "Keep your head up, okay? The mind-fuck is still weird, but I'm getting used to it. I feel a little like Hannon around you, I think."

"He keeps going on about a mind-fuck," I murmured as Weston tugged me with him.

"Is that why you got into an altercation with him earlier?"

"No. Well, yes, kind of. I think he was poking at me to see if I was being genuine, and I . . . snapped. Rather, my wolf did and I went with it. It took me a moment to come to my senses."

"He was impressed by how fast you moved."

"I doubt he was as impressed by the scissors sticking out of his leg."

"You don't know dragons very well." He stopped at the end of a corridor. The double door was painted a deep forest green befitting a wolf.

"No fuchsia?"

"Not in this life." He took out a key to unlock the door. "The queen was mystified at how you were able to get out of the tower. She was captive there for a time. She had to be let out."

"She was a captive? Is that the love language of you people?"

He didn't answer, instead pushing open the door and stepping aside. "Enjoy your snoop. I think I'll grab a book."

"Wow." The interior was enormous, at least twice the size of my cottage—and that was just the main sitting room and dining area. He had a sliding glass door that led out onto a little patio where I could see a tiny garden with vibrant pink and red and yellow flowers. Through an archway in the back was a large bedchamber and attached washroom. The bed was the biggest I'd ever seen, and from what I could see at this vantage point, the bath was just as absurd.

"Big enough for two dragons. In human form, anyway," he explained as he shrugged out of his dress shirt and draped it over the back of a chair.

"Sir." Entering the room was a man wearing one of the castle uniforms, this one in deep forest green, like the door. He was clean-shaven, with excellent posture, and bowed gracefully before Weston. "Do you require anything, Beta?"

"Send for dinner, if you would, Niles." Weston paused, looking at me. "Wine?"

"Yes, please," I answered demurely, smiling at Niles. "Thank you."

"Of course, madam." He bowed at me before retreating back into the hall, and I nearly laughed at the absurdity.

"If only my mom could see me now. She would think this was all an amazing treat, like my own little fairytale with an appropriately tragic ending. She had a dark sense of humor."

"Speaking of . . ." Weston entered the bedchamber. When he returned a moment later, he held in his hand a bound book with a lock on the front cover. "I got you another journal. I thought maybe you'd want to start fresh." He held up a little key with a heart-shaped metal handle. "It locks. To deter the snoops."

My breath hitched as I reached for it. The only gifts I'd been given since my mom passed had been from Granny, and I knew I'd never forget how dirty all those now felt. She'd manipulated me, using false pretenses to buy my happiness, my compliance.

This was . . . nothing like that. I could see it in the open way Weston looked at me as he handed it over. I could feel the warmth in the bond. There were no strings attached. No expectations. He was trying to do something kind. The little lock was a nice touch, emphasizing his apology while giving me an outlet, a fresh start.

It was endearing, touching, lovely, and, honestly, a little overwhelming. It was what I'd thought Granny's gifts had meant, though the bond proved his motivation was true. This gift held no illusions.

"Granny never said she was sorry," I murmured, feeling the soft cover before running my finger over the intricately decorated metal clasp. "She waited long enough after a punishment for the sting to go away, then she'd get me a present. The last one was that red cloak. She waited two months after I was punished for veering too close to the perimeter. It had seemed out of the blue, but after reading my journals and realizing her pattern, I know it wasn't."

"I hope you don't think this is me trying to gloss over the part I played in your journals—"

"No," I interrupted, laying a hand on his chest. "No, I don't."

"I thought maybe you'd want a fresh journal so that you could write down your thoughts and feelings, or even just memories of your mother, in a journal that hadn't been sifted through by others."

I smiled up at him, taking in his handsome face, his expressive gaze, as warm emotions rolled through me. "I know. It occurred to me Granny never apologized only because you have, many times. For many things. I was just thinking about how different it feels to get a gift from you than it did from her. Thank you. This is really thoughtful." I hugged the book against my chest. "I love it."

"I'll have your other journals returned to you tomorrow." He pushed down his slacks, and my gaze caught on the hard bulge between his legs and those powerful thighs. "The notes you were making . . ." He paused to turn and drape the pants over his shirt, and I caught sight of the scars crisscrossing his large back.

I reached out to trace one, as entranced as ever by his magnificent body, his perfect physique, but the need to understand his past pain and learn his tortured experiences tugged at me.

"A whip mark, right?" I asked softly.

He stilled against my touch. "Yes."

I ran my thumb across a small circle at the bottom of his back. "And this?"

"I'm not sure. A knife, maybe. Or a hot poker. I can't remember what it was. I just remember it went in deep and crippled me for weeks. I didn't mind it, though, because that meant they couldn't use me for their parties, their sexual desires. I spent my convalescence splayed on my stomach on the stone floor, torn between wishing for death and thinking of ways to burn the whole place to the ground."

I traced another line, thinking of what that must have been like. I'd been lied to and punished, but I'd had a bed and my own home. Sometimes it had gotten so bad that I'd wished for death, but ultimately, I had thought I could leave. Maybe that had been an illusion, but I hadn't actually been behind bars. I hadn't been in a little cell. The glaring difference between his past horrors and mine was that at least I'd had the impression of freedom. I'd had a lot of shit thrown at me in a very small span of time, but it was nothing like what he'd endured. I needed to remember to be thankful for that—thankful I was out of it now, thankful I could try to make things right.

"I'm sorry this happened to you," I murmured, my heart hurting for him.

He reached out, bracing his hand against his wardrobe. "Thank you for saying that."

Driven by impulse, I leaned forward and placed a kiss

between his shoulder blades, feeling more connected with him in that moment than at any point on our journey. I wasn't sure why, but I didn't want to ruin it by overthinking. Leaning away again, I dropped my hand and turned for his bathroom. Might as well start my snoop by investigating his hygiene.

15

WESTON

Dressed causally and sitting in my favorite chair in my living room, I held my book up as though reading it but instead watched my little wolf systematically move through my space. She'd been at it for an hour, reorganizing my washing kit and then my clothes, lining everything up perfectly so that things were easy to find. She wasn't so much snooping as setting everything to rights.

I'd never before left a lover in my quarters unsupervised. I didn't let women touch my things, let alone go through them. I'd thought this would be a lesson in humility, my secret spaces opened to investigation. Fair was fair, though, and I had planned to endure it.

Surprisingly, I hadn't had a single twinge of unease, not even when I stepped out to delay dinner so that she could finish her investigation without interruption. Organizing things seemed to put her mind at ease. She wasn't a person who liked to be idle. Not for long, anyway. Maybe she just didn't know what rest and relaxation felt like. As an alpha, I appreciated that. I never had much free time. It was good that she wouldn't expect it or want it, even.

More importantly, though, watching her leave her mark on my private sanctuary felt right. I wanted her touch on my things, her scent lingering in the air. I wanted anyone who entered to know she belonged here with me, that her intimate living quarters were also mine. The sight of it, the act of inviting her in, had peace blooming within me. My home felt more serene with her in it.

"You've never lit any of these candles." She surveyed the candelabra on top of a squat bookcase, the books in it either purchased because they were my very favorite or on loan from the castle's extensive library. "Why have candles if you don't light them?"

"Decoration. They look nice."

She gave me a flat look. "They look nicer when they're burning."

She dropped down to her knees to scan the titles, and I studied the gentle curve of her neck, her hair pulled away and piled on top of her head in a messy bun. She was such a delicate-looking thing.

Her size and the raging power within her made her unbearably fast, though. The king himself had commented on it after seeing her in the library. He'd never seen someone move so quickly: there one minute and out the door in the next. He'd admitted to being stunned, hit in the head with a book that he hadn't realized she'd thrown. He'd even tried the move she'd performed sliding down the stairs. He laughed as he relayed falling flat on his face.

"She would be a valuable addition to this kingdom," the king had said earlier in the day. "She has so much potential. This whole Granny mess is damned unfortunate."

He had no idea.

Aurelia leaned forward toward the books.

"No way! You have a copy of this?" She held out one of my favorites before leafing through the pages.

Usually, I'd tell a woman to put one of my treasured tomes down. She wasn't just "a woman," though. She was *the* woman. Mine. I would never think to spoil her joy.

"I loved this one," she exclaimed. "So exciting, and the hero? I swooned." She put it back and picked up another. "I didn't love this one so much, though. Kinda, well, boring."

"That one is a loan from the library. I haven't read it yet."

"Well, don't let me stop you from a boring time." She flashed a smile at me and put it back before touching a few more with the tip of her finger. Then she got up.

"You're not going to organize them?"

She shook her head, heading to my desk. "You have it the way you want it."

I furrowed my brow as I smiled. "How do you figure?"

"The really nice, shiny ones are a little removed from the run-of-the-mill, hard-used titles. The others are in between. You have it set up for what you love, what you want to read next, and what you'll get to, right?" She glanced up with pencils in hand, ready to put them in a new place.

"Right. But they aren't in alphabetical order."

"Cut me some slack, Weston. I'm not *that* anal."

But she *was* that anal. She was exactly that anal. She couldn't stop herself from lining things up perfectly—everything in its place at all times. I'd noticed it in her cottage and in her workspace, everywhere except the bedroom . . . where chaos reigned.

I found myself feeling . . . pleased. She'd correctly identified my books as something special to me, intimate, and allowed more leeway and chaos.

My need for her surged, overshadowing the fun of seeing her work through my space. My passion, my adoration, was suddenly too strong to keep attached to any sort of leash.

"Come here, Aurelia," I said with a hint of command.

She stilled in organizing my papers, slowly looking my way. A note of defiance tightened her shoulders and prevented her from immediately complying.

A little thrill ran through me at the desire to force my dominance. I loved these games. Apparently, so did she. I could feel it in the bond now, her craving for me rising.

I stared at her, my power swirling, and slowly lifted an eyebrow.

Her hunger coursed through her now. Still, she resisted.

I got up slowly, straightening to my full height. "When I tell you to come to me, Little Wolf, you do it."

The papers lowered to the desk as she turned to me in needy expectation.

"Now . . . *come here*." The command was evident this time, all my power sunk into those last two words.

She moved hesitantly, as though she couldn't help it. As though she couldn't stop herself, even when she tried to resist. Her desire was eclipsing all other emotions in the bond now. My cock was throbbing.

She stopped in front of me, her power merging with mine through the bond, boosting me higher. I felt like I'd been elevated, feet in the clouds, swelling with might. Fuck, that felt good. I felt like a god, my goddess alongside me, our wolves entwining.

I reached out and took her chin between my thumb and forefinger, looking down into her expectant sunburst gaze.

"I heard you were wandering the grounds today without permission," I said in a low, deep tone. A spark filled her eyes. She knew where this was going.

"Yes, Alpha," she said demurely.

"You know you aren't supposed to wander, don't you?"

Her breath sped up, her hands at her sides.

I laid my hands on her shoulders. "I warned you what would happen if you got caught, didn't I?" I slid one hand along her collarbone to the front of her throat and gripped firmly. "Didn't I?"

She licked her lips, drawing my attention to her mouth. "Yes." It wasn't more than a breathy whisper.

"Yes, what?"

"Yes, Alpha," she said, stronger now.

"Good girl." She shivered. "Now get on your knees and worship your alpha's cock."

She sank down gracefully in front of me. She pulled down my sweats and reached into my briefs, capturing my cock with her dainty hand. Moisture beaded at the tip, and my cock throbbed within her touch.

"Taste it."

She leaned forward, one hand on my cock, the other braced on my thigh.

"Eyes on me," I commanded.

Her eyes darted up as her tongue ran along the seam of my cockhead. She pulled the beaded liquid into her heart-shaped mouth and issued a throaty moan. A mate wasn't supposed to taste like candy until after two people imprinted, but she had always been delicious, from the first time I'd met her. Clearly she felt the same about me.

"Suck it in," I said greedily, and watched her lips wrap around the tip.

She did as I said, sucking my cock deep into her throat until my balls butted against her chin. Not many women could take my size, and truthfully, not many wanted to try. Aurelia had always been the exception, in everything. She sucked like it was her favorite pastime, pushing her lips against my base, her eyes watering, gagging on my length. She wanted this; I could feel it. She wanted to give me pleasure with the same urgent desire I felt toward her.

She moved a little faster, stroking as she sucked, watching me watch her. Pleasure flowed through the bond from both sides, passion running between us, building us higher at the same time.

"Touch yourself, Little Wolf," I told her, stripping off my shirt so she could see the torso she liked so much.

She groaned with the command, her eyes sliding along my body to take in the view. I let her, feeling more powerful under her wanton gaze. Her magic surged with mine.

Her hand pushed down into her leisure pants, brought to her earlier by Leala. I could see it moving in the fabric, dipping low, her fingers plunging.

"Are you wet, Little Wolf?" I asked, my tone rough and thick. I wrapped my fingers around her messy bun. "Are you wet for your alpha?"

"Mm-hmm," she moaned around a mouthful of cock.

I yanked her hair back, pulling her from me. "What did you say?"

"Yes, Alpha," she said, her eyes lidded as her hand worked her body.

"Let me taste."

Desire once again eclipsed all else in the bond. She pulled out her hand, her fingers glistening, and held them up for me. I grabbed her wrist and wrapped my lips around each one, sucking them clean and groaning at the salty-sweet taste of perfection.

"I need more." I barely contained my growl.

I reached down for her, lifting her up to her feet before walking her back toward the dining table. I didn't want to waste time getting to the bed. I stripped off her clothes and guided her backward. Her butt hit the polished surface and she lay back on the table, her knees falling wide. I bent to her pussy, licking up through the center and savoring the incredible taste. There was something special about this woman, or maybe our connection. Regardless of the circumstances, despite this push and pull we had or the hardship surrounding our introduction, I thanked the gods to have met her. To know these feelings and experience this incredible sexual high with her. This was heaven. *She* was heaven.

I sucked her in, circling her clit with my tongue. She arched on the table, threading her fingers into my hair and fisting. The bite of pain made me groan. I curved two fingers into her, pumping them as I continued to suck in pulses.

"Holy—mmm," she said, writhing beneath me. Her hips bucked and rolled. "Oh . . . fuck. Yes, Alpha, *yes*!"

I reached up with one hand and slid it over her breast; the peak grazed my rough palm.

"Holy—!" She jolted and then screamed my name. Incredible pleasure rolled through the bond, coating me in it, sharing her orgasm. I pulled my fingers away to taste, to drink her in.

I stepped back and removed the rest of my clothes before pulling her to her feet and spinning her to bend her over the table.

"Yes, Alpha, put that thick cock in me," she moaned, her hands splayed on the surface. "Fill me up."

I ran my tip along her glistening pussy before thrusting inside her. She enveloped me tightly, groaning with the sensation. I held myself deep as I leaned over her, my chest to her back, my lips against her ear.

"I am going to stuff you so full of my seed that whenever any other male stops to talk to you, they smell my scent leaking out of you." I pulled out before roughly thrusting back in. Our wolves were pushed right near the surface, basking in the glow of my dominant possessiveness. "I'm going to mark you so often and so deep they will know that you are *mine,* and mine alone."

I moved within her, deep, rough thrusts driving my point home. She panted with need, pushing her ass back into me, craving it.

I braced a hand on her hip, the other in her hair, my lips still on the shell of her ear. "This little pussy is owned by me. Do you understand, Little Wolf? I'll pump you full of my release as often as I need to prove that." I shook her a little. "Do you understand?"

"Yes, Alpha," she mewled, spreading her legs a little wider, trying to take me deeper.

"Good girl," I said, pounding her, nearly there.

"Oh, gods. Fuck me, Weston. *Please,* fuck me harder," she begged.

I did, leaning back a little to watch my dick disappear repeatedly inside her. I wouldn't knot her yet, though. I'd wait until we were in bed and had all night. For now, I'd give her another orgasm or two, maybe feast on her pussy, and then call for dinner.

With that thought, I came inside her, roaring my release. I basked in the afterglow, in the exquisiteness of the heat of her skin against mine. I took a moment to catch my breath, and then began showing her exactly how good I could make her feel.

In the days to come, if she felt a need to chat with Hannon or anyone else, I'd allow her the freedom. As Hadriel had said, this was all new to her. She needed time to accept no one else would ever be enough for her, not after me. Once she realized that—and I doubted it would take long—I'd end all threats to my claim. Permanently. No one would ever be able to take her away from me--not the dragons, not Granny, and certainly no other male.

This little wolf was mine, and I couldn't wait to prove it.

16

AURELIA

As usual, I woke at dawn. Only a thin sliver of light filtered through the thick curtains, but my body knew it was time to get up. Weston curled around me, holding me tightly, even in sleep.

I stayed like that for a moment, brushing my fingertips along his forearms, content to be held and warm. He'd ordered dinner brought to the room last night and fed me bits from his plate. After, he'd had a bath drawn and gotten in with me, content to lounge. Well . . . content to dominate me by fucking me senseless, and *then* to lounge. Gods, the guy was amazing in bed. He seemed to know exactly what got me off, and consistently delivered in a truly spectacular fashion.

I watched the dust motes float lazily through the stream of light, feeling his heartbeat against my back and the steady rise and fall of his chest as he breathed. I felt . . . peaceful. Cared for. Cocooned in his strength, held close to him like I was something precious. A lump formed in my throat, this blissful feeling creating a deep warmth within me, suffusing my body.

In the next moment, though, my thoughts drifted to yesterday, to the dragons, the interrogation, the fairy, all that had happened with Granny . . .

My heart sped up, and I slipped from his embrace, scared to lose myself in that feeling, unable to really process my life right now. I had precious little time for anything beyond work; the dragons had started the clock.

"Where are you going?" Weston asked sleepily, reaching for me.

I avoided his grasp. "Time to get to work. I need to grab a few books before heading out to the garden. I need to make sure my flower is planted properly today. I just want to dash into the library before that terrifying king gets there. Can I assume I'm allowed to enter now?"

He propped up his head with his elbow, watching me dress. "You were always allowed to enter. He's intense, but he's fair, Aurelia. He's a good king. He won't hurt you just to watch you squirm."

"I'd rather not accidentally prove you wrong, thanks. That guy is a dangerous sort of unhinged. Even my wolf is fine keeping our distance."

"Yup," my wolf intoned.

"Vemar is the one commonly thought to be unhinged, you know." Weston grinned as I slipped into the washroom, needing to clean myself up a little. He'd made good on his threat to thoroughly mark me with his scent, and I knew today would be . . . interesting. "He thought he was going mad down in the dungeons."

Weston had rolled to his back when I returned, his hands folded behind his head.

"Then again, I think we all did," he said. "Vemar just admitted it."

"Vemar has zero fear of things that should make him

wary. He's not mad, he's courageous. And fun. I don't really know him, but so far I like his company."

Emotions flitted through the bond, turbulent but reflective. I waited for his comment. When it didn't come, I said, "What?"

He looked at me for a moment. "Nothing. I've requested to have all your things rehomed. Your glass . . . contraptions will go out to the work sheds, as you call them. You'll be working in a shed alongside the queen so she can keep an eye on you, as promised. The former queen is in that shed, as well. I know you are new to all this, but it is considered a huge privilege and great honor to work alongside those women. They are the best at what they do, not to mention they are royalty. Please be respectful."

"Of course I will be. I'm used to minding my own business and ignoring hostile stares from my coworkers. I doubt this will be any different."

"Maybe not, but I suggest you remain mindful about challenging the queen. You saw how eager she was to meet the last one."

"I'll say," I mumbled. She'd been downright excited that I should show a little fight. She would not be as easy to manhandle as Raz. I'd need to learn to fight before I messed with that woman.

"Your journals will be in your new room. The room will be prepared this morning and will be available for you this afternoon. I'll take you to it once I receive word it's ready. We can make any adjustments as needed."

"What sort of lock does it have?" I grinned at him.

His smile was a thing of beauty. The man was a stunner. "Probably one you'll have no trouble picking. It won't be locked from the outside, though. You are free to move around the castle. That does not include the grounds, however, and it certainly does not include the Royal Wood. You are being given time by the royals, but that is more time for Granny to locate you and make plans. You are safer here than anywhere else, but you are not safe, Aurelia. Not until we've dealt with Granny."

I sobered, a chill running through me. "I know," I murmured.

He surprised me when he said, "Later today we'll shift together." My wolf leapt for joy.

Good. Maybe she could take over things for a while. I could use the break.

He leveled me with a *look*. "Be careful until I see you again, okay? Stay out of trouble. Don't stick any more scissors into dragons."

I couldn't fully stifle my answering grin, so I leaned over quickly and pressed my lips to his in goodbye. There I paused, startled, not actually having meant to do that. Once there, though, it felt like the natural thing to do. I softened my lips, drawing out the contact.

"I'll miss you," he murmured against the kiss, his hand cupped gently against my cheek. "Stay safe, Little Wolf. Call for me if you need anything."

"Okay," I whispered, falling into those slate-gray eyes as I straightened. The warmth from the moment felt thick and heavy within me.

Somewhat dazed, I exited the room and then the apartment. Was that the primal bond creating those feelings, or just Weston? It hadn't felt like a dramatic tug like the sex often did; it felt sweet and serene, an extension of the night before.

Pushing it from my mind, I wrangled my focus. I needed to concentrate on my work, on stopping Granny. That had to be my top priority. People were dying; others were succumbing to the hook. I had to help. The true mate situation could wait.

The castle had less activity on this floor; very few people roamed the hallways. The stairways and foyer had more movement, but the doors lining the hall leading to the library were all closed. The library itself was a ghost town. Good news.

I looked for the book I'd thrown yesterday, finding a hole instead. Dang. The king hadn't returned it. That, or I'd busted it by throwing it at him. Either way, it wasn't the best start to my library privileges.

Hurrying, I started systematically taking down the other books in the area, one at a time, checking the glossaries. Any that listed Moonfire Lily, which were few and far between, I put in a pile on the shelf below. Once done, I picked up five books and straightened, intending to descend the stairs and hurry out of the library to look at them somewhere else.

Hurrying along, I saw the banister just ahead. I reached it and turned, lifting my eyes to trace my path.

My whole body jolted to a stop when I saw who waited at the bottom.

I gasped, backing up.

The king stood just off the last step. His expression didn't change; he was devoid of emotion. He held up the book I'd chucked at him yesterday.

"You forgot something," he said in a deep, raspy voice.

I swallowed and contemplated whether to take the first step. Weston had assured me there was no reason to be terrified of the man. Dante had said it yesterday, too. The royals planned to give me time. That meant he *didn't* plan to hurt me.

My wolf adamantly shook her head. *"Plans change. Don't take the chance."*

She had a point.

I stood there and stared awkwardly, frozen to the spot.

He noticed the other books in my arms. "Do you need help?"

"Uhh . . ." I cleared my throat. "No, thank you." It was a miracle my voice didn't waver. "I was just about to go. I've got them all, I think." I paused. "Except that one, obviously. Um, thanks. For bringing it."

He held it up for a moment before slowly placing it on one of the lower steps. "I'm leaving. You can look at these in here and put back the ones that aren't helpful."

I eyed him warily, nodding. I was definitely making this into a bigger deal than it should've been.

"No, you're not," my wolf insisted. *"With him, distance is key."*

Who was I to argue?

He took a step back, that golden gaze once again unwavering, before turning and retreating through the nearest door.

I got to work but didn't find as much as I was hoping. Only one of the other books had anything of note, and it was information I'd already suspected: the flower liked shadier areas, growing best when protected by nestling in among other, sturdy plants. I could relate.

After the books were put away and I gave a quick perusal to make sure I hadn't missed anything, I left the library, headed to the work shed. Vemar waited for me near the back door, leaning against the wall in another colorful jacket, though this one lacked dicks.

"Hello, Captive Lady." He pushed away from the wall. "How are you today? Nice and relaxed, it seems."

"Hi, Vemar. Not so relaxed, actually. I saw the king, who totally freaks me out. I'm just heading to the garden now."

"Fantastic. I'll be heading out with you. I'm your babysitter."

"Have you been waiting long for me?"

"An hour or so. There aren't a lot of jobs where you can get paid for standing around, but I managed to land one. Lucky break."

Vemar held the door open for me to exit first and caught up to me quickly with his long stride. "I'm not big on standing around. I always feel like I should be doing something. Hazard of my last job, maybe."

"You need to learn to relax."

I smirked at him. "Probably."

There were only a few people in the garden and buzzing around the work sheds. It seemed the residents of this castle didn't often get an early start. Maybe they tended to work later? I didn't know.

"Which shed am I— Oh." My stuff was all waiting outside the oldest of the sheds. Vemar and I walked to the door, and I peeked inside. Despite being the smallest by far, it still held several pots used to brew things and had plenty of empty counter space. In the corner on a cleared-off worktable I assumed was my workspace sat a few of Granny's products still in the wrappers with the fucked-up butterfly on the front. Alongside them was an assortment of my product, separated by type but not necessarily by dose. "Okay. Let's get to work."

Some time later, I had burns covering my arms, scrapes dripping blood, and smoke billowing up into my face, making me cough.

"Ugh." I gagged. "Fuck this stuff." At that moment, I registered a grumpy sort of presence.

I glanced over my shoulder to see the woman from

yesterday, Arleth, standing in the doorway. She didn't comment, so neither did I. Instead, I stood up to try to help clear the smoke for a minute before going back to the mess on the table, mashing up part of Granny's coating and putting it into the contraption that acted like a pressure cooker. I fixed my goggles in place and lit the flame, watching the reaction to the heat. As I expected, the coating blackened, bent, twisted, and started expanding.

"Vemar!" I shouted, standing and grabbing the contraption. "Vemar, hurry!"

My skin blistered as I ran at Arleth.

"Move!" I shouted, and thankfully, unlike Raz, she actually got out of the way.

"I've got it." Vemar met me outside with potholders taped up his arms, across his chest, and over his hands.

"Hurry, hurry, hurry!" I didn't let go but let him support most of the pressurizer as we moved outside.

He set it down on an exterior table away from the door, jarring what was inside. I launched at him, covering him with my body as the device exploded. Glass pelted my side, back, and down my legs. Hadriel was never going to lend me his clothes again. Heat seared my calf and parts of my back. Something sizzled, and I turned to find the little bit of coating left in a puddle of slimy goo.

"You shouldn't keep trying to save me, Captive Lady," Vemar told me, flat on his back. "It's a weird look for a gardener-prisoner to save a mighty dragon, even if that gardener-prisoner has a tendency to blow things up rather than create."

"It's not your fault you're in this mess." I patted his shoulder, getting off him. "Look at that."

I hunched down next to the goo, my contraption in pieces and now totally unusable. I'd have to beg Weston to buy me more parts so I could make another.

Glass crunched under my partially burned boot. Vemar got up carefully and then leaned next to me, looking down on it as well.

"Slime and goo." I studied what was left. "We haven't seen slime and goo before."

"No, I don't reckon we have. What does it mean?"

"It means we changed the properties. It's giving us a look under its skirt and showing us its secrets. We're on to something."

Vemar waggled his eyebrows. "I do love looking under skirts."

I laughed. "Fucking right you do." I stood up. "Let's do the same experiment but with a different contraption. I have an idea."

Vemar stood and gestured toward the pile of broken glass. "Good thing, because this one was blown all to hell."

"Yeah. Hazard of the trade."

"Is it really?"

"In the beginning stages, yes." I turned toward the door of the shed. "Come on, let's rig up another one."

"Just what do you think you're doing?" Arleth stood in the doorway with an indignant scowl just as the queen walked toward us. In a brown pantsuit with embroidered flowers giving pops of color, she fit right in with the garden.

I held up a blackened finger, and Vemar helped by picking out a chunk of glass. Blood oozed out. "I'm getting to the bottom of that coating. I have several ideas on how they create the chemical portion of it, and a few ideas on what the ingredients might be." A drop of blood went *splat!* on the floor.

"Great gods, what happened?" the queen said, hurrying over with Hadriel and Hannon in tow. "Are you okay?"

I glanced down at myself, cataloguing the scene: the

jacket tattered in places and blackened all across the back and down one arm, part of a pant leg missing, glass everywhere, and blood.

"Sorry about the clothes, Hadriel," I said. "I didn't realize that stuff would be quite this volatile."

"Who cares about the clothes! Fuck a limp turnip, look at you!" He stepped around the queen and held out his hands. "What are you doing to yourself?"

"Oh, I'm fine. I heal really quickly, so don't worry. I've learned that my body will actually work the glass back out. I don't have to bother picking it out."

Hadriel was now doing that for me. "You're like a pincushion. I know you have a high tolerance for pain, but this is beyond."

"It's not deep. I barely feel it, honestly. And it helps knowing that it's short-term. I'll be better in no time."

"She really is very nonchalant about danger," Vemar said. "Even as a dragon, I'm not used to it. It's a little unnerving."

I gave Hadriel a suffering look. "Vemar is helping me learn just how arrogant dragons tend to be." Vemar chuckled. "Right, okay, let's set up that other one—"

"No, you will not," Arleth said, her tone steely. "You will absolutely *not* set up something like that again. It's much too dangerous. You could get us all killed."

I paused. "I will admit, that's a fair point. It's no problem—I'll just go set up around the back, then." I paused for a moment, my lips pursed in thought. "That's better, actually. Then we won't have to carry it anywhere."

"I'm on it." Vemar slipped through the doorway to get more supplies.

"No." Arleth put out her hand to try to stop Vemar, but he was already gone. It was clear he was having a great time despite the danger. Actually . . . maybe *because* of the danger. "This is ridiculous. You'll kill yourself."

"All due respect, Queen Mother, but you guys are going to kill me anyway. What does it matter if it is sooner or later? Besides, I didn't get where I am—making the best drugs on the market, as the queen said—by going slow and being safe. Granny rewarded speed over safety, and trust me, rewards were much better than punishments. It's ingrained. Now, if you'll excuse me, I want to try one more thing before I hit the library again. Then I'd like to sort out that Moonfire Lily, even though it seems quite happy in its bucket."

17

WESTON

Dragons soared overhead as my wolf loped through the Royal Wood, using the pack bond to note everyone's locations. The sentry and patrol placements spread out in our shared consciousness like a map, each person like a glowing point. In our mind's eye, we added in the flight paths of the various dragons. They couldn't form a bond like wolves or some other shifters and had to rely on sight and sound. The sheer distance they could cover, not to mention their power, made up for it.

As we were identifying the few places where we could tighten up the patrol before moving on to the various villages, a disturbance lit up along the bond. Fancetta's route. Dante was stopped with her—he'd called my wolf through the bond, his request urgent.

No one else in the kingdom showed any signs of disturbance. This was good news. It meant whatever had drawn Dante's alarm was not widespread.

My wolf headed his way immediately, taking as straight

a path as the various trees and flora would allow. A wince of pain flashed through my mate bond.

"What could Aurelia be doing?" I groused as my wolf wound closer to Dante. We'd been feeling it for a few hours now; nothing too bad, but there were occasional flares from various places on her body.

"Whatever it is," my wolf replied, *"her wolf is delighted with it. She's having fun."*

The trees ended in a jagged line along a strip of cleared land with a road leading into the only city in the kingdom. It was a fraction of the size of the port city in the Red Lupine, the populace here having been greatly diminished during the decades-long curse. Even so, there was no city in the magical world that could boast the same level of cleanliness and finery. The dragons were pouring a substantial amount of their kingdom's profits into rebuilding, creating new homes, and extending their markets. It would take decades, but I knew eventually this kingdom would be the envy of the magical world.

Dante waited with Fancetta in the central market, a large, bustling affair with carts and stalls as well as permanent shops and extravagant merchant outlets. The brick-and-mortar sellers existed in organized lines and in orderly fashion, taking up about half of the current market. The rest, patiently waiting for more establishments to be built, set up temporary shops using any means necessary to catch the public's eye. The king's guard patrolled at all hours, ensuring there was no theft or vandalism, and even the smallest stalls kept to some sort of order within the bustling chaos. It was probably the safest central city market I'd ever been in, and because of it, commerce thrived.

Each wolf in the market wore a similar long slip. Clothes or fabrics were stashed in various locations in the kingdom so that official personnel could cover up in public.

"Beta," Dante said after I'd shifted. He stood next to an empty cart cleared of items holding a rolled-up piece of paper in his left hand. Fancetta handed me a slip.

"What is it?" I took the slip and pulled it over my head.

"This was a medicinal cart." Dante motioned at it, walking around to where the seller would've stood to do business. He looked down at what was probably shelving and storage within. "Vampiric medicines said to help improve sex drive or thin the blood, or various other things that may or may not have actually worked, especially for non-vampires."

"Were they legal?"

"Yes. Every one. The king's guard checked him periodically. He didn't offer many products or carry a lot of stock, but he often had a line, usually later in the evening."

The setup was simple. Little shelves at either edge of the counter were made for showcasing the product. A banner would've gone down the front, and little placards for product names were affixed in various places on the shelving, all of them currently blank. The cart itself was worn and weathered, the rain swelling the wood in various places and the sun fading it. Simple but serviceable.

"They found him dead two days ago in his living room," Dante went on, bending a little and reaching under the counter. I couldn't see what he was doing. "Overdose on Granny's product. They found two wrappers and a dozen or so of her other products, all intact. Given the cart itself was rented for the market, it was assigned to someone else. When that seller came to clean it out and set up shop, he found this."

Dante reached into the cart, and something popped

within its bowels. He stepped away, the expression on his face telling me I should take his place, which I did.

All the storage had been cleaned out. In the middle, directly under the counter and built into the wood framing, a little door had cracked open.

I pulled it wider, finding a little cubby that would've been impossible to see unless I'd specifically looked for it. Within, neatly organized, were the familiar black and purple packages.

"The new cart owner found it when he was giving it a good scrub," Fancetta added. The tan-skinned woman with long brown hair and a square jaw was a dependable and loyal wolf, one I was glad to have in my pack. "Claimed he had heard of cubbies being built into carts like this and grew suspicious when cleaning it." She raised one eyebrow in a skeptical expression. "Said his rag caught on a crack or something. It wasn't clear."

"It wasn't meant to be clear," I growled, pulling out Granny's product and spreading it across the counter. "It's obvious this is a secret within the market seller community. He likely only told us because he was too afraid of anyone thinking this product was his." I pulled out the rest of the packages. "Contact the king's guard. Perform random inspections. Search for more cubbies like this. Not just in carts, but in stalls as well. I want a detailed report of everything they find."

"Yes, sir," she said.

I pushed Granny's product toward her a little. "Get that to the queen. She'll want to keep it with the others. Hunt down the original seller's contacts and try to find out how it got in."

"Yes, sir." She bowed and started collecting the product.

"Beta, a word?" Dante motioned me away from the cart.

I went with him, walking down a side street away from

the market. He handed over the rolled-up paper as he did so.

"Found that in the side of the cubby. The new stall owner, once he saw Granny's product, didn't proceed any farther. He called the king's guard over immediately. They took him in for questioning and then called us. I was the one that looked inside. I found that."

I unrolled the paper. The texture was more like parchment but thicker, with a glossy shine. It was made for traveling, less likely to get damaged in transit and more expensive because of it. My stomach dropped out.

Aurelia's likeness was drawn on the page, her loveliness, her outstanding beauty, captured perfectly. The streaks of white, so like Calia's hair color now that I thought of it, were placed in the right locations. Granny had done a marvelous job explaining her charge, and whoever she'd gotten to draw it up had done so in meticulous detail. At the bottom was listed a substantial sum as a reward.

"I figure something like that was what got Aurelia caught in the Red Lupine town," Dante murmured, his eyes straight ahead.

It surely was. The stall owner in that town had mentioned someone was asking the wrong sorts of questions, and the town guard had easily recognized her from this drawing. There'd be no doubt. Even her beautiful eyes were captured perfectly. Granny left no details to the imagination. She wanted back her prize, the backbone of their operation, and badly. Just as the queen had said.

"You're the only one who has seen this?" I asked, my wolf pacing within me.

"Yes."

"Did you look through his house? Was there anything else?"

"I was told there wasn't, but I figured we should go over it in greater detail in case something was missed."

"Do it." I stared at the likeness for another moment before rolling it back up. Myriad emotions rolled through me: fear, anger, urgency, frustration. Granny had her hooks in almost every kingdom, every market. It had only been a matter of time before someone drew Aurelia's likeness and sent word.

I wasn't sure why this felt so jarring. We'd known this would happen. I needed to shore up our defenses to make sure that even if they knew where she was, they couldn't slip through the cracks and grab her.

"Check all the carts and stalls in every city, town, and village. Make sure the guard is thorough."

"Yes, sir."

"I'll talk to the royals about doing a search in the castle, just in case."

"Begging your pardon, Beta," Dante said, "but maybe Hadriel is the best bet. The royals will make people rush to hide things. Hadriel has that way of digging in the right places without raising suspicion."

This was true. There was no sense in creating intrigue within those who didn't already know what was going on. They'd just gossip, and news we were looking for intel would spread more quickly.

"Given the timeline of the merchant's death, this had to have been sent before our arrival," I said, thinking everything over. "It must've been disseminated when the one in the Red Lupine town was. It was part of the wide net Granny first cast after we discovered Aurelia and the village. Given how hard people who distribute Granny's products in this kingdom are punished, and given the way this was stowed away, there is no way Aurelia's face would be displayed anywhere public. That means only a select few will have seen it, and those are all people who keep their heads down to avoid the dragons' wrath. Unless we find something in the castle, she is safe. For now."

For now.

Was that truly even the case? And if so, how long would it last?

Dante nodded, slowing to a stop. "I heard how it went with the dragons. The dragon queen is ruthless when someone threatens her people. Hadriel thinks she can be reasoned with, though."

"It's too early to tell, but let's hope so."

Dante faced him directly, his gaze intense. "Just know, if they are unreasonable, I'm with you, sir. Getting her out would be the easiest course of action, but whatever needs to be done . . . I'm with you."

I held his gaze for a moment but didn't nod, looking away before Dante was forced to drop his gaze. Basically, letting him know that the sentiment was appreciated without putting a voice to it. This conversation was dangerously close to treason.

I hoped it wouldn't come to any of that.

"Get after those markets," I told him. "I'll talk to the royals and employ Hadriel. Let's button this kingdom up."

"Yes, sir." Dante turned back the way he'd come without another word.

I walked for a moment longer, turning over the many possibilities. The queen was ruthless when protecting her people, that was true. She was renowned for it, exceptional because of it. Stubborn about it.

Aurelia needed to become one of her people, turned from the enemy into an ally. Then maybe Hadriel and I, and maybe even the king himself, could talk her down from her wrath.

We had to try. My true mate—and the whole kingdom—were at stake.

I disrobed and handed the slip off to the first guard I saw before shifting and heading back to the castle.

Time to see if they had any Granny-sized rats lingering around.

Aurelia

I felt the warning as the emotions registered through the bond, frustrated anger mixed with fear. It was the second time in the space of an hour, once when he seemed pretty far away, and this time within the castle somewhere. A moment later, Weston was on the move.

"Vemar, go," I said quickly, motioning for him to put down the books he carried. We'd been in the library since the last contraption had exploded, killing any further research I could do until I could replace my materials. I'd had to really juice it up to get a reaction.

I now knew the boiling point of Granny's concoction, and I knew that the toxicity was a by-product of heat. What's more, I had a strong suspicion she was taking my preliminary drug-making methods and then amping them up with extra, heat-altered ingredients. I also had a strong suspicion how she'd gotten the idea. Her clues were easy to spot once you looked, and her finished product lacked any sort of finesse.

She'd hired hacks, and why? Because she must've known that I would not intentionally make this stuff. I would've told her how dangerous it was, how it would ruin the product, and refused. I'd done something similar when

I accidentally made the concoction that I bet had given her the idea in the first place.

If I'd had any doubt all this was my fault, it had now been laid to rest. I was the mastermind; she'd just done a piss-poor job of replication. The proof made me want to break down and cry.

"Put them anywhere—just go." I waved at Vemar again to put down the books. "Weston is pissed, and I'm the problem. Ugh, I bet Hadriel told on me."

"My little buddy might seem like he doesn't give two shits about anything, but he actually has a very big heart. And yes, unlike you, he tattles if he's worried about someone. I've been told on several times. I take it as a very annoying act of love."

"That's awesome, but you still need to go." I took the books from his hands and put them on the table. "We don't need Weston thinking you had anything to do with this."

"With what?"

I gestured at myself. "With what looks like a body chewed up by monsters and then spat out again. He hates when I get hurt. He's going to freak out that I did this."

"That's sweet of him." He smiled serenely. "It must feel good to have an alpha wolf like him treasure you."

"I—" I furrowed my brow. I hadn't thought of it like that.

I wouldn't be able to now, either. Another feeling rattled my heart, like a drum-beating rallying cry. Something mighty and mean was headed my way, and only one thing made my wolf curl up in a little ball and try to hide.

Panic skittered through me from my wolf, hazing my ability to think. Only one need clawed into my awareness. *Flee!*

"Shit!" I yelled, shoving at Vemar. "The king must be with him. Run! Hide!"

"What the fuck?" Vemar braced against my push, his muscles going taut. He looked every which way. "Who are we fighting? What is happening? It feels like dread, like an enemy is descending upon us. Captive Lady, are you mind-fucking me again?"

I couldn't stay to wonder at that. I scattered, my body going one way and my brain another. All logic had gone, and my wolf's frantic power jumbled everything else up. I couldn't contain the overwhelming, desperate urge to flee. It rattled my nerves, sending my senses haywire. Fueled by terror, I had one goal and one goal only: get the fuck out of there.

I looked for an exit that wouldn't land me out in the hall, but they all inevitably did. My best bet was the windows. The ones on the second floor sometimes led to the roof. I could get on the roof, skirt across to the other side of the castle, find an open window—

"Go, go, go!" my wolf yelled at me.

I darted around Vemar and headed for the stairs.

"No, Aurelia, wait! What are you doing?" He ran after me, his long legs able to take two stairs at a time.

I clambered up the ladder against the stacks on the second floor, finding the first window. The window didn't open and the roof was too steep anyway.

"Bugger." Back down the ladder, then I ran to the next.

"Lady, the king won't hurt you just because you hurt yourself. This mind-fucking makes no sense."

Weston's wolf fed me more power. If his wolf was trying to help me escape, that meant bad news.

"Hurry, hurry," my wolf begged, dumping even more power into me. I felt stuffed with it, hazy.

The next window did the trick. I struggled to flick the old, unused lock, but once I did, I cranked the handle and turned, opening it slowly.

"Come on, come on."

"Captive Lady, I can't let you go out that window," Vemar told me, reaching for my ankle.

Weston's power started to pump now. He came faster, running, probably. That presence with him, the thing that had to be the king or something just as dangerous, was moving fast, too. Keeping pace? Ahead of him?

"Run! Faster!" my wolf pushed, wishing she was the one in charge, able to move better, escape faster.

"I have to go," I cried, kicking down at Vemar frantically. "I'm sorry, I have to escape! Fuck!"

The window now open, I hurried to crawl out. Long arms wrapped around my middle. I snarled and turned to snap at him, realizing my teeth weren't quite right. My magic bloomed, pumping strong, urging me on. Weston's was flowing within me through the bond, increasing my potency.

"I'm having a hard time holding her," Vemar shouted. "Careful, her mind-fucking is really powerful right now. I assume that we are not actually under attack."

I kicked off one of his hands and was about to shake off the other to slide out the window when I felt Weston's presence.

"Aurelia, whoa! Hey, it's okay." I stilled, and Weston's hand replaced Vemar's. "What are you doing? Where are you going?"

My wolf simmered down inside of me, feeling his wolf and taking comfort. Her near-takeover of my body and the desire to bite with significantly sharper teeth subsided, allowing for a little logic to trickle back in. I heaved a deep sigh and flattened against the ladder.

"I'm here, Little Wolf. It's okay." Weston's body brushed my heels as he climbed up behind me. He hooked his arms under me to brace on either side of the ladder. "Where you headed?"

"Oh, you know, the usual. Just heading out onto the roof so that I could find some other open window and escape some sort of unknown terror coming with you. Nothing big."

"I'm afraid to lean against you. Are these . . . burns? Is that a piece of glass?"

I rested my chin on a rung. "They haven't all worked their way out yet."

"How— Why—" I felt his sigh against my neck. "Let's get you down, okay? Let's not flee some unknown terror by climbing out the window."

"It's the king. I don't know who is more terrified of that guy, me or my wolf, but *he* is the unknown terror. I can't get around it. He makes me lose my senses."

"He's a very powerful alpha. I think that's what the problem is. He's the alpha of a place in which you don't feel safe. Your wolf—probably you, too—feel the threat of his power, and, knowing you can't fight it, you run. It's primal, baby. We're going to ease all that in a few hours when we shift, okay? We're going to work through that."

"I don't feel that way with the queen."

"The queen does not view all outsiders as an inherent threat. The king does because of his life during the curse. It'll wear off, I promise. Let's get down."

I let him help me down before he looked me over, his expression pained. "Gods, Aurelia, what have you done?" He pulled out a piece of glass before bending around me to check my backside. His angry eyes belied the frustrated pain coming through the bond, and he shook his head at me. "Stop this. I won't have you hurting yourself like this."

"It's okay. It's doesn't hurt, honest."

His gaze bored into me, intense and penetrating. He

would know I spoke the truth because he could feel my lack of pain through the bond. Still, he was not pleased in any way.

He put his fingers under my chin and tipped it up so he could plant a soft kiss to my lips. His soft growl sent shivers through me. "You still smell like me. Good."

Holding me by the hand, he walked with me along the second-floor balcony landing and to the stairs.

"He's here," I warned, embarrassed by my lack of courage.

"Yes. When he heard what state you were in, he wanted to come see for himself. Finley didn't do you justice."

"The queen told on me?"

"Yes. Why, who did you expect ratted you out?"

I didn't say, and he didn't push. We reached the bottom of the stairs and found the king waiting. He wore a plain black shirt, faded blue jeans, and worn black shoes that had long since lost their shine. His hair was in messy spikes, and a dark shadow dusted his defined jaw. His predatory eyes tracked my movements, and I stopped where I was. Honestly, whatever the reason, it was just fucking madness to get too close to that guy. Madness. He could snap me in half, and he seemed too unpredictable to gauge if or when that might happen.

"Aurelia," the king said, his hands behind his back. "I'm Nyfain. My mate has expressed some concern that you are going to kill yourself before we can do it for you."

He gave me what appeared to be a genuine half-smile, his eyes glimmering with humor to sell it. He was using Hadriel's joke. Coming from him, it wasn't all that funny. Still, I could tell he was trying to put me at ease, a kind thing for a king to do.

I played along. "Nah. I've learned how much dragons like violence. I wouldn't want to rob you of the pleasure."

His smile increased and he nodded. "Much appreciated. You have glass sticking out of you, like a porcupine."

"Yeah. It'll fall out eventually. Don't worry, I'll pick it up once it does. I don't leave it lying around or anything."

"It's the truth," Vemar said from the table where my books were stacked. I hadn't noticed him heading that way, but I'd still been on the ladder, trying desperately to climb out a window. "Very considerate, this crazy wolf. Very considerate."

"And the burns—did you need some salve for those?" Nyfain was scanning my limbs.

"Oh no, it's fine. I heal really fast now. Except for this whole need-to-climb-out-of-windows nonsense, the magic is really great."

"Yes." He twisted so he could see Vemar. "Where are your scrapes and bruises?"

"Nothing to see here. She made sure I had armor while she played hero. I'm right as rain."

Now the king focused on Weston. "You didn't send someone after her about this?"

"I did. Me. Finley was the first I'd heard of it."

"Don't you share a bond now? Didn't you feel this?"

Weston glided his fingers over the back of my neck, standing close but not touching anywhere else. He was probably afraid he'd encounter glass. "Barely twinges, like a paper cut. Her tolerance for pain is . . ." He shook his head. "She endured the same sort of abuse Finley and I did, but at a younger age. She taught herself to go numb against it."

Nyfain's power seeped out of him, giving me those flight butterflies. His gaze was severe. "Aurelia, there is a difference between suppressed healing and magical healing. You might heal quickly now, but that does not mean you are immune to life-threatening or permanent ailments. You still need to take care of yourself. Please be more careful in your pursuits."

"I'll do better," I said automatically.

His power relaxed a bit, my answer sufficient.

"I know the answer, though," I murmured, not wanting to look up and meet his eyes again lest I get the urge to take off. "I did this. I created that coating—the first layers of it, anyway. A while back—years ago—I accidentally made a product with chemicals that made it more habit-forming than the others. Raz was a nightmare. He kept hounding me about it, and he threw up in the work shed more than once. Rather than just fixing it, I asked Granny about it. She then asked around and came back with reports that it was making people feel sick. But we had more orders for it. I fixed it shortly thereafter, and sales fell back to normal. Not right away, but the uptick we'd seen died away. I bet you anything that is what gave her the idea. She's smart. She would've put two and two together."

"But she didn't ask you to change it back?" Weston asked.

"No. I won't put out a product that makes a person feel sick. I might have a shit job that is on the wrong side of the law, but I take pride in my work. Addiction and pain are not what they are for. She clearly took my methods and employed someone else to work them."

"She knows your methods?" Nyfain asked.

"She has a write-up of every new product I make. I turn it in with each crate of that first batch."

"We didn't find anything like that in her city residence," Weston said, looking at Nyfain. "And we didn't hear anything about the second production village until Aurelia was captured. We have no idea where it is."

"The write-up for Project X is at the bottom of the crate, under the product. That's a first batch headed to market. The write-up goes under so it won't flutter away when it's wheeled out to the pickup point. We learned the hard way. As far as that production village . . . give me time." Determination fueled the fire within me. "My journals seem like only feelings and bad days, but they are helping me remember periods that I clearly didn't want to. I didn't write down a lot of Alexander's news, afraid of the retaliation I'd get if he ever found out, but I remember bits and pieces. I'm trying to remember more. I'm hoping there will be something useful."

The library was quiet for a long beat as everyone looked at me.

"What?" I asked, lifting my eyebrows. "Oh, right. Depressing life. Sorry. Usually Hadriel is on hand to make fun of it and cheer everyone up. Where is he, anyway?"

"He had to see to the queen," Vemar said. "He handles a lot of her day-to-day affairs."

"I must confess," Nyfain said after a beat, "I didn't think you'd try very hard to find a cure knowing a nasty punishment awaited your success. It seems I was wrong. You not only started working at the crack of dawn, you blew yourself up and are reacquainting yourself with a depressing past to accomplish it. It's . . . well, shocking."

"It's really not. I spent the first part of my adulthood working as hard and diligently as I could to keep from being thrown out with nothing. I'm now spending all that energy to keep from going back to that place and that life. My motives might have changed, but my work ethic has not. I've been trained to grind, been punished if I slack. That sort of mentality doesn't go away overnight. Punishment is just"—I shrugged—"part of life."

"A very depressing life, yes," Vemar said, still looking through the books. He stage-whispered to me, "I'll keep trying to fill in for Hadriel and think of some jokes about it."

"Gee, thanks," I murmured, but couldn't help a smirk. It did actually make things seem less tragic.

The king studied me for another long moment.

"I understand all too well," he finally said. In that moment, all my fears about him relaxed. In that moment, I could tell he knew my struggles and appreciated the hustler, the fighter, the person who didn't know how to say die. It felt like, somehow, we had that in common.

And then Calia ran at me with a knife.

18

WESTON

"Watch out!" Vemar shouted, but Aurelia had already twirled and stepped out of the way, sticking out her hand to harmlessly shove Calia past. Nyfain did the same, his expression blank, his movements graceful despite his size.

I put my hand in front of Aurelia to tuck her behind me safely, but she caught my forearm.

"She doesn't mean any harm," she said, watching Calia turn.

Calia pointed at Aurelia. "You must feel the emotions of others. Or motive, maybe? I have not heard of that."

"I just feel danger, Calia," Aurelia said patiently. "You weren't exuding any."

"She feels danger, all right," Vemar murmured, organizing the books. "Then she blasts that feeling until everyone loses their minds and someone tries to crawl out a window."

"Or sends half the castle running down the hall and out the back of the castle," Nyfain said thoughtfully. "I've never heard of a shifter doing that."

"Have you ever known a shifter that has been suppressed for as long as I have and that has struggled to survive?" Aurelia lifted an eyebrow.

"Yes," Vemar, Nyfain, and I all said together.

"Right." She winced. "Well . . . I don't know, maybe I just got more creative in my survival skills?"

"No, that's not it." Calia held out the knife, hilt first. "You are something. I don't know what it is yet, but it's something. Whatever magic it is has been bastardized because of the wolf."

Aurelia huffed and rolled her eyes. "My wolf seems to think killing everyone is the answer. Except Nyfain, obviously. Him, she clearly just wants to avoid."

"Smart wolf," Nyfain replied.

"Here." Calia shook the knife she held out. "Since you know I didn't intend to actually stab you—yet—you can hold the knife."

"No, thank you." Aurelia still held my arm, pulled in now at my side.

"Just hold it. It'll only work for a person with a decent amount of fairy magic."

Aurelia hesitated taking what looked like a very pretty knife. The coral hilt gleamed while the metallic blade etched with scrolling runes had a muted shimmer. "How does a knife not work for someone? Even if the point dulled, if you stick hard enough—"

Calia huffed and handed the knife to Nyfain. "Show her."

The moment her touch was gone, the blade retracted into the hilt and the coral lost its color and luster, turning a drab sort of whitish-brown with darker brown spots.

"Whoa," Aurelia said in wonder. A delighted smile worked up her face. "How cool are fairies?"

"Whoever said dragons are the most arrogant of

magical people," Vemar drawled, "had *clearly* never met a fairy. They only design stuff like that to distinguish themselves from others."

"You *clearly* wish you were half as ingenious as my kind," Calia replied with a smirk.

"See?" Vemar said.

I took the knife from Nyfain. The blade didn't reemerge. I then held it out for Aurelia, curious to see what would happen.

"I assume Granny hasn't messed with this," Aurelia said, looking at it, "and that you aren't all in on some kind of joke at my expense."

"None of those things. That is my personal knife," Calia said.

Aurelia let out a slow breath. "I know this is ridiculous," she murmured, and I surmised she was answering her wolf.

From the bond, I felt trepidation mixed with hope. She was unable to deny her desire to call herself a fairy, even without the magic. She could no longer hide that from me.

Her fingers brushed mine, and a jolt of electricity surged through me. She swung her gaze my way even as the blade slid out and the hilt regained its beauty.

I held her gaze, our fingers entwined on the hilt, her hand starting to shake.

"It can't be true," she said on a release of breath. "It's impossible. My grandparents were definitely wolves. They could shift. Unless my birth father somehow has ties to the fairies?"

"Or unless your wolf grandmama had a dirty little secret involving the fix-it man and his lovely, popping pecs," Vemar said.

"Okay." Calia nodded with a smile, entwining her fingers in front of her. "That answers that. You definitely have the blood. Those blades do not lie. I will be able to prove it with a magical blood test when my things arrive. In the meantime, we just need to figure out what type of magic you have. For us, it is not as easy as shifting and determining an animal. For some, it is more like a gathering of clues."

"Arrogant and complicated," Vemar murmured.

I let go of the blade so Aurelia could hold it on her own, watching her marvel at its beauty. She hesitantly gave it back, clearly loath to let it go. I was suddenly determined to buy her one of those blades. I was sure Calia would help me get one and teach Aurelia how to use it. It suited her.

I had no clue what fairy magic would mean in the long term. Maybe nothing. But what if it was something? I didn't think it would become dangerous—Calia didn't seem concerned, just curious—but what if Aurelia became valuable for whatever it was that she could do? Would her situation get that much more complicated?

I pushed it out of my mind. At the present time, it was the least of our concerns. I'd mentioned the drawing of Aurelia we'd found to Nyfain, and how that had played out in the Red Lupine kingdom. He'd agreed that, for now, Hadriel was probably the best to gather information within the castle. The queen sent for him right away, and he'd been quick to know what to do.

Now we had to wait. Wait to see if anyone else had damning knowledge. Wait to see if anyone had sent word to Granny. Wait to see if Granny showed up to claim her prize.

Wait . . . and hope we had what it took to capture Granny before she captured Aurelia and escaped to a packaging village hardly anyone knew existed.

I ran my hand down Aurelia's back, unable to help hooking it on her hip and dragging her a little closer. She complied, watching Calia run her finger down the right side of the hilt and tapping the bottom twice. The blade slid back in, but the hilt maintained its luster. She slipped it into a pocket in her dress.

"If Granny knew I was a shifter, the lantern told her I was also a fairy, and my mom had no magic at all, you'd think she would be so horribly confused about my origins." Aurelia shook her head, looking up at me. "I mean, what the hell am I?"

"Did you tell Granny about your bio-dad?" I asked her.

"Yes. I told her as much of my history as I knew."

"Then I doubt she was confused."

"She probably knew she'd found a diamond in the rough," Nyfain said.

"Not a diamond in the rough." I shook my head, placing my hand below the back of her neck now, stroking the bare skin within her jacket collar with my thumb. "A treasure she made sure was locked away. She wasn't just isolating a village for her operation—she was hiding a woman from anyone who might have an interest."

"Why would anyone have an interest?" Longing filled her eyes. The world had convinced her that she wasn't wanted. It must've been surreal to learn that she was not only wanted, but hunted by several factions.

Fairies kept track of each other. The fairy king was going mad that he didn't know where Calia's sister had gone off to. They kept tabs on babies and powers, levels and status, making sure they were connected to any potentially potent or rare magic. Most of the kingdoms did. Bloodlines kept a kingdom strong.

Then there was her shifter side. Her bio-dad might not have wanted offspring with a woman with no magic, but he would have definitely wanted a connection with a child as powerful as Aurelia. Being a true mate to a wolf as powerful and high status as I was would also be an incredible perk. He'd want to stay close, able to keep an eye out for our brood, trying to entice them to Granddaddy's kingdom and court so the bloodline could be re-established there.

"I'll explain everything later," I told her. "Let's go see your new room."

"I think I should be in on that explanation, old friend," Calia said, her eyes narrowed at me but gleaming with mirth. She wouldn't get cutthroat until she knew what Aurelia's magic was.

"What about these, Captive Lady?" Vemar gestured at the books he'd stacked and organized.

"I'll grab those." I walked toward the table.

"I'll help." Nyfain met me, taking six of the ten Aurelia had chosen, looking them over as he did so. "I didn't even know we had books about this in the library."

"It's interesting reading," Aurelia said. "Creating and working with chemicals is way more fun than working with plants. For one, they explode or catch on fire way more often."

Nyfain quirked an eyebrow, clearly not quite sure what to make of that. "I'll take your word for it."

We headed down the hall, people respectfully keeping their eyes on their tasks or straight ahead, the castle's version of giving us our privacy. They often glanced at Aurelia, though, their cursory gazes sticking, traveling over her flashy, too-big, ruined clothes and the various burns and cuts and random pieces of glass on or in her person. She was an absolute spectacle, and though I could tell she noticed them looking, she showed no sign of it, a behavior befitting a member of the court. Her years of ignoring those she made uncomfortable had trained her for a life of high status, should she want it. What a change an invasion had made.

It also meant that she wasn't blending in. That made Hadriel's job that much more important. And probably easier. But it also made the danger more palpable.

When entering the back wing where many of the larger rooms and apartments were housed, we heard, "Da-da! Da-da!"

The tottering feet of the princess thumped the floor behind us as she ran for her daddy. Her chubby little arms outstretched and pure joy raced across her little cherub face. "Da-da!"

"Oh gods, how precious!" Aurelia squealed as she caught sight of the little girl, one little tuft of hair caught in a pink bow on the top of her head. She quickly fell to one knee, her expression showing the same kind of joy as the princess, Tabitha. "Hi, little lady," she said in a high, child-like voice. "Did you find your dada?"

The nanny waited back a little, knowing full well that when Daddy and daughter caught sight of each other in passing, they always stopped and cuddled for a moment before they each departed on their way.

Tabitha slowed as she noticed Aurelia, the child utterly fearless in most things but always wary of people she didn't know. She walked closer, and Nyfain took a step toward her, his power promising pain to anyone even looking cross at his daughter.

"It's okay, Daddy," Aurelia said without looking up.

Unlike any other time she'd been in Nyfain's presence, Aurelia had zero fear in her voice. In fact, it was almost like calm waves drifted from her, safe and comforting and happy. That was the mind-fuck Vemar was talking about, something she'd always done to some degree. When I first met her, it had so often been distress, and far less potent.

With her newfound access to her wolf, it was much more powerful. Aurelia was creating a child-friendly environment and nothing mattered, save her interaction with the little girl.

"I won't touch her. I just want to see her cute little face, don't I?" Aurelia said. The last part was said to Tabitha as Aurelia smiled big, sitting down on her butt to be at the level of the little girl. "Ouch!" she said comically. "Silly Aurry just sat on a bunch of glass. Oh no!" She balled up her fists and pretend-cried.

A smile worked at Tabitha's lips. The little girl stomped one of her feet and bent a bit, starting to laugh.

"She sat on glass, oh no!" Aurelia pretended to cry a little more before pulling her hands away, her smile so bright I couldn't look away. "Did you come to see your daddy?" she said, slower than usual.

Tabitha stepped closer to point at a hole in Aurelia's jacket.

Aurelia looked down at it, touching it with her finger. "Uncle Hadriel is going to be so mad. Look what I did to his jacket!"

Tabitha babbled solemnly. Though unable to say many words just yet, the tone made it clear she had something to say. Aurelia listened attentively, leaning forward, matching Tabitha's seriousness perfectly. I noticed Nyfain looking at me, and spared my focus for a moment to glance over at him.

"She's clearly good with children," he murmured.

"That is because I just *love* children," Aurelia said as though talking to Tabitha. "They are sweet and cross and sticky and judge a person solely on how that person treats them, not on what that person is. If they are angry, they get mad. If they are happy, they laugh. It is all very simple, isn't that right, Tabitha?"

Tabitha babbled a reply, nodding very seriously.

"Yes, that is what I think, too." Aurelia nodded adamantly before relaxing her expression and pushing to her feet. Blood spotted the floor. "Oops." She stuck out her hand to prevent Tabitha from tottering over to her. "No, no, careful. This is dirty. Yuck! Don't walk right here, okay? It's icky."

Tabitha looked at the floor and tried to edge around, grabbing Nyfain's pant leg for balance, clearly not ready for Aurelia to go.

"I'll see you again, okay?" Aurelia said, bending a bit, hands on knees. "I have to go now, but I'll see you again soon." She waited for Tabitha's response with a wide, sparkling smile, before standing and sighing. She reached for the books Nyfain held. "She is absolutely glorious, Nyfain. You are so lucky. I'll take these. Your baby girl wants a moment with her daddy. Sorry about your floor. But at least it's wood, right? It'll clean up."

"It's seen worse." Nyfain handed over a couple of the books, giving the rest to me. She stepped away, waiting, and Nyfain turned and lowered his voice, murmuring, "Put a baby in that woman, Weston. She's ready."

Fire surged through me. I realized that I wanted to do exactly that. I knew, without any shred of doubt, that she was *it* for me. My mate. My life. My future. I had no reservations. I had no hesitations. To add children to that dream, to have a family to love and protect . . . There was no sweeter destiny, not for me.

Nyfain scooped up his daughter, who said, "No, Dada," and pointed over his shoulder at Aurelia. "No, Dada!"

"Bye, sweet girl!" Aurelia waved before putting her whole hand to her mouth and then blowing a kiss. She did it again, and the little girl soon stopped protesting, instead imitating the motion as Nyfain walked her away, Vemar following behind them.

"That is the cutest fucking thing I have seen in my entire life," Aurelia said, continuing to watch and wave. "A little princess in the arms of a huge, ferocious dragon. My life has been made."

She gave me the sort of wistful smile that proved Nyfain right. She did want children—that was clear. Dreamed of them, maybe. It was sweet and charming and hit me deep, bringing forth devoted tenderness and an eager desire to get started immediately. Now more than ever I wanted all this shit circling Aurelia to disappear so that we could get on with our lives.

Feeling it through the bond, she turned to me. Our wolves pushed near the surface, the true mate bond singing, all of us longing for what could be. What we wanted as a whole.

Her glittering gaze connected with mine, and her smile slipped. Heat flared in her eyes. I could almost see her wolf moving within her as the primal longing raced through the bond: raw lust, unchained passion. *Need.*

My wolf pushed harder, so close to the surface, influencing me. It felt too good to back down.

"Do you want a baby, Little Wolf?" I asked in a deep, rough voice, my cock straining. I could barely think through the desire. Through my wolf's primal surge. "Do you want to be bred by your alpha?"

She gasped, her pupils blowing wide. Her arousal flared, and that primal need blossomed through the bond.

I nearly groaned, my cock pulsing now, painfully hard.

"Do you?" I pushed, taking a moment to set down our books before I stepped toward her.

She took a step back, looking up at me, daring me to chase.

This was in large part a game. A sexy, primal, intoxicating game. But at the root of it was truth. She wasn't ready for the next stage of her life yet, I knew, but in this moment we were sharing our heart's desires. Expressing what we wanted was at the very core of our four-way connection, the wolves pushing, the humans unable or unwilling to let logic interfere.

I stepped closer again, feeling my grin as she once again stepped back. Once more had her bumping against the wall, nowhere to go. The people in the hall faded around us. I knew nothing else but her—the proximity of our bodies, the electricity surging between us.

"I want you badly, Little Wolf," I growled as I put my palms against the wall, caging her in with my body. With my power. "I want to dominate that little pussy, locking you to me and pumping you full of my seed."

"Oh gods." She quivered, clutching my shirt and yanking me a little closer.

"Tell me," I commanded, our lips inches apart, heating the air between us. "Tell me what you want," I whispered. "Tell me what you dream of."

"Children," she breathed. "I've always wanted children, but never thought I could. I would never have brought a child into my old life. But now . . ."

"But now?" I murmured, kissing along her jaw and down her neck as she moaned.

"I want them," she said, almost like a confession. "I want you to put them in me, Alpha."

My body was a literal flame. I deepened the kiss, and she whimpered again, her hands shaking as they met my shoulders. She pushed up onto her tiptoes, and I knew she wanted me to lift her, to wrap her legs around my waist, to fuck a baby into her right now.

Gods, how I wanted to. I wanted to fall into her and

never come up for air. I wanted to drown in her perfect bliss.

Normally I'd quench both of our needs with a quick fuck, but this time was different. This was still a game. A game of primal need, of human longing. If I pushed now, when her overall comfort level in this new life was shaky at best, she'd rebel. She'd dig in her heels, and it would take longer for her to come around as she tried to make sense of everything.

I'd have to wait until we could make it a reality.

Because we *would* make it a fucking reality. I *would* secure our future. Nothing would stand in my way.

"Patience, baby," I murmured, my lips against hers. "Patience. When you're ready, nothing will stop me."

I pulled back slowly, and she mewled her displeasure. The cold air rushed to fill the gap between us. She shivered, her pupils constricting. In a moment, that big brain of hers started to churn, laboriously at first, in a daze of proximity and passion, but then sped up until a crease formed on her brow.

Here comes the distance, my wolf said.

Reality was about to steal the moment. She'd need to process. That game had been primal, yes, but within the game had been her truth. She knew it. She'd know I knew it. She just had to accept it.

"Let me just grab those books," I said, trying for cool and unaffected, but my voice was rough and my cock throbbing. Until this desperate feeling wore off, it was going to fucking ruin me. But it would ruin her, too. We were in this together.

She watched me heft the books, her eyes a little lost.

Yes, we were in this together.

I jerked my head for her to start walking.

Her movements were halting, her face flushed.

"Uhm," she said softly, clearly trying to get herself back on track. I could feel the confusion through the bond. I couldn't tell if that was related to her state of being, or because I hadn't pushed intimacy a moment ago. Maybe both.

"Uh . . ." She cleared her throat and smoothed her hair. Sweat glistened on her brow.

I waited silently as we walked, also too stiff. My throbbing cock was not making movement easy.

"Do you want help? Here." She grabbed a couple of the books, hugging them close. "Um . . . what I said just there. About the kids . . ."

Yup, here came the detached logic. She'd clearly gotten good at it with Granny, cutting off the hurt or the pain or the longing so that she could function in the terrible conditions she'd been forced to live. That mentality would need to be chipped away at slowly. Her wolf would help.

"You don't want kids, then?" I asked, nearly nailing the light tone I was going for.

"I do. I mean—" She made an annoyed sound. "I always have, yes, but before now there was the issue with my magic and my wolf. Now I have a death sentence hanging over my head. It's clearly not in the cards."

"You won't get a death sentence."

"Right, sorry. I wasn't supposed to mention that."

I stopped outside of the closed door to her new living space and turned her to face me, looking her in the eye. "You will not get a death sentence. Besides the fact that I'd never let that happen, the king does not tell me to put a baby in you if he thinks there is a chance his kingdom would kill you. Stop thinking like that."

Her pupils dilated again. Hunger flared through the bond and heat danced in her eyes. She didn't speak, fighting the urge, clearly trying desperately to hold on to reality.

"I probably shouldn't have mentioned that," I backpedaled quickly, feeling her conflicted emotions raging in the bond. I needed another angle this time. "His admission gives me hope, though."

"Hope of what?" she whispered.

Hope of winning you.

Hope of starting a family with you.

Hope of killing any fucker who ever dares touch you.

19

WESTON

I settled on: "That you will go on to live a happy life with as many children as you want."

It would do.

For now.

Her smile was intimate and grateful, her eyes open and hopeful. She didn't comment, so I handed her the books, stacking them so high she could barely see over them, and opened the door while she laughed.

"Welcome to your new lodgings." I chuckled as I took all the books so that she could go in first.

"Crap, it's huge."

"I know, but what do you think of the room?"

"Har-har." She paused briefly. "Your dick *is* huge, though. Not sure I ever mentioned that." She gave me a naughty, heat-soaked look.

"You didn't have to mention it. You were wincing when I first put it in you. Want a ride?"

"Meh." She shrugged a shoulder. "Maybe later."

The bond betrayed her unaffected tone, as it did mine.

Another game—this one trying to pretend the other person wasn't affecting them—equally as fun. *Who would break first?* I wondered.

Her quarters were nowhere near as big as mine, but still lavish for a visitor of mid- to high status, with plenty of space and all the essential furnishings.

"This is what we did to create a makeshift kitchen."

I showed her the large boiling pot over the fire, a setup for pan frying, and a very small wood-fueled oven. Rooms in the castle weren't really outfitted for people to do their individual cooking—we had a fully staffed kitchen for that —but Burt, I mean Sylvester, had come through. He'd rigged this up. It should work for her needs.

I put my hand on a large counter space where lady's maids usually assembled or prepared the breakfast trays, snacks, and other comestibles. Along the back were two blocks of knives and various other gadgets Sylvester said he knew she'd want.

"I had your spices put here. The ones we had in the kitchen were restocked, and anything we didn't have has been ordered. Most we had to order. We did have some that you didn't, however, so I had a second rack installed so that you had everything available. If you find more you need, just let me know."

Her expression was blank as she looked over the new selection. The bond was colored with too many emotions to process, so I moved on, strangely nervous now.

"I didn't know about décor." I motioned to the pillows and various art on the walls. "I guessed your style based on what I saw at your cottage, but you can change anything you want, just let the staff know. They have standing orders to charge anything you require to me. Don't worry about spending too much—it's yours." I stopped at the sliding glass door and looked out at the colorful but small garden with the little iron table sitting on the adjoining terrace. "The staff will keep the flowers alive for you." I grinned at her, but her expression was still unreadable.

In the bedroom, I stood against the wall and cleared my throat. We couldn't derail the tour here. I had one important thing to show her, not to mention she was covered in glass and burns. She needed some medical aid or time to heal before we wrestled in the sheets.

"The bed isn't as big as mine, and neither is the bathtub. This suite is for visiting non-dragons. The sizes are proportioned accordingly."

"Is the bed as soft as yours?" she murmured.

"Yes. Every bit. I made sure of it. Same bed linens, same fluffy pillows. I know you like that."

She looked around. Still, she showed no reaction, though I felt a plethora of emotions in the bond.

"Clothes are coming." I opened the armoire. "There are some things in here that Leala guessed might fit just to tide you over. You're technically a captive, so you don't need fancy dresses yet. It's mostly working attire. Although there really is no telling what Cecil is making. He apparently had a flash of inspiration from you and is working on a wardrobe. Everyone is annoyed because he delayed their orders. We'll get you into the new dressmaker as soon as she has an opening. Right now she's tending to everyone Cecil is shrugging off, but she's curious. That's probably a good thing for you. She'll make time."

I closed the armoire and pointed at the washroom.

"You have the essentials, and I ordered a few extras I thought you might like. You can have Leala change out the fragrances and everything as you see fit. I believe there are a lot of options. I've never really paid attention."

I edged over to the closed, sliding double doors.

"And there's one more thing." I started to sweat a little. "Oh, actually, two things. The bookcase is empty because I thought you'd like to fill it yourself. The library is huge. The fun is in the hunt, right? So you can take out any book as needed as long as you stop throwing them at the king."

Her grin was slight, but it was there.

"Okay, the last thing . . ." I grabbed the handles on the double doors. "Usually the rooms have more pieces of furniture—armoires, dressers, trunks, that sort of thing. Since you don't currently have much, I figured we could leave this area for . . ." I pushed open the doors, first one and then the other, stepping back into the bedroom instead of crossing the threshold. "This."

Inside waited various stands and easels, racks for paints and charcoals, colored pencils and pastels. Containers held instruments with which to draw, and blank canvases leaned up against the wall. A desk in the corner had her new journal, opened to the first blank page, a quill and pot of ink beside it. It was how the writing station in her cottage had been set up.

A few of her renderings from the village were set out on the stands to show her how that would work, and a couple I'd had framed. They leaned against the far wall, out of the way.

"I thought maybe . . ." I wiped my brow, still so unbearably nervous. I wanted to make this perfect for her. To give her the makings of a home, a comfortable place where she could rest and relax. I wanted to impress her. To please her. "I know you said your art was private, but I'd already had it packed up and brought with us before you said that. No one looked through it, though, after loading it up, I promise."

"Why?" The word was so faint I barely heard it. I turned

to look at her then. Her face was pale and her eyes were wide. "Why did you bring it?"

My chest tightened with something like dread. "This work, and your cooking, seemed like passions of yours. I thought . . . I just thought . . ." I cleared my throat again. I was sweating like some sort of farm animal. "I thought that maybe you'd want them with you. If I had created such beautiful art—if I had put the amount of passion and heart into them that you have—I would want to keep it."

"But you thought I was evil, a killer. You were taking me captive. To kill me. Why go through the trouble?"

I searched for something to say but came up blank. "I-I don't know. It just . . . felt right, I guess."

"Because of the true mate bond."

"Likely. Should I have it removed? This room is intended to be dressing chambers. If you don't like it, I can bring back the furniture I had removed. We can get you those dresses, if you want, and we can have dinners in our rooms or out in the garden . . ."

I realized I was basically babbling and stopped the onslaught of words.

She looked at her work on the stands and then skirted along the perimeter of the room, running her finger across one surface and then another. Only once did she push something back a little, just that tiny bit out of place, until she reached one of the containers on the desk. I'd left that one obviously and wildly out of place on purpose. I watched her ear lift, a smile, before she slid it in line with the others. She'd caught the joke.

Finally at the framed pictures, she turned and pointed, eyebrows raised.

I needed to stop clearing my throat. "Those were my favorites. I'd already looked through everything, so I figured the damage was done. It was to show you the framing options for any of the finished pieces you'd like to preserve."

She turned back to them, four in all, pulling one of the frames away to look at the work behind.

"If it's too much, I can have it all removed, Aurelia. Just say the word."

Her emotions were still too frenzied to read. She turned and finally faced me, her lips quivering.

"You organized it all just how I like it. You knew."

The tension in my shoulders eased a little, though I was beginning to feel a bit sheepish. "Yes. Except the bedroom. I know you prefer a little more chaos there, but, well, that's kind of hard to stage. It needs to be used, lived in, for the sort of chaos you like."

She laughed a little, and her eyes filled with tears. "I didn't even know that about myself. Did you do all this?"

"Yes. Well, no. Sylvester basically put the kitchen together. I didn't know how to go about that. The garden was there. I wouldn't have a clue on how to deal with that. Liron, the painting instructor here, helped me with the things you were likely to need. The bed was just ordering the right stuff from the laundry—"

"No, I mean . . ." She licked her lips as a single tear spilled down one cheek. She wiped it away. "No one else went through my cottage in Granny's village to help you piece all this together?"

"Helped a little, maybe, but no one was allowed to peruse. They took what I told them to grab and they got out. I didn't let anyone else snoop, Aurelia, I promise."

She shook her head. I still didn't understand; I couldn't tell if she was angry or happy or sad. "You hated everything I stood for, yet you took the time and effort to bring with me the things that meant the most to me in the world."

"Not technically. I'm sure there were gifts from Granny I missed."

"You know me so"—her lower lip trembled—"so, so well. You've tried so hard to know me and you've"—more tears fell—"you've nailed it. This is the"—she choked back a sob—"the nicest thing anyone has ever given me. Ever. It's the most . . . perfect, most magical space I've ever had. In a dragon castle, no less." She laughed through her tears. "My mom would . . ." She choked back another sob. "My mom would be so happy for me," she whispered, trying to get a hold of herself. "I could die tomorrow, with nothing else in the world, and I would be happy that I could recount all this to my mom."

I went to her. "You'll have many more stories to tell her, baby. I promise. But not for a long, long time. She'll wait for you, happily."

She put her hands on my chest. "I don't know you well enough to pull off something like this, and I feel awful about it. Why don't I have the same instincts with the bond that you do? Why doesn't it hurt me when someone mentions you in pain the way the bond hurts you?"

"She's too locked in her logic," my wolf said. *"Her wolf is frustrated by it, but I think you're right—it's a coping mechanism. She's trying to limit her wolf's influence so she doesn't do things like crawl out second-story windows. But it's stifling the true mate bond."*

He wasn't wrong, but I understood. *"She's always used logic. Her feelings—and her magic—were locked away. It's how she survived Granny. She won't submit to me simply because her primal urges tell her to; she'll submit to me because she loves me, all on her own. This space was the first step in showing her how perfect we are together. We now have more time than we thought we would. We just need to keep at it until she finally sees what we've known."*

In answer to her questions, I smiled down on her. "I had to read your journals, remember? We had to hash out your life. I looked through your things and remembered what I saw out of duty; I was on the job, and I'm damn good at it. You're just playing catch-up. You organized my whole room but left my books alone, right? You clearly knew I didn't like those messed with."

The wheels turned behind those beautiful, glistening eyes.

"And you would've withheld from the royals that I let you escape on our journey, even though the king threatened to make you talk." I kissed her nose. "You didn't feel hurt because you planned to take the pain instead of letting them go after me. Give yourself a break, Little Wolf. This is all new to you. Take it slow."

"Patience," she breathed, using the word I had with her earlier. She looked at my lips. "I have to pick out some glass, but then I want—no, *need*—you to take me slow."

I kissed her, long and languidly, afraid to run my hands over her lest I make it that much harder to take out the shards of glass. I couldn't imagine having glass sticking out of me and just leaving it there because I knew the healing process would inevitably force it out. I couldn't imagine ignoring pain of that magnitude.

"She'll be dangerous to herself in battle," my wolf said. *"Her wolf won't feel pain like other shifters and has an incredible drive for action and violence. I think she wants to make up for all the memories of the abuse she suffered in human form when she was suppressed and had no choice but to take it."*

"You know all about that."

"Many years of experience have taught me to temper it, same as you. She is fully grown, with a lot of power. She's going to be a handful."

"That's your problem. I look after the human, you look after the wolf."

His growl made me smile.

"What?" she murmured against my lips as a knock sounded at the exterior door.

"Expecting someone?" we asked together, and she laughed.

"Obviously I wasn't. I didn't even know where I lived." She pulled out of my arms and, with one last longing look at her new artsy sanctuary, headed for the door. "I'll need food to cook. Oh! I need to get some books on baking. I used to love bak—"

Her words cut off, and I saw why. Hannon waited at the door in a smart dress shirt that showed off his broad shoulders. His snug pants showcased his powerful legs. He didn't have my stature, but he was no slouch.

My wolf prowled restlessly, but only recognition came through the bond. Her smile was friendly. I tempered the urge to rush forward and throw him out of here on his ass.

"Hey." Hannon's smile was intimate. "Arleth would like to plant that Moonfire Lily, and asked that you come and give your insight. I believe you have some time before your first shift?"

He looked at me then for confirmation. There were no obvious traces of rivalry, but he was clearly paying no mind to my primal true mate claim. It was a dangerous line to walk in the shifter world.

"Oh . . ." Aurelia glanced back at me, traces of guilt in the bond, looking suddenly unsure.

"Go." I stopped beside her, my hard eyes on Hannon, and bent to kiss her head. "Have fun, baby. I'll see you later. Stay safe—no more glass explosions."

She laughed, relieved, watching me go. "See you later."

I winked at her. Outwardly, I remained unaffected by

another male vying for her attention. I didn't want her to think I was trying to cage her as Granny had done. If she needed to flirt and see what was out there, I'd endure it for her sake.

Inwardly I wanted to rip his pretty face off and shove it up his ass before killing him again, and again, and again, waiting for him to come back to life each time before re-teaching the lesson: do not fuck around with *my* mate. Touch her and you will fucking *die*.

20

HADRIEL

It was my turn for Aurelia duty, and I was more nervous for it than I'd ever been. She used to be so easy to watch, pliant and mostly placid, doing what was necessary and mostly following the rules. Now that she had her wolf, everything had gone tits up. I didn't know my head from my balls at this point, not to mention she got up at the ass-crack of dawn and had more energy than a vibrating demon butt plug set on high. I wasn't made for a detail like this. I was supposed to have retired when Finley had settled down. Thank the gods that Vemar had no trouble handling things, or I'd be in over my head.

"Where's the captive?" I asked the first gardener I came to. Aurelia needed to shift, and time was of the essence. I had more work to do on my hunt for castle gossip about Granny. I hadn't found squat so far. People were acting cagey with even the most benign lines of questioning. It was making me nervous. We had been gone from the kingdom for a while. I was starting to worry that one of her minions had sneaked in and compromised some of the castle inhabitants. Assuming I found them, the dragons would not deal with them kindly.

Poor Aurelia. That poor woman could not catch a break in life. It was beyond depressing at this point. Her first shift wouldn't even be normal.

Instead of having calm and sensible wolves on hand, they were bringing in a bunch of dragons. The powers that be worried Aurelia's wolf would go nuts and fight everyone or try to wrestle the bond away from Weston. Aurelia's wolf was an alpha, after all—one with substantial power. Without training, they could be unpredictable, and therefore, a real big problem.

It was probably a wise move. Her wolf seemed volatile and, honestly, foolish. Crawling out of a library window? Who did shit like that? Encouraging half the castle to run down the hall from an unseen foe? It wasn't helping Aurelia's image.

The gardener woman pointed to a crowd at the corner of the Everlass fields at the edge of the woods. A canopy of trees loomed over them, providing shade.

"Right, okay." I marched that way, mopping my head with a handkerchief because of the heat. Today was a terrible day to shift; it was much too hot. My wolf was not looking forward to it. I'd volunteered, though, wanting to see if Aurelia could assume control over my bond from Weston.

Okay, I had to admit it, I was fucking excited. I'd never in my life heard of a wolf as powerful as Weston. Some came close, but even those that we'd met hadn't had his natural finesse. I wondered if she did. She certainly had the determination. If anyone could best him, it would be her. And I was *here* for it.

I shouldered into the quiet group, all of whom were looking down on the glowing pink flower nestled within four Everlass plants. That they'd allowed her to plant an unknown flower amongst their precious Everlass was . . . surprising. Fucking shocking, actually.

The flower glowed, the intensity of it strengthening ever so slowly.

I found myself watching just to see when it would actually peak, then shook my head because the plant had just turned me into a zombie like everyone else.

"Hello?" I said to Aurelia, who was opposite the group from me.

She looked up in surprise. "Is it me you're looking for?"

I hooked a thumb behind me. "Time to shift."

"Oh." She nodded, looking down at the flower again. "Okay." She straightened slowly. "Okay, hopefully it makes it."

The flower did look dramatically droopy.

"We can call in Nyfain and Sable. They can sing it to better growth," Arleth said, staring at the flower like she was transfixed.

"You guys are all fine with the flower being in the Everlass, huh?" I asked as Aurelia stepped away.

"In the *dragon weed,* you mean?" Arleth cocked her eyebrow at Aurelia, her lips pursed in obvious scorn. A couple wolves in the group snickered. Aurelia must've dropped her nickname for it accidentally.

"The roots of this flower are shallow and fragile." Delaney, once Arleth's lady-in-waiting and now her best friend, straightened up. "Apparently they rely on the roots of the plants around them. We're not sure exactly how that occurs. This one was found between four Everlass plants. Even though *someone* trampled all over those plants, they survived and didn't seem troubled to have this plant in their midst. None of the other plants in the field were at all disturbed. We've never seen that happen. Usually—"

"It's okay, I don't need to know the details." I waved her away. "I wasn't that interested. Well, I hope it goes well. Aurelia, my love, we need to go."

I tsked when she walked around the crowd, her clothes still a mess, burn marks and all manner of things still evident.

"This is why you wore drab clothes, isn't it?" I said, cutting across the grounds toward the area where she'd be shifting. "You exploded yourself too much for nice things."

"Sorry about these." She plucked at the ruined jacket. "I haven't exploded things while making product in . . . well, years and years. Not since the beginning, really. It'll be worth it, though, you'll see."

"I also see you're getting quite familiar with Hannon." I watched her reaction closely as I lifted my eyebrows, having heard from various sources that the beta's true mate was seen walking, sitting, and conversing closely with a prime eligible bachelor. Everyone wanted to land that phoenix, but he was incredibly selective. He didn't usually give anyone so much attention. "What's that about?"

She looked over her shoulder; he had been in the crowd of people and now watched her go. "He's really nice. And smart. And easy to talk to."

He was also, quite obviously, smitten with her. He was doing nothing to hide it. She didn't notice the signs. Because of an upbringing where no one wanted to talk to her, let alone woo her, she was completely oblivious. It made the whole exchange fascinating to watch.

And poke a little fun at . . .

"And handsome," I drawled. "With a nice body. And big . . . feet."

Crimson spots bloomed on her cheeks. "He's friendly, that's all. He listens really well. He always gives me his undivided attention, like he's fascinated by every word that comes out of my mouth." She shrugged. "He's a friend. I hope. He's someone I'd like to be friends with, anyway."

"A handsome friend."

The blush intensified. "It's just . . . There's no history, you know? It's nice getting to know someone that doesn't already know so much about me."

"Ah," I said, nodding. That made sense. If I had a history like hers, and with the reactions we'd all given her, I'd probably want to start from scratch as well. And honestly, after the curse, I kind of did, didn't I? We'd had a big influx of new people who'd had no idea what it had been like before. I remember it being . . . refreshing. I could relate to her on this one.

Just for a little extra poke, though, in the name of fun . . .

"So it has nothing to do with how handsome he is, then?"

"His appearance is just . . ." Another shrug. "I mean, fine, sure, he's nice to look at, yes, but so is the king—" She shivered. "The king is too scary. I take that back. But so is Vemar—he's really handsome. And so is that dragon commander, even though he looks like he wants to punch everyone he sees. And Finley is really beautiful; Calia too—there are a lot of attractive people here. He's just another one of them."

"First, I am hurt that my name wasn't mentioned in that list . . ."

She nudged me with her elbow. "Of course you're on the list. That goes without saying."

"I'll accept that. So, to summarize, he's nice to look at, but you don't want to fuck him."

Her whole face was beet red now. "I'm just trying to get

by. I'm not looking to bang my way through the castle. I wouldn't even know what to do in an orgy."

"Orgy?" I put a hand on her shoulder to stop her. "Who said anything about orgies?"

She rolled her eyes, brushing past. "It was that cornhole guy—Liron. He stopped Hannon and me on the way out to the garden and asked if we'd like to attend. Thankfully, Hannon got a little scary and shut him down, so I didn't have to deal with it—"

"That fucking toolshed." I rolled my eyes with her this time. "Don't worry about that. Hannon likely solved the problem."

Hannon was as easygoing as they came, hardly ever ruffled, but when he reacted to a threat, it was extreme. Liron had probably shit himself. Served him right.

"Yeah. It's actually kind of nice that he can read emotions," Aurelia said. "I didn't have to say anything. When I got uncomfortable and started arguing with my wolf, who wanted to kill him, Hannon stepped in."

"Then you must also enjoy the four-way bond." Again, I watched her expression closely. "Since, you know, Weston will always do the same thing for you."

Her expression softened, her posture suddenly demure, a little smile playing across her lips. "Yes, that is nice, actually." She was also smitten, but not with Hannon. She was starting to come around.

I pushed a tree branch out of the way. "Now, I want to switch gears for a moment. What the fuck is with you blowing things up and getting glass embedded all in you? And what, gods help me, is up with wandering around covered in glass and blood and *burn marks*, of all bloody things, like some sort of horrific monster? You look scary enough to make iron stomachs churn. You've scared the whole fucking castle, my darling. Don't bother walking around with a knife—people will fucking run from you. Thank the gods' left nipples that Leala is your lady's maid. She is incredibly turned on by your high threshold for pain. She's itching to use that whip, I tell you, but don't let her. She'll fuck you with the handle, and you *really* don't want to know where it's been."

"Goodness gracious." She gulped and tugged at her collar.

"Exactly. Oh, and also, don't mind her if she lingers when the beta starts hammering that cock into you. I told her how spectacular you guys were to watch. She wants to see. She's not intrusive, though, so don't worry. She'll wait to wank until after she's left the room."

"*Leala?* She seems so nice and sweet. And normal."

"She is, love. Just very kinky, too. She'll get the whole room fucking if you let her. Now, here we go."

The beta waited in his birthday suit in the middle of six shifted dragons. One was the huge golden dragon of the king and another Vemar, who was curious to see how all of this would go. The others were of various power levels. Two were new to their forms because of the curse, and the other two from different kingdoms, therefore without the hardships the rest of us had faced. The king wanted a range of backgrounds to see how they and Aurelia would respond to each other. I got the feeling he was sizing her up.

As promised, no other shifters were in the area, save me.

"I'm going to go ahead and shift now, love, okay?" I stripped out of my clothes. "The beta will talk you through some things, and then the two of you will shift together."

She gripped my forearm, her nervousness palpable.

"No, no." I removed her fingers and stepped back, seeing the beta's frame tighten with thick cords of muscle I did not want coming at me. "Do not touch the Hadriel when he is removing his clothes. The Hadriel does not want his head pulled off in a fit of alpha wolf rage."

"Why do you all switch between calling him alpha and beta?" Aurelia asked, picking absent-mindedly at a nail and looking around at all the dragons. Her eyes widened when her gaze drifted over the king, who stood waiting patiently.

"Just to confuse you. Go now, he's waiting."

She did, slowly, getting more and more languid the closer she got to Weston. He watched her quietly, the sort of focus a true predator was known for. Now it wasn't only his muscles that stiffened.

When she stopped in front of him, he said, "Are you ready?"

She took a deep breath, laid her hands on his chest, and nodded.

"Okay."

He slowly undid her jacket, pushing it off her shoulders and tossing it away. The thing was utterly ruined; they may as well just burn it. Her shirt was next, then he leaned forward to take her lips.

I quickly finished undressing and shifted, letting my wolf take over. I didn't want to inadvertently start jacking off and draw too much attention to myself. There were rumors going around that I had an obsession with my dick, and while that was true of any man, at least to some extent, I was tired of defending the legitimacy of it.

When her chest was bare, he ran his hand down to cup a breast, still kissing her. She didn't seem to notice or care that people were watching. If not for the true mate bond, she'd probably be embarrassed as hell.

He worked at her pants, leaning back so that he could look down as he peeled them off her bruised and battered flesh. He didn't say anything, just worked them off gently, pulling out the larger pieces of glass that were still embedded in her skin. Mad, that woman. Pure madness.

On his knees now, he looked up at her before leaning forward to lick at her center. She threaded her fingers through his hair, widening her legs and leaning her head back, enjoying his slow, methodical touch.

"He's very . . . passionate," my wolf said, lying down, watching in interest.

Yes, he was. Pity I'd never gotten to sample it.

He licked some more before sucking, sliding his hands up the sides of her thighs and holding her hips. Slowly he rose, kissing up her skin as he did, back to her lips and sharing her taste. Aurelia moaned, and suddenly, for the first time ever, I was actually a little uncomfortable. This was insanely hot—enough to kick off a huge orgy—but also incredibly personal. Intimate. He was relaxing his mate, claiming all her focus before he guided her through her first shift. It was . . . touching. I was fucking touched, damn it.

Weston

"You feel me through the bond," I murmured, my lips against hers, feeling the nervousness still coiled within her. My wolf reached through, connecting with hers, readying to help her into the world.

"Yes," Aurelia answered, breathy, her eyes closed. Her focus was acutely on me, my ministrations having blurred everything around us. Except for the nervousness, she was in a good headspace.

"Keep that contact through the shift. Feel how I distribute my power and how I give control over to my wolf, okay? Once you start to release control, you need to —as the human—clear out of the way. Your wolf will rise and take over. It might feel weird at first, but you need to let her. I'll be right here. We'll do this together, okay?"

Another swirl of nervousness. "Okay."

I kissed her again, holding her hands, before stepping away. Her eyes opened slowly, meeting mine. We stared at each other for a moment, feeling our connection through the bond: her growing fear and uncertainty, my steadfast loyalty and support.

"I'm here for you," I told her, grounding her within our bond.

She nodded, and my wolf rose as slowly as he possibly could, showing her wolf how. Eyes never leaving Aurelia, I waited for the last possible moment before I got out of the way. He yanked power from them at the pinnacle moment, helping them feel the timing, sharing with them the pain, and then we were shifting, dropping down on all fours with scents and sounds rushing in to color the scene.

With another flutter of nervousness Aurelia began, following our lead to the letter. Her wolf rose to the surface, pulling power, more than she needed, wobbling as they passed each other in consciousness and control.

"Steady," my wolf murmured, stabilizing them through the bond, feeling her wolf clutch him as she tried to navigate.

She was in full control, using the power at the right moment to begin the transition. Pain pounded through them; it was always the hardest when the body morphed for the first time. Each consecutive shift got easier and easier.

My wolf braced for her wolf to reach for him in panic

or alarm, but they sailed right by, shrugging it off and completing the transition as though it had been painless.

He didn't say anything, but I grinned at the humbled feeling. I'd had the same reaction after she was worked over by Alexander. Those wounds would've put me down for days, but she'd pushed through.

"She's beautiful," my wolf breathed, in complete awe. I had to agree.

The black fur on Aurelia's head ran down her back and dusted the tops of her legs. A deep gray, similar to ours, dotted the black in places and flowed down her neck to her chest. It was her wolf's face that was unique: her muzzle, mostly white, had a streak of brown on each side with a black stripe running between them. Her ears were mostly gray with a little of the brown at the base, and her eyes shone hazel. She was striking and interesting, just like the human.

The wolf immediately lowered to her stomach, her muzzle on her paws, looking up at us.

"What's she doing?" I asked my wolf in the equivalent of a whisper.

"A wolf usually shifts for the first time when the human is going through puberty, remember? The human is growing, awkward and gangly. The new wolf is the same, needing to learn their new body. In the pack, though, everyone is doing it together, young, and there's a community-wide learning curve. Aurelia knows her body well, though, and her wolf is with experienced creatures. If it were just us she'd probably try out her new legs right away, but the king is watching, as are the other dragons. She's proud. She is trying to process her new shape before she attempts to use it."

Just like the human, then. She wanted to size up the situation before she dove in.

We watched patiently. Her cute little nose twitched as

she took in all the new smells. Her ears moved, processing the enhanced sounds—her wolf form was able to take in so much more information than her human ears. Her power throbbed within her, allowing my wolf to pull it to him before she accepted it back gracefully. He'd been worried she'd be unable to maintain the equilibrium of it in a new situation, worried she'd clutch it, hoard it. That she didn't was a very good sign.

Another good sign was that she was not reaching with it. Hadriel's pack bond pulsed nearby but remained connected to me. She could instinctively feel it; she could feel the bond to the whole pack in me. Most new wolves tended to grope for it, trying to find a lifeline. New alphas often felt it out, those with something to prove usually grabbing hold of it to see if they could wrestle it away from the more established alpha. Not once did she so much as think in that direction.

"She's worried about disrupting the pack bond," my wolf murmured with a note of pride, still watching her watch him. *"She is getting her bearings before she seeks our guidance. She's keeping her power as contained as possible, keeping herself firmly under control, to ensure she doesn't jeopardize the pack."*

She wasn't worried about herself and her shift now—she was worried about my people.

My heart swelled.

My wolf waited for a moment longer before bending his head toward her, about to nudge her along like he would a shy, new wolf.

Her lips pulled away from her teeth in a silent snarl. He backed off immediately. She would not be rushed.

I chuckled as he went back to waiting without a word.

Finally, she lifted her head. And then rose to her feet. Her wolf wasn't as small as her human, nor was she as slight. She was average for a wolf, about the size of

Hadriel. She'd be able to hold her own in a fight. Not that she couldn't in human form. What she lacked in size, she more than made up for in speed.

Hesitantly, she stepped forward. My wolf couldn't contain his pride as he circled her, watching. She stepped again, and again, walking in a straight line, nowhere near as wobbly as a normal first-timer. After a moment, she tried moving a little faster, the equivalent of a brisk walk. Her movements were halting at first, but she quickly got the hang of it. Then she went a little faster within the circle of dragons, up to a light jog. She didn't attack anyone as some had feared, and I still hadn't felt her reach for Hadriel's bond. She had control—of herself, and of her power.

"She's a natural," my wolf said as we felt her elation through the bond. He beamed with pride now, watching his little mate practically prance through the wild grasses and budding flowers.

He ran to join her, unable to help it. He licked her muzzle in a show of devotion before running his face over the back of her neck. She stretched for him, angling her face back to him as he ran his muzzle toward and over her shoulders. Heat worked through the bond as both of them reacted to their proximity for the first time.

"Uh . . ." I said, a little confused. *"Besides the fact that we're here to shift, not fuck, I thought this didn't happen until the female entered her heat . . ."*

My wolf didn't respond. He stood with his head braced over her, an indication of his claim, as was the beginning of her mating ritual: her tail swishing for him, leaning toward him, her head curved around submissively.

"Chill out," I told him. *"We've got business to attend to."*

He knew I was right and pulled his head from over her back, turning until he was standing beside her. Fuck's sake.

It wasn't as bad as crawling out of a castle window without wings, but this wasn't a great time for him to lose control.

We looked at Hadriel's wolf lying on his stomach. His ears suddenly flattened—he was clearly unsure what would happen next. The plan had gotten as far as using him for bait to see if she would usurp the bond, but she'd passed that test without even flexing. It was time to push her a little more and see how she reacted.

My wolf directed the bond toward Aurelia's wolf, magically guiding her to it, the task so much easier with the mating bond. We'd try to handle it together and see what happened. It was a gamble to bring in a powerful, untrained wolf in a situation like this, especially one who had the potential to snatch away the bond.

The only alpha true mate pairing I'd ever heard of were the king and queen, but they were dragons. They had a mating bond, yes, but dragons didn't form pack bonds. Their agreement to share leadership was verbal.

An alpha wolf pair leading a pack was different. They had to hold the bond together, working cohesively to balance the power dynamic. Their mating bond had to flow freely at all times, and sometimes compromises needed to be made in a fraction of a second. I'd never heard of an alpha wolf pair leading successfully for an extended period of time.

But I'd also never heard of an alpha true mate wolf pairing, period. I had to assume nature had gotten it right.

The sensation of her wolf taking hold of Hadriel's pack bond was featherlight, soft and serene and full of trust that my wolf would steer her. Then the bond swelled with power, a wave of it rushing through the pack bond straight for Hadriel.

His wolf whined, standing quickly and backing up. His lips pulled back from his teeth and his hair puffed, his fear of the power bearing down on him evident. Wolf and man tensed up; I knew Hadriel was probably screaming inside.

Nyfain's dragon, reading Hadriel's cues, took a step forward. A wave of panic swept through Aurelia, but my wolf gripped her power tightly, reclaiming her focus, staying the course.

The power washed over Hadriel's wolf, sloshing around him, probably dragging him under. The wolf growled, braced himself . . . and then the magic settled. The same iron hold still tethered us to Hadriel, but now Aurelia's connection existed all around, too, the soft sort of embrace something I'd never felt before. If I was the hard ground under their feet and the hot sun beating down onto their flesh, she was the bees buzzing around the flower petals and the birdsong high overhead. It was peaceful and tranquil.

Perfect, just like her. Just like us together.

"This is natural," my wolf said, leaning against her side and rubbing his face against her head. *"This is what wolf leadership was always meant to be. A true mate pair holding the bond, both nurturing and guiding the pack. Both of us, working together in perfect unity."*

I felt every reverent word he said deep in my soul. But just as Aurelia had taken one step at a time, so must we. I brought out the hard truths we'd have to face.

"She can hold a bond, but can she work with one? She can run, but can she fight? I have trained all my life; she has just met her wolf. She has the power and blood of an alpha, but she does not have the experience or know-how. We don't know if she'll work as half of our alpha pair."

He didn't comment, probably because he didn't want to admit I was right. He wanted to bask in the glory that was this moment, sharing it with our true mate. Just as Aurelia had said, my wolf was instinctive, and I was the logical one. We had work to do.

"Pull her back now," I told my wolf. *"Make sure she will disengage."*

He hated me for telling him to do it. He hated his duty more. But he was an alpha, and he would do right by his pack.

The swell of magic receded gradually, so incredibly smooth, as Aurelia's wolf took his guidance as truth. It showed how much trust she had in him. How easily she ceded to his dominance and leadership.

"The bond was more than twice as strong," my wolf said. *"The true mate pairing doesn't just double in power--it grows it exponentially. It's not in the actual bond, though, but more like . . . in the protection of the bond."*

He was right. If the initial bond was a rope connecting us all, Aurelia's added power covered that rope in an iron crust. It would be much, *much* harder to break or rip away.

"We didn't try communicating through it," I mentioned.

"Maybe we would have if you hadn't rushed us into tearing it down."

It was annoying when he was right.

"Now . . ." My wolf licked his muzzle uncertainly. Aurelia's wolf looked over to gauge the unsettled feelings through the bond. *"We need to see how she reacts to her worst nightmare."*

21

HADRIEL

Once the power had fully receded, the beta glanced the king's way. Nyfain's great gold dragon roared, deep-throated and vicious—a challenge.

"Oh shit . . ."

Weston's hackles rose and he turned toward the dragon, stepping in front of Aurelia protectively. He must've known this would happen, but his instincts had taken over anyway.

The other dragons roared. One lifted its shiny black head into the air and spewed fire. The impatient dragon pushed into the sky, moving into position as though planning to dive and snap Aurelia up.

My wolf bared his teeth, hackles rising. Aurelia's hackles rose, too, the threat obvious.

The king dashed forward, faster on the ground than anyone would expect he'd be. By nature, dragons were clumsy on land, but he'd had a shitload of practice. Weston dodged to the side, and Aurelia darted in the opposite direction. Despite being new to all this, she was still faster than Weston's much larger, more experienced wolf.

Weston sprinted between the dragon's legs, gnashing his teeth along the back of an ankle. It was one of the few vulnerable spots a lone wolf could reach; to defeat a dragon, a pack needed several strong wolves to bring the dragon toppling to the ground, where the rest of them could then get at the softer underbelly and throat. Weston was showing Aurelia, already training her. He wasted no time.

She followed suit but didn't go out the other side, instead systematically darting between his legs, over and over, sometimes barely missed by his stomping feet or swinging tail. Weston yelped at her, trying to get her away. Nyfain roared, turning as the other dragons began stomping into the fray.

"Oh shit, oh shit," I said, feeling our heart picking up pace. *"Go help! Get her out of there!"*

"She has to heed the beta's training," my wolf gritted out, his body tense. *"We can't get involved unless he calls for us."*

He wanted to, though. I could feel it in his coiled muscles, in his quivering haunches.

Weston's ears went back flat. He darted between the dragons, trying to get to his mate. Aurelia didn't relent. She was working Nyfain, gnashing at him. The relentless determination she'd shown in her work earlier that day was just as evident now.

The huge golden dragon stopped and then dropped into a crouch, as though going down onto his belly. He stopped at his knees, though, his control incredible; most dragons were not able to complete that maneuver. He was doing it so as not to crush her.

He wouldn't have.

She darted out like she'd been on four legs all her life, spun, and launched up. Her jump was clumsy but still high, and her teeth sank into his belly.

"There she is," I said in a hush. *"There's the crazy bitch Vemar said was in there."*

Nyfain roared, standing again. Aurelia didn't let go, somehow hanging on with her fucking teeth and now scrabbling with her legs, trying to claw through his underside.

"Fuck," my wolf said. He rarely swore, but this situation definitely called for it. *"I've never seen anyone do that. How's she hanging on?"*

"That woman is cunning as fuck. She's no joke when she's in survival mode." This was her wolf's equivalent of climbing out the fucking window.

Nyfain swung around, thumped his tail, and then roared in frustration. He spewed fire, nearly scorching us, and hopped around a little while Aurelia ripped at him in a feat of acrobatics that was as unbelievable as it was impressive.

Another dragon collided with Nyfain, knocking her off. She twisted in the air, but she was no cat. She fell on her side and Weston was there, standing over her, growling at the stomping dragons.

She didn't stop.

She was up in a moment, limping a little, running at Nyfain again. A swell of power rose through the clearing, and then a strange feeling came over me. It was a panicked feeling—a warning of danger, of an enemy in our midst. And then it was a strange sort of magical call to *attack!*

My wolf launched forward in a frenzy. Three of the five dragons on the ground immediately stopped stomping and shuddered. A moment later they were running at Nyfain, smoke billowing up from their mouths, teeth bared. The dragon in the air dove down, scraping his claws across Nyfain's back. The king was no longer their ally—he was now their enemy. Their target.

Only one dragon didn't join in. Vemar pushed back from the crowd and lay down. He knew the feeling for what it was: Aurelia's magic. Her mind-fuckery, as he called it.

"Don't attack," I yelled at my wolf as the magic drummed around us. I'd never felt it this strong. She must've been pulling power from Weston through the bond to enhance this other facet of her magic. *"Remember when I randomly took off running with her the other day and you called me an idiot? Well, now* you're *the idiot. Don't attack!"*

The dragons closed in on Nyfain, backing him to the edge of the clearing. He could've fought them off, but he clearly didn't want to hurt them. The one flying swooped down.

Weston's wolf tackled Aurelia, rolling her over with his larger body and then grabbing her neck in his teeth. She struggled to get free, to get out from under him. Her power kept throbbing in the clearing. That type of magic didn't come from her shifter blood. It couldn't; I'd never seen or heard of anything like it. Weston tightened his hold, growling, leaning half his body on top of her to pin her.

Her whine was barely audible over the sounds of the attack, and then the power in the clearing dissipated as fast as it had started. As it died, the dragons slowed, then shuddered again before looking around in confusion. Vemar lifted his head as the airborne dragon tilted wildly in the air before landing clumsily, sliding a few feet on his face.

Weston continued to keep Aurelia pressed to the ground as the dragons drifted away from the fight. They resumed their starting positions, heads bowed a little, clearly having no idea what had just happened. Vemar pushed himself to a standing position, waiting patiently.

Nyfain dripped blood from his belly and took halting steps. Aurelia had clearly had an effect.

"The beta will be proud of her," my wolf said, flattening to his belly as Nyfain huffed smoke out of his nose.

"If he doesn't get chewed out for this."

"He won't. She's an untrained asset. Just think of how effective she'll be when trained up."

"She's a captive. We need to address that first. People who've lost loved ones are calling for her head."

The situation was a mess. The king sympathized with Aurelia, but the queen still wasn't sure. Then there were the people. They didn't give a shit about her story, what little of it they knew. As far as they were concerned, she was Granny's drugmaker. A killer. They wanted justice.

The royalty might come around, but in some cases, they had no choice but to answer to the populace. Even if the king and queen agreed with each other, their hands could be tied.

I didn't even want to get started on the pack situation. It was no secret that Aurelia was Weston's true mate. It was also no secret how a true mate would react if his other half was threatened. Word was that he would leave, that many of his most powerful wolves would go with him, and the act would rip this kingdom apart from the inside out.

In the eye of the storm, just trying to do the right thing, was Aurelia. Slapped around from birth, hated for something that wasn't her fault and wasn't even true, she was now an enemy of the people for doing what she'd been told so her parental figure would love her. To try to keep a safe home. It broke my heart. All of it. That this was working out so horribly had me literally losing hours of sleep.

I'd fix this. Somehow, I would figure this out. I had helped get this damn place out of the curse, and I'd keep it away from boiled destruction as well.

Weston pulled away from his mate, turning to face the king. Aurelia rolled over slowly, staying on her belly for now, head on her paws. She had been chastised, forced to submit, and she was showing her subservience to the king. Perfectly handled. Thank all the fucks.

The king's large dragon form morphed back into a man with blood dripping down his stomach and his ankles and wrists all fucked up. He didn't show the pain as he looked down on Weston and Aurelia.

"Go," he commanded, waving the dragons away.

They took to the air, Vemar roaring as he took one last look at Aurelia before soaring away.

"Shift," the king told the two wolves.

They did.

Aurelia didn't stand after she'd regained her human form, sitting on her butt with her knees up, her arms draped around them. She studied the ground, head bowed.

The beta stood beside her, his shoulders straight and head held high, facing the king without remorse. That spoke volumes. He didn't give a damn what the king might say. It would not diminish Weston's pride in her. My wolf had been right.

"What was that?" Nyfain asked Weston before looking down on Aurelia.

"I'll do better," Aurelia said in a monotone voice.

My heart ached. There was no way I could be sure, but I'd bet my left nut she'd said those words, in that tone, when Granny scolded her and told her she'd be punished for what she'd done. Her response seemed practiced. Pitiful.

"Aurelia, look at me," Nyfain said.

She looked up dutifully, her eyes devoid of emotion, ready to face what came.

Nyfain took a knee in front of her, wincing as he did so.

"I wasn't scolding you, Aurelia. I challenged you, and you answered that challenge in a way none of us expected. You did well here. You need training, that's all. My mate was a handful in the beginning, too. What I meant was, what was that magic? What did your wolf do?"

"Panic, mostly."

"You don't know how you turned the dragons against me?"

She shook her head slowly. "My wolf wasn't really . . . thinking things through. She mostly just reacts, and you're mostly just terrifying, more so in dragon form. She used everything at our disposal."

"And that magic, that mind . . . spin you used on my dragons, that was at your wolf's disposal?"

She shrugged. "I had the thought we needed help. Then . . . we got help. I'm honestly not sure how. I've never been in that situation before."

Nyfain looked up at Weston for a long moment before he reached out and placed his hand on Aurelia's shoulder. "Do not beat yourself up over this. You didn't do anything wrong. In fact, when Weston called you down, you submitted. That was the right response, and very well done. We can build on this."

She nodded, looking up at him with large, glassy eyes. "Thank you."

My heart felt like it had been kicked around the floor. My wolf's ears drooped, and if we'd been in human form, I'd have been sobbing.

A crease formed between the king's brow as he studied her, truly seeing for the first time what Granny's treatment had done. It was one thing to hear it while the woman was confidently and defiantly answering questions, but it was another to see this puddle of human. This strong woman was so used to getting beaten down, she simply sat there quietly as she waited for the blows to come.

He didn't comment further, just patted her shoulder before standing again.

"Hadriel," Nyfain said, "take her back to her room and get her a hot bath." To her he said, "No more working today. Bathe, and eat, and relax. I won't keep your"—he paused—"Weston long. I'll send him to you in a bit, so you can talk through it."

"Okay." She pushed to her feet, and Nyfain stepped back to give her room.

Weston stepped in front of her, placing his hands on her shoulders. He bent, his lips near her ear, whispering something I couldn't overhear. She nodded once, and then twice. After that she was on her way, her eyes down as she crossed the clearing.

I shifted and hurried to grab our clothes, stomped and kicked around and crushed into the dirt though they were.

"Well, now I'm glad you didn't change and ruin another of my jackets," I said, picking up her things. "How do you feel about just walking back naked? These are terrible."

"It's okay, I'll wear them." She put them on silently without looking up, and I knew she was ready to break.

I was breaking just watching her.

No one was challenged like this their first time; no one was usually challenged at all. This had only happened because she was the alpha's true mate and posed a risk to the pack. Pushing her like this—bringing out that strange magic she didn't know how to control—wasn't fair, not for someone who didn't know the culture. Not for someone who had only ever known a life of being abused when she wasn't absolutely perfect. They needed to handle her differently going forward, something I thought the king had made mental note of. If he hadn't, Weston surely had.

They were two great leaders, and I had faith they'd guard her better going forward.

In the meantime, I would do my best to bolster her back up until the beta could join her and offer her the support of a true mate. I'd had plenty of experience helping her navigate through the stories of her depressing life. This experience would not be going to that pile. This would be a heroic moment in her journals, her bravery and tenacity and magical abilities recounted in vivid detail. I'd make sure of it.

"To the bath," I said after I'd put on my dirty clothes, pepping up. "Just in time, too. My lord, you're dirtier than a demon's dick. Let's get Leala to get you some really nice bath salts and petals and all that extra shit that makes us feel like royalty, shall we? There are perks to living in a castle."

I hooked my arm within hers.

"And a nice meal, too." I licked my lips as we walked. "I could go for lamb. Do you know how to make lamb? I'll steal all the supplies and you can make it. Sound good?"

Weston

I watched Hadriel guide my mate to the castle, wishing I could've been the one to walk her back. I knew she regarded this situation as a failure, when in reality it was anything but.

"Well?" Nyfain asked me, ducking behind a tree to grab our clothes.

I took a deep breath. "Well."

He laughed once and nodded. "Let's start at the beginning. The shift seemed like it went well."

"The shift went fine. There was a moment of confusion during the transition, but we managed it."

"Grabbing for control?"

"Not even a little." I told him about how she managed her power, keeping it banked to protect the established pack bond.

"Sounds like the makings of a good alpha." He paused. "A good mate."

"Yes, it does," I said quietly. "I merged our power and tried a direct pack bond with Hadriel. I wanted to see what that might look like."

"And?"

"She strengthened the pack bond in a way I can only describe as pleasant. Really fucking pleasant. Strong, too. If we can train her to apply it to the rest of the pack, it'll be the most intense pack bond I think anyone will have ever felt. Unbreakable."

"Do you foresee having a problem giving commands with her in the bond?"

I ran my fingers through my unruly hair. It needed to be cut, badly. "I don't think so, but I can't yet say for sure. That sort of thing is what usually tears down an alpha pair. Our bond is new, our wolves are new to each other . . . I really can't tell yet how that will play out. Aurelia can be stubborn as all hell. When I tell her to do something, she pushes back. I don't know yet if her wolf will be the same way. If so, it's not a good recipe for a pack bond."

"I think you're forgetting the type of mate I have. I know something about stubbornness, pushing back, and refusing to do as she's told. When it's important, they usually make the right choices. If they are a strong leader, it'll help make you better. Make us all better, as a kingdom.

Our alpha pair leadership works. There's no reason yours couldn't."

"I'm hoping so. I—" I clenched my jaw against my swell of longing. The future I imagined with her was something I was scared to admit. I'd done such horrible things in my life. Lived such terrible experiences. Often it felt like I didn't deserve true happiness, that I shouldn't have my dreams answered. But damn it, I couldn't deny how badly I wanted her, wanted our messy yet perfect love. A family.

"Speak," he said, studying me.

I made busy doing up my buttons. "I really want this," I admitted. "I want her as my mate. I want her to lead your pack alongside me. I want to be the strongest commander in the magical world, and I want her help with that."

"You want it all."

"Yeah, I suppose I do."

"There's just one problem."

There was a helluva lot more than just one problem.

"What is that?" I asked.

"The fairies are going to make a play for her. That magic . . ." Nyfain shook his head, a warning in his eyes. "That magic was not shifter magic. We already know she has fairy blood. That magic was powerful and has the potential to be devastating. My own people turned on me. They would've killed me if given the chance. That magic would be dangerously destructive in battle. She wouldn't even need to fight; she could have the enemy do it for her."

"Did you note that Vemar didn't succumb?"

"I did. Vemar is known for his inability to be manipulated with magic. His mind is strong. Most aren't."

"She's your prisoner. How would the fairies get her without stepping on your toes?"

Nyfain laughed, heading back toward the castle. "Calia seems sweet and nice, but she is cutthroat. If she deems

Aurelia's magic valuable, she'll offer Aurelia the world. If Aurelia accepts, Calia will take her out of here right under our noses. She won't even say sorry when I call her on it. I know this because if the roles were reversed, that's exactly what I would do. Inter-kingdom politics are a battlefield, and though Calia is a strong ally, she also makes an excellent foe. As for the shifter element of Aurelia's magic, I'm guessing her power is as strong as yours."

"Yes, and when we merge in the bond, our combined power doesn't just double—it grows exponentially."

"We're looking into her father. My mother has already identified a few possibilities. She sent a note to her contacts to get more information, as did Hadriel. It's safe to say it is someone powerful."

"Yes."

"They'll want her bloodline, and they'll pay handsomely to get it. She'll have a real family again—a biological family. That'll be attractive for someone like her."

Cold dread seeped through me. "This is turning into more than just one problem."

"I'm bad at counting." He paused, then looked me in the eye. "I need to know, Weston. If she goes to another kingdom, will you go with her? I'll do everything in my power to keep her, but you know the reality of her situation. The people here . . . aren't fans."

I didn't want to be anywhere else. I'd found a home here, a job I loved, people I was honored to serve. The fairy court was sly and crafty and wouldn't want me to lead anything. The other wolf kingdoms were shortsighted, and ruled by leaders I didn't respect. I wouldn't be happy in any of those places.

But she was my future. She was so close to realizing it. I wouldn't say no to her.

"I don't know," I answered semi-honestly. She would

still have to ask me, and she wasn't there yet. Not quite. "She might not even want me to go. She isn't ready to accept my claim. I'm not rushing her. I want her to come to me on her own."

"Noble. A word of advice—be nice to her. Show her how much you like her. I know from experience that running hot and cold just pisses them off, and Aurelia is not one you want to piss off." He smirked. "She'll have the whole fucking castle trying to kill you."

22

AURELIA

I felt worlds better after the bath and the pep talks from Hadriel and Leala, who hung around as I soaked. It helped that they told me stories of when the queen was new and giving the king hell. Really helped, actually. I wasn't nearly so bad by comparison.

A knock sounded at the door, and I found myself hoping it was Weston despite the lack of sensation in the bond. Turned out it was Dante, book in hand, annoyance on his face.

"Really?" he asked as he barged in. "You'd rather spend all day blowing yourself up instead of finishing this book? We're halfway in—we need to see what happens!"

Tanix, Sixten, and Nova followed him in, looking around as they entered.

"Sweet place," Sixten said, plopping down on the couch. "It feels like you. Did the beta set this up?"

"Yeah, he decorated and everything." I peeked out the door to make sure no one else was there before I shut it. A maid down the hall saw me and startled, clutched some sort of fabric to her chest, and hurried away.

That couldn't be good.

"He's thoughtful like that," Sixten commented, fluffing a couch pillow.

"Stop." Dante froze, staring at the kitchen, book in hand with thumb in its crack to mark his place. "Stop right there. What is happening?"

"Ooooh." Tanix clapped Dante on the shoulder as he neared, staring at the kitchen. "She's cooking. Good call on barging in, brother. This is officially your best idea."

"She's cooking?" Nova, who'd been busying herself by looking through the opened book on my dining nook table, walked over. While the beef braised—Hadriel had gotten yelled at and chased out of the kitchens for trying to steal some lamb—I'd been doing some necessary research. I had a million ideas racing around my head. "Is there enough for everyone?"

"If not, I'm happy with just a bite." Dante raised his hand. "Just a little morsel would be fine for me."

"There's . . ." I pursed my lips as I thought over everything. "There'll be enough for an appetizer if we all share. I want to save a plate for Weston, but Hadriel and I can get dinner from the kitchens."

"No, Aurelia." Tanix gave me a stern look. "You're not going to do all this work just to feed everyone else and not yourself. We'll eat from the kitchen."

"No, no, it's really okay. I love cooking—it relaxes me. The castle has plenty of hot food. It'll be great. I have a hankering for cheese, anyway."

Tanix gestured at Nova.

"Cheese, bread, nibbles, on it." She took off out the door.

"No, really—"

"No, *really*." Tanix arched an eyebrow. "It's good. Let's get to reading. Do you have time?"

I glanced at the books on the table. I had plenty to get me started for tomorrow morning, and it had been a long day. I could really use some wind-down time. Besides, people actually wanted to hang out with me when they didn't have to? That was a treat in and of itself.

"Of course. I'm . . ." I pointed toward the bedroom. "You guys all know I draw, right? It's not a secret?"

"We're not supposed to mention it or speak about it in any way, lest you think we invaded your privacy," Dante said, grunting as he sank into the couch. "But we do know, yes."

"Way to call out the beta, dick." Sixten punched him in the arm.

"She's not stupid, vadge," Dante replied.

"Okay, well . . . While you read, do you mind if I try to paint? I've never had paints and it'll probably be a mess, but I thought I might give it a go."

"All the gold you made for Granny and you never had paints," Dante murmured, shaking his head as he spread open the book.

Sixten rolled her eyes. "Ignore him. Yes, paint, absolutely. Can I try, too, if you don't mind? I suck at it, but it's fun."

"Need help?" Tanix paused in the process of sitting.

"I got it." Sixten waved him away.

"You should take Liron's class," she told me as we entered the bedroom. "Oh shit, good thing Tanix didn't come back here. The beta would lose his shit if that male entered your bedroom."

I led her through to the art area.

"Oh wow, look at this." She nodded as she looked around. "The beta did all this?"

"Yeah," I said sheepishly, gathering the supplies. "He

was nervous to tell me about it, as though I wouldn't like it."

"That wolf is thoughtful as shit," she said under her breath.

Butterflies once again fluttered through my belly. My face heated and I shrugged, all warm and tingly inside. "It's probably just the true mate bond," I said to deflect.

"No, girl. No." She shook her head adamantly. "The true mate bond would usually have him moving you into his room and trying to keep you there to best protect you. The true mate bond should have him claiming you the second he had access and killing anyone who looked at you. I've seen lesser wolves, male *and* female, lose their minds with just a claiming. This?" She gestured around, not just at the art, but the room as a whole. "Allowing you your freedom speaks to the control that he's known for. The art, though? The kitchen? That speaks to the man. You wouldn't know because you haven't been around any decent shifters, but trust me, *this*?" Now she gestured specifically at the art space. "This is courting-type stuff. Milk this shit. Milk it for all it is worth, girl. You've clearly got your own control. Use it."

I was reflective as we moved the supplies into the front room, setting up to paint as I mulled over what she'd said. No one had explained the difference between the bond and the man. Or even how extreme the bond made some people, and how much Weston *wasn't* acting on that primal pull. He was holding back, actually, giving me space. Giving me the freedom I'd requested. The freedom to make up my mind. His actions weren't because of the bond —they were despite it.

My belly fluttered, the warmth and affection that had been growing for him since the start of our journey infused within me. He might've noticed the things I liked because of his job and the bond, but he'd gone out of his way to use that knowledge to make a home for me here. He'd held back with me earlier this morning, controlled himself when I hadn't even known up from down . . .

My lack of knowledge about the bond had made it seem limiting, burdensome. My heart continued to soar as I felt those shackles loosen, cut free. I felt lighter. Released, almost.

A timer dinged, snapping me out of my reverie just as Sixten let Nova back in the room. I stopped to check on the food. The beef was steaming away and the vegetables were ready to go in. Nova had come back with a huge assortment of cheeses and assorted nibbles, including bland chicken wings, little pieces of pork on too-soft bread, and some sort of tomato-cheese thing with the wrong seasonings.

I didn't mention any of my criticisms, of course. Getting used to someone else's cooking was going to be an adjustment. Figuring how to get food I could cook myself from the kitchens was moved to the top of my to-do list.

Dante began reading, and Sixten and I painted. Two chapters later, three quick knocks sounded on the door just before it opened, and Hadriel walked in. "What the fuck is all this?"

Everyone looked up with food in their mouths.

"It is a collection of highly intelligent individuals enjoying a sophisticated read and a bite to eat." Dante gave Hadriel a haughty look. "Now, where was I?"

"You were not going to get to the part where the very interesting villain gets the girl," Tanix said, crossing his arms. "The book is poorer for it."

"Aurelia, love—suck my balls, what is *this*?" Hadriel leaned over my shoulder, looking at my painting.

"Yeah." I lowered my brush. "I'm not really getting the

hang of mixing the colors. I need to see about Liron's classes, assuming he doesn't invite me to any more orgies. Or see if there is a book on it."

"Do not bother with that cornholing jackass. Or, if you must, spend your time painting dicks in his class. That would be good enough for him. No, love, despite the questionable color choices, this is . . . fantastic. I love it! Once you figure out the colors, do it again and present it to the king."

"What is it?" Dante lowered the book, and Sixten stopped in her progress to lean around my canvas.

"You knew it was supposed to be the king?" I'd tried to paint him from earlier in the day, when he'd been at his most terrifying. He'd frozen up my wolf at first, appearing as big as the world, blotting out the sun, eclipsing the trees. It seemed as though fire had rolled across his glittering golden scales and the ground had shaken under our feet. Most of that was terror turned imagination, but I'd tried to draw it all, purging the feelings onto the canvas.

What I'd ended up with was an orange-yellow lizard creature with crimson fire and blue trees. Not great.

"Yeah, bro, that's cool." Sixten looked back at her canvas. "I fucking suck at this."

"Lemme see." Hadriel moved to behind her. He patted her shoulder. "Well, it's lucky you have other strengths."

"Oh, fuck off," she grumbled, looking back over at my canvas.

I laughed and got up to shut the door, finding Vemar just down the hall, sauntering toward us.

I paused and pointed within. "Are you coming in here?"

"I would love to, Captive Lady. I just came to make sure you planned to get up early. I don't want to bother you if you want to sleep in."

"I don't really sleep in."

"Neither do I. I'll be waiting for you down the hall first thing in the morning." He glanced into the interior of my room. "Oh! I see we have a party."

He slipped inside, and I finally closed the door.

"Oh no, not you too!" Hadriel exclaimed. "You eat like a fucking horse. Now there'll never be enough."

"Enough of what?" Vemar asked, looking at my painting. "Is this some sort of dreamy landscape or something? That's supposed to be the king, right?"

"Here, look at Sixten's—it makes Aurelia's look better," Dante said, having gotten up to see the paintings.

Sixten twisted to look up at him. "Let's see you do it."

"Can't, I'm afraid. Someone has to read, and only one of us knows how."

"Would you like something to eat?" I pointed at the various options. "I have braised beef and vegetables cooking—they're almost done—and some salad to go with it. I'll have enough salad for everyone, but sadly, the beef will just be a taste."

"It would've been a big meal for four until all you fuckers showed up," Hadriel groused.

"You thought you had a nice little secret, didn't you?" Dante told him. "You didn't mention the kitchen to anyone. Very sneaky."

"That wasn't *my* secret." Hadriel put his hand on his chest. "That information is between her and the beta. What's the beta going to eat now?"

"Oh, he'll have his full meal, don't you worry." Tanix clapped a hand on Hadriel's shoulder, making him jump. "You, however—"

"I would advise you to remove your hand from my little buddy," Vemar said, darkening the room with his building rage.

"Okay, okay." I put up my hands. "Let's all mind our

manners. If you guys want, I can cook a big stew tomorrow and we can all have some. Or, if you can somehow procure a pig, I can roast it in the ground early tomorrow morning and we can have a small feast tomorrow night for dinner. I have all these new spices to try, so I'm happy to make enough for everyone."

Everyone looked around at each other. "Pig," Sixten and Tanix said together.

"Pig," Dante repeated, nodding.

"Definitely the pig." Hadriel clapped. "I'm on it." He turned to go.

"Wait, who was the fourth?" I called.

He paused. "Anyone who wandered in, smelled what was up, and stayed for dinner."

"Smart," Sixten murmured, back to her painting.

Once the beef was done, I set aside a plate for Weston and handed out portions to everyone. The new spices I'd used were a little off and my critique of it made everyone angry, so I used my new journal to write down how I'd prepared it and make notes of things I would change for the next time.

After everyone had eaten their bites and cleared the trays Nova had brought, Dante put a placeholder in the book, put it in my bookcase, and everyone said their good-byes. The glow of their company lingered in the silence of their wake. This evening had been truly exceptional. The food had been decent at best and the painting was a mess, but the friendship and camaraderie would be cherished for the rest of my life.

I checked the fire in the stove. It was slowly dying, the oven losing its temperature. Soon Weston's food would go cold.

Full night had fallen. Bedtime was close. He would've come by now if he'd planned to.

"Go to him," my wolf pushed, anxious to be in the vicinity of her mate again.

I rested my hand on the door, thinking about it. But honestly, he had never been shy about stopping in when he wanted to see me. He'd had long days since he'd gotten back. He was probably tired.

I slid my hand away, feeling a strange hollowness inside that he hadn't come. I didn't like it. Gods, what if he was meeting with another woman? What if—

Panic seized me, along with anger, and I spun for the door again. Only when it was halfway open did I pause, breathe, and slowly unwrap my fingers from the handle.

What he did in his free time was none of my business. I'd been the one to create distance between us. We were lovers. We'd been forced into proximity on the trip, but now we had our own lives, our own struggles. I couldn't stop him from finding a mate. I shouldn't. It wasn't fair.

"You're his mate, you fuzzy-minded cow," my wolf barked at me. *"*You *are his mate. The human wants you. Go to him."*

The human was giving me my freedom. I couldn't, in turn, strip away his.

I closed the door slowly, heart lodged in my throat, fighting against my instincts. Fighting against my wolf.

Through deep breath after deep breath, I put everything in the kitchen back in order before tucking away my art supplies. I placed my journal back on my desk and wrote a quick entry about what I was feeling: missing Weston, wanting to be with him, kicking myself for this frustrated fear of being trapped into a life I hadn't expressly chosen. At the end I put in a memory of my mom, and then spoke directly to her, wishing she was here to give me advice. Wishing she was here to meet the man that didn't exactly fit the fairytale mold, but would if the villain could turn into the good guy.

When I was finished, I straightened my desk, pushing a stray container back to its place, and noticed a slip of paper sticking out from under it. Pulling it out to put it away properly, I noticed what was on it.

Weston's neat writing filled the page.

If you need anything, even just a warm body to sleep next to, come to me. Anytime. X marks the spot.

A smile stretched across my lips.

X marks the spot?

I looked around my art room but knew there was no X in here. I would've noticed—just like I'd noticed his cleverly hidden note under the thing he'd moved, knowing I wouldn't be able to relax until I'd put it back in its correct place. Nothing in the front room, either; I'd been through there.

In my bedroom, I looked around my bed, creased from when I'd sat on it earlier. My wardrobe was closed. My shades had been drawn by Leala, who'd gotten things ready for bed before being released for the evening. Near the back corner, though, I found a piece of paper taped to a panel next to the stone hearth. After peeling it off, I found a tiny indent, nothing more than a compressed part of the wood.

Frowning, I scratched it, and then pushed, trying to figure out why X marked this spot.

Pushing did the trick.

A *click* sounded from behind the panel and it popped open.

"No way . . ." I said softly, pulling the panel open and peering in. A small stone tunnel ran along the back of my room, clearly a secret passageway. "This castle just keeps getting better. Dragons *and* a secret passageway?"

Another note waited on the ground featuring an arrow to point me in the right direction.

Hurrying now, I ran back inside the room and grabbed Weston's food and the leftover bottle of wine from dinner then sped into the passageway, leaving the panel open just in case. Little tunnels led away from this one, each lined with alcoves that must have led to other rooms throughout the castle. At every intersection I came to, there was another note with an arrow. Two notes up and the arrow pointed right. I stopped in front of the alcove with a note taped on, the arrow pointing to a little keyhole. There was no key.

Giggling to myself, I set his food down and retraced my steps back to my room, finding tools that would work in no time. I closed my panel, finding such a keyhole on the backside and marveling that you couldn't see it from the front. At his door, I made short work of the lock and pushed my way inside, stopping to grab the food and closing the door behind me.

In any other situation, I would've been worried this was a trick; a woman had to be wary of randomly being lured into someone else's bedchamber. I knew, though, without a doubt, that this was Weston. No one else would know I'd find those clues, as subtle as they were, as perfectly placed.

In his huge bedroom, his bed had been turned down and the curtains drawn. Soft indigo light, now reminding me of Calia's eyes, glowed from atop a trunk at the far side of the bed. He'd retrieved my lantern. He must've had her turn it on for him.

Shadows from candles in the candelabra flickered throughout the space. I thought back to our conversation the previous day and warmed at the thought he'd paid attention to what I said. I took several steps toward the front room and spotted Weston. He was sitting in his well-worn chair, dressed in loose, comfortable pants and a plain, snug shirt, feet propped up on an ottoman. A soft light glowed from behind him, illuminating the book in his hands.

He glanced up when he saw me, eyes creasing at the corners with the beginnings of a smile.

"Hey, baby," he said affectionately, no note of surprise that I'd come. He noticed the items in my hands. "What've you got there?"

I released my breath into a smile and walked forward. "A lukewarm dinner with an odd use of spices that has probably been sitting too long. A few of the pack members from our journey stopped by. Hadriel was upset that he only got to eat just a few bites rather than the full dinner he thought he'd stolen. The others gave him a lot of shit for it, too."

Weston smiled and put down his book. "I heard the commotion as I passed by. I figured you were having a good time."

"Why didn't you stop in?" On impulse, I walked directly to him and waited for him to set his feet on the floor. I sat on his lap and pulled the cloche off the serving tray to show him the meal. "Crap, I forgot a fork."

"It's okay." He leaned back and settled one of his hands on my lower back. "Fingers are fine." He dropped the other hand to my knee. "I didn't want to ruin the fun."

I hesitated. "Are you not hungry?"

"On the contrary. I am very hungry." He waited expectantly.

My stomach fluttered with the desire to feed him. It felt more intimate than a kiss, somehow. More poignant than verbalizing my growing feelings. More sensual than eating usually would. I wanted to take care of him, to nurture him maybe, as he had done for me. Creating a home had been his way. Making him dinner, and now feeding him, was mine.

I hesitantly plucked a potato from the plate, never having done this before. As when he'd washed me that time in the port city, I was strangely nervous, unsure what to do. I put it to my lips for a moment to test the temperature before reaching it out. His eyes bored into mine. He wrapped his lips around it, grazing my fingers in the process, before chewing.

"Mmm," he said, his thumb stroking my knee. "Delicious."

"You people have no taste buds," I murmured, grabbing a carrot this time.

He smiled. "Maybe we aren't as fussy as you are."

"You should be. Good food is one of life's great pleasures."

"So it seems."

"Here." I grabbed his hand and shoved the plate into it as heat dripped down into my core. "You need to be the table so I can use both hands for the meat."

His eyes were so intense. He did as I said, eating whatever I gave him, even closing his eyes at one point to savor the taste. After trying the bland chicken from the kitchen earlier, I understood why people would think even incorrectly used spices were a treat. He finished every bite and pulled me closer for a kiss when he was done.

"That was delicious, baby. Thank you. Do you need help cleaning your place up?"

"No, that's all done. Listen . . . I know you give the pack room so that they can relax, but maybe . . . Can you hang out more and show them that when you're not on duty, you're a little more chill?"

He took the plate from my hands and set it on the side table. He pulled me closer, tucking me against his body. I curled my legs into his lap.

"It doesn't really work like that. I can relax with the royals to an extent because we all understand each other. I know my place, and they never have to worry about me forgetting it. Hadriel and Vemar, who are a bit removed from everything with the pack, are fine. Everyone else, including the dragons, tend to forget themselves at times. They might get too drunk, feel my power, and want to take me on just to see how it would go. They might get too friendly and think they don't have to treat me as a commander, wanting allowances for friendship. There are a great many ways things can break down when in my position, and it is safer for everyone if we maintain the status quo."

"So you can't ever hang out with me when I'm with them?"

"I can hang out when everyone is minding their manners. I have to excuse myself if things start to get rowdy."

I traced my fingers along his neck and then his chin, feeling the rough stubble. He ran his palm along my back.

"That life sounds lonely," I whispered.

"It's the job, and I love my job. I handle the setbacks in order to do it."

I pushed up so that my face was even with his, sucking in his bottom lip. "Do you want me to get more wine so that you have someone to get drunk and rowdy with? I might feel your power and want to take you on, but that usually ends in a real nice time."

He smiled against my lips. "Not tonight. I promised I'd take you slow, and I intend to."

He held me close as he deepened the kiss, lightly

cupping my jaw. I fell into the warmth against my skin, the warmth within my heart. He stood with me in his arms, stopping by the candles to blow them out before walking me into his room.

"Fire hazard," he murmured, his lips curling against mine.

He let me drift down his body until my feet hit the floor, then used both hands to cup my face, his kiss languid and soft, gentle and full of feeling.

Something moved within me, way down deep. The warmth from a moment ago started to blossom, spilling into my body, out through my lips. I was high on it, enveloped within it, connecting with him now in a way I hadn't before.

I pushed up his shirt, needing to feel more of him. He yanked the fabric over his head quickly so that he could return to our kiss. I pushed down his pants as he lifted my shirt over my head. By the time I'd stripped it off, he had his pants on the floor and was working my trousers off.

"Weston," I murmured urgently, a plea, a feeling, my hands all over him as he guided me backward onto the bed.

He kissed me as he slid onto the bed with me, his lips never far from mine. I groaned as his hands ran up my chest, over my skin, between my thighs, his tongue chasing mine.

I gripped his shoulders as he settled between my legs, fisted his hair when I wrapped my legs around him, closed my eyes in ecstasy as his cock found its home deep within me.

"Weston . . ." I said again reverently. Needing him. Wanting him. On the verge of choosing him. I just needed a push. A way to get around my fear of giving my heart to another after it had been trampled on so thoroughly.

He moved within me, his kiss so deep, his body in mine deeper.

"Aurelia," he whispered against my lips, his fingers threading through mine, his strokes long and slow.

I whimpered, writhing under him, feeling his raw emotion through the bond. His honesty. His devotion.

Tears caught in my lashes with the sweetness of his lovemaking, genuine, unapologetic. I opened myself to it, to him, soaking in the sensations, expressing the emotions.

His lips still touching mine, he breathed heavily as he stroked, our bodies working to get closer, climb higher.

"Oh gods, Aurelia . . ." His moan sounded like a victory.

I clutched him now, digging in my fingers, not wanting to let go of the moment. Of him. Maybe ever. He wrapped his arms around me, his lips never leaving mine, sharing our passion. He reached one hand down to the swell of my butt, wrapping his other arm around my shoulders, holding me put as his knot butted against me.

"Gods, yes," I breathed, lifting my head to get at his lips.

He thrust himself in fully, his movements getting smaller so he'd stay lodged inside, his arm around my shoulders shifting to cup the back of my head.

He pulled back a little now, his beautiful gray eyes looking down at me, into me. I met his gaze, opening up just that little bit more, finding myself at a precipice but scared to teeter over.

A little smile curved his full lips. His nod was slight yet confident. He clearly knew what I felt. He didn't say a word.

He didn't have to.

He kissed me again. All-consuming, pulling at my soul until he could entwine it with his own. My world unraveled until this moment consisted of only him and me, our bodies, our hearts.

"I'm scared," I admitted, knowing he would understand what I meant.

"I know. Don't rush it. Let it come naturally." He nipped at my lips. "Just feel it."

And I did. With him guiding me as his wolf guided mine, I gave myself over to the emotions coursing through the bond. Through my soul. I allowed them to sweep me away, trusting he would keep me tethered.

His movements became faster, his kiss deeper. His arms wrapped tightly around me like he wouldn't ever let me go. I lost myself in his embrace and the delicious friction our bodies created and hit a high that stole my breath.

I cried out, shaking against him. His answering shudder echoed through my body, and the admissions I'd made earlier in the day came rushing back to me. Some had been in the heat of the moment.

All had been true.

Another shock of desire coursed through me, and I gripped him tightly. As I continued to rock against him, I knew I might not be totally ready yet, but I was almost there. I knew it wouldn't take much until I was lost forever.

23

AURELIA

Sometime around midmorning, the first gardener entered the work shed. Delaney, a middle-aged woman with brown skin, a moderate build, and zero tolerance for me, stopped at the end of my table. She was an incredibly smart person who knew an impressive amount about plants and various elixirs.

She ignored the glass canisters all simmering along the workstation and said, "I'm supposed to be nice to you."

Vemar glanced at her, quirked an eyebrow, and went back to watching the end canister, which was turning an alarming shade of red.

"My old coworker said that to me once," I replied. "He then went on to a lifetime of regret and misery. You may as well just be grumpy and try to ignore me. It would be better for us both."

Vemar started to laugh silently.

Delaney stared at me for a moment, seemed to realize I was dead serious, and nodded. "Works for me."

I'd have to ask Weston who said she was supposed to be nice to me, and why.

Arleth came in not long after Delaney, giving me a curt hello. I responded in kind, and then we ignored each other as well, going about our work in peaceful harmony. Except for one thing, of course: it seemed my work was a helluva lot more volatile than theirs. I'd never worked with anyone else, but my style seemed somewhat dangerous compared to theirs. Smoke and fire and fizzing happened all the time when I was creating. They kept looking over at me and at each other. I could tell they were wary.

Sometime around noon, after Vemar had brought me some lunch and ate beside me, Delaney looked around in a huff. A cursory glance didn't offer much insight, and Vemar ignored it entirely, so I went back to my work. After a foot stomp, though, I figured it was better to break the silence.

"Is something wrong?"

She was looking out the opened door. "Someone is supposed to be here to relieve me. Arleth is in a meeting. She won't be back in time to complete this elixir."

I hadn't even realized Arleth had left. But now I saw her corner by the two bubbling cauldrons was empty.

"Can I help?" I asked.

Her gaze was annoyed and speculative. "Can you follow directions?"

"Yes."

She pondered it for a moment. "Pay attention. Write this down."

Without looking up, Vemar held out a sheet of blank paper. I took it, readying my pencil. "Ready."

"In ten minutes, these dried leaves here"—she pointed to a dish on the table—"need to go into that cauldron there." She pointed again. "Those leaves"—point--"go into that one. Got that?"

I spoke as I wrote. "Ten minutes, put . . . leaves . . . next to cauldrons . . . into cauldrons. Got it."

"You do not stir them. You just drop the leaves on top of the boiling water and let it seep in by itself."

"Drop leaves . . . into pot. Do not stir. Perfect."

"The water needs to keep its slow boil. It's absolutely necessary."

"Tend fire. Okay."

"Can you handle that?" she asked me in a firm tone.

It was very hard to keep my sarcasm in check on this one. "Setting a timer and throwing some leaves into a pot? Yes, I can handle that."

"Even I could handle that," Vemar murmured.

Her look said she wasn't so sure, but she left anyway.

"If I was guarding one of them, I'd be bored out of my fucking mind," Vemar murmured. I laughed.

Before the timer had run out, another presence pulled my focus away from what I was doing.

I glanced up to find the queen, dressed down in her "work" attire that was still nicer than anything anyone in Granny's village had owned. Behind her came Hannon, his eyes filled with a strange sort of intensity, and it made my gut pinch. Something about it felt . . . that we were *more* than mere friends, somehow. More expectant, maybe. Deeper. The feelings made me pause, and my wolf growled within me.

The memory of last night was still so fresh, so delicious. The way Weston had left those secret hints to help me find him had been perfect. The new insight about his thoughtfulness. And the way he'd made love, so tender and careful and devoted, had swept my breath away. Something about Hannon's behavior right now felt disrespectful to that. It felt invasive in a way I didn't like.

He caught my wary look immediately, surely feeling all

of that. His eyes were as soft as his smile, his understanding plain. It was really handy that he spoke in emotion.

"I'm sorry," I told him, thankful I didn't need to explain. I wouldn't even know what to say. It wasn't like he'd done anything specific.

Finley looked at me in confusion before realizing I was speaking to her brother. She furrowed her brow at him, shook her head, and went to check on the elixirs.

"Don't be," Hannon said. "I enjoy your company. Nothing has to change but the intent."

"And the flirting," Finley murmured.

Hannon laughed. "Fine, maybe the flirting. I look forward to our continued non-flirting friendship, Aurelia."

I stared at him with my mouth open. Was it rude to say I hadn't been flirting? I didn't think I even knew how. I'd never done it before.

He laughed again, so I just dropped it. I was relieved he understood, because I really did love talking to him. He was such a rock-solid human.

"I do too, Hannon. I mean that," I said.

"Her very first real friend was Hadriel." Vemar lifted his eyebrows at Hannon. "Let that sink in."

Even Finley laughed at that, and then looked around. "Where is everyone?"

"Gone." I pointed at the doorway as Hannon did a sniff test of the air.

"What's that smell?" Hannon asked.

My timer dinged, and I got up. Vemar immediately occupied my place and tended to the fire on the glass canister.

"That, my friend, is poison." I excused myself around him, then Finley, and reached for the leaves.

"Whoa, whoa." Finley put her hand out to stop me. "What are you doing?"

"She's fucking the leaves into the pot," Vemar said.

"Per Delaney's instructions," I added.

Finley's brow furrowed, but she let me, watching as I dropped the leaves into one cauldron before moving to the other. That done, I checked the fires, just to reiterate to everyone that I was paying attention, and went back to Vemar.

"Look at you! You got the hang of that no problem," I told him, patting him on the back. "You're a natural."

"I think I have found my calling," he responded.

"Don't say that—you'll be killed for it."

"I'd like to see them try."

"Sorry," Finley interrupted, "did you say that smell was poison?"

"Oh. Yes." I sat down next to Vemar, pulling away the pot lid so the interior could cool. "The toxicity is at a much lower level now, though. It'll be fine for you to breathe. We haven't thrown up in . . ."

"A couple hours," Vemar supplied.

"Yeah, a couple hours. It was a little unbearable earlier, but we made it through using your cure-all dragon weed—"

Vemar held up a finger. "Respect the dragon."

I laughed. He was fun to poke. "Sorry, cure-all Everlass elixir. Arleth and Delaney left for a bit, but once those products were finished, we were able to air out the work shed. I do think it might be better to put me elsewhere, though. I think I'm too disruptive for their style."

"It's good for them. Tell her about the taste of the cure-all," Vemar said.

"Oh, right. Honestly, I think you should put some spices in that brew. It is *incredibly* bland, and the aftertaste is not great. A few spices shouldn't change any of the properties and would make a world of difference on the palate."

"She would know—she's an excellent cook," Vemar said. He leaned back. "There. I think that's it."

"Awesome." I checked his work, agreed, and pulled off the top of that pot to reduce the temperature.

"Sorry . . ." Finley braced against the table and cocked her head. "Can you just . . ." She pointed between all my stuff. "Just take me through all this, would you please?"

"Yeah, of course." I explained what I'd surmised about Granny's coating, how she'd gotten the idea, and what I thought she'd likely used to re-create it but make it stronger. "Basically, they just doubled up on some of the ingredients. I *think*, anyway. I've got these here to test." I pointed at one of the finished products. "I've got a lot of other tests, as well. Different ingredients, different amounts. Once I get a similar recipe, I'll start to refine. Now, the problem is going to be the finished product. I will very likely make a better version of Granny's coating. It will either be less poisonous or not poisonous at all, and either just as addictive or more so. This is because I know how to do my job, and whatever hack she is employing does not."

"Wait, how do you know what the poison is? A better question is, how are you making the poison?"

I explained the characteristics of some of the chemicals and how they reacted when heated, their properties changing from something that'd make a person mildly sick to killing them outright. The amount of heat and pressure applied was the catalyst.

"Previously I had thought it was the accumulation of the coating's chemicals building up in a person's body," I said. "And that is still true. But I also think it depends on the batch. If the person making it isn't careful, that product could be a killer all by itself."

"Is there a way to tell?" Finley asked, looking over my setup.

"For me? Yes. I just need to get some new supplies. I blew up all my others. For the person buying the product? None. And that doesn't factor in that semi-toxic coloring. I'm not sure what that paint is supposed to be used for, but it shouldn't be on fucking food. I have no idea what Granny is even thinking. Has she lost her mind? Her pure ignorance means she's creating problems that shouldn't exist!"

"Breathe," Vemar said slowly. "Breathe."

I took a deep breath as instructed. "Right. Sorry. Anyway, I can probably make something to test the toxicity level, but what's the point? It's just one more thing for people to buy that they very likely can't afford. I'd rather create something that can eat away that coating, thus making the product safer. But again, what's the point? It's yet another thing to buy, it'll make the product soggy and gross, and there might be some lasting toxicity. Those aren't realistic solutions."

Finley put a hand on her hip. "Then what is the solution?"

I shook my head, waving my hand to clear smoke. "Find the culprit and kill them?"

"Sounds familiar," Vemar murmured.

I huffed out a laugh and scratched my head. "Maybe I can create something that works much faster to stave off the addiction. But then again, it's not actually a solution. The danger is still there. Maybe people won't buy as much, but they'll still buy it."

"Can we negate the danger?"

"Possibly. Or maybe *you* can, if I find a better way to

explain what creates it. You're the medicine woman, not me."

"Or . . ." Vemar leaned back and put his hands behind his head, flaring his big arms out like wings. "You flood the market with safe, non-habit-forming products that look messy but don't kill anyone."

"Non-addictive? Some products *are* habit forming for some people . . ." I muttered.

Finley scoffed. "We are not going to fight drugs with more drugs, Vemar. Don't be daft."

"Why not?" he asked. "Make it cheaper and make it a competitor to Granny. It'll dry up her business. Combine that with her not having quality product—since we kidnapped the original drugmaker—and that might just put her out of business. I mean, look. Some of the stuff Aurelia makes might as well be medicine. A relaxant? I tried one and barely saw a difference."

"You're pretty calm when you're not in a rage," I told him.

"And why would I want to calm a rage? I wouldn't. The replacement for the pregnancy tea? Not a drug. The product that makes you happy? I hate it. It made me very lovey, and I am *not* interested in hugging Liron, who immediately got the wrong idea. But if distributed by the right people who handle the more dangerous medicines? I can see it being necessary for some people. Then just throw the hallucinogens into the shadow market, put an actual warning on them, instructions on the wrapper that tell you how to get out of a bad trip, and you're good. I really don't see the problem here. Aurelia's product has been around for years. No one cared until three years ago when it started killing people."

"He really does make a lot of sense," Hannon told Finley.

She chewed her lip as she looked at her brother.

I pointed at the fire beneath the cauldrons. "My instructions note to tend that fire. Also, you all have modern materials in the other work sheds. Why are you still stoking fires here?"

Finley didn't answer me, just stood looking out the door.

"Look." I held up my hands as Hannon stood and headed for the cauldrons. "That is a pretty radical proposal. Let's just leave it in the air for now. Let me first figure out how to make the coating, okay? There could very well be a solution I haven't yet thought of. Or maybe I'll find something in my journals that'll help us locate the other production area. We can try to get records of cure-all Everlass elixirs being sold."

That snapped Finley out of her reverie. "Why would that be relevant?"

Vemar looked at me with raised eyebrows. "She didn't see us throwing up all over the place earlier."

"Whoever is making Granny's coating is doing it at the expense of their personal health," I told Finley. "They will need large quantities of something to reduce the sickness, or Granny's people would be dying. And honestly, maybe they are. If we can figure out the general vicinity of the production area, large shipments of elixir should lead us to the target."

Finley turned to me with an unreadable expression, and, for some reason, the hairs on the back of my neck stood on end.

24

VEMAR

Later that night, I joined a bunch of others at the impromptu pig roast. Captive Lady sure could cook. Hadriel's raving hadn't done her justice—not even close.

Calia walked over to me, the roll of her hips indicating she believed herself the prize of the party. She sure was pretty.

"Hello, Kind Lady," I said, a name I'd given her when we met in the demon dungeons. "What can I do you for?" I popped a bite of pork into my mouth. I offered her a morsel from my plate.

She hesitated, probably running through the rules in her mind. If a wolf or other shifter offered food, accepting it meant you wanted to head to the sack—or to eternity—with them. When a dragon did it, we were just being polite. We didn't need to trade food for sex—we got laid just by being us.

She gave me the sort of smile that said she wouldn't be opposed to heading to the sack this evening, and reached for a bite. I wouldn't say no.

She tossed it into her mouth. "Everyone has been somewhat tight-lipped about what happened yesterday when the new . . . castle inhabitant shifted for the first time."

"Yup. King's orders—"

"What . . ." Her brow furrowed and she stared at my plate. "What is this?"

She looked around at the crowd of people gathered. There were more people here than Aurelia had been expecting. She'd planned on doing just one pig, but it seemed my little buddy, Hadriel, had correctly surmised the word would get out. Aurelia had prepared more food accordingly.

"The Captive Lady did a little cooking for the friendlies." I put another bite into my mouth.

"Aurelia did this?" She reached for pork this time, watching me as she chewed. "This is delicious."

"Yes, it is rather good."

She took a root vegetable and looked it over for a moment before eating it. "Mmm." Her gaze turned intense. "The first was pork, but what is this?"

"That I do not know. Something edible that grows around here in great supply, apparently. I've never had it before."

"How'd she know about it?"

I shrugged. "Apparently she went through long periods of not having enough food and figured out a solution. She knows a lot about foraging and natural foods. I'm sure the locals know what it is, but the castle cook isn't the type to go traipsing through the woods looking for vegetables."

She grabbed another type of vegetable, surveying it first and then sliding it into her mouth. She sucked on her finger, and I started salivating.

As was usual for this female, she didn't voice what she was thinking, her gaze far away while her wheels clearly turned. She issued a soft grunt, coming to some sort of conclusion, before refocusing on me. I continued to eat, and she continued to help me clear my plate.

"I got wind of an emoting situation," she told me. "Yesterday, I mean. She emoted very strongly. So strongly that very loyal dragons turned on their king."

Who'd been talking, I wondered . . .?

"I didn't turn on anyone," I said.

She studied me. "I remember you from the demon parties. It took a lot of magical effort on their part to get you to . . . perform."

"That is because I don't like people pulling levers in my brain without my say-so."

"You killed a lot of their demon guards."

"Not as many as Micah, but I did all right."

She paused for a beat. "Aurelia doesn't affect you."

I wasn't supposed to talk about yesterday, that was true. None of us were. The king wanted to keep the Captive Lady's talents close to his vest. She was valuable to a kingdom because of her bloodline, her power, and now this new magic. Granny had been keeping a tight leash on a very interesting sort of shifter. It spoke to Captive Lady's talents and intelligence that Granny hadn't capitalized on her beyond making the drugs. Aurelia was turning out to be a treasure, and the king was a political animal. His mate might want to bring this lady to justice to appease her people, but he wasn't so considerate. If Aurelia wasn't careful, she'd become a pawn in the scheming of kingdoms.

So no, I wasn't supposed to talk about yesterday, but no one said anything about any other time I'd spent with her. I wouldn't sandbag her ability to have a better life.

"I wouldn't say she doesn't affect me," I said delicately. "I would say that I choose when and how she will affect me."

Calia's eyes gleamed. "How strong is she?"

"She is completely untrained and has no idea what she is doing, but when she really panics and she thinks survival is on the line, she'll rattle your brain with the need to do as she bids." I put my plate forward for Calia to grab another bite and listen in a little closer. I lowered my voice. "She needs training, Calia. Are fairies the only ones who emote?"

She chewed slowly, her gaze going far away again. Her tongue slid across her bottom lip, lifting any juice she might've missed.

"Because you are being honest and forthright, I will too."

I snickered. This woman was a spy for her court. We all knew it. She didn't hide it. Her friendship with the royals was based on the understanding that politics would forever be mixed in their affairs. They'd all found a way to work with that. If she was giving me information, it meant it helped her cause in some way.

She went on, "Some demon magic includes emoting. That's what we experienced in the dungeons."

"They only have the one form of it, right?" I asked. "Forcing sexual desire?"

She narrowed her eyes in thought. "I can't recall if there are others. I have to look. I've kind of . . . tried to block all that from my brain."

I didn't much believe her, but I went with it. That was a very dark time in all our pasts. "I know what you mean."

She nodded. "Vampires can hypnotize, but that's not the same thing. Goblins can deflect, in a way. They can make people want to turn around and leave a cave, for example. But to the best of my knowledge, it is just demons and fairies."

The beta was being really chill about the whole Hannon

situation, the only wolf that probably had the control to do so, but he would never, not ever, no matter how much she pleaded, allow his mate to be subjected to sex demons. Never. And if he relented, I'd step in. And if I relented, the royals would step in. No fucking way. They were not welcome in this kingdom, thank the royals.

The only choice for training was the fairies, at least according to Calia.

"How rare is someone who emotes?" I asked, wondering if she'd tell me now, or if I'd have to make her tell me later by edging her for a couple hours and making her beg me to come.

That gleam was back in her eyes. "Not rare at all. We have many who emote. It's a trait that has appeared frequently."

I stared at her. She stared back and popped another bit of meat into her mouth. This little fairy wasn't giving anything away. Too bad I knew how her wheels turned. They might have a lot of people who emote, but judging by her interest, they didn't have anyone strong enough to turn a dragon against their king.

The fairy king would give his left nut for that ability. The dragon king scared the crap out of that ol' fairy. He'd shit himself for a way to keep Nyfain minding his manners.

I laughed. "Keep your secrets, little fairy. Let me sweeten the pot, though. Captive Lady made the queen's head spin earlier today. Your courts' fairies have magic to make potions and whatnot. The queen has an aptitude of her own, I've heard, helping her connect dots that normal plant workers can't. Aurelia, though?" I shook my head. "She is doing things with plants that no one has ever thought of. Ingenious things. It's not magic, either—it's brainpower. She's more than just someone who can emote.

More than a powerful shifter and true mate. She's a genius, and given half the chance, she's going to change the shape of the market."

Calia slowly stopped chewing, studying my expression. "What's your angle?"

"Aurelia has had it rough, and she doesn't have a support system like we do. No one has been in the trenches with her. No one knows what her trials have been like. She's been on her own for most of her life. I want her to have the best chance possible at a bright future, and whether she goes or if she stays—whatever she does—I will be there, guarding her asshole."

It was a figure of speech, one I'd used for my little buddy. Well . . . for him, it was also literal. He'd been in some precarious situations. Hadriel was doing just fine now, though. He had his community, he had support, and he had powerful people to protect him. He didn't need me, and neither did the royals, not anymore. Everything had settled down. My position with them was redundant.

Aurelia had nobody that would drop everything and see where this journey led—besides the beta, of course. But the beta was a rule follower. He believed in his superiors. It was what made him damn great at his job.

I, however, didn't give two shits about authority. Aurelia needed someone at her side who was happy to blow shit up just to see what made it tick. I hadn't figured out all her bells and whistles just yet, but I was learning. In the brief time I'd known her, I was positive she was someone I wanted to stand beside, and I knew Hadriel would be happy I took the job. At the end of all this, whatever the outcome, Aurelia would know she was wanted, and she'd know she was in charge of her future. I couldn't wait to see her sparkle.

Calia studied me for a long moment, grabbing more

food. I'd always thought she wasn't a big eater; apparently, she just didn't like the castle's cooking. She was certainly cleaning my plate in a hurry.

She opened her mouth to speak, but then her eyes widened. *Ooohs* and *aaahs* came from the gathered eaters looking all around. Little light bugs were drifting in slowly as the night settled over us. Not just a few, like I'd seen in the woods, but hundreds. They filtered through the trees and spread out over the grounds, drifting in the air like dust motes. They moved and swayed almost as one, lazy and tranquil, utterly magical.

I lowered my plate, entranced.

"This always happens around her," Dante was telling someone close by. "When we were traveling, a day or so after abducting her, these bugs were always around like this. They are her warning system. If danger comes, don't worry, these fuckers take off. Aurelia knew a damn bit sooner than the sentries that we were going to be attacked. No shit."

Calia turned, paused in her eating, to look Dante's direction. She stared thoughtfully for a moment, and then chewed in a hurry.

"Excuse me, I need to go." She hurried by me, brushing my shoulder before starting to jog back to the castle. The bugs swirled in her wake.

I'd never seen her frazzled. Something about a bunch of pretty bugs hanging around was apparently the proof she needed, and I knew it could only signify one thing:

Power.

25

AURELIA

"What are they?" someone asked, noticing the emberflies drifting in.

The insects had found me, it seemed. I'd wondered if they would. I hadn't seen any since we'd gotten here. I hadn't been sure this place even had any, and it was a comfort to see they did. It meant I'd get some warning if or when Granny's people came for me.

I wondered if she'd realized whose ship I was on. Where I'd been taken. It wouldn't be easy snatching me from a palace with dragons soaring overhead.

I sure fucking hoped not, but knew deep in my bones it wouldn't deter her. It might take her longer, but she'd find a way. Her determination rivaled mine.

"Are these insects not usually found here?" I asked Sixten, who was working on her second plate of food.

She shook her head, watching them drift in across the grounds. "Not like this. We have them, sure. I've seen a few hanging around the woods. But they have never gathered like this."

"Really?" I frowned at that. I'd never seen them *not* gather like this, not since I could remember, at any rate.

"I wonder if that's a fairy thing. Bug charmer." She grinned at me.

"Somehow I have a feeling they won't be in any hurry to get me a special fairy knife for that type of magic."

"Then we will just have to steal one." She winked. "Oh, the beta showed up."

I followed her gaze, and my stomach dropped out. I barely recognized the man who'd taken me from my village. He'd cut his hair, the sides short while the top was kept longer, styled in a sort of sweep so the ends spiked up. The change let me see more of his face, highlighting those sharp cheekbones and the delicate curve of his eyebrows. His thin nose cut down to his deliciously lush lips, and his almost severe jaw was dotted with a dimple in the center of his chin. He wore a crisp black top with gold embroidery around the collar and along the shoulders, while charcoal-gray threads swirled around his torso. The perfect cut of his black slacks showed off his muscular thighs, ending in shiny black shoes. He walked with confidence, his presence authoritative, a commander amongst his subordinates.

I'd known he was handsome—of course I had. I'd stared at his face often, traced the lines of his body with my eyes, my hands, my mouth. But my appreciation had been tempered by an initial meeting seeped in dislike. My perception of him had changed, but I realized that, before now, I hadn't entirely gotten over the feelings from our first encounter.

Seeing him now, like this, was like looking at a completely different person. Someone new, a comfortable stranger. That fact scared me for a moment, like I was losing the man I'd grown to know, the man I missed every time we were apart and the one I enjoyed waking up next to. The one I chatted with so easily, whom I was learning about gradually while being in his space and hearing about his life. I didn't want to lose that man, even to this handsome stranger.

"You're a fucking idiot," my wolf said, her frustration with how long I had taken to get to this point at an all-time high.

I couldn't blame her. It *had* taken me a long time. A really long time, maybe. I'd been downplaying all the amazing things he'd done, all the ways he'd tried to care for me. But now, *right now,* I knew, without a doubt, that I approved of nature's plan. I approved of my primal desire for him. I agreed with my wolf. I was no longer teetering; I was ready to fall.

His gaze zeroed in on me almost immediately, and he ignored anyone saying hello as he moved through the crowd. I started forward, butterflies swarming my belly, really hoping he hadn't had a personality change to match the image change. People cleared out of the way, giving us space as we met near one of the fires.

"Hey, baby," he said, sounding fatigued. "I can't stay long. I just stopped by to grab a bite, and then I need to go speak with the royals."

"Is everything okay?"

He traced my jaw and slowly shook his head. "I can't say more just now. Can you show me around?"

I grabbed him a plate and walked him to the roast, where Burt piled on some meat and then gave him a dash of vegetables. He looked at me. "Have you eaten yet? We're running low on veg."

"Oh no, that's okay. You go ahead and serve—"

"No." Weston handed me the plate. "Aurelia, this isn't your old village. You don't have to go without here. We have plenty of food in this castle. If you run out of something you have cooked, then they can eat elsewhere."

"It's fine—"

"It's not fine." His look was stern. "It is not fine. You need to eat."

He was right, and I was hungry. I relented, but handed his plate back. "I can't eat all of that."

"Here." Dante reached for an empty plate. "Hi, Beta. Here, Aurelia, use this."

"Thanks," I told him. He'd been trying to push food on me since I arrived.

Burt gave me too much food, despite my protests, and Weston led me away from the others to a chair, somewhat off to the side of the group. He was probably right in that people would stiffen up if he was in their midst, especially when he looked like this.

"We have to eat with our hands because Burt didn't bring enough utensils," I said as Weston sat down. He used one hand on my hip to tug me down onto his lap.

"I doubt anyone cares." He groaned softly with the first bite, closing his eyes, and then gave me a funny look when he ate one of the cut-up vegetables. "What is this?"

I paused in eating my own, assessing the flavors. "Some books call that a rune carrot, while others just a wild carrot. They are all over this wood. I would've expected the cook's crew or the garden crew to have picked them all by now."

"Cook has his own gardens for food. He doesn't grow this, though. Not that I have ever tasted. It's good."

"It's strong. You have to simmer it down. It's best in stews."

"I see." He smiled and continued eating. When he was done, and after a severe look at my half-full plate, he finished what I couldn't. "Delicious, baby, as usual."

"Weston."

Hannon walked up quickly, and Weston stiffened. Frustrated rage filtered through the bond, his hand on my hip tightening for a fraction of a moment before I could feel his concerted effort to relax. He put our plates on the ground before gently nudging me up and standing up beside me, stepping back to give me some space as Hannon approached.

My heart hurt at the amount of effort I could see and feel. It also swelled. Sixten had been right—he'd gone against his instincts to make sure I was happy. He'd said to take my time, to figure out what—and whom—I wanted, and he'd meant it. He'd allowed me a choice—something Granny never had. That was incredibly honorable, and I felt so fucking lucky. I would treasure him for that always.

"We should've been claimed by now," my wolf groused.

Hannon stopped in front of us, and I stepped closer to Weston, wrapping my arm around his waist.

A shock of desire rang through the bond as he realized what I was doing. My choice had been made in front of everyone: him. Only him.

He wrapped his arm around my shoulders possessively, pulling me in tightly. He turned to face me, ignoring Hannon, and tilted up my chin to kiss my lips. His eyes were hard and fierce.

"Are you sure? You need to be sure, Little Wolf," he told me softly. "I've been holding off my possessiveness. Once I commit, that's it. No more Mr. Nice Guy."

"Commit," I told him, closing my eyes, feeling his lips. "I'm sorry it took me so long."

"Don't be sorry. You had to rebuild your trust in me. I accept that. I'd rather you take a moment and be sure you have no regrets than live a life you aren't sure about." His kiss was long and deep.

Only after he released me from the kiss did he turn to Hannon, his alpha power pumping out around him. His possessive aggression sang through me in delicious ways I did not expect—primal ways that bubbled up my middle while sending molten heat to my core.

Hannon's eyebrows rose a fraction. He took a step back.

"What is it?" Weston growled.

"The royals need you. Both of you. That shipment we heard rumors about? It wasn't just rumors, and the supply was dirt cheap. Drinks were spiked in a few of the taverns. Half the villages are having problems, some with very powerful shifters. We've got people dispatched to the villages in case there is sickness, but we need to do something to calm down the powerful shifters without bloodshed. It was mentioned Aurelia has a way to do that. My village is requesting her presence, but that isn't the worst of the problems right now." He paused, his gaze on Weston poignant. "Micah partook."

"Fuck," Weston said, slouching a little. "What was he thinking?"

"Who's Micah?" I asked. His name was familiar, but I couldn't place him.

"The dragon commander," he replied. "He has the same rank as me, and a lot of power."

"He'd heard that a few of your sub-pack, and then Hadriel and Vemar, took product and were fine," Hannon said. "He was confused between her product and Granny's. He's sick—very sick. They're worried about him. He won't let anyone close enough to give him something to cure him. The king has asked for a solution that doesn't involve him forcing the issue. He's afraid this will turn into a dragon battle, and his dragon has had a longstanding . . . problem with Micah's."

"I know—"

"Wait, Granny's product?" I asked, aghast.

"Yes," Hannon told me. "Her product arrived on our shores and was put up for sale for a fraction of the price. Dirt cheap."

"Why would she do that?" I asked, but I knew the answer and so did these guys. "She's trying to flush me out."

"We found two posters of your likeness, with the promise of a large reward, tucked into hidden cubbies in market stalls or carts," Weston said quickly. "One of the stall owners died. He wouldn't have been able to send back word of your arrival. The other was thoroughly questioned earlier this evening. He got the likeness a while ago, days before you arrived, but hadn't thought more about it. He didn't send word you'd arrived on these shores. I'm almost certain Granny doesn't yet know where you are. She's probably doing this across the other kingdoms she thinks you could be hiding in. Her spies will be watching, and we don't know who they are. If you help, she'll get word. She'll know where to find you."

"All the other kingdoms have supplies of the elixir that saves lives," Hannon said. "What will tip her off to Aurelia specifically?"

"Because I know the fail-safes, and she knows I'll help people use them. It's clear she never passed those instructions to the traders." I started forward. "Yet *another* lie," I said through gritted teeth. This one was just as unforgivable as lying about my wolf. I started to jog.

"Where are you going?" Weston called after me.

I stopped and turned, noticing Vemar and Hadriel hurrying toward us. "It sounds like I'm not going to be able to force some of these shifters into closets. I'm going to need some dragon-sized tarps. I'll meet you . . . Where should I meet you?"

"Billiard room."

Hadriel slowed and then pushed Vemar on. "Go with her. I'll get a plate for the king and queen. If they eat this food, maybe they won't be so mad about her product fucking things up again."

"I'm on it, little buddy!" Vemar jogged ahead, putting on a burst of speed when I started running.

Weston

"She didn't pause," Hannon said as we started hustling back. We couldn't be seen running—we didn't want to frighten people. "She had no regard for the fact that helping Micah and the others would out herself to the person who supposedly imprisoned her. She wasn't concerned, even a little, about putting herself in danger."

"She's not thinking about Granny right now. She's thinking about her product and how to help people through it. She'd do it at any cost."

"She said that and I believed it, but now she is proving it. I think this will go a long way to convince the court of her position in all of this."

"She was bound to prove it at some point. This is a clever move on Granny's part to find her location. She clearly wants her drugmaker back, and she'll do whatever it takes to get her."

"It is. She's known for being cunning." He paused. "Listen, Weston, since I have you—when I first met Aurelia, I didn't know about the true mate bond. I'd only heard about her connection to Granny."

"And after you found out?" I growled.

If it wasn't for the current situation with the kingdom, that smile would've been enough to send me over the edge. She'd accepted me, and now I would allow no challenges to my claim. None.

"Simply put, she needed the connection, and I was happy to provide it. She wasn't ready for your bond. I assumed you knew that."

He'd feel my affirmation, so I didn't bother voicing it.

He nodded. "I welcomed her attention not just because . . ." He cleared his throat. "Well, not just for personal reasons, but because I didn't want her to bestow attention upon someone else who was too afraid of you to let her. They would've turned her away, and I felt like she'd had enough rejection in life. Ultimately, I gave in to my own desires because I knew it would also help her. If I'd been interfering, I would've bowed out before she asked me to. Please believe that."

I stopped and faced him, unable to help it, unable to contain my boiling rage.

"You gave in to your own desires? What the fuck does that mean?" I took a step forward. "Did you touch her?"

He flung up his hands. "No! Not at all, no. Nor did she want me to. I gave in to my desire to talk to her and flirt. I did not touch her. I knew that would be crossing the line. She's a remarkable woman, Weston. I've never before been jealous of any man in my life, but I am jealous of you. Take that as the compliment it's meant to be."

It took every ounce of strength to stand down.

I let out the breath I was holding. "She's made her choice. The flirting is over."

"Agreed." His hands were still raised. "It's over. We *will* still talk, as friends, but she made it clear that she has no interest in anything else, and I respect her wishes."

I stared him down until he lowered his eyes, submitting, before I turned.

"You walk a very fine line, Hannon."

He caught up with me, so fucking nonchalant. He always had been, even before he'd known he couldn't stay dead.

"Sometimes that is on purpose," he said. "I did it with the king, as well. Power feeds me, as you know. Sometimes, I do it for someone else. This time I did it for her. She needed an outlet. I was happy to provide it."

"She seems to have created a lot of loyalty in a short period of time." I couldn't help feeling pride in that, and I hated that my connection to her could possibly undermine the truth of that statement.

"She'll make an excellent half of an alpha pair if you'll trust her with the role."

And now he was telling me my business, sparking my longing for exactly that. It was not easy being around a phoenix when you'd spent most of your life concealing your emotions. It felt like there was nowhere to hide.

"What's taking you?" Hadriel asked as he half jogged by. "Fuck, I'm running again. Clearly something has gone wrong with my life when I find myself exercising."

The royals were in the dining room, Arleth and Delaney included. Half-finished dinners had been pushed away, and Finley had her elbows on the table, her head in her hands. No matter how hard she tried to eradicate Granny's product, it always seemed to work its way back in.

"Hey. Cheer up." Hadriel put a plate of Aurelia's cooking in front of Finley and one in front of Nyfain. "Eat that, it's delicious. What's going on?"

Finley summarized what Hannon had told me, ending, "Micah heard about all your exploits, Hadriel, and wanted to join in on the fun."

"What fun? Granny's?" Hadriel asked, picking up the fork and putting it in Finley's hand. "Eat that, love, trust me. It lifts the spirits. Did Micah not actually listen? Everyone knows it wasn't Granny's drugs, but Aurelia's product."

"No, actually, they don't, Hadriel, and now he's sick and in need of help, and Nyfain doesn't feel comfortable giving it."

"I don't want to accidentally kill him," Nyfain said, leaning over the plate but staring at nothing. "Micah has been pushing the limits again, his dragon more so, and my dragon is ready to force dominance. If we do it like this, that could get ugly."

Micah had been pushing the limits since he'd first arrived in this kingdom. He didn't like the title of beta. He wanted the alpha spot, like in the town or village he'd grown up in, in another kingdom. He'd tried to settle into a commander role, but it chafed, especially with a wolf, me, at the same rank but much better at the job.

"What about Vemar?" Finley asked.

"Not quite strong enough," Nyfain said. "We'd need two dragons against Micah, but there isn't room. We need to get him outside, and then we can deal with him."

"Is he in human form now?" Hadriel asked, using Finley's hand, fork in her fist, to spear a vegetable.

"Yes," Nyfain replied. "Inside the billiard room."

"Okay then, no problem. It'll be fine. Here we go, love. Treat this thing like a kingly dick and shove it in your mouth. You'll thank me."

"Explain," Nyfain said as Hadriel practically forced the food into Finley's mouth.

Hadriel stepped back, looking at her chew. "Simple. Aurelia will handle it."

Finley's eyes lit up, and then her brows drew together as she looked down at the dish. "Whoa, this is good." She waved it away, though, obviously worried about her kingdom. "My village reports that the woman Hadriel brought into town has a way of putting drug users to sleep. There are several eyewitnesses. It's why I asked for her. But Micah is . . . much more dangerous than anyone she would've encountered in my village."

"And right you were." Hadriel winked. "I was one of those witnesses. Don't worry about the danger. She can handle it."

"You are part of this problem of Micah's," Finley groused, spearing a hunk of meat. "I'm too annoyed to cut this."

"And that is why you pay me the big piles of gold that you do." Hadriel stepped toward her again, treating her like a child. "You're hangry. Come on, keep eating."

"Well, hell, I'm curious." Delaney leaned across the table and speared Nyfain's dinner with her fork.

"And where is—"

He cut off as Aurelia jogged in carrying an armful of folded tarps. Vemar was right behind her, carrying even more.

"Where to?" Aurelia said.

I led her to the large billiard room. Micah was taller than Nyfain, though not as robust. His brown eyes were wild, and each large hand gripped half of a broken pool stick. Balls littered the ground. Several people stood in there with him, hands out, trying to calm him down. Their power pumped through the air, while tempers ran just as high. Dragons were terrible at handling things in a calm, collected manner. Micah was just about to go berserk.

"Oh yeah, this is great." Aurelia slipped in through the large dragon males, a tiny figure with zero fear. She glanced around as Micah tensed his whole body and roared at the sky.

I was about to shoulder through to her when Hannon put out his hand to stop me. Nyfain was already moving, yanking the dragons out of the way, taking up residence just inside the doorframe.

Micah zeroed in on him, and more power seeped into the air.

"Get him out of here." Aurelia spun and pointed at Nyfain. "Get the fuck out of here. You're making things worse."

"What did—"

"Go, baby." Finley slipped by me and grabbed his arm, pulling at him. "Go, my love. She's right. He'll challenge, and you'll answer. Go, go. Step out of sight. I'll handle this."

"You can't handle him in human form."

"Would you guys get the hell out of here?" Aurelia shouted, looking around the large room. "All of you. He's not in human form, he's in drug form. It's fine. I've got this."

"Go." Hadriel shooed Finley back, Nyfain with her. "Go, seriously. Trust her. She's very good at knowing what she can handle."

There was no fucking way I was stepping back. I wouldn't leave her to a dragon like Micah. Most of the time he was a good commander, but we'd never gotten along. Trust was hard won, and he'd never tried.

The big dragon shifter stared at me, his face sweaty and pale, his brown hair standing in all directions, eyes manic. He gripped his sticks, leaned back, and roared again.

As the noise died down, a hum in the same pitch rose, the sound calming and tranquil.

Micah cocked his head and turned, finding Aurelia at the back of the room, taking things out of the supply closet. She hummed that tune, keeping his focus and finishing her task quickly. Then she stood in front of the opened door and started a roar of her own, weak and almost silly. He matched it a moment later, suddenly entranced, all his focus on her as she ended in that hum.

Then she picked up a cue ball . . . and threw it at him in such a fast movement that he had no time to react. It hit him square in the middle of the forehead.

"Oh shit," Hadriel said softly.

Vemar shoved to get past. "He's going to go for her."

Too late.

Micah was closer, he was pissed, and she was his target.

26

AURELIA

The dragon roared as he ran at me. That big fucker probably moved fast when he wasn't sick and drugged out. He might've moved faster than me before I had an animal. Now I could catalog his jerky movements, his halting steps. He was trying to move in as straight a line as possible, but his body was off. He wasn't doing great. That product was either shit, or he'd taken a lot of it. He'd need some cure-all.

But first he needed to chill the fuck out.

He appeared with his sticks held out, probably forgetting they were in his hands. The bitch was, he wouldn't fit into the closet with those stupid things swinging.

"Aurelia, no," Weston yelled, terror in his voice.

I ignored that as the big dragon bore down on me. He bent with his mouth open, as though he was trying to eat my face or something. You never knew with a bad journey. People got some crazy ideas.

I feinted to the side, knowing he wouldn't buy it and would assume I'd dodge the other way. There weren't many options for an opponent his size. I, however, wasn't his size, and planned to use it to my advantage. He stepped toward my feint, saw I didn't go through with it, and stretched out the other hand to capture me.

I ducked and rolled through his long legs. I clipped one of them as I did so, making his knee bend. His weight shifted dramatically, an effect of the product, and he fell forward. His shoulder slammed into the edge of the door, and those fucking sticks hit the frame.

At his back, I grabbed his arms and twisted, bending them behind him. He struggled—and so did I. He was fucking strong. *Really* fucking strong.

"Fuck," I grunted, hurrying, trying to get those damn sticks out of the way so I could get his big, dumb body into the closet.

"I got him, I got him!" Vemar came running. He punched one of Micah's fists, forcing the other dragon to drop a stick.

Weston was at the other side, shoving me away. He grabbed the dragon's other arm and continued twisting it, ripping out the pool stick and bending it behind the dragon. He waited for Vemar to bend the other arm, all of them struggling.

"What do we do with him?" Vemar yelled.

"Shove him in and shut the door." I shoved all of them. "Get in there, dragon. Time for night-night. Get the fuck" —I shoved all of them harder—"in your cave. Sleepy time. Get into your fucking cave, you bastard."

Micah roared, but Weston and Vemar had him, the three of them half falling forward as I rammed them from behind. They shoved the dragon in, then backed out fast.

"Shut the door," I yelled, though Weston was already grabbing it. "Night-night, dragon. Go to sleep in your cave on your piles of gold."

Weston swung the door closed and leaned his shoulder

against it, pushing hard. Vemar joined him, his back to the wood, applying all his weight.

The dragon roared and thumped within. Thank the fucking gods Raz hadn't been a dragon. That would've made my life much, much more dangerous.

"Is there a key?" I asked through labored breaths.

"No." Weston eyed the door. "No key. What do we do?"

"Get a chair to brace against it. That's all he needs—the small, dark space is going to send a signal to his brain that it is sleepy time. He'll get drowsy, probably get enraged, because dragons are clearly nuts, stomp around, and bash things, but eventually he'll quiet."

"He's strong enough to get through that door," Nyfain said, coming up behind us.

"He won't." I motioned for Hadriel to grab the chair to my right. "Products that cause this reaction cut down on thinking ability. My old coworker could've just walked out the back door at any time. Instead, he stayed in the supply closet, sometimes smashing all my stuff and writing mean things about me on the walls, until he drifted into a stupor. When he woke up, he left. I don't advise waiting that long with this guy. He didn't look good. He needs help. Wait until he quiets—maybe another twenty minutes after that for him, actually—and then inject him, if at all possible. Then get out again. If you have to use liquid, go slow. Coax him to swallow. Or maybe just call me. I can work with him after he calms down. I can probably get him to swallow just fine. Once he's out of it, he'll probably just knock on the door and ask to be let out."

More than one person was blinking at me.

"How . . .?" Finley shook her head slowly, looking at the closet door. The dragon was in there howling, banging on the wall, tearing down whatever was left from the shelves.

"How could you possibly know how to . . . do that? Create a drug that operates one way in one situation, and then another way in another situation?"

"Books. There is some fascinating stuff out there about the magical brain. They're all a bit different. I kind of stumbled into it, asked for more books on it, and then figured"—I shrugged—"if I can work that in, that would be good. But there's a downside to this fail-safe. If a person is trying to take the product in secret, like away from their wife or something, they won't get much out of it before they go to sleep. That's then a waste of their money."

The sounds within the closet started to quiet. His thrashing slowed.

"I can't believe it," Arleth said quietly, also watching the closet. "I've never heard of anything like it. And this . . . effect has always been present?"

"She discovered the first traces of it at about eighteen," Weston said as he motioned for us to get moving. "I remember reading it in her journals. Don't we have a lot more people to see?"

We did, as a matter of fact, but it wasn't at all the long night I was expecting. It turned out that Vemar and a handful of other dragons came in quite handy. They were amazing at forcing people into closets or small spaces or into little balls on the road, where tarps would then be put over them. The way they went about it was a little comical, too, with chasing (by the dragons), screaming (by the dragons), and occasionally nets just for funsies.

I handled anyone dangerous and high-powered enough that might result in someone getting hurt, but mostly . . . I just chatted with the people watching, some of them angry their mate would take that stuff, some sad that their mate was at it again, and some laughing with how people were being rounded up. I spoke to those who were sad, heard stories of addiction and underlying problems, and did the best I could to console them.

An amazing bit of information kept cropping up—Vemar had really been onto something. A group of people habitually using the product were not doing the fun stuff, like the hallucinogens. They were taking it to help them sleep, or battle mental health issues, or various other things as a way to self-medicate. Small groups of those people knew to scrape off the top coating and get at the meat, as they called it. The addiction and sickness didn't trouble them much, as they were only exposed to the remnants from bits of coating they'd left behind.

I tried to remember everything I heard, especially as it pertained to making my product better, but there was too much. I really only caught what was often repeated. I needed to visit another time with a pencil and paper. That was if the queen would allow me. I loved the challenge of doing better, but after this, I doubted she'd love my desire to try.

The queen's village was the last, and the dragons were annoyed to find that it was under control. They'd gotten tired of waiting and taken matters into their own hands, mostly successfully.

On the way back, riding behind Weston on his horse, I wrapped my arms around his torso and leaned my cheek against his back.

"It seems like she unloaded a lot of product," I said, looking out at the emberflies floating lazily.

"Yes, it does."

"I didn't see anyone obviously watching as the night progressed. I didn't feel threatened or in danger. Do you think her people are here?"

"I had the pack check out all the traders' carts. Homes,

too. The one that had your poster—the one still alive—was only selling small quantities of Granny's product. He's in the dungeons at present. He couldn't have released all this, at least not alone. We didn't find anything else; not one wrapper. Not one stray drug. Someone got in and unloaded all this product, in all the villages. Likely many people. We have no idea who. Or how, or when. No one saw anything—not anyone that is talking, at any rate. Yes, I think her people are here. I think they are watching. I'm going to check in with the other kingdoms and see if they were hit in the same way. If so, I'll ask how it was handled. From that we can determine if Granny will have learned anything from this . . . episode."

"If she has people watching, she has the drawing of my face in their hands. It won't matter if I helped—it'll matter that they recognized me. Soon she'll know where I am."

It was only a matter of time.

Weston ran his hand along my arm and entwined his fingers with mine. "This is true. We'll need to assume that word will reach her about where you are. Who you're with."

I hugged him a little tighter. "How long will the news take to reach her, do you think?"

"With a fast ship, a few days."

"Can't you dock all the ships? Delay them?"

"We can make up some reason to delay people getting to their ships, but we can't keep them forever."

"Then the countdown has begun." Fear trembled within me, but I shoved it away in favor of determination. I had precious little time to find a solution to the dangerousness of her product. I'd focus on that and let Weston focus on protecting me. He had the army of a kingdom at his disposal. I would trust him to use it.

He squeezed my hand. "We'll handle this, okay? She won't be able to get to you."

I closed my eyes, my cheek against his back. I would not live in fear of her, not anymore.

"I'd like to learn how to defend myself," I said in a small voice. "In both human and wolf form."

"Of course," he replied.

We'd need to start training soon.

After the horses were handed off to the stable hands, the stable guy from our journey nowhere to be found, we made our way toward the castle, behind the king and queen. We were nearly there when the queen stalled, looking back at us.

"Thank you," she told me, falling in step. I paused, and Weston moved in beside the king to give us a moment. "I realize what your help means. Please rest assured, we know what threats you will face if you were to fall into Granny's hands, and we are keenly aware of the threat we all face if that were to happen. We have a solid defense in this kingdom. You'll be protected."

I inclined my head, letting the sentiment drift by me.

"I'd like to learn how you make your product," she said.

"Okay."

"I assume I don't have to impress upon you how quickly I want something to combat Granny's poison."

"No, you don't. I'll find you a cure, if not a solution. Just give me the supplies I need."

She paused for a moment. Finally, she said, "We're not going to kill you, just so you know. I know you had doubts. I thought I might put your mind at ease. We'll probably have to whip you or make some show of things, but . . . your life isn't in danger."

I laughed without humor. "Your Majesty, it wasn't what you would do that troubled me. It was always my past becoming my future again, and you just saw the lengths she'll go just to know where I am. But thank you, that . . . is nice of you to say. Sort of."

"The whipping . . . isn't necessarily great news."

"No," I breathed. "It isn't."

As we reached the castle doors, the attendants pulled them open for us. The queen looked across at Weston, her eyes hard and troubled, before she nodded and led the way across the threshold.

"Did you want to stay with me tonight?" Weston asked a few moments later as we walked down the hall.

"Yes, please. I just . . . Could I have a minute to write in my journal? I heard quite a lot today, and I'd like to write it down while it's fresh."

"Of course. Come over when you're ready."

He was where I'd seen him the night before, book open, candles lit.

"You don't have to light those for me every night, you know." I gestured at them as I made my way to his lap.

His smile was soft. "They're nice. They soften the space a little."

I nestled against him, loving how his arms felt as they wrapped around me. "I'm sorry."

"Don't be." He paused. "For what?"

"For making you wait. I . . . was lost. I'm not anymore. I'm sorry for causing you pain."

"*I'm* sorry," he said.

I furrowed my brow, sitting up so I could see his face. The candlelight flickered in his beautiful gray eyes.

"Don't be," I said. "For what?"

"For snatching you from your home without interrogating you first. For making you share a stranger's bed as a captive. For making you a captive here again instead of a true mate, or even as just a pretty stranger who needed help with her animal. I mean, need I go on? For ripping your life apart without mercy. For saying you can go free but then shoving you off into a foreign town without any sort of protection. For not telling you about Granny sooner." He shook his head. "Giving you a little time to figure out your life is hardly a big ask, now is it? Not after what I've put you through. It is also well within your right. I haven't claimed you, and even if I had, you are free to choose whoever makes you happy. Nothing is forever unless you wake up every day and decide it will be, over and over, until the end of time."

I ran my thumb along his jaw, feeling a little stubble. "I would've lost it if you'd been with another woman."

"Good. I like my mate possessive."

"Is that what I am now?" Butterflies filled my belly. "Your mate?"

"Yes."

I kissed him softly. "Can I ask you a question?"

"Yes?"

"Do . . . Will we . . ."

"Spit it out," he whispered with a smile.

"Mates claim each other, right? Eventually? Or . . ."

Hunger flashed in his eyes, and I felt him harden beneath me.

"Yes," he said. "Mates claim each other. We're in a unique position, though. We need to wait a bit longer."

"For what?" I asked, desire pooling in me. I leaned forward and kissed his lips as I reached down between us, rubbing along his hardness.

"For your world to get more complicated and for you

to choose a path." He grabbed my waist and lifted me so that I could settle a knee on each side of him.

"I don't know what that means," I said against his lips, working at the buttons on his shirt.

He undid my pants, reaching in and feeling along my wetness. He groaned at how ready I was.

"You will soon enough," he murmured, stroking me as I finished undoing his shirt.

I kissed down his chest while I undid his pants, pulling out his sizable girth. He stopped me from sucking it in, though, reaching forward to yank down my pants and underwear and pull me toward him. "You looked really handsome tonight."

"This is my professional attire."

"I like your professional attire." I shrugged out of my shirt and leaned forward so that he could suck in the peak of my breast. I ran my slick sex against him before lifting up and rubbing his tip along me.

"I like you riding my cock." He grabbed my hips and pulled while thrusting upward, driving home. I groaned as he put one of his hands to my cheek, keeping my lips close. His other hand stayed on my hip, lifting and pulling in time with his strokes, sliding out then back in hard. "If it were up to me, baby, I'd have you claimed and bred by now."

I groaned against his mouth, those dirty words lighting a fire deep inside of me. Kindling a need. We breathed the same heated air, full of want.

"I walked out onto that path the first night," he murmured, "because I couldn't help myself. You called to me. Everything about you called to me. From that moment until now, I've wanted you with every fiber of my being, even when I thought you were the enemy. I lingered at your work desk, looked over your art, riveted. I was there to get clues to Granny's operation, but I wanted to learn about *you*. Your loves, your quirks, your interests. Everything about you has me entranced. I hate how we met—well, after that first night—but I'm so glad my journey led me to this moment. I will choose you, every day, for the rest of my life. I love you, Aurelia."

The words sent a shock into me, like a spear through my chest, breaking everything away until the sentiment lodged deeply into my heart. I could feel Weston's truth rising within us, our wolves fusing, our hearts joining. Only my mother had ever said those words to me and meant them. I knew in my soul he meant them now, and that he'd felt it for a while. Like bubbles, all those feelings rose to the surface.

Tears dripped down my cheeks. My body moved on top of his.

"I—"

He stopped me with a kiss, stealing the words with my breath.

"Not yet," he murmured, emotion making his voice wobble. "Not yet."

I didn't know what he was waiting for. What choices he thought would come before me. Maybe the problem was with the towns and villages, where people might not trust the beta to have a mate who'd been responsible for the drugs infiltrating their safe spaces. Maybe it would be a black mark on the pack, or the royals. Whatever the reason, I trusted him. He'd waited for me; I would wait for him. It wasn't any great hardship. I'd still see him, get to be with him, get to call him my mate. It was more than I'd ever expected out of life. I was blessed to have gotten this far, to have this much of a fairytale, as fucked up as it had been.

I rocked against him, and he worked my clit, bending

me back so that he could roll his tongue around my nipple. He drove deeply, trying to work in that knot. Trying to lock me. I didn't want that in this position, though. Not tonight. Tonight, I wanted to fall asleep with his knot lodged in deeply, him not able to go far.

I pushed off his chest, climbed from his lap, and turned, bending over. He was up in a flash, arm around my waist and lifting me. He dropped me on the couch, my knees on the cushion, elbows along on the back. He shoved his cock in hard, all the way to the hilt. I bit my lip with the small ache and felt his growl of triumph dance up my spine. His hand fisted my hair and his other snaked around me, his finger massaging me right where I needed it most.

I bucked against him a little too hard, sending pain flaring again. He let go of my hair and curved his arm around my chest, holding me in place as he pumped in shallow movements. His finger worked my clit. His teeth scraped along my shoulder.

"Please, Weston," I begged, rolling my body.

His teeth lingered, and I felt his power building. Felt his need rising. My wolf was right near the surface, desperate for this, wanting their forever mark. His wolf snarled, though, pulling back at the man. Refusing to commit. I wondered why the sudden change in the wolf.

"Fuck," Weston growled, and his mouth found my neck instead as his fingers pinched a nipple.

An orgasm exploded through me. His pleasure tumbled through the bond a moment later as he shook with his own release. Back and forth the pleasure went, chased by power, by a deep feeling that welled up so big it consumed me.

I couldn't stop the tears, but fuck it, this was heaven. I knew he didn't mind.

I snuggled back against him, feeling fatigue come over me. "Can we go to bed and do this until we pass out?"

His answer was to lift me and move locations. Once we'd gotten under the covers, the process a lesson in teamwork, he curled around me just the way I liked. With his lips against my ear, he whispered, "I love you," one last time, and then we slowly fucked our way to sleep.

27

AURELIA

In the week that followed, I attempted to keep my regular hours—the ones I used to employ in the village. It soon became apparent, however, that those hours made everyone nervous. On day three the queen herself tried to chase me out of the work shed, telling me I was going to burn myself out.

I'd stared at her stupidly for a moment. "I've been keeping these hours for . . . over ten years. I'll be fine, I promise. I'm used to this."

The look she'd given me—the look everyone had given me—was full of sorrow and compassion—and pity. That part made me highly uncomfortable. Just to get away from it, I'd excused myself as though I were taking their worry to heart. Instead, under the guise of resting, I'd gone back to my journals, attempting to pinpoint where the other production village might've been. That, or I hit the books in the extensive library, working on several things to keep my mind fresh on any given product or counter-product.

When it was time to wind down, I decided to look into a painting class and learn about mixing colors. The teacher, Liron, was a donkey's twat, a colorful term Hadriel had taught me, but he did know his stuff. Most days, at some point or another, one or more of my reading crew would join me in the work shed, out of the way of the others, and read while I worked. After that, I lost myself in cooking, ate with Weston, wrote in my journal, then usually made love to Weston and went to bed.

I'd never felt so fulfilled. Previously, I'd done all of this alone or with a coworker who distrusted and disliked me. Being around people I enjoyed and respected—having real friends—was a sort of happiness so big I didn't know it could fit inside me. My heart was continually bursting, making me tear up randomly, touching a shoulder in thanks or hooking an arm through Hadriel's or Vemar's as we walked. I loved it.

I also loved my new coworkers. The women hadn't thawed so much as I'd just learned how they worked. They were like a dance, moving around and within the work shed, humming often and chatting seldom, content to work the plants and make their brews. They'd spend time in the garden every day, manhandling their Everlass and checking on everything else. They were all great with greenery, though none so diligent and thorough as the queen. They even nursed my Moonfire Lily into blooming health, the slow throb of color illuminating the dragon weed every night amidst the speckles of light from the emberflies.

Then there was Vemar, the new guardian of my asshole. I had no idea what that meant, only that it was a kinda-sorta, half-literal inside joke with him and Hadriel. Vemar was the best coworker I could ask for. He flowed with me like a synchronized dance. I barely had to ask for things; I could just look up for what I needed and he'd fill my hand with it. When he needed something, I reciprocated. He worked our contraptions right alongside me, learning the craft in no time, completely unafraid and constantly inquisitive, getting the handle of the heat and quickly understanding my instruction. He spoke when it felt right and was content to work in silence when the mood called for it, his finger on the pulse of those around him. In just that week, I knew I'd be lost without him.

At the end of the week, I was finally ready with my Granny lookalike coating. It was time to unveil it to the queen.

I let myself out of Weston's chambers, where I now spent my nights. The hall was deserted, as it was most mornings.

Constantly rolling around inside my head were various ideas of things I could improve, things I could attempt, and various new insights I'd gleaned from working with the genius that existed in that work shed.

I'd been so caught up in my work that it took me a minute to notice the presence behind me, a soft footfall on the hard wood.

I glanced back, vaguely recognizing the uniform colors —burnt orange, which meant food collection for the kitchen staff. What were they doing all the way down this hall? Usually, Burt took care of that at a "decent" hour, finding me in the work shed or tracking me down in the library, but maybe they were changing things up. Were they sent to inquire personally if I needed anything?

Slowing a little, I started to turn to ask just that.

The man, not much taller than me, with a slight build—definitely not a dragon—had slicked-back hair, allowing me to see his pockmarked cheeks, indicating bad skin in his youth. Which was . . . odd for a shifter. Maybe he'd been here during the curse, suppressed within the castle and unable to heal.

He slowed with me, his head tipped down and his dark eyebrows lifted so that he could peer at me from under them. That was usually the sign that the staff didn't want to be intrusive.

So then . . . not here for me.

Frowning, wondering if maybe he was dropping off an early dish for someone's valet or maid, I turned back around and picked up the pace again. His footfalls sped up as well, though he kept a respectable distance.

I resumed thinking about my concoctions, but the ideas were splintered; I was too distracted by the man to regain my focus.

"Something isn't right with that one," my wolf said, pulling forward what was niggling at me.

His gait had been off for a member of the castle staff, hadn't it? His lack of poise.

Often workers in the castle had straight posture and an air of busy importance, or so I'd always thought. Even the people who dusted and swept seemed to embody the grandness of the establishment. This guy sort of . . . lumbered, his shoulders rounded and his weight shifting from one foot to the other with each step, as though he were looking for a street brawl.

I glanced back again, finding his red-brown eyes focused on me. A sudden wave of unease washed through me right before his gaze sliced right and he dropped his head again, slowing his walk.

"I don't sense danger," my wolf said.

Neither did I. But all the same, thoughts of Granny flashed through my mind. There hadn't been any other instances since the drugs flooded the market a week ago, but that didn't mean she'd retreated. She would have people watching, wouldn't she? Keeping tabs on me?

My breath came faster as I debated what to do. Should I

just accost him, maybe? Ask his name and demand to know why he was in this hall? It might be as simple as his being someone's bed bunny and trying to get out before he was noticed. Then again, it could be someone learning my schedule.

What if he had a weapon, though? What if he had backup waiting around some of the corners I had yet to turn down or pass? I had barely started training. I was in no shape for knife work if he had one on him. Right now, he was keeping his distance. I had room to run.

Biting my lip in indecision, I waited a little longer, until I was near the foyer. If I got into trouble, someone would see me.

I slowed, then stopped to turn. His footfalls lightened and then stopped. I had spun just in time to see his clothes hit the floor, as though the person inside them vanished.

"There!" my wolf shouted as a bit of fabric moved.

A rat ran out of the neck hole, scurrying away down the hall at blinding speeds. I didn't even know shifters could be rats. Or that rats could run that fast.

"Move!" my wolf shouted, tearing at me to get out of the way. *"Let me out. I'll catch him."*

I ripped at my clothes, barely getting them off before my wolf had taken over. She put on a burst of speed, sprinting down the hall in the direction the rat had run. In the moment it took to shift, though, we'd lost sight of him.

She stopped at his clothes, picking up his scent before taking off again.

"What if he's leading us into a trap?" I said frantically as she reached the first corner and sniffed.

"Our mate is close, and a host of wolves and dragons surround us." She reached the next corner and caught the scent to the right. *"If they take us, they won't get far."*

She was fine being bait, it seemed.

That wasn't a pleasant realization.

Down the corridor, the scent started to disintegrate. By the time we got around the next turn, we could feel Weston on the move, clearly having felt our emotions and hurrying to investigate or help.

Another turn had us staring at a small exit up ahead glowing with the watery light of the misty morning.

"Shit," my wolf muttered, speeding to the door as the lingering scent began to drift away.

She moved aside so that I could resume our human form. I pushed open the door and hesitantly stepped out into the chilly morning air. A wide gravel path curved away through leafy bushes glistening with moisture. Visibility was cut down to just this little stoop, where none of the flora so much as shivered with the passage of a body, big *or* small.

"Do we follow?" I asked out loud, my senses in human form not as keen, unable to tell if there was a scent trail to pursue.

"No. We were already losing him. Out in nature, there's no chance. A wolf or larger animal might've raised notice with the patrol, but a rat? He'll be able to hide easily and sneak out with any deliveries or castle visitors. He's beyond us. Let's tell our mate so that they can search for the scent inside. Perhaps it will lead us to others."

I turned and started to run, smacking into a body with an *"Oof."* Leala bumped back, staggering, the tip of her whip shivering as she struggled to stay on her feet.

"Sorry." I grabbed her.

"What is it?" she asked before she'd even regained her balance. "I saw your discarded clothes and followed your scent. What'd you see?"

It seemed as though the first person to find and help us was my lady's maid—and her trusty whip.

"He's gone. Let's get Weston."

It turned out that uniform had gone missing several days prior. No one had remembered seeing a person matching the man's description. No one could remember coming across his scent, left behind on his discarded clothes. Weston had distributed those clothes so that the patrol and guard could track him down as he inevitably tried to flee the kingdom, but nothing turned up. He'd been a ghost—a ghost that had gotten into the castle unnoticed and been able to gain access to me. While I was alone.

My wolf trusted that our mate would've intercepted if the rat had been able to drag me away, and I agreed with her. It was one thing to visit the castle and slip into the kitchens, keeping one's head down and even roaming around. One guy minding his own business wouldn't really be noticed, especially on food collection detail. Grabbing the resident captive and wrestling her out of the castle, across the grounds, through the woods? That was another thing entirely.

That was not good enough for Weston. That morning, with the king's blessing, he started an overhaul of the castle's security. His goal was to ensure something like that could never happen again.

Watching my mate, thorough and excellent at his job, had filled me with pride.

Now, though, as I finally got to my work—with no strangers allowed within the vicinity of the garden—the reality of the morning's events seeped in. Maybe that guy wasn't one of Granny's, and maybe it wasn't even me he was after, but it was a stark reminder that I wasn't safe here. Maybe I wasn't safe on my own. I needed to heed the warning.

"Walk me through it," Finley said, leaning over the table to look at my five little balls of beige product. She'd been all business since I arrived, having heard what happened but not commenting. I was grateful. She seemed to realize losing myself in work and pushing away the fear that Granny would force me back into the life I'd left behind was the thing I needed most right now.

I pointed at the first. "The most like Granny's"—I pointed at the last—"what she was going for"—I pointed at those in between—"and my trial and error. It took me a while to create something shitty enough to resemble what Granny's people did. Then, because I couldn't help myself—"

"You didn't want to help yourself," Vemar supplied, quietly enraged that I'd had to deal with that guy this morning on my own. Even just sitting next to him raised the small hairs on my arms. I had a feeling he was about to get a lot more intense in his bodyguarding duty. He reached up to grab one of our contraptions now lining the back shelf.

"Fine. I wanted to see if I could make something that wasn't shitty. Anyway, this last product should create the hook in half the time while creating almost no sickness. It's safe. It won't kill anyone unless there is a *lot* of it in the bloodstream."

"I didn't feel any sickness." Vemar sat back down.

"Me either. The build-up effect was drastically cut as well, hence being able to have a lot. Have five in a twenty-four-hour period and you're going to throw up. I don't know how many it would take to die. My product would be very bad for the mind if someone were to take more than five doses in a short period of time. I doubt anyone would or could."

"Wait." Finley held up her hand while squeezing her eyes shut. "Are you telling me you ingested this stuff?"

I frowned at her. "Of course. I had to test it."

She pointed down at the last beige round. "You ate five of these in twenty-four hours and just, what? *Hoped* you wouldn't die?"

"I was on hand with Hannon's special brew." Vemar winked at Hannon sitting in the corner. His face was devoid of his usual good-humored expression. Instead, his blue eyes had a poignant sort of focus. His lips were pursed in a straight line, his body relaxed but expectant, as though he might be called upon to battle at any moment.

No one was taking the security breech well. I was quickly learning that the dragon kingdom might sparkle and shine like a well-polished gold coin, but the people here had grown up fighting. Struggling to stay alive. They were ready, able, and more than willing to defend their homes, and would do so with a vicious sort of aggression I likely couldn't comprehend. I could be in no better place to face the threat of Granny.

I had to keep reminding myself of that, lest the fear start picking away at my courage to push on.

"It should be me trying those things," Hannon responded.

"Nah." Vemar waved him away. "Then you'd have this horrible itch to consume more of it. It's not pleasant."

"Yeah." I wiped my face. "That elixir you guys make to stave off addiction is much too slow."

"*Much* too slow," Vemar agreed.

"How do you test your products?" I asked them. Arleth and Delaney were gathered around the table as well.

"On people who need it," Finley responded as though I were daft.

I lifted my brow. "You give test samples to your patients? Isn't that . . . dicey?"

"If we don't have the ailment that needs to be cured, how will we know the product worked to cure that ailment?" Finley returned.

Vemar and I shrugged at each other. She had a point.

"Right. So." I blew out a breath. "This is what we're working with. I have a lot of ideas to counter this stuff. It should work on Granny's coating like a dream. I'll test that, obviously. If I am captured by her and forced to work because she threatens children or something—which doesn't seem above her, to be honest—you will know how to counter the best of my addictive products."

Vemar's rage spiked, sending the other dragons into their own hum of aggression. Hannon adjusted in his seat, leaning against the wall projecting pseudo-calm. The guy seemed to always look unruffled, and I had a feeling his killing you would then be quite the shock.

"No one will capture you and live to tell the tale," Vemar growled. The women nodded, Finley's intense agreement sending my stomach rolling.

Taking a page out of Hadriel's book, I said sarcastically, "Great. What a load off." Hannon started to laugh. It made me realize I hadn't yet seen Hadriel that morning.

"Does Weston know you took these?" Finley demanded, obviously stuck on our testing practices.

"No," I answered, organizing the samples out of the way. "He'd be pissed. It would be nice if you didn't tell him. I'm fine. Vemar is fine. All is well. The worst is over."

Finley looked at Arleth, who was studying me. Neither commented.

"Great. That's that, then. You guys wanted to learn how to make the product on the market, right?" With a cleared workspace, I pulled a list over. "Let's start with Product X.

That's the stuff to stave off pregnancy. People here have a lot of sex—a lot more than in my old village. My own stock is running low, and I don't want to resort to that horrible tea. Here's a list of ingredients. I'll let the gardeners among you collect them while I pull out the right contraptions."

"Which we don't need yet, but it's a good excuse not to have to help them," Vemar mumbled. I elbowed him. That was supposed to be a secret.

After they'd looked over the list and checked the things they currently had cooking, Arleth and Delaney opted to collect the ingredients.

"So, all of this is made with Everlass, huh?" I pointed at the many steaming and cooking items around the room. Special vents had been put in the roof of the work shed to whisk away all the smoke and scents.

Finley didn't glance behind her. "Almost all of it. What are those?" She pointed at the contraptions I'd pulled out.

"It's easier just to show you. So how do you work those leaves? I saw you dry them. Then you . . . what, just boil and steam them?"

"Dry them at different times of the day, inside or out, to alter the properties as we need. Then we boil or simmer or cold-brew them and mix them with various other ingredients that further enhance the properties."

"Ah." I nodded. "I knew there was some complexity to it. So, you really need a vast understanding of plants."

"Yes."

"Gotcha. Have you tried burning it?"

She stared at me for a moment. "No."

"Freezing it? Pressurizing it? Lighting it on fire and then quickly freezing it?"

Still staring. "No."

"Micro-blowing it up?"

"What is that?" Vemar leaned over.

I grinned at him. "You'll love that. No glass to pick out of one's person."

"No," Finley responded.

I nodded as the others walked back in, placing down bunches of greenery without a speck of dirt in sight. "Think of all the possibilities left for you to explore. What is this?"

Arleth and Delaney paused, Arleth still holding the list. She frowned, looking over it and checking what was on the table. "The fresh ingredients are there"—she gestured at the pile—"and we're grabbing the dried ones now."

"The dried ones?" I picked through the "fresh" ingredients. "This is undoubtedly a dumb question, but is this their natural color? I assume the vibrant green probably is, but the flowers of this one are blue. I thought they were supposed to be a light sort of purple?"

It turned out Raz and his helpers were very bad gardeners, and Vemar and Hannon thought my confusion—especially as it concerned the necessity of drying plants—was hilarious.

"At least I don't have to wash off the dirt," I finally said. "Thanks for that. Time saver. Okay, let's get started with the expectation that this might go horribly wrong with these healthy plants and I might need to tweak the instructions."

Thankfully, I didn't have to tweak as much as I'd thought. In fact, in many cases the plants were easier to work with, probably because they weren't half dead and had more moisture with which to reduce the heat. I didn't have to be nearly as careful.

When I'd finished the instruction, Finley looked at the others, eyebrows raised. "That was . . ."

"Technical," Arleth said quietly.

"Complicated." Delaney shook her head.

"What happens next?" Finley asked.

"Oh. Well then I just do it again and again until the order is filled," I replied. "For this one, I'll use the plants up, since they're picked. You can decide if I keep it all for myself or if you trust me enough to let others consume it. For the other products, I guess I'll just show you how with a sample, since you don't want to do anything with it?"

We did several batches of the next products, and each time only Finley seemed to catch on—but only moderately so. It was clear these ladies' talents were in experimenting with various plant properties: how best to grow them, how they were used best and what for. I was better at the more technical applications of pressure and heat, and had to rely on books to tell me the facts they had in their heads. All of it was just as complex, but a completely different facet of production. It was fascinating. I couldn't wait to learn more.

At the end of my agreed-upon day, I tidied everything up and started on the labels for what we'd finished but hadn't cut into batches.

"What are you doing?" Vemar looked over my handiwork. Finley turned to see, pausing in hanging something on a line to dry.

"Just labeling so we know what is what tomorrow morning."

He watched for a moment, his version of trying to figure out what I'd said. "Why?" he finally asked.

I paused and then half straightened up. "Oh." I looked at Finley watching me, and then the workstations of the others who'd gone out for a while. "Uh . . ." I dropped my hands. "Force of habit, I guess. In the village I'd label the product just in case Raz whirlwinded through and ransacked my desk for items I might use to kill him with—the drugs made him uncommonly paranoid. Or maybe I did. Either way, I always labeled the products so I'd know what was what after he'd scattered it around."

There was that damn look again.

I hated that look.

"Never mind." I bent to continue the labels.

Vemar's hand covered my wrist. "No, Captive Lady," he said quietly. Compassionately. "You don't need to do that here. If you are hiding things with which to kill us, we will laugh with glee when you try to use them."

I huffed, chuckling and pulling my hands away again.

"Yeah, I guess— Actually, no." I pushed his hand gently away and went back to my labels. "Sorry, this is part of my process, and it'll mess with my head if I don't do it. I'll spend all evening worrying about it and end up here in the middle of the night writing out labels because the job wasn't finished."

Vemar straightened up. "Well then, is it going to fuck with your noggin if I help?"

"You really don't have to—"

"That's not what I asked."

I gave him a crooked smile. "No, it'll just make the job go faster."

"Great." He set to work alongside me even though he thought it was a frivolous effort.

"Thank you," I told him, tearing up again. Damn these people and their touching qualities.

He shrugged. "There's an art to guarding assholes. You never know when you'll meet a broom handle."

Finley snorted a laugh, and I could only imagine how those two things correlated.

The next day, I had barely sat down to my journals and

more depressing memories when an angry knock sounded at the door.

I froze. A flashback of Alexander doing the same thing caused a spike of fear.

"I can get that, miss." Leala came from the washroom, where she'd set down some new bath items to try.

"No." I stood quickly and stuck out my hand to stop her.

It couldn't be Alexander. The entire castle had been checked over yesterday and throughout the night, to make sure everyone in the castle was supposed to be here. They hadn't found anyone out of place or any lingering scents that didn't belong. They'd even sent a small shifter through tight spaces. All visitors now had to be logged in, and there were more guards stationed around the grounds. In addition, likenesses of both Granny and Alexander had been drawn and posted, as well as any known employees. The castle was locked down. It couldn't be Alexander at my door.

Knowing that still didn't do much to slow down my rampaging heart.

I wiped the sudden perspiration from my face. "Sorry. Old demons, as they say. I'll get it, just in case it's"—I shrugged—"dangerous."

Her smile was confident as she stepped around my hand. "I can handle it just fine, miss."

I followed her anyway. I would never forgive myself if this was an unwelcome surprise and she was caught in the crossfire.

Cecil stood in the hall, his hands on his hips and his face screwed up in annoyance.

"Yes?" Leala said.

"Yes?" Cecil repeated angrily. "*Yes?* I tell you *yes*. She has ordered clothes and no pickup. Where has she been? They are just waiting for her, all the time. Just waiting."

Before I could step in, Leala tilted her head. "And did you send word to me that I should bring her up to get the final fitting?"

He froze with narrowed eyes.

"Exactly. We can't read your mind, Cecil. When would you like her to come up?"

"She comes now. Come, come." He took a step away, waited a moment, and then gestured harder. "Come!"

Leala turned back to me. "You do need clothes, miss. The ones you brought are threadbare, and Hadriel's don't fit you properly."

"Yeah, it's okay. I'll go. Do I need anything?"

"You need just yourself," Cecil said. "Come!"

"The guards are posted in the halls, but I'll still go with you, just in case." Leala smiled at me, stepping out ahead of me.

"Okay." I hurried after Cecil, who was already walking down the hall.

When we were nearly to the main staircase, little feet caught my attention. There were very few children in the castle. Sometimes visitors would bring them, but to my knowledge, Princess Tabitha was the only child in residence. I had only really seen her in person the one time, otherwise getting glimpses as she ran through the halls or was helped up the stairs or was in Mommy or Daddy's arms. Each time I'd stopped and watched; I'd always enjoyed seeing children's joy and love. When I worked for Granny, I'd gotten to play with a few in the village square —their parents turned a blind eye to it when they wouldn't dare talk to me themselves. I cherished the time and always had so much fun. I never stayed too long, though, not wanting to press my luck.

I paused and watched the little girl tottering. I'd been told she was just over a year old. She evaded her nanny's grasp with a hand stretched out and a "No!"

"What are you doing?" Cecil stopped just ahead. "Come!"

Tabitha caught sight of me and slowed a bit, sticking her finger in her mouth. A moment later, a look of surprise and delight raced across her little face. She put out her hands and said, "Ah!" before running in my direction.

I bent to one knee, unable to help my own wide smile, waiting for her to get to me.

"Hi, Tabitha!" I exclaimed, keeping my hands down so that she didn't get confused and think to hug me. The king's body language and general scariness made it pretty clear he didn't want strange women touching his daughter.

She didn't slow, though, barreling into me and laughing.

"Oh, whoa!" I lost my balance and tipped over, falling onto my butt. I made an *oof!* sound for fun, but tried to discourage her from coming closer. "Oh no, honey, no, you can't climb into Aurry's lap."

She did a toddler wrestle, wiggling into my arms and sitting down between my crossed legs. Immediately she started babbling as I looked at her nanny in alarm. Leala crossed to the woman immediately, unease in her expression as well.

The nanny waited to approach. Was this why they weren't worried about Granny? Did they know I'd end up dead at the hands of a big gold dragon?

28

HADRIEL

Now that the docks were open again and ships were coming and going, there was work to be done. I waved the report I'd just been handed. The royalty had made up some scare about a sinking vessel or some load of bullshit to then search as many people waiting for their ships as they could. They didn't find anything, though, and they couldn't detain the vessels any longer.

Fucking Granny! She was as sly as they came. I mean, fuck, there had been a trespasser in the castle, and I still had no fucking clue who it had been! In the last week I'd been busting my balls trying to work the gossip network, sharing everything I could think of, prying in any way I could imagine. I'd come across plenty of people that seemed like they'd had secrets, but when I'd hashed those out, it was stupid shit like cheating on their spouse or stealing from a merchant or raunchy thoughts about Granny's worker.

I needed to hit the taverns in the towns. *Someone* had to know *something*. I wasn't above bribing people.

In fact—yes. That would be my next tactic. Bribing.

Granny was not smarter than me. Her talents might reside in her cunning, but mine were in my ability to expose that shit. Her people had infiltrated this kingdom and were hiding in the shadows. I'd find them.

And while I was out there, I'd work on the problem of people still hating Aurelia. The queen had come around, thank fuck. After seeing Aurelia nearly work herself to death and hearing some of her awful stories, Finley had finally accepted what we'd all been saying.

But the general public were kept at a distance. Obviously, it was necessary, what with Granny's people lurking around, but it was still a problem. We needed to figure out a way around it.

"You were the cause of this, I know you were!" Liron cut diagonally across the hall, hitting several people with a large canvas, and stopped right in front of me.

I stuttered to a stop, rolling up the report and lowering it so that he didn't get the bright idea of trying to stick his dick in it.

"What?" I demanded, annoyed at his interruption. I was already late for the king and queen's meeting with Weston.

Liron held up the canvas, shoving it toward my face. "You did this! That woman has talent. You are killing her chances of doing anything with it!"

"What woman? What are you talking about? Get—" I pushed the canvas away a little so that I could see what he was talking about. Without a good reason to shoo this guy away, he'd just follow you, chattering the whole time. It was annoying as all fuck.

The canvas was alive with color. An abstract design in angles and lines filled the space.

"It's good," I said as each shape and color pulled my gaze around the canvas. "But what does it have to do with me?"

My words trailed away as I saw it, an angular dick jutting into the middle, disguised by the busyness around it until you actually made it out, and then there was no denying it. Near the tip was a collection of different colors in triangles, just as cleverly depicting a vagina.

I laughed so hard I wheezed, now realizing what he was talking about: Aurelia had drawn a dick into her design.

"If she had just taken this seriously, she could've gone somewhere." Liron shook the canvas at me.

I took it from his hands. "She's the beta's true mate and connected to two other kingdoms through magic or blood. She makes drugs and cooks like a goddess. I doubt art is the thing that would've gotten her ahead, you cumgoblin's wet dream."

I huffed in annoyance and continued down the hall with my new favorite painting. As I rounded the corner and nearly arrived at the stairs, a big shape caught my attention. The king was standing idle with the beta, looking at something farther down the hall.

It had better be a grizzly fight, because they should be in a meeting.

"What are you guys—" I caught sight of what they were looking at.

Aurelia sat on the ground with little Tabitha on her lap. Aurelia's hands were out in front of them, opened like they held a book, her lips moving and focus on her palms, as though reading. Tabitha was utterly engrossed, looking at the hands and then twisting to look up at Aurelia's face. Whenever she looked up, Aurelia would take a hand away and run it over the air, directing the little girl's gaze into the sky as though watching a painting unfold in front of them.

"Not that that isn't the cutest fucking thing I have ever

seen," I said, watching Tabitha crack a wide smile and bend down, giggling, "but what is going on?"

"We can't get Tabby to sit still long enough to get through a book," Nyfain said, riveted to his daughter in the arms of a near stranger. Shockingly, the guy wasn't running down there, ready to tear off Aurelia's face. "She always wants to move. Yet here she is, in the lap of her new best friend, reading a book that doesn't even exist."

"Well . . . that's probably it, isn't it?" I held up the painting for Nyfain to take. "Aurelia is making it a lot more fun than some words and a picture. She's turning it into a live-action, imaginative event. She'd certainly know how. She makes the fucking stuff." I pointed at the canvas. "Check that out. Also, Finley is going to anger-fuck the shit out of you later if you don't hurry up. She wants to watch the trial runs of Aurelia's new product batch. She wouldn't let Vemar take it yesterday without someone on hand in case something went wrong, so we are going to do it tonight. Also, I need to head up a drinking session—"

"*We?*" Weston cut in without tearing his eyes away from Aurelia. It was perfectly clear what he was thinking: he was ready for that to be their child.

"Yeah. You know, Vemar, me, Leala, no one else of consequence. By the way, Aurelia is going to be sick later. She'll be indisposed. Don't check in on her. Doctor's orders. Anyway—"

"This is neat. Why am I looking at it?" Nyfain said, frowning at the canvas. "Actually, it would go in our sitting room. The colors match."

Fucking dragons were always very calm when there were giant problems and insurmountable odds. Was I the only one cracking up from stress? The fucking waterways were open again. Granny's people knew, without a doubt, that Aurelia was here. They'd either heard about her presence, witnessed the fail-safes helping people, or seen her in the towns—or worse, *in the fucking castle.* They'd be on their way to tell Granny *right now*. She'd be showing up to collect *very soon*. We needed to get into that meeting and talk about all this silly shit before the chance to stop it slipped away entirely. I'd made a good friend, and I would not see her taken back to that hell pit.

"No, probably not your sitting room," I said, feigning patience so that I didn't yell at him and get my arm ripped off. I mentally amended my previous statement: dragons were calm in a crisis until directly provoked. And I did not want to be the one provoking.

Belatedly, I noticed Cecil standing off to the side, looking quite impatient. It was clear he wanted Aurelia to go with him but was not brave enough to interrupt the princess when she was having fun, especially not with the king standing down the hall, watching.

What's his game? I wondered. He didn't tend to have secrets, but he'd been awfully secluded lately. Now he was getting the captive in person? Since when did he bother?

"Is that . . ." Nyfain looked closer, pulling me out of my reverie. He pulled it back to look farther away. "Is that a cock and balls?"

Crisis or not, I burst out laughing again, drawing the notice of several people, including Aurelia. She looked at Weston, her smile holding all kinds of messages, and then at the king, with probably no idea he was looking at her art. She pointed Nyfain out to Tabitha, urging the little girl to get up and go to her daddy.

Nyfain spat out a laugh and then wiped his mouth with his sleeve. "This painting is hilariously lewd. It takes a while to notice, though."

"That's the beauty of it," I replied.

Nyfain passed it to Weston. "That shit is funny," he told his beta.

"No!" Tabitha shouted as Aurelia tried again to get the little girl to stand up.

"I don't see—" Weston huffed. "Ah. Clever. It's pretty well hidden." He turned to look at me then. "Did you do this?"

He passed the painting back to me. "No, actually. Your lady love did. Liron is pissed. He thinks I put her up to it."

Nyfain glanced over at Weston as Aurelia stood with Tabitha in her arms.

"A woman of many talents," Nyfain said.

"When you grow up with zero friends, you get good at hobbies." I beamed as little Tabby got closer. "Hello, sweet girl! Come here, come to Uncle Haddy!"

She didn't pay me any attention, not when her daddy was in her sights. She beamed at him, reached for him, and then thought better of it. Her little face screwed up in anger and she pointed at his face. "No!" Her babble was serious and commanding, and she was every bit her father's daughter.

Aurelia

"I really need to go get my clothes, or Cecil is going to pop a blood vessel in his face," I whispered to Nyfain when I approached. "I'm sorry, I tried not to touch her, but she tackled me."

"C'mere, baby girl." Nyfain reached for his daughter. She continued to point at him and opened her mouth to yell, "No," but he blew a raspberry against her neck and made her wiggle and giggle in his arms.

My heart squished. I'd never get over that big, fierce man so ardently loving his little princess. It was the sweetest, cutest, loveliest thing.

A tapping foot invaded the moment. Cecil was not holding it together well. He really wanted me to see those clothes.

I noticed what Hadriel held, though, and paused.

"Why do you have my painting?"

"Because you pissed off Liron, and I love it."

I turned my eyes skyward, my remembered annoyance flaring. "Yeah, he kept overexplaining like I was an idiot and then condescending to me. I got what I needed from him. I can go to the library for the rest. Sorry to say, but he's not worth dealing with."

Hadriel held up a hand. "I understand all too well, my love."

Cecil's foot was still tapping. Hadriel frowned as he looked that way.

"I'm coming, I'm coming," I told Cecil to keep the peace, catching Weston's eye and feeling the warmth radiating through my middle. He looked down on me, his eyes so soft, so deep.

"Hi," he said, his voice rumbling in his chest.

I smiled as I ran my hand up his chest and around his neck, angling up for a quick kiss. He complied, his lips lingering as I melted. The warmth overflowed, filling my heart and making my belly flutter once again. I'd never get enough of this alpha, I knew that now. I wanted each moment with him to last forever, each moment apart to be cut short.

"Hi," I murmured against his lips, wishing it was him I

was handing a cute little girl to, watching as her daddy hugged his little princess close. *Our* little princess. "I have to go." I gave him one last kiss, my emotion throbbing within me. "I'll see you later, okay? I love you."

I turned to walk away as affection exploded through the bond. It took me a moment to realize what I'd just said, something I'd been feeling but waiting for the right time to say. It had just slipped out.

I faced him with what I knew was an *oh, shit!* expression, wondering how he'd take it. I'd just thrown it out there, in front of his king, in front of Hadriel—in front of the damn seamster, for fuck's sake!

His expression melted from stoic to soul-warming devotion. He reached for me, pulling me to him.

"Gods, I love you, Aurelia," he said before kissing me, fiercely at first, then backing off into a tenderness so sweet I wanted to cry.

I guess any time was the right time when your feelings for your mate could no longer be contained.

"Oh my—was that the first time you said it?" Hadriel whisper-yelled. "Baby girl," he said to Tabitha, "we are witnessing the first 'I love you!' Oh my . . ." He waved air at his suddenly glassy eyes. Tabitha turned to grin at him. "Isn't this amazing? I love when beautiful couples with a lot of privilege and clout share their first, most intimate moments publicly. It makes me so happy to live in the castle."

I laughed against Weston's lips and then let him hug me, rocking me a little. Somehow, an audience was actually perfect. We'd gotten to know each other with an audience, fought in front of one, fucked in front of one . . . and were now officially in love in front of one.

"I love you," I whispered, glad to finally say it. To finally feel it. To have taken the fall and been held safe in the landing. "I choose you, every day, for the rest of my life. You're my forever."

I sealed it with one more kiss before I ripped myself away and went to Cecil, tears in my eyes and a smile on my face.

"If you take much longer, I die from boredom," Cecil groused, shooing me along.

I laughed, because that seemed perfect, too.

Hadriel

Cecil was all but sprinting. Why was the guy in such a fucking hurry? They were clothes. It wasn't like they would go bad.

"No, no." I pushed the painting at the king, then realized what I was doing. I nearly shoved it at the beta but figured he was just as scary since learning his mate's whereabouts had been officially confirmed, and decided just to take it. Cecil was hurrying Aurelia away. "Leala, hurry, catch up to them." I stepped in front of the king. "Start the meeting without me. I want to . . . check a few things out."

No sense in alarming them. Not yet. Cecil had never given me cause for concern before. I would hate to have him hung up by his toes for . . . whatever his secretive urgency with Aurelia was.

Shit. Was this a bad idea?

"No, is okay, we no need him," Cecil said. Leala hurried to catch up to them, clearly intuiting my concern. Her hand dropped to her whip.

"Yes, you do need me," I shouted, jogging after them.

After quickly stashing the painting at the bottom of the stairs, I climbed them and caught up with the small group. Cecil hadn't stopped, determined to hurry.

"What's up?" Aurelia asked, looking back at me.

I put on a cheery disposition. "Not a thing, my darling. Was that your first time declaring your love? I am gushing."

Her cheeks turned crimson, and a soft smile covered her face as she turned to continue up the stairs.

Leala put her hand to her heart. "I teared up just then." She paused. "No claim, though, huh?"

Aurelia shrugged. "He said we had to wait."

"Oh. Hmm," Leala said thoughtfully, indicating she didn't know why. "He probably wants to wait until the patrol is a little more settled with their new routines so he can take a couple days off to, well . . ."

Aurelia shrugged again as we reached the second-floor landing and headed toward the next set of stairs. Staff bustled by in a line carrying the new chairs for the banquet room. I grabbed Leala's arm to hold her back, allowing them to pass and putting a bit of distance between us and Aurelia so I could have a quick chat without losing sight of Cecil.

"What's going on?" Leala asked quietly.

"What's the deal with Cecil? Since when is he in such a rush?"

She dragged me forward through a break in the line. "I don't know. Seemed odd, so I thought I'd better come along. I can't imagine Granny got to him, though."

"Why not? She's got deep pockets. She'll probably pay better than the royals, and he'll be able to get out of here."

"He can already get out of here if he wants." She hurried us along, closing the gap between us and Aurelia. "He went through the curse. He witnessed the demon battle. He's seen the king, the dragons, and Weston's people all in action. Do you honestly think he'd stick out his neck and risk receiving their wrath? Finley alone would strip off his skin if he betrayed this kingdom. He's not that foolish."

"Well, someone sure is. How the hell else are Granny's people operating in the shadows? We have a loyal fucking kingdom, Leala. How are Granny's people functioning here?"

She didn't answer, her brow pinched in concern.

"Fuck this stress," I said as we reached the third floor—just in time to see Cecil's door shut. "Fuck!"

Leala reached it first, grabbing the handle and wrenching, clearly thinking it would be locked. It turned easily, though, dumping her forward.

"Keep calm," I whisper-yelled at her, taking a step up. "Don't alarm Aurelia until we know for sure something is going on. There's no telling what that mind-fuck magic will turn into."

Or what *she* would do. Or, hell, if she got scared, what the beta would do.

I missed the days when watching Aurelia felt easy.

The room was the same mess of color and fabric as usual. Cecil stood in the corner, bent over a table with a pile of clothes on it. Aurelia stood in the middle of the room, her hands on her hips, looking out the window dreamily. That woman's head was currently so far in the clouds she could easily be blindsided.

"How do you feel, love?" I asked as I edged into the room, commanding everyone's focus so Leala could poke around. The windows were all closed and latched, the room as stuffy as ever. We were the only four in the room; no one waited in hiding. "Are you desperately in love, or are you mating him for his gold? I get it. I'd mate that man for far less."

Leala slipped behind me, latching the door. Good thinking, just in case Cecil was the distraction.

"Why doesn't that make me insanely jealous when you say it?" she asked as silver glinted in Cecil's hand, catching my eye. He tossed it on the floor.

"Because you know I'd never be dumb enough to touch an alpha wolf, let alone *your* alpha wolf. Besides, he's much too headstrong—almost like a dragon, but more sane. My darling, talk to me. Tell me everything."

I meandered toward her, checking out the corner and not-so-absently kicking a pile of fabric. It gave way; it was a mess, not a hiding place.

"He said it"—she paused, clearly thinking back—"a week ago now, I think it was? He wouldn't let me say it back, and he doesn't want us to claim each other for some reason. Do you really think he's waiting because he wants a few days together for it?"

I fake sneezed just to turn my face away. I hated lying to her, but this was for the best. If the beta could practice that level of unbelievable self-control and refrain from claiming his true mate, I could keep my lips shut. "Definitely. He probably won't be fit for public. Much too possessive."

Leala quirked an eyebrow at me, and I bared my teeth in response. Yes, it was a stupid fucking lie, but Aurelia didn't know any better. Her gaping lack of knowledge about shifter life was a travesty, but for the present, I'd use it to my advantage.

"You made a big stink about getting her up here, but you don't have everything ready?" Leala tsked at Cecil, crossing her arms over her chest as she strolled along the windows, looking out.

I didn't know what she was looking for. Only fliers

could get Aurelia out, and no dragon would be stupid enough to betray Nyfain and Finley.

Cecil ignored her, finally pulling out a monstrous pile of clothes, all in browns and beiges with one article of cream clothing.

"Ugh," I said, the pile stealing my focus. "*That* is your inspiration? The most boring, drabbest colors you could possibly find?"

He turned to me and held up a finger in warning. "You shut mouth, or I stick dick in it."

Leala spat out laughter.

"Chew bark," I told her.

She batted her eyelashes at me. "Swallow a thumbtack."

"You think this is boring, yes?" Cecil spread his arms for Aurelia. She looked between us all, wary. She didn't know what to say.

"That means yes," I helped absently.

Leala glanced back at the door before continuing her pursual. I kicked another pile of fabric or dresses or whatever it was. I had to say, I wasn't seeing anything.

"So boring I almost fall asleep making it." Cecil shook his hands at the sky. "But you were a captive, and now we want you to stay, but the kingdom hates you. What do we do?"

"Certainly not break it to me gently," Aurelia muttered.

He wanted her to stay?

Leala turned toward him slowly, her expression quizzical.

"You can't have nice things. You cannot do flashy. No. So we do boring, fine. Look the other way, people, don't notice me. That's what we do."

I couldn't fault his logic, but I could tell from his tone he wasn't done.

"But . . ." Cecil lifted one of the garments and held it closer to her.

But what?

Cecil's eyes sparkled. "If you look . . ."

She bent closer. "Are those . . .?" She started laughing. "You put dicks with wings on it."

"Drab *chic*, yes? That is what the little pencil-dicked critter calls it?"

Leala straight-up cackled. "He called you a critter!"

"Drab *chic*," Cecil reaffirmed. "Drab with dicks. Yes? This is what works."

"Do they all have dicks?" Aurelia gingerly leafed through the contents of his pile.

"Not all." Cecil shook his head, showing some with other patterns, most fairly hideous, though I didn't totally hate the polka dots.

"Wait. Wait a minute." I tilted my head as I desperately tried to process this new turn of events. "First, I think I speak for all of us when I say that no, this is not what works. But . . ." I puckered my lips, looking around, wondering what sort of ass-backward situation I was in. "Did you practically drag her into this room to show her a bunch of heinous clothes with dicks in your haste to . . . help *absolve* her of her crimes in the eyes of the people?" I widened my eyes incredulously. "So you not only want to clear her name, but your plan to do so is to dress her in drab clothes with dicks on them? Am I getting that right?"

Cecil gestured at the clothes, his tone full of righteous indignation when he said confidently, "This is what will work for now. I do other stuff for later."

I lifted my eyebrows at Leala. Since when had Cecil given two shits about anyone? He'd never helped a soul in his life. Back in the day it had been because he was too busy surviving. Since the curse lifted, he'd been more focused on his job. Sure, he liked Finley and had made some great clothes for her, but he'd never practically dragged her up here by her hair with a half-baked plan to help her find her way.

Then again, Finley hadn't needed it as badly as Aurelia did.

"Just . . . so I'm absolutely clear." I chewed my nail, watching his every movement. "You are trying to help her by making her look ridiculous?"

He scoffed at me, his bushy eyebrows forming a V. "This is why you should stay to the chicken coops, yes? No vision. Useless. She is captive, okay? She has to fit in with the people. Be one of them. She's not royal, no. She just trying to get by, like them. Like us. These clothes, they will work."

I shook my head in bewilderment, turning to Leala and putting a hand on my chest. "Am I unpardonably jumpy, or is he nuts? Because I have a meeting to get to, and I don't want to leave you with any surprises."

"What surprise?" Cecil grumbled, approaching Aurelia with the first horrible garment to try on. "You find your small dick, *that's* the surprise."

"Both," Leala answered, giving me a small nod to release me.

If a dipshit like Cecil could fool me, it was no wonder I couldn't find any of Granny's people or learn her secrets. Or did he just confuse me? Either way, this was not my best moment.

I gave Aurelia a commiserating look before motioning at Leala. "I'm going to leave this to you. Use the whip if you have to."

I closed the door amid Cecil's protests and hurried to the place where I really should've been this whole time. At least I'd gotten to see a lovesick Aurelia for a bit. That had been sweet. She and the beta deserved this happiness. If I could only get my finger out of my ass and come up with a better plan than Cecil to ensure they kept it.

Down on the second floor, I headed to a mostly unused section of the castle, reserved for privacy when meeting with foreign leaders or dignitaries. There were no eavesdropping holes in the walls or drafty tunnels where someone might overhear what was going on.

The royals were present, along with Arleth, Hannon, Weston, and a still-very-reserved Micah. He and the king were not on good terms, but he was the commander of dragons. For now. He had to be in on this.

They stopped talking after I walked in. There were no staff on this side of the door, only a pitcher of water anyone thirsty would have to pour for themself. Until the door was clicked shut behind me and I had settled into a chair at the table, the king busied himself by shuffling some papers around.

"Micah, I'll expect a report when you've got the dragons better aligned with Weston's new strategy," he said, pulling a piece of paper in front of him.

"Yes, Your Highness," Micah answered, his tone flat.

"Now, Hadriel, this report you have," the king said, looking at me. "The findings are similar to my mother's, but with a lot more history. Who gave this to you?"

"I made friends with a sexually confused scribe while he was traveling. We've kept in touch. He has access to the archives."

Arleth flared her hands and sat back. "Then he would know."

"So, if I'm reading this correctly . . ." The king looked through the report. "At the time when Aurelia's mom would've been in the court asking for help, her father would've been four levels down from the beta, correct?"

"Yes." I entwined my fingers on the table. "He had more power but less experience than his superiors. His lower standing but stronger power made him perfect for seeing cases of suppression. She would've been directed to him, and given Aurelia's age and some guesswork, they would've been within five years of each other, give or take. Aurelia is beautiful, Eldric is still good looking, and her mom drew his notice, so she was probably also beautiful. A little proximity, and whoops! Banging, then baby."

Nyfain put his finger on the page. "It says here that he has two children. One is twenty-five, one is twenty-nine, and his current mate is the mother of both."

Weston tensed. "Aurelia tells it like her mom was in love and thought the relationship would go somewhere. If she knew he was cheating, she didn't pass the info on to her daughter. I'm not sure we need to mention that part."

"That woman has the most fucked-up life I think I have ever heard of," Finley said, "and *my* past is pretty gruesome. At least I knew where I stood. For her, the hits just keep coming."

"It's not any more fucked up than ours," Nyfain said. "All of us in this room have difficult pasts. She has been operating with incorrect knowledge, and the bad shit keeps piling up. It's why she belongs here."

"In a kingdom full of people who blame her for the drugs that killed their loved ones?" Micah quirked an eyebrow.

"We're working on rectifying that." Finley entwined her fingers. "We just need a good story to merge it all together. Bringing her here as a captive didn't help. It didn't set the right tone."

If the situation wasn't so serious, I might've injected a little humor by mentioning Cecil's plan . . .

Weston looked completely torn up. "I wasn't thinking."

"You were doing as you were told," she responded.

"I know. Like I said, I wasn't thinking," he growled.

A sizzle of power gave me goosebumps. The last thing we needed was the beta and the dragons to fall out and for the fairies or wolf kingdom to take both Weston and Aurelia. Vemar would go with them, and likely a bunch of wolves, too. This kingdom would go from the best to limping along. We needed to keep things together.

"Right. Fine." I shrugged, emulating nonchalance. "We have to spin a story. Whatever, we can figure that out. We do, unfortunately, have to mention to her that her father has a mate and two other kids, though. Can you imagine going over there to connect with dear old Dad and realizing you're the kid of the other woman? Not so awesome."

"Not so awesome, indeed," Nyfain grumbled. "It seems highly likely he is her father. He rose through the ranks fairly quickly and is only one step down from the beta. At that level, they don't challenge for placement. It's all about leadership and politics. Mostly politics."

"He is very politically savvy," Arleth said. "He's the protégé of the current beta, who is now up in his years. When the current beta steps down, which really could be any time now because he's having health issues, Eldric is all but assured the position of beta, defender of the throne."

"My rank," Weston said.

"You share your rank with a dragon," Arleth countered, "in a small and previously hobbled dragon kingdom. We are a young kingdom, since we have been reforged. Eldric, once ascended to the position of beta, will hold more clout because he is in a longer-running, prosperous kingdom. Your power, and previous second-in-command position in the Red Lupine kingdom, is the only thing that gives you anything close to a level playing field when it comes to status."

"Our kingdom will mature," Nyfain said.

Arleth nodded. "In time."

"It's more prosperous than theirs," he replied.

She tilted her head. "At present. As I said, it is a young kingdom. The trick isn't gaining income in one ruler's reign. The trick, as the late king proved, is keeping it over time. The Flamma kingdom has shown its resilience. Our kingdom has not."

"And why does any of this matter?" I asked, utterly lost.

It was Finley who explained, as she was better at breaking it down in layman's terms.

"They are considering Aurelia's possible status. It is based on her blood, and we must consider the various factors that may tempt her over to the Flamma kingdom."

"Oh." I laughed. "She won't give two shits about status and clout and whatever else. Not two shits! But did you see the bit about his kids? Their mother is powerful, their match was a great one, and yet both kids—a girl and a boy—have only about half, maybe three-quarters of his power."

"Aurelia will have more than him, plus fairy magic." Nyfain looked at his mom. "Her blood will build her status and her power will solidify it. Not to mention, she is one half of a true mate alpha pair. If she stays with us, that is worth a lot."

Finley clasped her hands and leaned forward, bowing her head. She was not great at hiding her emotions. Something was up. I was dying to know what it was, especially given the way Nyfain's brow furrowed with whatever he was ignoring through the bond. Forget anger-fucking tonight; they would full-on rage-fuck.

"Speaking of the fairy blood," Arleth said. "What do we know?"

Weston leaned to one side and pulled something from

his back pocket. He pushed it toward the royals, and I could tell he really didn't want to.

"My people intercepted Calia's note. We're going to have trouble with the fairies."

My fucking heart dropped so fast it nearly punched my dick.

29

AURELIA

Over a week after I'd received the oddest clothes I'd ever owned, I was hard at work and closing in on some truly amazing discoveries. Arleth and Delaney had been lecturing me on plants and their properties, and also about their complex creations. It was like getting that journal all those years ago, except better, because I could ask questions and dive deeper into anything that struck my fancy. My need to create more product had blossomed—truly blossomed. I was like a woman possessed.

First things first, though. I'd needed to do my duty and cut out Granny's threat.

The addictive element of that coating had proven easy to formulate, and therefore easy to counteract. They already had something to combat it, it was just too slow. After some analysis and trial and error—using increased pressure to force the plant elements to break down more and then adding a few different elements Delaney had come up with—we had something that prevented the addiction from forming. Take it with the drug—even the one I'd devised that worked really quickly—and there shouldn't be a problem. Done.

The sickness had been a little more elusive. It was caused by a poison the taramore root created when it was broken down—Arleth had known that one. The dragons had a brew called the nulling elixir that was essentially the cure-all Vemar and I had been using. It worked, but wasn't quite powerful enough to counteract a deadly dose of Granny's poison.

After a ton of trial and error, I found that the Everlass leaf was just fine with lots of heat—it was dragon weed, after all, and those fuckers blew fire. It was *made* to handle heat. I also found that it performed best when under duress. I threw everything I had at it: pressure, heat, ice, water. I even tried to find a way to get lightning to strike it until Weston had tramped out into the field in the middle of the night in a thunderstorm and dragged me back to bed. Vemar was still in trouble for letting me do it, though he'd been just as keen to try.

In the end, and with the dragons hovering over me like a bunch of nervous mamas, I'd found the right balance between pressure and heat and cracked the secret of the crowded Everlass plant, something they grew in such a way that it was very potent and thus very dangerous.

They could've spared me a lot of fucking time by mentioning that up front.

They hadn't felt comfortable with my recipe, worried that if I didn't do it exactly right, I'd kill myself or someone else. They worried doubly so for anyone else who might try to re-create it.

It had been a good point.

I'd backed off the potency of the Everlass, a little *too* crazy under duress—much like dragons, actually—and given the Moonfire Lily its first chance to shine.

And shine it did.

I picked it at night, because Arleth and Delaney had read somewhere that it popped up in places where wolves roamed, much like the way Everlass grew near dragons, and they believed it would be stronger and more potent when picked within the glow of its namesake. I made them gasp the next morning when I lit it on fire.

"It's a simple plant," I told them, breathing in the heavenly aroma of its perfume. "Its favorite things are in the name."

The addition of the Moonfire Lily to the mix had worked just right. Perfectly, actually, on the first try. Easy to work with, like wolves. The final concoction was even pink! Not so bright as Granny's crap, but still really pretty.

It wouldn't only work on Granny's product, either. They tried it on someone with food poisoning, and it had worked like a dream. It didn't have to be made as needed or heated in order to use it. All you had to do was store it in a cool, dry place and it would last for . . . some length of time I had yet to determine.

Addiction? Sickness? Problems solved. The relief I felt at having made something to counteract the coating eased something inside me. It eased the burden of guilt I'd been carrying since I learned the truth about Granny and her organization.

Feeling emboldened, I added, "Do you know what else will solve the problem? Scraping off the fucking coating. That's all anyone has to do. Spread the word and there you go."

They hadn't appreciated my candor, apparently. Or Vemar's laughing.

Goal achieved, and glowing from Weston telling me how proud he was of me, I now had time to take all I'd learned and really play with things. I had a whole list of stuff I wanted to try using the Everlass and the Moonfire Lily and the dangle root and some sweet flower that tasted really good and smelled even better.

"Aurelia—" Finley, finding me in the work shed surrounded by a dozen contraptions and with tubs and bowls and finished product ready to be tested, stopped dead in her tracks in the doorway.

"I can explain," I said quickly, my hands out, knowing I was not supposed to have woken up before dawn, and was definitely supposed to have stopped working hours ago.

She was afraid of burnout. I was afraid of the drug I'd tested earlier, the one that was supposed to give a burst of energy and instead was making me zoom around, jittery. I was working too fast and was high as a motherfucker. I needed to take the Moonfire Lily out of this one.

She looked over my workstation, noticing which plants I was using, the things I'd finished, and the chunk taken out of the sheet in the container labeled *Test*.

Vemar was right—I needed to stop labeling things.

"That creation, whatever it is, is denied," she said smoothly.

"But." I held up a finger, then launched into a very long-winded explanation about nothing relevant while looking in random places around the room and occasionally laughing for no reason.

She watched me silently, waited for me to finish, and said, "Was that an argument or your agreeing with me?"

"That question is a test, isn't it?" I nodded too fast and too much. "Agreeing. Did you need something?"

"Rid that stuff from your mind. We have something we need to do, and then I am going to force-feed you your sleep aid so that you will stop working. This is getting ridiculous, Aurelia. You *cannot* keep up this pace. I've let you extend your hours a bit because you showed no signs of fatigue, but eventually you will crash. Also, where is your protection? Where's Vemar?"

"I wouldn't let him try this product, and he did, indeed, crash. I'm good, though. I used to work from dawn until dusk, then cook, then do my art or read or—"

I held up a finger to pause myself, then my other pointer finger . . . then started drumming them against the edges of the table in a too-fast rhythm. My foot got going and my body followed, bobbing along to a beat that was probably so erratic it matched the pace of my heart.

"This stuff might cause heart attacks. Denied."

I shoved my finger into the air, saw Finley bristle, and decided enough was probably enough. She was getting ready to force-feed me that sleep aid.

"Okay, okay." I nodded. "Okay, okay. Whoooeeee! Moonfire Li-lyyyy!"

Finley, now officially unamused, sent out a burst of power and growled, *"Now,* Aurelia."

Thank the gods she had a lot of power and an alpha's command. It helped clear my mind long enough to slip into my alternate headspace and clear these chemicals from my consciousness. I'd learned after nearly dying from Granny's product, though, that the effects would stay in my bloodstream.

"Do you know what we need?" I said as I came out of it.

She was watching me. "Something to slow down your thoughts?"

"I have that. No, we need a way to test the potency of stuff."

She motioned around the room, and I stared in blind terror at the mess in front of me.

"I can't leave this mess. Crap, what . . .?" I grabbed the sheet from the test basket and turned to throw it into the garbage. "The last thing we need is a dragon getting hold of that and going on a tear. Just hang on a moment while I set everything to rights."

She did, stepping out of the work shed. Once I'd finished—my area was now organized but packed full of stuff and therefore ridiculous, and I knew Vemar was going to make fun of me—I met her outside. My heart was beating too fast and I was sweating.

"You okay?" she asked, studying me.

"I . . . am not sure, actually. I guess we'll see. As I was saying, it would be helpful if we had some way to evaluate how strong the mixtures are. Like some sort of solution you could drop a test product into that would change color depending on the potency. The more potent, the less we ingest when testing." I paused. "Should we be leaving the castle grounds this late in the day?"

"I'm not the sort of person Granny wants to capture," she said in a low voice, walking to the stables.

"Oh, someone should've told you . . . I don't know how to ride a horse. I tend to jump off, they try to kick me, and it's a whole thing."

She shook her head and looked away. A moment later, her shoulders shook and she lowered her head, laughing silently. Then louder until it was echoing across the grounds.

"Was it something I said?" I muttered.

That just made her laugh harder until she stopped, bracing her hands on her knees.

"The thing is," she said, "I'm supposed to always show decorum and maintain the prestige of my post. Arleth has spent a lot of time and effort—continues to spend time and effort—drilling proper etiquette into me. But you're just so fucking hilarious, made funnier because you don't realize it. Aurelia, tell me, how the leaping fuck are you so naïve? How is that possible? Hannon says you are every bit as genuine and honest and . . . wide-eyed as you seem, but I've heard your history. You're a survivor, like me. How are you so . . . like . . ." She made a flowing sort of gesture with her hands, swaying from side to side.

"I don't know what that gesture means."

She shook her head again, smoothing her hair into a ponytail. "Well, what do you want to do, then? I ride the horse and you run in wolf form? I fly and you run? I fly and my dragon carries you in her mouth?"

My wolf piped in then, growling, *"Nope."* I could only assume she was responding to the last one.

"Just so we're all on the same page here," I said, "Weston knows you are taking me away from the castle, right? Into the wood? Without a guard or anything . . .?"

She studied me for a moment. "You're a rule follower, like him." It almost sounded like an accusation. She was definitely irritated about it, that was clear.

"You seem to have forgotten threatening me with death for my involvement in the drug trade. But no, following rules right now is not my main concern. My fear is that Granny has someone hiding in that wood, and when I pass by on my own, they'll trap me and take me back to her. Weston's rules are an attempt to keep me safe. I very much want that safety."

She chewed her cheek, still analyzing me. "Fair."

Clearly this queen was not in the habit of following rules. Interesting she expected people to follow hers.

"You'll be on the ground," she said, "and I'll be watching you from the air. Weston's people are covering every inch of that wood in anticipation of this outing—or they will be in a moment. I told him not long ago this was happening. We've got you, Aurelia. You're good."

I nodded, having no problem trusting her. If she'd wanted to kill me, she could've ordered it done weeks ago.

"How about I'll just run, and you can do whatever you want?"

She looked out at the wood, at the shadows elongating and deepening as the sun lowered. "Yeah, fuck it. Let's see how fast you are."

We picked up a sack from the stables to put our clothes in. She held it in her mouth as she shifted, growing and growing until she was huge, burgundy with golden dusting, as beautiful in dragon form as she was in human form. She took to the sky immediately, and my wolf took off running as fast as she could, a thrill zipping through us as she did. Scents drifted by and the cool night ruffled our fur. Her paws barely touched the ground, zips of lighting in the growing night.

I'd shifted again since that first time, and I'd run with Weston, but his wolf had always been close, monitoring my wolf's progress. She had been afraid to do something wrong and hadn't let loose. She hadn't gone wild or pushed her limits.

Now she did, leaving the path and sprinting through the trees. Another wolf with a scent she recognized joined us from the right, and she leapt, her feet landing on his back and rolling him across the ground. Her yip conveyed her playful intentions, and the chase was on, with him coming after us with everything he had.

She was faster, but not only that, she was cleverer.

She slowed just enough to let him catch up, then she darted right, ducking between two reaching trees and dodging left around a boulder. Another wolf ran out, and mine opened her mouth and ran her teeth across the other wolf's back, shaving a bit of her tail in the process. That wolf started after us, too, and then another, our mad dash zooming in and out of various guard posts and attracting their chase.

A roar sounded overhead. Fire blew across the tops of the trees. The failing sun streaked across gold dusting.

Finley was probably trying to tell us to stop playing around and get a move on.

We were going the right way, though. I had zero sense of direction, but my wolf was not so unlucky. She used smells and markers and whatever else to remember her trek on the way to the castle. She cut across the land, nearly bowling into a big black wolf with silver tips on his ears. Its scent registered immediately: Dante.

Another thing registered, too: his wolf's magic reached toward us in a familiar way, trying to pull us into the pack bond. Weston could do it easily—or maybe it was that my wolf always wanted him to, allowing him to suck me into him magically and holding me close. Dante, though, didn't have nearly enough power.

My wolf slapped his attempt away and bent, taking a nip at his chest.

His wolf growled, spun, and lunged. We were already gone.

I internally laughed with glee, riding up close to the surface of my wolf, taking in all the smells with her and the delirious, amazing feeling of running through the woods with the pack on our heels. We weren't united, and my wolf wouldn't jeopardize the pack bond or Weston's trust, but even just having them with us was a thrill unlike any other. I understood why everyone had gathered to hunt in the old village, even when they usually didn't come back with anything. They wanted this feeling of running together, of working as a unit, as a pack.

More wolves ran out, and my wolf dodged. Still more joined us, only one getting close enough to nearly trip us up: Nova. She had great instincts. None of them could catch us, though, not until we finally crashed through the trees and met the big queen dragon waiting on the other side.

Her fire blistered the air, and my wolf was already dodging the blast when she realized it wasn't directed at us. In fact, it was up into the air, over the trees. The wolves behind us slowed at the tree line, watching my wolf for a moment before silently turning and drifting away back into the wood. Once they were gone, Finley shifted, ending up crouched over the pack holding our clothes.

My wolf cleared out of the way, and I shifted into human form, panting with the effort of the mad dash.

"Weston has been babying you too much." Finley handed over my things.

"He's trying to get my wolf used to the bond and her body and all that stuff."

"Yeah. Slowly, right?" She lifted her eyebrows. "He's babying you. Mates tend to do that. You need to flex or you're never going to learn."

"I think I just did."

She laughed. "Damn right you just did. Felt good, right?"

I had to admit it had. I also had to admit that her strength and boldness set a fire burning within me. A lot of dragons just seemed out there. I liked them, but they were on a level all their own. She seemed . . . accessible, somehow. On par with me, as ridiculous as that notion sounded.

She nodded as though she knew it. "Don't let him hold you back, Aurelia. Mates like yours—like mine—want to protect us at all costs. That is super sexy, but it can also be smothering. Don't let him put you in a gilded cage and fluff your pillow as he shuts the door. You gotta fly free and experience life. Or, in your case, run wild and call your pack. You're a natural at it."

I thought about that as I dressed, about the joy I felt that they had run with me. That they had played.

"By the way . . ." She gave me a side-eye. "If Weston finds out those wolves left their posts to chase you, they'll be in some serious trouble. They broke the rules for you."

"I'll do better," I said automatically as I fastened my shirt.

She froze and then pushed the edge of her hand against my arm, leaning toward me. "Ew, what? You'll *do better*? Gross, Aurelia. No, you won't do better. You already did great by breaking the rules so that you could flex and learn your wolf while she learned her pack. What I mean is they won't tell on themselves or each other because they won't want to get in trouble. If you tattled on them, it would ruin the bond you're just starting to build."

"Oh." I huffed out a breath. "Sorry, I'm not used to a superior telling me that it is okay to cause trouble. No, I had no intention of telling and getting anyone in trouble, myself included."

"Good. I figured, because you ate that poisonous stuff and didn't mention it to Weston, but you never know. Right, you ready?"

I shrugged because I had no idea what we were doing.

"Good enough." She started walking forward, her stride long and determined.

I hurried to catch up.

"Do you know this village?" I tore my eyes away from her commanding presence. There were probably few things more awkward than walking beside someone, staring at them bug-eyed while struggling to keep up for all you were worth. My weirdness probably made her nervous.

"Yours, right?" I said. "Didn't Hadriel say that?"

"Yes. I grew up under a curse where everyone around

me was dying—my mom, my grandma. Toward the end, Hannon and I tried to keep our family going and keep my dad alive while we stared death right in the eye. It was a miserable existence. A traumatizing one."

I nodded as we crossed the dried grasses to the lane I'd traveled before, leading into the center of the cute, homey village.

"It was also this weird sort of social time freeze." Her gaze skimmed over the houses we were coming up on, and I realized I was staring again. "The women here all wore dresses, tended house, cooked meals, looked after their mates. Hell, their whole world revolved around getting a mate and then looking after him. My strengths were more in hunting, fighting, weapons . . . It was no secret that I wanted more than that provincial life. But not following norms—wearing pants when I should be in a dress, putting my life on the line to get food when even men wouldn't, shopping while covered in dirt—all that was seen as . . . different. 'Not right.' And different here was seen as threatening. Hannon, too, didn't fit. He liked tending house and looking after our younger siblings. He cooked and patched me up. He was the rock our family clung to. He was mocked for it. Ridiculed."

Her gait slowed as the village neared; she was not ready to cross its borders.

"We were seen as odd, both of us. Our whole family, really. We didn't have friends, and while we could've had suitors because of our looks, we weren't respected. They tried to beat us down to make us conform, and treated us harshly because we wouldn't."

She fell silent for a moment, and I could tell it was cathartic to talk about it.

"Even with all that," she said, taking a deep breath, "I worked my plants and helped the village stay alive. I worked day in and day out trying to find a cure. I taught people how to work the Everlass and delivered any extra food to those too sick to hunt for themselves. Despite being an outcast, I created a cohesive community out of sheer . . ."

"Bullheadedness?"

She spat out a laugh. "Yeah, I guess. I mean, when I spell it all out like this, I'm like—why did I fucking bother? But honestly, at the time I just could not bear to see people suffer. I did not want my community falling down around me, because the unity of a community—of a pack—can help everyone thrive. The strong lift up the vulnerable. The able help the ailing. At the end of the curse, it was my village—poor, out of the way, and with no real resources—that was the healthiest. Why? Because we worked together."

"Or because one of you was a genius with plants and also a strong enough personality to force everyone to fall in line to save themselves." She looked at me out of the corner of her eye, and I shrugged. "I know from experience that people will overlook their prejudices to save their own lives or those of their children. Hell, the nastier ones will prey on your generosity out of pure selfishness, usually while also calling you names. But I get your point, even though I don't have any experience with it. I've never really been part of a community."

"Did you not give up food to help them thrive?" she asked. "Get punished but refuse to relent?" I found myself frowning at her. "Weston filled us in on your past. As did Hadriel, albeit in a much, *much* more colorful way. You stood your ground to take care of the children, often at your own peril. It isn't just one of us that is bullheaded."

"They're children. They deserved better."

"And the adults you sacrificed for? The meals you made for the sick?"

I hadn't remembered talking to anyone about making meals. It had been in one of my journals, though. Weston must've ignored the part where I was venting about being called names when delivering the food. That still annoyed me.

"I wasn't part of a community in the pleasant way, either," she said, "but I was still a part of it. I lived here, it was mine, and I protected it as best I could under the circumstances. I still would."

She really was tenacious.

"Fine. There are parallels in our histories," I relented grumpily.

She chuckled. "There are parallels, even if you don't fully grasp them all yet. Aurelia, my point is . . ." She faced me. "When I took my place at Nyfain's side, it was to fight for this kingdom. It was to fight for what I believe in, for a better place, a stronger, more cohesive community. Every day I work toward this kingdom's prosperity. I want everyone well, want everyone as happy as possible. I want this place to thrive. When you ultimately choose your path, you need to choose what will make you the happiest. You need to choose what you're most passionate about. With hard work and perseverance, everything else will fall in line."

She paused, making sure she had my full attention.

"Don't settle for what is handed to you. Take what you want and make no apologies about it to anyone."

30

AURELIA

She stared at me poignantly, and goosebumps covered my body. Suddenly I wasn't at all sure what we were talking about.

Without another word, she turned and started walking.

Damn her long stride. I had to jog to keep up while trying to stare at her beautiful, impassioned face and trying not to trip. It was a lot to handle.

Before I could even think of which questions to ask to get a better handle on this very personal conversation, she had stopped at a little house on the outskirts of town.

"I remember coming back here with Hadriel," she said in a hush, stepping up to the door. "It was before I was queen. He was in one of his very colorful outfits, and the people here had no clue what to make of him." Her face broke into a huge grin. "He lost a shoe going over a fence and freaked out about it." She began laughing. "Those were good times. I mean . . ." She raised her hand to knock. "Shitty times—the literal worst, actually—but there were some gems amongst all the horror."

The door swung open to show a frail man with loose

jowls and white stubble along his jaw. His eyes widened when he saw who was at the door, and he held on to the knob as he tried to bow. "Your Majesty."

"There's no need for that," she said with compassion, putting up her gloved hand to stop him. "I have been informed that you habitually take Granny's snacks, but to make it safer, you take off the coating."

The man froze, his eyes suddenly wary.

"I've not come to punish you," she said smoothly. "In fact, I've brought the drugmaker." She indicated me. "Aurelia does not make that coating—that is Granny's addition—but she does make the product itself. She is very passionate about it. She has expressed an interest in meeting with people like you to see what might be improved. Do you have time to speak with her?"

I jerked my head to look at the queen in dismay.

Shortly after the fiasco with Granny's cheap drugs, I'd asked Hadriel to ask the powers that be if I could return to the villages to take more notes. No answer had come, so I'd assumed they weren't interested. It had been a long shot, after all.

To hear that I not only got to make those notes—with a royal escort, no less—but might also be able to actually improve upon my product?

I knew my smile was giddy.

"Yes," I gushed at the older man. "The queen is correct. I heard some feedback the other day and wondered if you'd be willing to share some more? Maybe you could gather all your like-minded friends together, and we can get into it."

"Oh . . . yes." The man looked back and forth between the queen and me as though this might be a trick. "You're the drugmaker, you say? That captive they got over there at the castle?"

"Yes." I clasped my hands in front of me. "I am being

made to repent for my sins as part of my punishment. I am eager to clear my name, and am working on a way to make recreational and medicinal products safe for all. Part of that, per the queen's orders, is to address the woes and concerns of the people in this kingdom. Please, help me repent."

I wasn't sure where all that had come from, wondering if maybe I hadn't evacuated all of the trial product from my system after all, but the man seemed to thaw.

"Oh, right." He nodded. "That makes sense. Yes, of course. Here, come in, come in. Have a seat, please. Can I get you some tea?"

"Maybe just a glass of water?" I asked politely. "And something to write with. And on. Thank you."

"Sure, yes." He hesitated, doing a double take at my shirt. "Are those penises on your shirt, young lady?"

"Um . . ." I looked down at myself. "Yes?" I grimaced. "It's part of my punishment."

His frown was clearly meant for the queen. "Some punishment," he muttered.

He collected a few people from within the village. All of them were eager to share feedback, and I was just as eager to write down the things they had to say. We visited one other house before we traveled to another village, and then a town, my wolf running straight there, keeping in line with the dragon flying slowly overhead. Her annoyed roar when my wolf passed through the middle of an Everlass field made me want to snicker.

Wolves ran forward to greet us as we traveled the wood, the full night no longer a hindrance to my wolf's vision. They didn't run all the way with us, though, instead staying at our flank until another wolf took up the position. It was clear they were offering themselves as our protection, and each one of them extended the bond for us to grab on to. Given their offer wasn't grabby like Dante's had been, my wolf didn't slap it away. Instead, she did the equivalent of politely refusing, veering a little to bump into their sides to ensure there were no hard feelings. Flexing was one thing, but disrupting the bond of the pack was entirely another. I was sure Finley would agree.

After visiting a few houses, it quickly became apparent that I wouldn't need to visit every village or town in this kingdom to get a good idea of things that weren't working or that needed to be fixed. Most of the issues that were cropping up were universal. The few that weren't? Well . . .

"I need something for pain relief," one woman told me. "My back is always hurting me."

"You already have access to something for that," Finley replied. "There are many remedies for various types of pain, all of which use Everlass, which grows just . . ." She twisted and pointed. "Just in the wood there. Any of your neighbors, I'm sure, can help you make it. It won't cost you anything. Everything you need can be collected in the wild."

"I have that. But . . ." The woman had issued a dramatic sigh. "You have to boil the water and pour it in and wait for it to cool . . ."

"Your solution to that is to stop being so lazy," I said without thinking.

The other people in the room laughed.

"No," the woman persisted, "it's not just all the work. I mean, just popping something into my mouth would be much easier, but it's not just that. The Everlass pain formula doesn't work very well with the Dream Scape. My back ends up being much worse."

The Dream Scape was Granny's name for one of the stronger hallucinogens.

Finley tilted her head in that way that said the woman's

information was noted. She waited for me to write it down.

I didn't bother.

"If you take something like Dream Scape," I told the woman, "you're going to be twisting and turning and doing weird stuff that your back is not going to appreciate. You either need to take care of your back and work on fixing it, or you need to feel the pain after taking a drug. I am not going to help you ignore a physical problem so that you can make questionable choices and end up crippling yourself for life. If you want to cripple yourself, you're going to know about it. Stop treating me like a common fool."

Everyone gasped. Silence followed. I stared at her stubbornly.

"Well, you're wearing dicks on your clothes," the woman had muttered, crossing her arms over her chest.

"My willingness to wear dicks on my clothes but refuse your request should tell you how absolutely absurd said request actually is. Next?"

If I'd stepped out of line, Finley hadn't chastised me for it.

"Do you think you have enough information?" Finley asked as we left the house and headed toward the center of town. It was the fastest way back to the wood.

A small collection of emberflies drifted through the quiet lane. The silver moon shed its light overhead.

"Yes, I think so." I organized my collection of papers. "Question, though. Will I actually be reformulating any of these products, or am I just getting a fun brain teaser?"

"We will sit down and talk over your thoughts, and then choose one or two things that you can fix. We can think about putting them into the local market. We'll see how that goes. If it goes well, we can improve and/or expand. If not . . ."

"The axe, I get it." I nodded, thinking about, not just the things I'd heard, but the various other problems people had described. "I like this," I murmured as I took in the dwellings. The buildings were larger than those in Finley's old village but similarly maintained, with window-box flowers and manicured front gardens. Cobblestones didn't line this street, not until we neared the square, but the fine rock and hard-packed dirt did the job, the road smooth and well maintained. Every town we'd been in was the same. It seemed the royalty took care of their whole kingdom, not just the castle.

"What's that?" she asked as raucous laughter drifted into the night. Glass shattered and Finley glanced toward the sound, but it must've been behind this row of little storefronts with hand-carved signs of scrolling text.

"Talking to people, finding ways to help them . . . I've always liked this kind of work because of the challenge, but . . . I don't know, I guess I just like helping people. That sounds a little trite, but it feels like a better purpose than just trying to make gold."

She raised an eyebrow at me. "That's because you've never gotten to reap the rewards of that gold," she said.

"That's true, I guess. Hard to miss something you've never had."

She side-eyed me again. She was doing that a lot tonight. "You're so . . ."

"*Pliant* is the word used most often, I think. *Boring* is another one. Dragons tend to think I am too agreeable."

"Yeah. Why are you so agreeable?"

"I'm open to new ideas, but more importantly, what's the point of arguing when it's not going to get me anywhere? I'll argue if I can change the outcome of a situation, but there really is no point in expending energy just to be right about something that doesn't actually matter. It just takes longer."

"It takes longer for what?"

"To be left alone."

She stopped and put her hands on her hips. "Fuck, man. That's really fucking tough to hear. It's one difference between us—"

"I'd imagine there are many. Like height, for example."

"You were never on equal footing in Granny's village. Not ever. You were young and small, and you weren't trained to fight to compensate. You didn't have the strength and speed and ability to heal as everyone else around you. You were mercilessly bullied, right?" She didn't wait for an answer. "But there was fuck-all you could do about it. You just had to take it. Right or wrong, you had to silently take it." She shook her head and turned away. "Fuck that shit. That really pisses me off. Fuck those people." She turned back and put a finger in my face. "You're on equal footing now, do you hear me? You will learn to fight, you will join the fucking pack, and if I need to take over your training to make sure you are pushed, I will. Flexible is good; being pushed around is not. We need to make sure you are never pushed around, not ever again."

Swearing under her breath, her rage clearly needing an outlet, she turned and screamed into the night. A light clicked on down the lane, and I shrank back, not really wanting to be implicated in the madness. Somewhere not too far away, a scream matched hers, deep and guttural and clearly wild. And sounding very drunk. The town tavern, or one of them, was clearly over there.

I stared at her with a quickly growing fondness. She was the sort of wild my wolf craved, and had the sort of passion that spoke to me. She made me feel better about life, mostly because she made me feel better about my future. She was the sort of person that lifted up everyone around her, and I wasn't above admitting that, at times, I needed that.

She began ambling up the lane, and I jogged out of my hiding spot to catch up to her again, glancing back to make sure no one had come outside to check out the disturbance. I mean, I was with the queen, so it wasn't like I could get into trouble, but still.

She lifted her hands and twirled, and the emberflies scattered away from her reaching fingers. She dropped her arms again and watched them for a moment, and it occurred to me that she was stalling going back. Her duty was over for the night. She clearly wasn't in a hurry to rush back to it. She probably didn't get much time for herself where she could truly let go.

"I can't get enough of the light bugs," she said, her voice hushed.

I walked over to a shop, lowering myself onto the little two-seater bench out front. "Emberflies."

"Right, emberflies. I've never known the name. I've seen a few here and there within the wood, but this . . . They are so beautiful. It's like walking within a tranquil sea, slowly floating and swaying and drifting. Do they follow you everywhere?"

"They don't follow me. They just kinda . . . congregate."

"Around you." She wandered over to me slowly.

"No, around peaceful places."

"There is nothing peaceful about dragons. We had almost none of them before you came. Now we get to exist in a fairytale."

I scoffed. "A dark fairytale, maybe."

She laughed and took a seat next to me. "Is there any other kind? Mine was dark as fuck. Worth it, though." She was quiet for a moment, watching the glowing lights. "Listen. I'm going to be brutally honest with you. Magically speaking, you don't only need training as a wolf. You also need training in that other type of magic you have—the emoting thing. It's fairy magic, and we simply can't help you with that. As much as it pains me to admit it, you are going to need them. We can train your wolf, but they need to train the fairy part of you." She held out a finger. "Neither camp owns you. Okay? Weston is your true mate, and I know you love him, but he—and this pack—aren't entitled to you. They don't dictate your life. The fairies don't either. If help comes with strings attached, that's not help, that's a contract. Don't enter into anything you can't easily walk away from unless it is *your* choice. Remember what I said? Don't allow anyone to push you around."

I nodded as the emberflies shifted and moved. Loud talking approached from around the corner.

"If you get stuck," she went on, "Hannon can get you free, even just for some space in which to think. He has a soft spot for you, and you two are very alike. If you need to get out, ask him. He can leave at a moment's notice, and he will, to help someone in distress. He'll get you out."

"I don't think—"

"That's not to say I don't think Weston will do right by you. I know for a fact he will. You've made him question the rightness of the orders he follows. Given his past, that is a very good thing. It's annoying Nyfain right now, but he'll come to appreciate it in the long run. It's just one more guarantee that this kingdom will do right by the people it governs. And I'm sure Weston is making plans of his own."

"Plans for what? Why are you telling me all of this?"

"I am not telling you *any* of this. We are talking about plants and improvements and things we need to look into. This whole outing has been to get information from the people. I've said absolutely nothing about anything outside of that. I haven't even sworn. I've been distant and aloof and royal, as I am expected to be until things are decided."

"What things are decided?"

"I'm not at liberty to discuss. Neither is Weston, so don't ask. Just remember this: *you* are in charge of your destiny. *You* make the decisions. The days of people pushing you around are over."

She patted my shoulder and moved to get up, but paused.

"One last thing," she said. "Weston is a damn fine alpha, but he's an even better human. You got lucky with him. Whatever you need, whatever you want to do, he'll stand by your side. I hate telling you that, but sometimes doing the right thing is sticking to your roots. My roots, not yours. Yours are fucking depressing."

I huffed out a laugh. "That sounded like something Hadriel would say—compassion steeped in crass humor."

She nodded, then paused, looking at the emberflies.

"Maybe just sit here for a moment," I murmured, taking a deep breath to lead the way.

She laughed softly. "You're going to be a damn fine alpha someday, too." She leaned back, her muscles loosening. "You're doing the emoting thing to force me to relax."

"Sorry. I don't know how to stop it. Or start it. Or even that I'm doing it."

"I know." She sighed. "In this moment, I like it. And in this moment, you've clearly realized I need it. It feels good to just sit here in anonymity and stare at the pretty light bugs."

"Emberflies," I whispered.

"Emberflies," she repeated, just as softly.

A shadow blotted out the light of the moon, moving

across the street. A great green dragon curved through the sky as the patrol did its checks.

A moment later, a loud belch announced a man coming out of an alleyway up ahead. He staggered to the right before turning, his top half swaying a moment before his bottom half joined in. He worked at his pants, moving like he was on the deck of a ship at storm, before untucking himself. A steaming stream of urine splashed against the shop face.

"What the . . ." Finley surged upward, striding over to the man and grabbing him by the collar.

"Wha—" He flailed, letting go of himself. The stream went wide, spraying the sidewalk as Finley flung him into the street. He dribbled the rest across his pants as he rolled across the ground.

"How about a night in the dungeons to sleep it off, huh?" Finley stalked after him.

"Bitch," he growled, rolling over and pushing shakily to his feet. "Fuck you."

He swayed and staggered as he tucked himself back into his pants, watching her approach.

"Stupid bitch." He didn't bother buckling his pants, instead clenching his fists, clearly ready to fight. He couldn't have known it was the queen.

Finley's wide smile made it clear that was the best news she'd heard in a long time.

"Or maybe you'd like to spend the night facedown in the gutter, knocked out? What do you think? I'll leave you lying near all that piss so you can clean it up tomorrow."

He swung at her, his movements slow and jerky. She hardly moved, dodging easily, circling him. The emberflies started to clear away from the disturbance. He growled, a line of drool escaping his mouth, and swung again, way wide.

She dodged and slapped his fist before throwing one of her own. A jab only. It smacked him in the jaw, and his head snapped back.

He wiped at his face and swore before launching at her.

I was distracted from the fight when I realized the emberflies weren't fleeing from the disturbance—they were headed that way and beyond, fleeing from behind me.

My heart jumped into my throat, and I spun around just in time to see a large shape pull away from the corner where it had been watching me. It dashed between the shops. Shadows moved over the form, the person dressed in black, my night vision unable to pierce the gloom enough to discern if it was man or woman, young or old.

"Finley!" I shouted, up in a flash and rushing that way.

"Let me do it!" my wolf said. *"I'm faster!"*

"It will take too long to shift, just like with that rat."

I slipped between the buildings, following the sound of fleeing footsteps ahead of me. Feet scuffed along the gravel just as the shape disappeared around a corner.

With a burst of speed, I was there in an instant, grabbing the edge of the building and swinging myself around it. I slammed into someone, knocking the wind out of me. Hands grappled at me, spinning me around so I couldn't see his or her face, a thin arm holding me put, a glint of metal catching my eye.

A knife!

Panic surged through me, enhancing my reflexes.

"Stall so the dragon can catch up," my wolf yelled. *"You have hardly any training and don't have a weapon, but a knife in your stomach won't kill you. Play defense!"*

I took the suggestion, slapping at the hand with the knife and throwing my head back to smash it against a chin. Still the person held me, but their movements turned sluggish. They stabbed at my side again, so slow it almost seemed like a joke.

"Aurelia?" Finley called, panic lacing her tone—panic and blistering rage.

"Here!" I yelled, smashing my fist down on the person's wrist to try to dislodge the knife. They held on to it, but their other hand started to loosen from around my waist. They were aiming to release me, trying to get away from the dragon queen.

She turned the corner in a moment, power blazing through the air, her eyes on fire.

"There's a knife," I yelled, latching on to that loosening arm as Finley barreled into him.

She tackled him to the ground, and I was jerked down with them, wrestling with the weapon as she punched him. The person yanked, trying to free the weapon and stick it into Finley. I held on, just barely, until Finley hopped over to his other side and jostled me in the process.

My fingers slipped from the person's sweaty skin, and the knife was suddenly freed, but their muscles still coiled in the struggle. It slashed through the empty air where Finley had just been. The person, slow to process her movements, followed through on their swing, still sluggish. The knife sliced through empty air until the blade slid into their neck. They ripped it out again in confusion. Blood spurted from the wound.

"No! Fuck." Finley reached out to grab the knife and toss it away. Blood splashed across my face. She pushed her hand to the person's neck to apply pressure to the wound.

A wolf tore around the corner like a phantom. It pushed into me, separating me from the fray. Another was right behind, teeth bared, striking for the person's wrist and pinning it to the ground as blood pumped between Finley's fingers.

"Stand down!" she yelled, moving to crouch over the injured person. "Back off. I've got it. Get some elixir. We don't want them to bleed out. We need to question them."

The wolf released the person's weakly flailing hand. They feebly kicked at the ground.

"Fuck," Finley ground out as blood seeped all around her fingers. "How the fuck did you make him stab himself?"

"What? No, I didn't. He did that by accident!" I bleated, even though I hadn't actually realized we had been trying to keep him alive.

"Some fucking accident," she muttered, looking behind her and then back down at the man. "And making him slow?"

I winced, remembering what my goal had been. "I might've done that. I was trying to stall him until you got here."

"Well . . ." She tilted her head and huffed out a laugh. "Looks like you managed that just fine." She looked at his stilling feet. His hand went limp. "Dumb fucking luck," she whispered. "You're lethal even when it's just dumb fucking luck." She pulled her hand away, looked at the wound for a moment, and then sat back on her heels. "What the hell happened?"

I explained about the emberflies and the chase that followed as two more wolves showed up. I felt Weston through the bond, concerned but stoic, clearly concentrating on his job, sending people to check on me. He would not be pleased about this.

Finley sighed and pushed to standing before reaching down a bloody hand to help me up. I grimaced as I took it.

"You probably shouldn't have given chase," she said, her

hands on her hips as she looked down at the body. "You don't have enough training. Weston will scold you for it. For my part, I say that you did a good job here. At least we have an identity. We can look into him."

"What if he was just watching you handle a drunk?" I asked in a small voice, realizing that I'd acted before logic had a chance to filter through. "I personally didn't feel any danger."

She glanced at me and then did a double take. In a moment, she shook her head.

"Come on. Let's get you back to the wood and close to the bulk of the pack." She walked me that way, her pace much faster than earlier. "You're new to this kingdom, so maybe you don't know this, but you do not run from dragons unless you know you'll be chased if spotted. You certainly do not run from the dragon queen when you possess a knife unless you know your life is on the line. That's just a recipe for a horrible death. If he was watching me, he wouldn't have run from you. And he wouldn't have run from you unless he didn't want you to see his face." She paused. "I do wonder why he waited for you, though. Maybe to render you ineffective so he could escape before I caught up to him."

"Very likely."

"Yeah. Idiot." She scoffed. "He definitely does not know this kingdom." She put out her hand to stop a wolf that was about to jog by. "No, you come with us. Aurelia needs to go back to the castle. She's going to need a guard when she runs."

He slowed and turned to fall in behind us as we left the edge of the town and headed toward the trees.

"You didn't sense danger because he hadn't originally planned on attacking you," she said, peering into the trees up ahead before looking to both sides, assessing the danger.

It almost felt like she was *hoping* people came after us.

"That's a guess, obviously, but it stands to reason, since he ran. They're watching and reporting. Keeping an eye on you. Probably trying to learn the schedules—yours and the castle's schedules of patrols, guards, etc."

She stopped at the edge of the wood. A wolf stepped out of the trees, clearly waiting for us.

She nodded and then turned to me with a smirk. "We have the best alpha wolf in the world, and Granny has just shown us her cards *twice*. That's all it will take, mark my words. Granny is outclassed. She won't ever nail Weston's schedules. She won't ever find a hole in his planning after tonight, because there won't be any. The only reason that person got close is because Weston hasn't put his fortification plans into full effect. He's been rolling it out in stages. That, and the fool hadn't meant you harm. If he had, we both would've felt him long before you noticed him, and it would've been me who'd gotten there first."

A shiver ran through my body at the rage burning brightly in her eyes. She really, *really* would've liked to have gotten there first. That thought was both exciting and terrifying. Also a little endearing. She was providing safety for her people, not just for me. There were no strings. She enjoyed meeting danger head-on. She belonged with that golden king; they were both clearly a little unhinged.

Or maybe they were just dragons.

"I'm going to fly ahead," she said. "I can feel Nyfain's suspicion through the bond. I'm going to go antagonize him so that he forgets how long I was with you and fucks the hell out of me instead. Weston's got you covered. He had the pack watching you closely through the woods earlier. He'll be having them guard you now. I'm sure I'll get an ass chewing about stalling with you in the town, but . . ." She shrugged. "I'm the queen. I do what I want."

She made like she was brushing off a speck of dirt from her shoulder before winking at me.

"Hand over your clothes. I need to go." She put out her hand.

Trying not to be self-conscious in front of the wolf still waiting near the trees—I was really trying to desensitize myself to nudity, since I shifted a lot now—I stripped out of my things and handed them over.

"No dallying this time," she said, stuffing everything into the bag. "Straight back to the castle. Take the main roads. The pack will guide you in." She paused, looking me straight in the eye. "You reacted well tonight. Remember I said that. You have excellent instincts. We can build on them, and next time you won't need to stall. You'll just need to kick a little ass."

She shifted before pushing off into the sky.

31

WESTON

My wolf lay on the castle greens, trying to keep his composure. We both were. I'd known the ladies were going to the towns and villages and had prepared, but when the worst happened, the pack wasn't there in time.

Again.

It had happened twice—once in the castle, and now this. It would not happen a third time.

There would've been no point in sprinting through the wood trying to get to her. By the time we knew something was happening, it was a moment from being over. A mad flight to her location would've been seen for what it was: panic. That wasn't something an alpha should show his people, not in this situation. It would make them worry our perimeter wasn't secure and their loved ones were in jeopardy, and for what? Our mate was fine. There had been no pain, no real fright. There had been a thrill of surprise, determination, and a cool-headed decision. She and the queen had handled it.

Instead, out of respect for Aurelia, we'd stayed right

here, now facing the direction where she would likely emerge from the wood.

She trotted along in wolf form. I felt each member of the pack drawing close to her and then pulling away again once they reached the edge of their security zone. With each greeting, an offer was extended for her to join them, to join the pack. They really shouldn't have. That wasn't something a pack extended to an alpha; it was something an alpha extended to potential members of a pack.

It was especially risky because she was considered a lone wolf. Usually, lone wolves would either leap at the opportunity to join a pack or vehemently reject it, choosing to stay on their own.

She did neither, politely refusing with a soft touch. *No hard feelings.* Even after a situation where it would've been safer had she been in the pack, able to call people to her aid immediately, she was careful not to damage our internal structure. She did what was necessary to preserve it.

Finley's dragon appeared over the tree line. She caught sight of us and blew a puff of fire before circling, fluttering her wings to land beside us. She reduced down into a woman and brought over the sack that had been in her dragon's mouth.

"Here's her clothes." Finley dropped a messy pile beside my wolf, who didn't bother getting up. "She was fine. She was in no danger."

She told me what happened, surprising me with the details about Aurelia's magic. I'd felt her panic, and then her confusion. That must've been when it happened. Like how she reacted with Nyfain, she seemed to reach for the fairy magic when she was at her most terrified.

"She has great instincts, Weston. I know you want to wrap her up in a blanket and lock her in a gilded cage to keep her safe, but that's impossible with your position—

and her personality. She'll be safer with training and the ability to use it."

Now I was thankful to have stayed in wolf form to monitor our mate. I wouldn't have to be obvious about refusing to answer Finley. She was right, I knew, but still . . . Stashing Aurelia away in safety sounded so much better.

"Overall," Finley went on, crouching down beside my wolf, "she did well today. She even created a story about a sort of . . . quest for redemption that people seemed to buy. We might try to build a strategy around that, because—and I've thought a lot about this, and talked it over with the others—we're going to release some of her products. Just a couple to start, but Vemar has been right all along. The things I asked her to do weren't solutions, they were patches, and not enough to put Granny out of business. It's time we think differently about this."

She pulled her own clothes out of the sack.

"I haven't told you this because I wasn't really supposed to get involved, but . . ." Finley shrugged into her shirt. "She's fucking *amazing*, Weston. She's as hard to ruffle as you, with company as easy to keep as yours. She's much, *much* smarter than you, though. Good thing for you everyone in her life has always taken that for granted, or it might've been a problem. A beautiful, intelligent, hard-working woman with a knuckle-dragger like you? *Someone* got lucky with their true mate."

My wolf growled softly with the dig, showing his teeth. Finley laughed delightedly as our whole world lit up in pride. I'd known all of that, of course, confident in how incredibly lucky we were to have been paired with such an intelligent, enchanting woman. Hearing the queen say it, though, hearing her compliment our mate, knowing she could see the things we always had but that Granny had taken for granted or ignored . . . It was beyond special. Beyond magical. It felt like Aurelia was coming home.

"But seriously, she is really, *really* fucking smart, and she really wants to help people. After all she's been through, that's an admirable quality. It's an alpha's quality. I hope it works out for you, Weston. I really do. You both deserve to see some happiness."

She paused there for a moment, watching the ember-flies float over the grounds.

"Okay, seriously, did these bugs just start heavily procreating for her specifically? How are there now so many?"

I would've laughed if I could've.

She pushed to standing, finished dressing, and gave her farewell.

Aurelia's wolf came jogging out of the woods not long after Finley had said her goodbyes. Her wolf's tongue lolled from her mouth and she panted, having run hard. My wolf rose to his feet, eager to see her but holding his position only because her clothes waited beside him. She caught sight of him and put on a burst of speed, closing the distance quickly.

Her smell hit us when she neared; it was mouth-watering. My wolf ran his face along her neck and over her shoulders, breathing her in, feeling his ardor rise. She stood still as he nibbled along one of her shoulders, able to claim her right now if he wanted to. Wolves could do it as well as humans. He wanted the pack to bear witness, though. He wanted to make his choice—and her choice—known for all to see.

Instead, he pushed in close behind her, feeling the warmth of her body. Her tail swished and she moved, looking back over her shoulder.

"She's not in heat," I said as he pushed his upper body closer.

"I don't care."

I did. I knew this was inevitable if I ever took a mate, but now wasn't the best time. But up he went, his paws on her back. He wasn't quite lined up, but it didn't stop him from ramming home. I could feel Aurelia's confusion as her wolf shoved backward against him, and then her extreme discomfort. I would've laughed if I could've. Being a dragon for this part would be so much better. They got to at least fly really high and then tumble through the air. We just had to sit here on the ground as our wolves rutted away.

"Don't knot her," I told him. *"I want to talk with the human."*

"You'll wait your turn."

Super.

I felt Aurelia sink down into the wolf body, grumpy, clearly trying to get away from something she hadn't been prepared for. Still inwardly laughing, I pulled her tighter within the bond, feeling her emotions as though they were mine. The pleasure of our animals pulsed through the bond. I cuddled close, letting it all seep through us. My wolf hit his stride, then his finish, and Aurelia's wolf followed not long after.

"I am not cutting it short for you," my wolf said, standing on his own again. *"I am doing it for her."*

He didn't elaborate, and I wondered which *her* he meant.

"That was . . . strangely erotic, but also gross," Aurelia said when she was back in human form. She reached down between her legs. "Yes, it was gross. I don't care about it being natural for you—I was not prepared." She paused again, obviously speaking with her animal. "I don't want to think about that right now. I'll deal with that when or if it happens." Her fingers came away wet, and I gritted my teeth against the wave of arousal.

She lifted her brow at me.

"That was my first time," I told her, because for some reason, that seemed important. "His first time, I mean. My first time witnessing him do that."

Her gaze dipped to my hard length.

"This is a result of you, uh, checking things out." I motioned to her fingers.

She dropped her hand. "Sorry, I just didn't know that was a *thing*. I mean, I wondered after the first shift, but . . . It makes me wonder what they were *actually* doing on their hunting trips in the woods when they came back without a kill."

"Usually it's only when the female goes into heat."

"Am I in heat?"

"No, you'll know when you are. I guess maybe true mate pairs do it any time? I don't know. I hadn't heard."

"Surprise," she muttered, lifting her fingers to look at them again. "Do I need to . . . Does that count as something that'll get me pregnant?"

"Yes. It's a wolf form originating from a human mind and body. Our shifted forms aren't actually animals, they are humans with magical shape alteration. If that makes sense. Same heart, same liver, stuff like that, just different placements. Same semen."

"Huh." She went about getting dressed. "It is kind of remarkable how curious I have not been. I never even thought to ask more about shifting and stuff."

"You never thought you'd do it, so why would you ask about it?"

"Yeah, I guess."

I couldn't help myself—I pulled up her hand slowly and

sucked her two fingers into my mouth. They were just as sweet as I was expecting, and her eyes flashed with sudden desire.

"Because he's hot and not even remotely as hairy," she whispered, moving in close and tiling her head for a kiss.

"You realize you're talking out loud, right?" I murmured against her lips.

"Yes. My wolf was saying some very dirty things when your wolf was going at her, and now I just kind of want to keep everything above board for a moment. I just want to be a little more public about thoughts and feelings for a short time."

I laughed and pulled away, heading to the place where I'd set my clothes. "Now I'm curious, but fair enough."

"It's too soon to talk about."

"I understand."

"Maybe I'll say some of those things to you later tonight. Then maybe it won't be so weird."

"I support that decision." After getting dressed, I wrapped an arm around her shoulders and kissed her on the head. "I heard what happened. Finley filled me in."

She sagged a little. "I probably shouldn't have chased him. She said you'd be mad."

"I'm not mad." And I wasn't. Scared for her safety, yes. Angry at myself for failing to keep danger away from her, absolutely. But I couldn't fault her for what Finley deemed were good instincts. I wouldn't want the inverse to be true. "I would like to ask you to stay out of the towns and villages, and especially the city, until I can get everything set up, though. There are too many holes in our—"

"Of course," she said. "But this wasn't your fault. It is nearly impossible to lock down a whole kingdom. The people shouldn't be penalized for my troubles."

I walked her back to the castle. "I won't be locking

things down—I'll be setting up better guards and patrols. That drunk shouldn't have been able to urinate up against a shop after such loud and drunken behavior in the tavern."

Finley had knocked him out before helping Aurelia, and my people had dragged him back to the castle to lock him up for public indecency. Tomorrow he could clean up his mess and do a little community service to atone for his crime.

"It was long overdue. I'd gotten complacent, having spent too much time chasing Granny's drugs. The people like to feel safe. They'll appreciate my providing that for them. The criminals . . . Well, I couldn't give two shits if I fuck up their day."

She bumped into me as we walked toward the castle steps, a pleasant hum in the bond.

"My whole life, I've longed for that," she said softly as the guard at the entrance looked us over. His eyes snapped straight in acknowledgment of who we were before he opened the door. "I've longed for that kind of protection. Granny traded me for it by using me. She gave me what I ultimately wanted, but in a roundabout way—you. Because of her, I got you."

Her voice drifted off as I scanned the interior of the castle, checking to make sure everyone was in their correct places. All the stationed guards inclined their heads at me.

We wouldn't need such extreme protocols after Granny was taken care of, but this was a very good test for any problems in the future. Given the sort of splash the dragons were making in the markets and with other kingdoms politically, I had a feeling we'd eventually need it.

"I do it because it is my duty," I told her, entering the hallway leading to each of our chambers.

"You do it because you enjoy doing your duty. You enjoy making sure your kingdom is safe."

"Yes."

"I love you for that. It's one more thing on the list of reasons I appreciate you. I feel like I've found my dream man."

I waited by her door as she opened it, and took her hand as I led her inside. Only Leala's scent filled the air, but I kept Aurelia by the door as I checked the interior anyway, ensuring there were no surprises.

"And I feel like I've found true love," I told her when I returned, wrapping her in my arms and kissing her deeply. "I love you."

She squeezed me tight, the feelings mirrored in the bond and overflowing.

"Just give me a few minutes, okay?" she said, backing off a little. "I just need to write in my journal and get ready and all that. I'll just be a moment." She gifted me a saucy smile. "And then you can take me back to your chambers, and we can give my wolf a run for it when it comes to talking dirty."

32

AURELIA

"Time to seize the day, Captive Lady," Vemar said a few days later, standing just outside Weston's door. He wore a sunny disposition and plain gray attire.

"You look fresh-faced," I said, closing the door behind me. "Why the drab attire?"

"These are my new work clothes." He smoothed the fabric down his large torso. "If I accidentally blow something up and ruin my clothes, new ones will be quick and easy to make."

"Makes sense."

"So, I hear you're the quickest wolf in the pack." He kept pace as I started walking.

I glanced at him. "Where'd you hear that?"

"A little wolfie told me. Apparently, it is a big secret."

"That you will keep, hopefully."

"Of course." He put his hand on his heart. "I am very discreet. Everyone says so."

I laughed, shaking my head. "Is that why you are so sunny this morning? Did you get properly laid last night?"

"Getting properly laid yesterday was more of an afternoon delight. No, I tested your new sleep product last night."

I frowned at him. "You know the rules. I'm supposed to test that first."

"You did test it first. You did it last night, right? I'm sure you popped it before I did."

I gave him a flat stare.

"Anyway, it worked like a charm. I slipped softly into z-land and didn't wake up until the usual time. No sleep hangover, no grogginess, nothing. I wouldn't make a habit of it because I don't like sleeping that soundly in case something happens, but for a one-off, I think you nailed it."

I nodded as we walked. I thought I'd nailed it too. The first change had made it so it took too long to get to sleep, but this time it had seemed natural and just right.

"I think I'll make one that doesn't pull you so deeply under—"

"Hello." Farther up the hall, Calia, dressed in a beautiful sort of shimmering robe with tassels down the front, pushed off the wall. Her hair was done up in blond braids with little wisps of hair falling around her face. She smiled, always a beautiful sight. "Good morning."

"Good morning." Her presence confused me, and I slowed as we reached her. "You're up early."

"Yes. I wanted to catch you first thing. Word came in late last night from my king. I wondered if you had a minute?"

Vemar pointed at me, stepping away. "I'll catch you later, Captive Lady."

He walked off down the hall.

"Yeah, sure." I entwined my fingers as nervousness simmered within me, the conversation with the queen the other night coming to the forefront of my mind.

"Fantastic." She turned, holding out her hand in the

direction we'd just come from. "Please, this way. I have a lovely pastry setup in my chambers."

"Oh. Sure." I let her escort me down the hall, turning a few corners and winding toward the backside of the castle. Near the end of the corridor, she unlocked then opened a door and stepped aside, allowing me to enter the lavish space with a large sitting room and decorated walls.

A table displayed various pastries, like she'd said, with tea laid out in a delicate porcelain pot with cute little teacups.

"Please, help yourself." She gestured at it, stopping behind the teapot. "Would you like tea?"

"Yes, please." I took a pastry out of politeness, setting it on a little plate that matched the tea set that I was worried I would inadvertently break.

Once the tea was poured, she crossed the room, her robe swishing around her legs. She sat on the couch, and I took a seat opposite her. The furniture was white and easy to stain. I leaned forward and set the plate down on the polished coffee table.

"I'm so sorry I haven't had time to speak with you properly," she said before sipping her tea. She set the cup on the saucer and the saucer on the coffee table. "I've had some pressing business to attend to. Every time I come here, it is always a working holiday."

I nodded politely, wondering what this was all about.

"As I said, I got some interesting news from my king last night." Her smile was friendly. "First, would you be so kind as to humor me?" She looked to the side, where a shelf held a little red box with a very cool design stenciled on the side. "I have the kit to determine how much of your heritage is directly connected to fairy lineage."

Butterflies swarmed my belly. "Sure."

The test required a sample of blood mixed with a potion made by fairies. After using a needle to prick my finger, she squeezed out a drop into a waiting glass vial. Lights danced in a little orb and then a single color illuminated the sphere: cherry red.

"An exact quarter." Her smile was jubilant as she tucked the test back into the box.

"So, one of my grandparents was full fairy? Or maybe two of them were half? Or three—"

"It is very likely one was full fairy, yes. It will take some time in the archives, but we should be able to establish who was traveling or living near your grandparents at the time of your mother or father's conception. Likely your mother's, since the wolf court of Flamma prefers its higher-level positions be occupied only by wolves, though I suppose the mixed blood could be hidden if the magic wasn't obvious. We'll look, at any rate. I'm sure you'd like to know."

My teacup rattled on the saucer, and I set it down. The idea of family ties to the fairies spiked my adrenaline. It was like living in a dream.

"Yes, please," I said softly, clasping my hands in my lap.

Her smile was genuine, and I felt a rush of warmth that she seemed happy I wanted into her society.

But really, who wouldn't? The fairies were such pretty, ethereal, magical beings. Anyone would want a family tree reaching back into their history.

"Now." She sat back down, clasping her hands like mine. "Let's discuss your magic. You are what is known as an Emoter. The effects of this magic are just what it sounds like: you emote your feelings into the space around you. Those feelings can affect people in whatever way you desire. I thought you might also have some empathic traits, but I believe you have developed a sort of sixth sense to danger based on your troubled life. That is commendable, but not a trainable magic. The emoting portion of your magic, however, is highly trainable."

"That's the mind-fucking Vemar talks about."

She inclined her head. "It is. A very powerful mind-fuck. We have a great many Emoters in our kingdom; it is not an uncommon form of magic. Through intense training and study, most Emoters only reach a passable level of service. They can change a person's mood, mostly, turning a happy man sad, for example. They can make an enemy more willing to give up their secrets, things like that. We do not have anyone with the level of power you possess, able to turn dragons against their king. Able to send people fleeing out of the castle. We have historical records of Emoters that strong, but there have been none in recent years. Until you."

I massaged my temples, starting to shake. It was hard to process what she was saying. I hadn't grown up sensing my animal, but I'd grown up amongst shifters. I'd had a frame of reference for their kind. I had nothing for this. It wasn't even making sense. Sure, I now had proof that I had fairy blood, but a strong magic as well? I simply couldn't comprehend it.

"Are you s-sure? My mother didn't have any magic at all."

"First, we aren't exactly sure about that, are we?"

I remembered what Hadriel had said, that maybe my mom's ability to influence people—they'd hated her one moment and fawned over her the next—might've been magic. She had been looking for shifter magic all that time, not fairy magic.

"For argument's sake, let's assume she didn't," Calia continued. "Mixing fairy magic and that of shifters can sometimes be . . . unpredictable. Usually, one of the magics will be at the forefront, whichever is stronger. That is the most common result. That is why it could very well be your father who has the fairy magic, hiding it from his court. And then sometimes the magics compete and essentially cancel each other out. If you mother truly didn't have magic, this is likely what happened. Rarely, sometimes the magics boost each other, making each stronger. This is what I think happened with you. Your shifter magic is as strong as it comes, as evidenced by your true mate. Your Emoter magic is incredibly powerful, something we haven't seen in a long time. The emberflies clinched it for me. You have created for yourself an advanced warning system, unconsciously drawing to you the elements that would best display danger. Through training, this can be achieved in a multitude of ways, not to mention the other uses of the magic. You are a gem, Aurelia. A fairy gem. And my court would love to have you."

I froze at the last line as she once again got up, moving to a little alcove with a desk.

"What do you mean?" Explosions of excitement and nervousness went off inside me.

Her indigo eyes twinkled as she handed me a folder, placing a wrapped present on the coffee table in front of me with the other hand.

"Just what I said." She resumed her seat. "We would love to have you. You will have a spacious apartment in the fairy castle and servants at your disposal. We have carriages at the ready for our castle residents, so you will be able to leave whenever you wish. No more being caged for you, Aurelia. Your life as a captive will end immediately. Our tailors are the best in the world, and our cooks just as fine. Your yearly income is noted in that folder and is negotiable, though I think you will be pleased. The situation with Granny will be a thing of the past. Our guards will hunt her upon your acceptance and end her threat to you forever."

"What . . .?" I opened the folder and scanned the contents, seeing a description of the apartment, drawn pictures, and a yearly sum so extravagant that it seemed like a joke. This whole thing seemed like a joke, actually. A prank, maybe, someone having a little fun at my expense. I closed the folder and looked at the present. "What will I do there?"

"You'll train your magic, of course. You won't just learn how to work magic—you'll also have access to tutors, a large library, and other professionals to help you on your intellectual journey. I know how much you love to learn. You'll assist the king and court but will still have ample time to roam the grounds and gardens, savoring each beautiful day. It is a wonderful area with pleasant, giving sorts of people." She tilted her head a little. "You will be welcome there, Aurelia. You will be a treasured member of the community. You'll be one of us. A fairy."

I let out a shaky breath, looking at the present, still unable to comprehend it all.

"Please." She gestured toward the present, indicating I should take it.

I did, pulling the ribbon and letting it fall to my lap before peeling away the paper. Inside the little box was a fairy knife. It immediately started to glow when I picked it up, the hilt a gorgeous moonstone—a clever nod to my dual magic. It was touching. I watched the blade spring out, slicing the air.

"A gift," she said.

Remembering how she'd put the blade away, I did the same, setting it back into the box and closing the lid. My whole body was shaking now, not just my hands. Adrenaline and longing pumped through my veins. I felt incredulous but excited—and so horribly confused about the sudden turn my life was taking.

"You'll want to think about it, I imagine." She reached for her tea as I sat with my hands on the box, looking down at a surreal situation. "But remember, we are the only ones who can train you in your fairy magic, Aurelia. Any shifter can teach you how to run and fight—and we can employ a whole pack to do just that—but the dragon kingdom doesn't have the means to train you any other way. You need to get a handle on that magic, and we are the only ones who can help you do it."

I didn't look up. "What about working with plants and making my product?"

"A wonderful hobby. The dragons have fashioned their gardens after what they saw in our kingdom. We can purchase anything you require and would just ask that you make whatever is safe and throw away anything that is not. We would not dream of asking you to stop an art you so dearly love."

I looked up at her then. "And Weston?"

She smiled at me warmly. "Has an open invite to join you. Your apartment has plenty of space for you both, and a family if you choose it. It would be a dream to have such a powerful alpha represented in our court. There, he would get to reclaim his true right—the title of alpha."

I nodded slowly and gathered up my things, putting the ribbon and wrapping on the coffee table. She stood as I did, her hands clasped in front of her and her smile so pretty.

"We could be friends, Aurelia," she said, and I could tell she meant it. Longed for it, even. "I don't have many because of my position. I can't be open with the people here because of it, either. My relationships are always strained, and with my sister gone, I don't have anyone to confide in. You'd be entering the court at a status similar to me. Your magic is that attractive to the king. We could be like sisters, open with each other in a way we couldn't be here. In a way the royals here can't be with anyone below them. In a way Weston can't be with the people below him —your fate should you become a beta at his side." She stepped toward me and put a hand on mine. "Think about it, will you?"

"Yes," I whispered. I couldn't believe I was getting this offer. I couldn't believe I'd have any sort of status in a fairy court.

In a fucking *fairy court*!

I'd dreamt of this. This was one of my wildest fantasies, and it had the potential to actually come true.

Was I dreaming? I had to be dreaming.

I didn't remember leaving. I didn't even remember the walk from her room back to mine to deposit the folder. The guards could've been gone and Granny herself could be following me and I wouldn't have noticed. I did remember taking the knife out of the box. I still held it as I walked out to the work shed, everything around me floating with a strange sort of surreal quality.

"Welcome back, Captive Lady." Vemar was working on making more of the sleeping product. Finley had yet to try it or approve of it, but it seemed Vemar was so sure it would pass that he was going ahead with it.

"You're late this morning," Delaney said, glancing over at me. She did a double take. I had no idea what sort of expression was on my face, but it was enough to make her study me for a moment. She then looked at Arleth, who had stopped to study me as well. They shared a look, and it was clear they knew what had happened. They'd known an offer like this was going to come, one with all sorts of perks attached, with promises of training and tutors and the sort of fairytale life that was not meant for people like me.

I started laughing as I got to work. A quarter of me was fairy.

I was a full quarter fairy, with fairy blood and fairy magic. Someone was playing a joke on me.

My day felt slow, but it was over in a blink. My mind just kept replaying the things Calia had said. Freedom to go where I chose. Room for Weston and a family. A promise of friendship.

I'd have a fairy bestie.

I laughed again as I was leaving the work shed, intending to head to my room and finish the last journal. I had all my notes, I had all my ideas, and now I just needed to put it on a map to see if it yielded any results. I didn't know much of the world, not even my home kingdom. I had names, a few repeated over and over throughout the years, but no real idea what those names meant.

Instead of heading that way, though, I found myself sitting on a bench, looking out at the wood.

Vemar sat down next to me. He crossed an ankle over a knee and laid his arm across the back of the bench, content with silence. The guy could really read a room.

"She said she'd take care of my Granny problem," I told him, assuming he knew the situation. He hadn't seemed overly surprised about seeing Calia earlier. "She said that if I agreed to her offer, she'd send guards to hunt Granny."

"I recall that we tried that, too. We found you instead."

"No, you guys found her—you just weren't quick enough to grab her. You were plenty quick to grab me."

"Ah. Well then, maybe they are quicker."

I shook my head, looking away. "They aren't. I know that they aren't. Weston and the dragons are having a hard time with her. I've spotted two of her people following me, but who knows how many of them I haven't."

"This is true, but Weston is on the case."

"I know. I trust him. He's the best, isn't he? Everyone seems to think he is."

"I don't know, but he is definitely one of them."

I nodded slowly, tears in my eyes. "I don't want Granny killed. I don't want her hurt. I know I should for what she's done to me, but tearing down her livelihood feels like enough. My act of war is enough. I don't want more."

"I don't know that you'll have that choice."

"I know," I said softly.

I closed my eyes as the breeze slid across my face. We fell into silence for a while as the afternoon waned. Butterflies fluttered across the greens, and I wondered if I could somehow gather them like I seemed to do with the emberflies.

"I'm an Emoter," I told him. "I'm a powerful Emoter. That's the mind-fucking. I don't know when I'm doing it. She said she'd train me. Well, someone would train me, I guess."

"An Emoter, huh? That's pretty cool. You get to be two things. I'm just a dragon. Of course, being a dragon is a privilege, so I would say I come out on top."

I chuckled even as I rolled my eyes. "If you were Hadriel I'd say, 'No, you're two things as well. You're also an asshole.'"

He laughed. "Good one. How does it feel to know you have powerful, in-demand fairy magic?"

I bit my lip. "Really fucking good."

"Fucking A." He bumped my shoulder with his.

"I want to be trained."

"I would, too."

"It sounded like I'd have to go there to get trained,

though. I'd be high status and have a bunch of gold and be in their court."

"Sounds like a dream come true."

"It does." I chewed my fingernail. "My job would be to emote. Making drugs would become a hobby."

"Fun hobby."

I squinted as I looked off to the right, to the sun blaring through the tops of trees. "She didn't say it outright, but she did give an example of an Emoter *encouraging* an enemy to divulge information."

"That would be useful."

I continued to chew my nail, not really liking the sound of messing with people in that way. "She said she'd bring in a pack to train me as a shifter."

This time he didn't respond immediately. When he did, I could only describe it as careful. "I don't know if that setup would fit your needs for a pack, but I could be wrong."

"I don't even know what my needs for a pack are. I still haven't experienced one."

"Maybe you should."

"I don't want to step on any toes or mess up what's already established."

He looked at me. "I get that, Aurelia. I really do. But you need to make an informed decision. You've been solitary all your life. You've existed without a pack bond. You know what that is like. Now you need to know what it is like to have one. If the desire to live with the fairies is more appealing than a pack bond, well . . ."

"Yeah," I said softly. "She said Weston could go. That he'd be an alpha there."

"Did you talk to him about it?"

"Not yet." I remembered Finley saying that he would stand beside me. "Calia said that here I would be kind of alone. The royals are a step above and don't really make friends below them, and I know Weston stays removed from the pack socially. She said she and I could be friends, since we'd be of similar status. Is that true about the people here?"

He adjusted in his seat, getting a little more comfortable. "Truthfully, I don't know. I can see your being friends with Finley behind closed doors. She wasn't brought up a royal, and she chooses when to follow those rules. I know Weston has a beer with them on occasion. I think Calia might've been painting a picture that's a little too black and white. But if you were to take a beta position, if that is something you're able to do, I know it'll get a lot more complicated with those below you. Weston stays removed for a reason. Whether you will have to do that as well, I don't know. He was raised and trained for the position he is in. You were not. That might make a difference with how each of you sees things."

He turned his head, meeting my eyes.

"What about you?" I asked quietly. "What about Hadriel?"

His answering smile filled me with relief. "We aren't the type to follow rules or give a shit about status. You don't need to worry about our friendship going to shit, Captive Lady. We're with you to the end."

I returned his smile and then went back to watching the trees sway in the wind. We didn't talk about it anymore, and when the light started to drain from the sky, I made my way to my room only to find Hadriel already there.

"Hey," I said as he and Leala looked up from the table.

"Hello, miss." Leala stood. "We got a note from the royals. They asked if you'd like to dine with them this evening."

More fireworks went off in my belly as I remembered what Finley had said: she wouldn't kill me, but I might need to leave to avoid a political mess. Would the royals of this court make an offer like Calia did? Or would they want to punish me for entertaining Calia's offer behind their backs?

Before I knew it, it was nearly time for dinner. I looked out the sliding glass door at the fading light. The first of the emberflies were making their way closer.

I summoned my courage. Suddenly I wanted to escape right now.

I finished off my daily journal entry in silence and then organized the notes I'd taken that day to make things more concise, noting I'd need to hit the library for a map. Then I made some food. The dish was fairly simple—roasted chicken and vegetables—but I worked with the spices, new and old, to see if I could make it more interesting somehow. Once it was done, I left it in the oven to keep warm for Hadriel or whoever barged in here with an appetite.

A short time later, Leala popped her head in the room and said, "Ready?" I'd put on plain black clothes—no dicks—and put my hair up, then added a touch of makeup.

I felt Weston through the bond, his emotions turbulent, matching mine.

Would he go to the fairy kingdom with me? Standing by me didn't mean he'd *want* to leave his home and his job and go somewhere without a pack. I wondered if he'd enjoy the chance to be around people of his status, to be able to open up a bit more and join the parties.

Maybe that was wishful thinking.

Was this why he hadn't yet claimed me? It wouldn't make sense to claim each other if I was going to leave and he didn't want to go.

My heart hurt with that thought as Leala led me up the

stairs and down a hall, stopping before a set of double doors.

"Good luck," she said, smiling supportively, and turned to leave.

The attendants opened the doors, and I stepped through, finding the king and queen already seated at the table. The queen sat at the head and the king was on her right, leaving an open place setting in front of him.

"Aurelia." The king stood as I entered, then circled around the table to pull out my chair.

"Thank you," I murmured, taking a seat.

Someone came around with wine just as Nyfain sat back down, pouring us each a glass.

Nyfain wasted no time getting to the point. "I heard you had a meeting with Calia." His gaze was hyper-focused.

"This morning, yes." I leaned back so the attendant could put my napkin in my lap for me—a little overkill.

"She identified you as an Emoter, correct?"

"Yes."

"And of course you know that you are also a very powerful wolf."

"Right. I need training for both."

The soup was put in front of us, and I reached for the salt without tasting it. The castle chef was pretty consistent with the lack of seasoning. Calia had said the fairy cooks were some of the best in the world. I should've asked her what she thought of the food here. I would love to meet with people with a similar culinary passion and trade secrets with one another. Another hobby, perhaps.

Nyfain delicately dipped his spoon into the soup and then ran the bottom of it against the far edge of the bowl. He brought it up to his lips slowly, then sipped from the side of the spoon daintily.

My stomach churned as I picked up my spoon. I'd never looked even remotely that sophisticated when I ate. I wouldn't even know where to start.

I noticed Finley staring at me. When I glanced that way, she winked before unceremoniously dipping her spoon into her soup, letting the drips on the bottom fall back into the bowl, and slurping it into her mouth.

I smiled gratefully and nearly laughed. Nyfain glanced up at me and then noticed Finley.

"Excuse me." He gave me a little smile. "I was forgetting myself."

He dropped the poshness immediately, and my anxiety eased a little.

"I'll just get down to it," he said. "I know what her offer was. We cannot match even half of the yearly gold allotment. This kingdom was ailing for many years. It's tiny in comparison to some of the other kingdoms. We are trying to expand and fortify. Most of what we make is pumped back into those efforts."

"We're looking after the people," Finley added, "making sure those without much have proper housing, medicine, and education. We're expanding communities—training teachers and healers, installing recreational centers and instituting various programs for the youth. We want to make this an amazing place to live, and the steps we are taking have been positive. Because of that, though, we have less discretionary gold. Nearly every coin is put to work."

I finished half of my soup and laid down my spoon. "I understand that."

"Your status here would be similar to what Calia is promising," Nyfain said.

"But as a re-established and therefore new kingdom, one with a common queen and a king without a longstanding royal bloodline, your status across kingdoms wouldn't be as high."

Nyfain's jaw clenched. He did not appreciate his mate shooting down his bartering chip.

"You'd be granted an apartment," Nyfain said. "Something large enough to house the family you so clearly want."

I felt my face redden as a server cleared our bowls.

"What about my status as a captive?" I asked. "What about my freedom? The fairies would let me come and go. Their kingdom doesn't despise me for who I am or what I've done."

"When they find out, and they *will* find out"—Nyfain gave me a pointed look—"they may very well despise you. You've created a lot of problems there, same as here. They might not say it outright, given your status, but you'll be able to tell that they are thinking it. You can't outrun your past with Granny, Aurelia. Here, we will help you work through it. We'll integrate you into our pack. You already know some of them, and they like and respect you. Weston thinks it would be an easy transition."

Finley added, "Though Weston is not sure how a true mate alpha pair will work."

Nyfain's eyes sparked fire as he looked over at her.

"I will not lie to her, Nyfain, or gloss over the truth." Her eyes sparked right back. "You and Calia are going to go to war over this, and that's fine, but she has a right to know all the facts. This is her life we're dealing with."

I felt a rush of gratitude that Finley was breaking things down for me. That she was trying to give me a fair picture regardless of what it might mean for her kingdom. Nyfain and Calia were focused on what I could give them—just as Granny had done. Finley was trying to help me decide what I wanted for myself. She was trying to look after me, her own interests be damned.

I also realized that this was what Finley had meant about my possibly needing to get away. Calia had been very nice, but she had hit all the hot buttons that could convince me to go. Nyfain clearly knew it and was prepared to play dirty in response. They were fighting over me. I went from a person no one wanted in their community to a person two kingdoms were fighting over.

I started laughing as a server refilled our glasses.

Nyfain turned his attention back to me. "Is something funny?"

"Yes. All of this." I gestured around the extravagant room with the well-dressed servers and all the utensils needed for just one dinner. "Did you know I used to dream that I was a fairy? I used to dream that I would meet a fairy prince and live in his castle with attendants and white horses."

An attendant bent to Nyfain's ear, whispering something. Nyfain nodded, then focused back on me.

"Instead, you've met your true mate," he said. "Something much more desirable than a fairy prince. Trust me."

"Calia mentioned that she would have Granny captured," I said, just to see his reaction.

Nyfain huffed humorlessly. "Calia is very good at telling people what they want to hear. We tried to hunt Granny and nearly caught her—I'm sure you remember. She's gone underground. None of our informants have heard a word about her."

"She sent her snacks to other kingdoms, by the way," Finley cut in. "Deaths were reported. It was mayhem. She unloaded a lot of product trying to find you."

"And she has," I replied. "She may not be able to get to me, but she knows where I am."

"You're right, she does." Finley inclined her head. "And though Hadriel is now working within the cities and towns trying to find both these elusive watchers and the people who brought in and released product right under our noses, he's only gotten a couple leads. No solid hits. That woman is incredibly cunning. I've never seen anything like it. Neither have the fairies. You can believe whatever else you want, Aurelia, but do not believe Calia when she says they'll capture Granny. She is being far too optimistic. We were at one time, as well. That is why you are here. We've seen the error of our ways."

Her words sent tingles down my spine; her statement was more poignant because of how truthful she'd been a moment ago.

"Unlike the fairies," Nyfain said, "we have Weston. He has devised a thorough defensive system that we are actively putting in place."

Finley murmured, "I mentioned that to you the other day." I nodded once, indicating I remembered.

"When we hear of trouble, we do not rest until we root it out," he went on, rage seeping into his voice. "It is why you were found. It is why we continue to support you in your quest to end Granny's dangerous products. We will not rest until your safety is guaranteed. We will protect you until you are trained enough to protect yourself."

His vow sent more tingles running across my skin, as did Finley's serious nod. Nyfain might've been playing with my emotions, having had access to my journals and knowing how desperate I'd always been for protection, but his declaration was still such a relief. The threat I faced now was different than it had been when I was young, but it was just as terrifying.

The next dish came out, and I was surprised to see that

it was the chicken and potatoes I'd cooked before coming here.

"How'd . . ." I stared down at it. "Why?"

"Hadriel had it brought up. He said it was too good for us to pass up." Nyfain scented the plate in front of him. "Smells delicious."

"It might be a little dried out because it was left in the oven to warm." I cut into it, slipping the bite into my mouth. I had to say, the spices really worked this time.

"Fucking hell," Finley said, chewing with her eyes closed. "This is delicious."

"What would my job here be?" I asked.

Nyfain glanced at Finley.

"We don't know yet," she said. "Obviously, we really hope you can work alongside Weston as a true mate pair. In a perfect world, you'd co-lead the pack with him. We'd like to train you for combat because of your fairy magic—"

"I don't know how to use it. Calia mentioned that I'd get training for it after accepting her offer."

Nyfain's lips tightened as he cut a piece of chicken. "We'll need to sort something out. The fairy king always has a price."

"What about making my products?"

Finley answered, "That would be one of your duties. Vemar mentioned that the sleep aid was great. I'll try it—"

Nyfain cut her off. "No you will not."

She gave him an annoyed look before turning back to me. "We'll go slow rolling them out, and some will be available only through our medics just to make sure nothing is being abused, but it seems there is a need for them. I'd like to fulfill that need. Here, and elsewhere."

"Listen, Aurelia, we know Calia's offer is incredibly attractive," Nyfain said. "It is a lot of gold. What her kingdom doesn't have, and what she comes here for, is our unity. Our pack is kingdom-wide. We've had a lot of hardship in this kingdom, and it has brought us together, strengthened by my mate and yours. We collectively understand what it is like being suppressed. Many of us understand the pain and degradation of being trapped and beaten. You wouldn't be an outcast with us—you'd be part of the family. My daughter loves you. My people respond to you. My beta has found his heart within you. I ask that you give us a chance to help you make this kingdom your home."

Hell. That was a good speech.

Finley pointed at her plate with her fork. "One of her duties needs to be teaching the chef how to cook."

"Agreed," Nyfain murmured around a mouthful of chicken.

"Now for the third option." Finley dabbed at her mouth with her napkin. "Your biological father. We have a pretty good idea of who it is. He holds a high status, and you are his blood relation. Despite not being one hundred percent wolf, they'd respect your lineage and your level of power. I'm sure they would welcome you into their court, though I have no idea if that would come with a job or annual gold. I will mention that your biological father has a mate and two kids. One of those kids is older than you. One is younger. You can do the math."

The reality of what it meant sank in.

"Fucking hell," I said, pushing my half-eaten plate of food away. "Did any of my family keep it in their pants? I've got fairy blood from a random addition to my family tree, and now it turns out my mom was a mistress?" I wiped my mouth and leaned back. "Clearly, that is why she was sent away. How the hell did she not know?"

"Trust me, I get where you're coming from," Nyfain grumbled, which made me incredibly inquisitive. "Just asking, how much would I mess up my chances of enticing you to stay in my kingdom if I ate the other half of your chicken? Would that be a serious *faux pas*?"

"Yes," Finley told him. "Eating off an almost-stranger's plate in a professional meeting is a *faux pas*. Your mother would freak out."

"Not if she tasted this chicken." He lifted his eyebrows at me.

I laughed and pushed the plate a little more. "Knock yourself out."

"There, see?" He half stood and speared the chicken with his fork. "Everything is fine."

"She probably thinks less of you now," Finley told him. "Hell, I think less of you, and I'm your mate. You take the food from her room and then off her plate? Disgraceful."

"I didn't take it from her room, I just let it be served." He sighed happily as he chewed and swallowed another bite. "No regrets."

"Disgraceful," she said again, her eyes sparkling. She turned her focus back to me, and my heart melted with the residual love I saw warming her eyes. "I'm telling you about your father merely to be open about the situation. I don't recommend trying to make that connection."

"I had no intention, even when I just thought he'd sent us away. Now I *definitely* don't want that connection."

"I don't blame you." Finley leaned back so her plate could be cleared. "You need to think about this, I assume."

"Yes," I said.

"You need to talk it over with Weston, as well. He knows about both offers. We wanted to be the ones to speak with you directly, though, so we told him to keep it to himself. I'm sure that couldn't have been easy for him."

I inhaled sharply. I'd had no clue he was keeping something else from me. But I realized I was glad he had. I was glad they'd told him to. I wouldn't have believed him or taken it seriously if he'd tried to relay all of this. I still didn't fully believe it, and I'd heard it from everyone's mouths. I was just having a hard time accepting it.

At least he'd already know the details when I sat down with him. I wouldn't have to try to recount all I'd heard and was having a hard time coming to grips with.

"What about my freedom?" I asked.

"What about it?" Nyfain, now finished with the dinner, leaned back and put his hand on his stomach. "Gods I'm full."

Finley scoffed. "You're a pig, is what you are." I couldn't help laughing. This wasn't at all the sort of regal behavior I'd been expecting. I appreciated it.

"I don't mind being punished," I said. "I'm okay with being whipped or whatever else you need to do. But eventually, once the situation with Granny is resolved, I would like my freedom. I don't want to be trapped again. I don't want the borders of my home to be closed to me. If I want to travel, I would like that option."

"You devised your own punishment," Finley told me. "Well, you and Cecil. Hadriel is pissed that the dick clothes helped you. As far as the people are concerned, you are making amends by working for free to try to help them. The word is spreading fast about your visits. It was a genius story you told throughout the villages, and when you deliver the product by hand, speaking with people about it and walking them through it, it will be further evidence of your atonement. After what I've seen and how hard you've worked to right any past wrongs, I'm content."

"But as you know," Nyfain said, "until we know Granny's intentions, you are not safe. You need training, you need to integrate into the pack, and you need to sort out your life. You're not out of the woods yet. But once you are, then yes, you can come and go as you please. As any of us can."

A silent moment passed between us.

"You have a lot to think about," Finley finally said.

"I need to choose a path," I said, alluding to our conversation the other night.

"Exactly."

"Do you have any questions about the kingdom?" Nyfain asked. "Any questions for us?"

I didn't. My questions were all for Weston.

33

AURELIA

Weston sat in his little garden, the doors opened behind him and the emberflies drifting in the night sky. He didn't look up when I came out, staring at nothing.

I pulled a chair around and positioned it right in front of him so that he had no choice but to look at me. When he did, his eyes were shuttered, his demeanor closed down.

"You need to make a choice," I told him, leaning back, suddenly exhausted.

Quietly, coolly, he said, "It isn't me who got the offers."

Emotion flared within me. "Like I said, you need to make a choice. Are you on my side, or are you on the royals' side? Because if you are on my side, it *is* you who got the offers. We both did, because we are mates. To me, being mates means we are a family, and I don't make decisions that will affect my family without consulting the other members of my family. If you are on the side of the royals, though, the way you have been up until and including this moment, then *I* need to decide if I can tolerate being left out and having information withheld from me by someone I love for the rest of my life."

I knew I was coming on a little strong, but I needed to make a point—one he couldn't avoid.

He didn't speak, watching me silently.

"You didn't claim me because you didn't want to send me away with your permanent mark, right?" I asked, my heart suddenly very heavy. "You didn't want to make it harder for me to find someone else."

It was hard to even say that last bit.

Through the bond I felt the pain pierce him, evidence he felt as hurt by that thought as I did. "I didn't claim you because I didn't want to trap you. I didn't want you to think you'd have to stay here with me. Or stay with me, period. You made it clear that you needed space to decide what you wanted for your future. If or when I claim you, it will be as an alpha claims his mate: in front of the pack, publicly, a statement. It will unify us all, you and me and them. You didn't seem ready for that before, and now you have other offers to consider. I won't join us all only to rip you or us away from each other, from them. It's not fair to anyone. In this, my wolf agrees. I don't have all the answers, Aurelia, but I'm trying to navigate this complicated situation as best I can."

I sagged against the chair. "It's complicated because you are trying to navigate both our lives without any input from me. Talk to me, Weston. Include me. Stop locking me out."

"This was the last time," he said sincerely. "The very last time, I promise. I didn't want to mention the message I intercepted from Calia because there was a chance her king would've changed their offer. Or denied it, even. I didn't mention Nyfain's intended offer because I didn't want to add my weight to it. I just . . ." He ran his hand down his face and took a deep breath. "Aurelia, I want you to be happy, baby. You fought so hard to survive, and then I ripped you from your home, your life. I want to make that right, to make sure you never suffer again. I'll do whatever you think will make you happiest. I'll go wherever you want to go. I'm with you, always."

My eyes were glassy as I resisted the urge to go sit in his lap and wrap my arms around his neck. There were still decisions to be made.

"So you agree, we're in this together?" I wiped the tears I couldn't stop from my eyes.

"Yes."

"Okay then." I nodded and crossed my legs, ready to get down to the nitty-gritty.

"You look really pretty, by the way."

I lit up inside and my heart melted, feeling the truth of his words through the bond. I soaked in his handsome face.

"Thank you," I murmured, suddenly bashful and feeling so in love with this man. "No one has ever told me I was pretty before. Well, except my mom. But she doesn't count. I never had clothes to dress up in in Granny's village—"

"This isn't you dressing up, this is you making do. We'll get you a fancy dress and sparkly jewelry and everything you could ever want to feel beautiful."

Resisting the urge to sit in his lap suddenly became a lot harder.

"Right, time to discuss those offers. Let's go in order." I cleared my throat. "What would be the situation with my biological father . . ."

"Without me, you'd be admitted to that court because of your power and your bloodline, but the fact you have fairy magic would dilute your bloodline in their eyes. Plus, you'd be a half-sister to siblings who don't know you exist and a horrible reveal to a mate who wouldn't want to see constant proof that her mate was unfaithful. Bottom line, you wouldn't be well liked or received, and would very likely be miserable." He paused. "Assuming you allowed me to go . . ." He smiled at me. It didn't reach his eyes. "I'd be admitted to that court and handed the beta job in a split second. I'd be offered a lot of gold. More than here. I don't know if they'd allow you to be a beta pair with me, given your tainted blood—"

"Just stop." I lifted my hand. "Stop, please. It was never even a consideration, but now it just sounds . . . awful."

"Your biological father and the current beta would try to sabotage me, as well. I'd be stealing their positions—"

"Stop, seriously. Just stop. It's a no."

This time his smile made his eyes glitter. "Good. I really didn't want you to think that was the most appealing offer."

"And you thought that was a possibility *how*?"

"Family. Blood relations."

"*You* are my family. Moving on." I inhaled deeply as his soft eyes drank me in with that comment. "Have you been to the fairy kingdom? The Narva kingdom, I mean."

"Yes. It's beautiful. It is stunning, truly. The castle is gorgeous, the grounds are amazing, and, despite her best efforts, Finley is failing to compete with their gardens. It's really annoying her."

"They said my drug making—because I'm not really a plant worker, more like a plant burner—could be a wonderful hobby."

"They want you solely focused on your magic, then?"

"Yes. But to receive training, I'd need to accept their offer."

He didn't react to that. He must've expected it.

"What are the people like?" I asked.

"I don't know many of them personally. I was in the demon dungeons with Calia and her sister. She is lovely. Her position as a foreign dignitary, which basically means a spy, doesn't allow her to be genuine with us about some things, but she makes it clear when she is acting in her professional role. The others I met seem . . ."

"Spit it out."

"Arrogant."

I scoffed. "Dragons are arrogant."

He laughed. "Yes, they are. Fairies are also snobbish. Status is a huge thing in their kingdom. If you have it, you are afforded a certain level of reverence and respect. You are seen as your position. You'd have it, so you'd get deference, the best placements at theaters, invitations to formal dinners, the works. You'd have the best clothes, the most servants, things like that. You'd be expected to procreate, and you'd be expected to don that arrogance if you met dignitaries and the like—which is guaranteed, because they'd want you to exercise your powers as an Emoter to influence outcomes. That would be your role, I imagine. You would help the king get what he wants. Don't hold that against him, though—all royals are the same. They play politics, always. It's their job."

Not the dragon royals, though. Not Finley, at least. She'd given me an out. She'd told me to be happy. Hell, she'd even told me that I could rip Weston away from her kingdom, that he'd allow me to do it. A move like that would cripple their pack, yet she was open and honest, wanting the best for me. Just as she clearly wanted the best for her people.

When I took my place at Nyfain's side, it was to fight for this kingdom. It was to fight for what I believe in, for a better place, a stronger, more cohesive community. Every day I work toward this kingdom's prosperity, not just for those with the most gold, but for all. I want everyone well, want everyone as happy as possible. I want this place to thrive.

She'd said it, and she'd meant it. She'd proven it in how she took me aside behind her mate's back, with how she'd given me all the information that her mate was trying to hide, and done it right in front of his face. She stuck up for what she believed in, and, in so doing, asked that I do it too.

Weston continued. "They are a long-established kingdom with a lot of clout. They are well run, well managed, and push for peace. Their army isn't great, but they've worked to build it up in the event the worst should happen, which it did over a year ago. This kingdom shouldered the bulk of that conflict. Still, they saw the need for improvement and are rising to the occasion. As far as leadership, they are one of the better kingdoms."

"And this kingdom?"

He took a deep breath. "I'm biased."

"Of course you are. Maybe your bias here will balance out my desire to be a fairy queen and rule the land with my crown and scepter or whatever they have."

"This kingdom comprises a lot of people who barely survived a very hard time. They're fighters, dreamers, builders. They are rough around the edges, don't follow the typical social norms of a court, and don't care who you are—just what you can do. Here, you prove yourself or you get out of the way. It's a kingdom that is making more gold than any other kingdom, but whose royals are not keeping it for themselves or their top people. You wouldn't get paid nearly as much here as you would with the fairies. Not even half, I think. They won't sacrifice the wellbeing of their kingdom to keep us—you *or* me. I respect that about them."

"You love it here."

"I do."

"Even lonely as you are."

"Even so. I owe Finley a life debt for getting me out of that demon dungeon. I count her and Nyfain as friends, something usually unthinkable with royals. They should be above me, but they've had it so hard that decorum often slips away when they are able to relax. The pack I've built is strong, and they let me lead it as I see fit. Micah and I don't get along well, but we've made it work. The kingdom is cohesive, solid. The dragons are a rush to fight beside. And when it comes to material possessions, I have more than I need here."

"You'd give all that up to go with me?"

"That's why I didn't mention any of this before now. I knew it would affect your decision. Yes, Aurelia, I would give that up to be with you. I love it here, but I want a family, our family. I want you as my mate, and, you and the gods willing, children. I want to watch you with our child like I see you with Tabitha. I want to watch as you hand our baby to me and say, 'Here's your daddy.' You've sacrificed so much to get to this point. I think it is only fair that I be willing to sacrifice for us to get to the next step."

I stopped resisting the urge and climbed into his lap, my legs draped over the sides of his. I slipped a hand under the hem of his shirt and onto his warm skin, tracing my fingers over the muscle I found there.

"I haven't sacrificed to get here," I murmured, tucking myself against his body. "I was stolen, and because I was stolen, I was saved. I have always wanted to live with the fairies, it's true, but I think it is enough that I am one."

He pulled back a little, just enough to look me in the eye. "You need to be sure."

"No, I don't. I don't assume this magic is going to go away. If I end up hating it here, I can always go to them later. They want me more than I want them."

"Aurelia, you need to be sure, baby, because I can't integrate you into the pack and then uproot us both if you decide to leave later. This isn't just your life we are talking about here—it's theirs too."

The gravity of his tone, in his eyes, sobered me. I licked my lips, thinking about this.

But what was there to think about, really?

"I say I've always wanted to live amongst the fairies because they seem so ethereal and magical," I said. "Which, honestly, Calia does a great job proving is the case."

"She does."

"But the other half of that dream was to have a little house all my own with a loving mate and a wagonload of children. It was to have friends who would sit with me in the garden, or to be cooking dinner for a large gathering. What I really wanted was a community that welcomed me. That was it. I latched on to fairies, I think, because I'd never met one. It was easy to dream that they would treat me differently than the shifters I met every day, and that they were less . . . icky than the demons or goblins or vampires. I latched on to them because they were my best hope at a community."

"You didn't even think about the dragons."

"I didn't." I leaned in and whispered conspiratorially, "Don't tell them. They'll just get pissed."

He laughed and kissed me. "They don't need much of a reason for that."

"No, they don't." I cuddled close.

"You have time to think it through," he said softly.

When you ultimately choose your path, you need to choose what will make you the happiest. You need to choose what you're most passionate about. With hard work and perseverance, everything else will fall in line.

"I want to make those medicines," I told him. Or maybe I was telling myself. "I want to speak with people and come up with ways to make their lives a little more manageable. I want to work with Vemar and play jokes on Hadriel. I want Leala to teach me how to wield a whip, because how cool would that be? I want a family with you, and I want to be claimed. The public part of that is a little daunting, but it's not like we haven't done it before. Do you know what else I want?"

"Should I be writing this down?"

I laughed and snuggled against his neck. "I want to create a business that eclipses Granny's. I want her to see that I wasn't just good at making drugs—I am good at many things. I want to show her that I have more value than what she gave me the barest of credit for, and I want to do it after I have driven her business—the business I was integral in building—into the fucking ground."

His lips crashed down on mine, and relief soaked through the bond. "Thank fuck. I was worried you'd want to go to the fairies."

"I mean, I do want to visit someday, if they'll have me. I want to see their land. It sounds beautiful."

"We will. Once life settles down and the threats are exhausted"—the last part was a growl, clearly referencing Granny—"we'll follow Calia home and let her show us the gardens and the countryside. Maybe we can keep you from meeting the king and tarnishing your love of the lands."

I laughed and smacked him. "You didn't mention that I wouldn't like the king!"

He chuckled. "He's fine. Like any other royal. Nyfain is

an exception." He kissed me again, gentler this time. "I love you. I need to organize the timing with the royals and ready the pack for it, but once the particulars are sorted . . ." He pulled back to look deeply into my eyes. I felt his heat run through me. "I will claim you for all to see and show the kingdom that you are now, and will forever be, *mine*."

34

AURELIA

The next morning, I was a woman on fire. I gave Vemar a thumbs-up as I exited Weston's room and passed him by.

"Hello, Captive Lady," he said, catching up to me with a laugh. "Damn fine morning, isn't it?"

"Damn fine." I stopped by my room and grabbed the notes from my journals. "Change of routine for today, Vemar."

"I love changes in routine."

"Take me to the royals."

"Very dangerous to disturb them so early in the morning." He pointed to indicate our new trajectory, and we started walking. "I can't wait to see what happens."

"Dragons," I murmured with a smile.

He took me right to their door, and I didn't miss the warning looks of those we passed on the way there. I knocked, hoping to holy hell I didn't wake the baby. If I were them, I'd punch me in the face if I did.

A fierce-eyed Finley swung the door open—hair wild,

robe open down the middle exposing bare skin, and war imminent.

"Is the king awake?" I pushed into her room, on dangerous ground. I was a fairy, though. It was my right to be arrogant. At least twenty-five percent so.

Vemar stepped into the room but stayed by the door. He wasn't a fool.

Clearly, I was.

"Sit there." She pointed at a couch in a finely appointed sitting room and continued farther into the large quarters.

In a moment, Nyfain walked into the room wearing his robe fastened at the waist.

"No, I meant I need to speak with both of you, not just you."

He glared at me and growled, "The only reason you should ever be here at this hour is if it is an absolute emergency. Because of your unique situation *in this moment,* I am allowing it. Do it again, and I will beat the ever-loving hell out of you, and then the hell out of your mate when he tries to come to your rescue. Do I make myself clear?"

His threat sizzled through me because of his intensity, but I could tell he didn't really mean it. Whether or not Finley would mean it, though . . .

"Clear," I said for the sake of appearances.

Finley joined us a moment later in jeans and a T-shirt, taking the couch opposite me, while Nyfain sat in a chair at the head of the arrangement.

"Why do you wake up this early, and why are you here?" Finley asked me, glancing at Vemar.

"I'm going to take your offer, but with non-negotiable stipulations." My tone made it evident I wasn't playing around when I said, "Give me what I want, or I walk."

Nyfain's brow arched. Neither of them said a word, so I just got into it.

"I want to create a whole line of products to sell at market and beyond. I want to corner the shadow markets, and I want the traditional markets and I want the medics. All of them. This is all under the banner of your kingdom, obviously. I'd like access to the people of your kingdom for ideas and to test the products you have deemed safe. The current products need a fresh look, and I'd like to design that. They work great but look lame. Granny has taught me the value of packaging. I'd like to create a dragon-centric logo for anything with Everlass in it. My logo would be different—I'd like to put a fairy on it, but I know that might be . . . touchy, since I won't be accepting the fairies' deal, so I'll have to think of something else."

I cleared my throat and took a breath before continuing.

"I do want training for my fairy magic. I think it would benefit us all. You said the king can be bought. Maybe he can get a percentage of proceeds from the product I make, or maybe they get a deal on it. I'm okay with offering twenty-five percent of myself, however that might work. Maybe giving some of my time to them? I don't like the idea of forcing emotions on people so that the king can get what he wants, but I'm willing to negotiate. That said, I am also willing to walk away without training if they get heavy-handed or ask too much, so please keep that in mind. I can probably learn to control it if I try. Training with them would be helpful, but . . ." I shrugged.

"Anything else?" Nyfain asked, his gaze piercing. Fuck, he was an intimidating bastard.

"I would like that apartment for me and Weston. If I'm able, I'd like to have children someday, and we'd need space for that. Though I'm fine to wait until we get to that point."

"Let me see if I'm getting this right." Finley crossed her

ankles. "Your demands are essentially that you want a job, you want to improve the marketing and sales of my products, you're willing to put yourself in a very precarious position with the fairies in order to get training to help *our* kingdom, and you want space for a family to continue a very powerful bloodline that will make our kingdom great for years to come."

I blinked at her as Vemar started chuckling. "In my head all that sounded way more stacked in my favor. Oh!" I held up a finger. "You do not get to tell me how many hours I will and won't work. I'll work as many as I want, which will be more than you think appropriate. I'll lay off if I need to, and take breaks when I want, which is not something I was afforded with Granny, but otherwise, I'll do what I'm used to."

"And you'll overwork yourself to benefit our kingdom," Finley surmised.

I curled my lips between my teeth.

She shook her head with a smile and looked at Nyfain, who was still surveying me.

"What made you decide to stay?" he asked.

"A few things. The work I'd be able to do here aligns with what I am passionate about. Weston loves it here and I trust his judgment, and I love the people I've met. I want to be part of the community you are building, and I truly want to help people . . . while also driving Granny's business into the ground."

"The yearly sum of gold—that isn't going to be an issue?" Nyfain asked. "We can match the other material things the fairies might've offered you, like clothes and jewels, but I need to know if the lack of gold is going to be a problem down the line."

I laughed and looked at my knees. "I first started toward this kingdom as a captive thinking I had no magic.

I thought I was coming to my death or some other horrible tragedy. To now be offered anything is . . . To be fought over . . ." I laughed again. "This is all surreal. I'd be happy with a place to live, food to eat, and a job that makes me relevant. Anything else is extra or unneeded. I'll take the gold to save for any children I may have, but I'm not concerned about it."

"And you'd take less for all you'd be doing for us." Finley smirked. "It's pretty apparent, Aurelia, that you will never, not ever, be in charge of negotiating for this kingdom. You should've sent Weston."

"She's certainly not going anywhere near the fairies to discuss this." Nyfain leaned back and rubbed his chin. "I'll handle those negotiations. We'll be able to figure something out. I assume you'd be okay with having a standing invite to visit any time you like? They'll want some sort of claim on your successes, and it sounds like you won't stop until you own the world."

"That would be . . ." I nodded earnestly. "That would be really great to have a standing invite, yes. I told Weston I do really want to visit."

"Of course you'll visit," Nyfain said, pushing to standing. "You just won't be allowed to go unattended, at least not until you develop some sort of clue as to how to negotiate."

"I doubt Weston would let her go unattended anyway," Finley said.

"And yet here she is, making the world's worst deal for herself. What does Weston plan to do about the pack, do you know?"

My face heated. "He said he was going to talk to you guys about the timing, but he plans to claim me in front of them. I think he might be planning to try to integrate me, though I don't know how exactly."

"Fuck's sake, woman," Finley spat, standing. "You need to take a firmer grip on your life."

"I am, just in the things that are the most important to me. I trusted Granny and I shouldn't have, but I'm not going to let her treachery close me off. Weston has things in hand, and if he goes too slow, I trust that you'll step in. Nyfain will handle the fairies. That's all sorted. Now I'll go start working on taking down Granny. Between all of us, we'll do what needs to be done. Isn't that what a pack mentality is—working together toward a common goal?"

I stood, and the two blinked at me before a smile spread across Finley's face. "Touché."

"I really do like her," I told Vemar after we'd exited and were halfway down the hall.

"It's hard not to. You're right, by the way. In trusting people. Those royals will look after you, as will Weston. As will I, and Hadriel, too. I would've gone with you regardless of where you chose, but I'm happy you decided to stay here. It's home."

I smiled at him. "You would've gone with me?"

"Of course. Someone needs to help you make product. You don't think those stuffy ol' fairies would have the first clue, do you? They cheat at their potions with magic. They don't know how to get their hands dirty like we do."

I nudged him with my elbow. "Thanks."

"No sweat. Gotta guard that asshole."

I parted ways with him to head to the library. Once there, I searched for the geography sections and grabbed all the books with maps of the Red Lupine kingdom.

Time to see if I could figure out where Granny was hiding.

35

AURELIA

A week later I sat at the table in my apartment with my journal, notes, and various maps spread around me. I rested my elbows on the hard surface with my head in my hands.

"Everything okay, miss?" Leala asked, pausing as she walked by.

I continued staring downward. "I've been all through these journals and all through my notes. I've pored over the maps. Alexander mentioned hills—really steep, treacherous hills—multiple times. I recall he once talked about damn near falling off his horse. I know he went to that location multiple times. That's the packaging plant, I'm sure of it."

"Well then, that's great!"

"I don't have a name, and there are somewhere between five and seven places that fit the description, given his propensity to exaggerate. And that's if I'm getting it right."

"Five to seven is something, and a lot more than they had to go on. Now you can compare those with the Everlass sales, right? Didn't you say that?"

I'd forgotten about that, so sure I'd find something to lead me to Granny's other location. "Yeah, I guess."

"Well then. You have something. And given the beta's tightening up of the kingdom, we have time to look into it. I've heard all his tests have gone smoothly—"

A gentle tap sounded at the door before the handle turned and Hadriel stuck his head in. "Oh good, you're here. Listen to this!"

He practically bounded into the room, took a look at all the stuff spread across the table, and pulled a chair back so that he wasn't right on top of it.

"I did it!" His large smile stretched his little mustache. "*I did it!*"

"Did what?" Leala crossed her arms over her chest.

"Saved the day. Well, there was the beta's expert setup and the fact that Micah finally came through, and the towns and cities were all locked down for the most part—but besides all of that, I have saved the fucking day."

I sat back into my chair, too grumpy to be excited by his glowing enthusiasm.

"As you probably don't know because I didn't tell you," he went on, "I could not get any sort of hint about how Granny's spies were getting into the kingdom. No one was talking! Not one to be deterred, I took to the second largest town. Why the second largest? Because they—"

"Skip forward," Leala said.

He frowned at her. "Well, that town has two taverns—"

"Let's just get to where you actually saved the day," Leala pressed, and I furrowed my brow to stop the smile that threatened to spread across my face.

Hadriel sent her a hostile glare for a moment before turning back to me with a haughty expression. "Well, I got talking to this one old woman, a real grumpy type who doesn't trust anyone. She would only talk to me because she thought I was part of the queen's guard—long story. Anyway, apparently she overheard two boys talking—" He put out his hand. "To her, 'boys' means anyone under sixty. *Anyway,* they were way back in the corner and didn't notice her lurking back there. I sought her out specifically because of her location. She's a regular—"

"Does this story have a conclusion?" Leala's continued annoyance made the fight against that smile even harder.

"I'm getting there, I'm getting there. She didn't recognize those guys from the bar. They weren't regulars. Well, she overheard them talking about a way to slip into the castle at the dead of night."

I lifted my eyebrows, suddenly all ears—and also concerned about whatever hole they might've found in Weston's defense.

Hadriel nodded with glee at our interest. "They haven't been back since. I got their descriptions and checked the other tavern. Nothing. Then I went to the other towns, the village—nothing. So, I got this bright idea—"

"To take a class in concise storytelling?" Leala said.

"I went to the squares and started loitering around the towns. And this morning . . . I found one of them!" He pumped a fist in the air. "He runs a stall in the city market. He sells baked goods!"

Leala dropped her hands. "Please tell me you told the beta instead of coming back here to gloat."

"Leala, my darling, don't be so dense. Of *course* I ran straight to the beta. I told him what I knew, and he had the guards grab the guy and do a sweep of his house." He sat back in the chair, face smug and his arms spread wide. "In a little cubby under the floorboards in the bedroom . . . were mostly empty crates of Granny's product!"

I gasped, adrenaline making my head feel light. "I thought they'd searched houses before."

"They did a generalized sweep, but the hiding place was hard to find—very discreet. The beta himself was the one to spot it. I gave the description of the other guy, but they haven't found him. Doesn't matter, though—they took the one I did find in for questioning. They'll get something out of him. It's only a matter of time before we start to unravel who else is working for her."

Happiness filled me, as did relief. She was still out there, but at least we were starting to close the door on how easily she could get in here. In the meantime, I'd been working diligently on fixing my product to get it ready for market. Soon we'd start edging her out of that, as well. Those efforts would buy me time to look for more clues to help us locate the packaging place. It was a start, at least.

"Excellent work, Hadriel," I said, my mood finally lightening.

He twisted and patted himself on the back. "I'll keep looking, just in case they can't get anything out of the guy in questioning, but this is good."

"What about the hole in our defenses, though?" Leala asked.

Hadriel shook his head. "It's a decoy. It's there precisely for this scenario. One of two. I'm telling you, the beta has thought of everything. He's fucking good. I mean, I knew he was good, but he's fucking *good*."

My admiration for Weston intensified, heightening my love, the feeling burning and throbbing deep in my middle. It bled down to my core, tightening me up and sending sparks of desire through the bond to him.

I felt him receive it, felt his body tighten, his ardor rise.

He needed something special tonight, like me waiting in his chambers, offering myself to my alpha.

"Okay, well . . ." Face flushed, body on fire, I stood, collecting everything and putting things away.

"What am I missing?" Hadriel half stood from his chair. "What happened?"

"I already laid out that little nighty that Cecil brought down this morning," Leala told me, clearly reading the situation. "It's on your bed. And make sure to dash into the washroom to freshen up."

"Ah." Hadriel finished standing. "Yeah, he deserves a good fuck for his talents, I agree. Suck him dry, love. Well, I'm off."

Leala had laid out a little satin nighty, draping the soft, shiny crimson material across the top of a bed I still hadn't slept in. Heat still coursing through me, I felt him start to head my way now, though from a great distance. He must've been visiting one of the towns or villages. I took a moment in the mirror to pay some attention to my hair. After that, I dusted my face with a little makeup and began to brush my teeth, noticing a pop of color in the washroom where it shouldn't be.

I reached for it, crinkling the paper as I pulled it off the shelf, and then slowed when I realized where it had been sitting.

I stopped completely when I realized what was missing from that location.

My gaze fell to the peach-colored paper and Weston's familiar scrawl.

The claiming is set for next week. I'm tired of waiting.
No more Product X.
Wait for me on our bed, legs spread.
It's time to start our family.

A surge of primal desire nearly stopped my heart. I wondered if he'd put this here after I'd left for the morning, but I realized he hadn't been near my apartment. He must've had Leala do it.

The dots began to connect: the nighty already set out, Weston starting back at the first sign I'd felt sexy thoughts, Leala specifically telling me to duck into the washroom . . .

Excitement and desire and more excitement and world-ending love crashed into me all at once. I clutched the note in one tight fist as I started to shake, my smile so big it felt glued on.

He wanted to make a baby.

With me.

Nature willing, I would get to have a baby!

"Leala!" I shouted, turning for the door and then stopping to rinse my mouth and make sure I'd wiped my face. "Leala—"

"Yes, miss?" Leala stopped up short when I nearly ran into her. She noticed the note in my hand and smiled. "Congratulations! Shall we get you ready? Maybe we'll tie you up so he can have full control and can do what he likes. Or maybe we'll have you defy him by sitting on the couch and running from him when he tries to make you do what he says. I think you'll be tremendously satisfied either way. What would he like best?"

I froze with my mouth open, unable to speak with the throbbing desire suddenly pounding in my core. My pussy was so wet it leaked down my thigh. I'd never dived headfirst into primal kink, or any kink, only following his lead when it happened in the moment, but there was no denying my lust or my sudden, desperate urge to do either of those things. Both of them.

"Hmm," Leala said, tapping her lips as she studied me. "He's going to breed you, and for that, I think he needs to chase and then dominate you. That sounds perfect for the moment." She winked at what was probably my stunned expression, because she'd nailed it. "I'm really good at knowing what gets people off. It's a gift. Okay, c'mon, let's go get ready."

Back in my room, she stripped me of the nighty.

"He wants you to wear this, and to start the fun, we will not be doing what he wants." She tossed a pair of red, lacy panties on the bed. "No crotch. We want to defy him, but we want him to turn to jelly when he finally forces you to submit." Then another nighty made of black silk, the material cut to drape down my body to my ankles with a slit up both sides to my upper thigh. "This will do."

Once I'd slipped the nightgown on, she mussed my hair just a bit, darkened the makeup around my eyes, and took me through the secret passageway to his chambers.

"How much time?" she asked.

Before I could assess how far away he was, the feeling in the bond let me know his cock was throbbing and he'd be wound up when he reached me. He was as eager, and desperate, for this as I was.

I couldn't stop myself from blurting that out, but quickly regained my composure enough to tell her that he was getting closer and coming fast.

"Then this is perfect," she said, letting us into and ushering me to the front of the room. His valet, Niles, turned when we approached. To his credit, he didn't glance down at my attire or waste any time asking what we were up to.

"I've put out some wine and nibbles," he told us, finishing the setup on the table. "I was just about to light the candles . . . but maybe you had other plans? I see you've changed the dress code."

He looked at Leala without expression or comment; he

was simply trying to gauge the new direction. They were both very good at their jobs.

"Light the candles, yes," Leala said, leaving me standing there stupidly as she adjusted the pillows on the couch. "Pour a glass of wine. Just one for her. Half full. Leave the bottle near the edge of the table, uncorked."

It was a good thing our situation started how it did and not in any normal way, because I wouldn't have had the first clue as to how to seduce him. Leala was doing all the heavy lifting.

He was on the castle grounds now. I could feel him winding closer.

"He's coming," I said, suddenly out of breath and incredibly nervous. I wasn't even sure what I was nervous for. I loved him, I wanted him, I wanted us, I wanted *this*. It was a dream come true to even try for a baby. To be with him, to have a warm home and all these fine things . . .

I felt like I was living in a dreamland.

Leala directed me to the couch and instructed me to lie on the pillows with my upper half propped up, my knees together and to the side, and my hair styled around me on the pillow.

"Now." She held out her hand while looking at me, and Niles filled it with the glass of wine. She handed it off to me, directing me to hold it near my lips, my elbow resting on the arm of the couch in front of me. She glanced around and then pointed at the light Weston used for reading. "Turn that one on. The rest go off."

Niles did as instructed before standing behind her, looking down at me as well.

"Perfect," he said with a nod. "He won't know up from down when he lays eyes on her."

A smile spread across Leala's lips. "Excellent. Okay, let's

get out of here and leave them to it." She winked at me. "Have fun."

They both left together, heading out the back way.

"But wait, do I"—I reduced to a murmur when the latch clicked on the secret door—"take a sip?"

Anticipation rolled through the bond as he drew nearer and nearer. I sensed he thought he was going to walk through the door, maybe grab two glasses of wine, one for each of us, and head back to his feast—me.

Instead, he was going to get a little sport.

My own anticipation kicked up, and my stomach started to swirl. He was closer now, in the castle. Even closer, now nearing the hall. Maybe in the hall; I couldn't tell. The bond was not precise when it came to distance, at least not for me.

My breath kicked up, the wine starting to roll around the glass as my hand shook. I didn't dare try to take a sip now. I'd end up wearing it.

Just outside, the key scraped the lock. The bolt clicked over.

The door swung open and he stepped into the doorway, all business, looking toward the table . . .

He froze, his gaze snapping to me before slowly sliding over my face and to the half-filled glass, down to my heaving bust and on to my closed legs. His movements turned fluid, graceful, as the predator emerged and he became the alpha someone had dared to defy.

He took one step into the room and closed the door behind him. The metal clinked over, locking us in. My swallow was audible.

"What do you think you are doing, Little Wolf?" he said in a dark, raspy voice.

It was almost like I heard Leala in the back of my head: *Now take a sip.*

Nonchalant, somehow no longer shaking, I did. The wine was sweet on my tongue; his eyes were fire as they watched.

"I *said* . . ." He took another step, and I could see his cock straining at his pants. Molten desire seared through the bond. "What are you doing? You're supposed to be on our bed with your legs spread, waiting for your alpha like a good girl."

My breath felt heavy, and my wetness dampened my thighs. "If my *alpha* wants me to do his bidding, he'll have to try a lot harder than leaving a little note."

His wolf pushed up close to the surface, so present I could almost see him moving behind Weston's intense, lust-filled eyes. Mine was right there, too, lapping up the intoxicating power and desire that kept flowing back and forth between us, wanting this with everything in her. She'd always wanted this: her mate, his brood.

"Is that right?" He took another step toward me, holding up his arm so he could unclasp the buttons on his sleeve, then undoing the other sleeve. Task complete, he shrugged out of his coat and draped it over the back of the nearest chair.

I raised the glass up to rub it against my lips once, twice, and then slid my tongue across. His whole body tensed; he watched the movement with a feral glint in his eyes. I pressed my lips to the edge and gulped down the rest, so bloody thankful Leala hadn't filled it all the way up.

I sat up and dropped my feet to the floor, my knees tightly pressed together, hidden within the fabric of the nightgown. Chaste. Defiant.

The bond pulsed power, primal desire, spiraling passion. And along with it, an alpha's need to force submission.

My stomach quivered with adrenaline, with nervousness, with the rush of pushing this man to his limits.

"Maybe you need to learn what happens when you stand up to your alpha, Little Wolf." He shrugged out of his shirt, his big, broad, glorious chest on full display. His power now pumped into the room, heady and erotic. "I'll give you one last chance. Spread your legs like a good girl and get ready for your alpha's thick cock. I'm going to pump you full of cum and breed that little pussy, and when I'm done, you're going to beg for more."

My breath hitched; I was on fire now. Somehow, I managed to stand without dropping the glass, my legs shaking with adrenaline, with the excitement of what would happen when his power and strength was unleashed and he took me, forced me to take his knot, rutted into me again and again.

"Or maybe it's you who needs to go lie on the bed and wait for your mistress to make use of you." I crossed to the table, setting down the glass.

Watching me with that predator's intensity, he worked at his pants. I stalled in getting more wine, watching. His power ratcheted higher, and suddenly I realized mine was draining. His wolf was sucking it all into them.

A flurry of apprehension ran through me. I wasn't sure if I should rip it back, stop the flow, or let his wolf take it all and then consume us. I'd lost track of the game as I looked into those intense gray eyes. All I knew was this feeling of primal lust and the sense of being caught in the snare of this powerful, dominant wolf.

"Are you nervous?" He dropped his pants. His large, thick cock sprang free. I salivated, almost wishing he would tell me to drop to my knees and worship him. He took a step toward me.

"No," I whispered, taking a step back, nearly daunted by

his size, by his slowly stalking toward me. I was so fucking excited for him to catch me.

"No?" Another step, corralling me into the corner. "Do you want me to take you against that wall there? I don't think that would be very comfortable, not for the first time we try for a baby."

Who gave two shits about comfortable? I'd fuck this man upside down if that was what he offered.

He prowled forward, closing down the space between us. My desire pumped higher as I retreated, stopped on my right by a small table and forced left. He took another step, shutting off any escape route, backing me against the wall.

"Nowhere to run, Little Wolf?" He grinned, looking down on me, stepping in close.

My chest heaved as I pulled in air. My core pounded with wild, raw, primal desire. With the need for his cock inside me, his knot locking me, his cum pumped in deep while he fulfilled my wildest dreams.

"That's right, baby" he murmured, placing his hand to the side of my neck and using his thumb under my chin to tilt my head up. He looked down into my eyes. "Stroke my cock," he commanded.

A breath tumbled over my lips as I gripped his length, sliding my palm against his smooth skin. Pleasure rolled over me as I submitted. He released my power, and all of it rushed back to me, my sweet reward.

"Good girl," he cooed, in control now. It was so fucking sexy. "What do you need from me, Little Wolf?" He dipped his head to the other side of my neck, skimming his lips along my skin.

I closed my eyes, in ecstasy. "I need you inside me. I need you to fill me up, over and over. Put a baby in me, Weston."

His arms came around me, bands of steel keeping me

put while he sucked on the skin of my neck. His teeth scraped the spot as one of his hands dipped under my fabric, his touch gliding to the crotchless part of my panties. Two fingers ran against my bare, sopping core.

He sucked a breath in through his teeth, probably because he'd expected there to be fabric and instead been presented with my arousal. "Fuck—"

His control shattered. He picked me up and tossed me over his shoulder, marching me back to the bedroom. Once there, he dropped me to my feet and ripped the nightgown from my body; silk tore and then pooled on the floor. His lips crashed down onto mine, and he plunged his fingers inside me, rubbing my clit with his thumb.

"You're so fucking wet," he growled, sounding almost pained. "You want this so bad."

"Yes, Weston, *please*," I begged as his fingers worked, making me whimper.

"I'm going to pound my cock deep inside of you, baby." He pushed me onto the bed, covering my body with his. "I'm going to pump you full of cum and knot you for hours to make sure it takes hold." He rubbed the head of his cock through my wetness before thrusting, letting out a groan, long and low, matching my moan. "Fuck, you feel so good."

He wasted no time in starting to move.

I strained up to him, feeling utterly bared.

"Oh fuck, Weston, please." I groaned, lost in the primal desire of it, struggling to get him deeper, gyrating against his thrusts, loving the wet smack of our bodies joining. "*Yesss . . .*"

His movements turned rough. His skin slapped against mine. I reached between us to massage where I needed it most. I rocked up into him, meeting him thrust for thrust. He kissed me as he cupped my breast and rolled his thumb over my nipple. I moaned into his kiss, rocking a little faster now, my pleasure building quickly.

He groaned as we worked to get closer. I held the side of his neck with one hand and bit into his skin with the other, marking him deeply.

"Yes, baby," he hissed, thrusting faster. "Show everyone what's yours."

The bed bumped repeatedly against the wall. I called out his name over and over as I rocked, gripping his body with my legs. He slammed down into me, his kisses deep, his cock deeper. I felt the base enlarge, butting against me, seeking admittance. Fuck, I wanted it bad. I wanted it seated for hours, nothing between us.

I resisted, though, playing at defiant again, making him chase it. I wiggled, trying to slide away, pulling back right as he tried to shove in.

His growl was carnal. He slid an arm around my shoulders and grabbed my waist with the other, holding me still while ramming into me. I struggled against him, making him tighten his hold even more, compelling him to overpower me. His thrusts were wild and deep as he forced that knot into me, grinding it there, biting down on my neck.

"Take it," he commanded, thrusting harder. "Take your alpha's knot. I'm going to breed you hard and make sure it sticks."

I whimpered at the onslaught. I clutched him tightly, lost in his body. In his movements. In the dream of what we were doing.

He pulled up so that he could look down at my lips, then into my eyes. "I love you, Aurelia."

He kissed me, his tongue delving deep before he lowered his body again, skin to skin, pounding hard. I still clutched him as I tightened up. I was almost there. His teeth scraped my flesh, and then I exploded, pleasure coursing through me. He groaned long and low as he shuddered, finishing inside me.

A surge of joy lit me up as I hugged him harder. A tear escaped from my eye.

He pulled back again, breathing heavily, looking down on my face.

"I love you too," I told him, stroking his cheek. "Thank you. Even if nothing comes of it, the act of trying is . . . more than I ever dared hope for. Thank you for making so many of my dreams come true."

He kissed my lips tenderly. "From now on, this stays inside of you." He pumped his cock, and I heard the wet sounds his release made as he moved. "If it leaks out of that pretty little pussy, I'm going to shove it back in with my fingers, tongue or cock, depending on how I feel."

I shivered, my pleasure starting to build again.

"This pussy is mine," he growled, pumping inside me again, the friction delicious. "You are going to stay full, do you hear me? When you need a top-up, you come and see me. Are we clear?"

"Yes," I groaned as he started moving again, working that knot, pulsing it within me.

"That's my good Little Wolf," he said, and pumped harder. "Let's see how long we can keep this going before we pass out from exhaustion."

36

AURELIA

A week later and I was still floating on a cloud. My nights with Weston were on a whole different level. Primal desire sang through all four of us, the wolves thrumming with need, the humans unable to keep our hands off each other. It was hot and passionate and wonderful and delicious.

We'd even tried the tying-up thing—first me, then him. Both were damn fun. I'd been a bit of a ghost toward the others, something Hadriel had given me shit for last night when he barged into Weston's chambers before we retired to bed. He was busy, too, though. He was still checking in the cities and towns, talking to people and learning all the gossip.

At least we both had something to show for it. They'd questioned the one guy he'd found, leading to two more. Hadriel had found another since, delivering her to Weston. One by one, they were ridding the kingdom of all Granny's spies. Anyone new coming in was watched, the reason plainly given: Granny's people are not welcome, and if you are with her, you are against us. People seemed okay with that.

Weston was always on edge, though. Constantly vigilant. He would not rest while she was at large. It made me swoon to think about. Granny would have a much harder time than she ever imagined trying to get to me.

I almost dared to dream she'd just give up and let me live my life with the man of my dreams.

"Good morning, Captive Lady," Vemar said when I stepped out the door. Dark circles ringed his eyes, and he had no pep in his tone.

I stalled. "You okay?"

He sighed and ran his hand down his face. "There was a serious party last night. I had way too much mead, one thing led to another, and suddenly I'm being pounded in the ass by the head maid's purple strap-on. That thing is unrelenting. Things got a little fuzzy after that. I think I stuck my dick in every single female in the castle, along with a few guys thrown in for good measure. I woke up spooning Calia. I'm hung-the-fuck-over and my dick is rubbed raw. How was your night?"

I blinked maybe a few too many times. "Quiet." We started walking. "Why don't you go back to bed? You don't need to keep my hours, Vemar. I'm used to this. I'm *not* used to having so much fun."

"Nah. I'll grab one of the queen's hangover elixirs. That'll do me. Oh, I heard they have people testing your products now."

"Yeah. We were phase one, I guess, and now the queen is passing them out to volunteers for phase two. If those work, we'll start trying them out in the various markets. Which reminds me, we need to stop by my room. I need to grab the packaging mock-ups. I want to see if the queen has any notes."

"You're on fire."

"Things go incredibly quickly when I have help. Did Calia mention anything about me?"

"Nope, but she was definitely working off some frustration. I don't think negotiations are going well between her and Nyfain. For her, anyway. Nyfain holds all the cards."

"That's probably my fault. I didn't even tell Calia I wasn't accepting her offer. I was so fired up about Granny that I wasn't thinking about the big picture."

"Don't worry about it. They both want you for their own reasons. Let them squabble. So you don't get training in your fairy magic—so what? You still have the pack, your plants, your food, your art, and your friends. You've got plenty."

I smiled and bumped his shoulder with mine fondly. I understood why Hadriel liked him so much and wanted to always work as a team, even if they were currently going in two different directions. He was kind and loyal and supportive while also being fiery and rage-filled and (still) supportive. Nothing fazed him until he was trying to bust a head in. He was remarkably calm for a dragon.

"This is true." I laughed.

As we entered the work shed, I noticed a weak, glowing throb of pink lighting up the interior.

"They must've picked another couple Moonfire Lily petals to work on," I said, glancing at the basket in the corner.

In order to gain experience about plants, the ladies tended to read everything they could—which wasn't much about the Moonfire Lily—and then heavily experiment. They tried everything: when to pick it, how to dry it, maybe not dry it, not burn it. I'd soon be enlisted to try things with my contraptions, adding to their compiled notes about the plants they used. They were a fountain of knowledge, loved their job, and were great at the work.

I was in fucking dreamland.

"The basket is empty," Vemar said, searching for the origin of the glow.

"Hello." Arleth and Delaney walked into the work shed, their eyes puffy and their hair and clothes not quite as pristine as usual.

"What are you guys doing up so early?" I asked, pausing in my pursuit of the glow with a hand on the desk.

"We knew that if you discovered Finley's new elixir," Delaney said, "you'd try it without preamble, but we don't know if it is viable."

Arleth looked at the ceiling as the next pink throb started, a smile spreading across her face. "Look," she breathed, pointing at the ceiling for Delaney.

"That's worth the experiment right there," Delaney said, watching the light climb in strength, hitting its zenith.

"Don't keep me waiting—is that an elixir that glows?" I half shouted, pushing forward to see.

Arleth laughed, crowding around the cauldron with me. "Finley has been thinking about the properties of that Moonfire Lily. It seems like an amazing way to strengthen Everlass without it turning dangerous. Using it is like making a maximum-strength elixir or something. Just as you can make various strengths to your creations, we can use the Moonfire Lily to make certain brews stronger."

"I need to design a new logo," I said wistfully, turning back to what I'd laid on the desk.

Finley walked in with brisk movements, glancing around the room upon entry. Hannon was at her back, smiling at me in hello.

"Hey, Hannon! Where've you been?" I asked, stepping out of the way so Finley could look at her elixir. I hadn't seen him in several weeks; he hadn't been wandering around the castle or stopped into the work shed.

"I was sent away for a bit to give you and Weston space." He grinned and glanced at his sister, who rolled her eyes.

"That wasn't why," she replied.

He quirked an eyebrow at her. "I can tell that you're lying."

Finley scowled at him. "Fine. It wasn't the only reason why. We needed you to speak with that court."

He winked at me. "I hear the fairies are after you."

Arleth scoffed. "*After her* is an understatement. They're at the stage of threatening to 'take what is theirs.'"

I turned toward her with widened eyes. This was the first I was hearing about this. The king hadn't been keeping Weston or me in on the negotiations, saying it was so that we could focus more on the pack and the product, that this was a matter of the kingdom and no longer an individual concern. I was more than happy to ignore it, but I didn't want to cause a problem for Nyfain or create a bigger problem for myself.

"What's that, now?" Vemar asked, pausing in getting his things ready for the day.

Delaney chuckled darkly. "Don't worry about it, Vemar. If that king wants to try his hand at attacking this kingdom, he'll be quickly reminded of which one of us is battle-worthy. He'll lose his ass."

"Don't feel bad about this, Aurelia," Hannon told me, feeling my turbulent emotions.

"I'm not trying to cause a war," I said. "I'm sure there's something I can—"

"No." Arleth held up a hand. "Absolutely not, no. You will not lower yourself to make nice with a court that is essentially threatening to abduct and imprison you. Well, except maybe with this court, but that was a totally different situation."

Finley started laughing. "Stealers, keepers, huh, Arleth?"

Arleth pressed her lips together primly, and Delaney started laughing with Finley.

Finley turned toward me, unconcerned. "Don't worry about it, Aurelia. This is good practice for Nyfain against a more experienced ruler. They've made trades in the past, but this is the first time both parties really want something. It's bound to get heated." She shrugged. "Besides, that fairy king can be a real dickhead. It's time someone gave him hell. Nyfain is giddy to have a reason to do it."

"What is it about you that everyone wants to abduct and imprison you?" Vemar asked me with a grin. Fire coiled in his eyes. He'd probably like it if the fairies came for me. It would give him the excuse to rage.

"They don't know who might've sired her," Arleth said, watching Finley stir the contents of the cauldron. "How could they possibly try to claim her as their rogue fairy? They don't even know which side her fairy blood might've been on!"

"Her mother's," Hannon said, and the others turned to look at him. He faced me, though. "Nyfain and Finley sent me to the Flamma court. I was there for various reasons—there is still a collection of dragon villages in the hills. I asked for, and was denied, royal permission to visit them. Those dragons are mostly ignored, but apparently the wolves don't want to lose any more dragons to this kingdom."

The world fuzzed around me as I waited with bated breath to hear what he had to say about my mother.

"Why didn't you tell me?" Vemar asked, sitting down to his work. "I still have a house there. They can't deny *me* admittance."

"This was a political move," Finley told him. "Our relationship is strained. We wanted to see just how strained."

"While I was there, I had a chance to speak to a certain possible biological father," Hannon continued.

Cold washed through me, memories of my mom when she spoke about my dad collecting near the surface. I couldn't deny my curiosity—what he might be like, if we shared any traits. What she'd seen in him, what had attracted her and held on. Forgiveness and my aversion to do so.

Hannon smiled kindly. "You have Weston and a budding family here, Aurelia. You don't need to trouble yourself with a man who isn't worth the fancy boots he walks in."

"I haven't heard any of this." Arleth put a hand to her hip as Finley sprinkled in some herb or other.

"Hannon debriefed us last night," Finley said. "We were going to have a meeting about it today."

"Now is as good a time as any," Delaney said. "We've got plans tonight."

Hannon glanced at me before looking at the ground. He sat in his usual seat in the back corner, crossing an ankle over his knee.

Finley looked over at him. "Go ahead and tell them."

"At first he denied any involvement with anyone other than his mate. Cheap words. He's known in that court for his wandering eye and having many mistresses. After some chatting and a mild threat or two, he started to be a lot more honest. He remembered your mom, Finley. He did a good job affecting sneers and disdain, but I had the sense he'd genuinely liked her. His memories were fond, even after all this time. His remorse at having sent her away was palpable. I highly doubt she was deceived in his regard for her."

"So, it is him, then?" I asked, my gut tightening.

Hannon inclined his head. "There's a likeness between you and him."

I released the breath I'd been holding, unsure how to feel. Hearing about a person from the past, one I was assured I'd never meet or know any more about, and then learning that he was not only flesh and blood, but had talked about my mother and me with Hannon . . . It was a lot to process. The whole situation suddenly seemed . . . really real.

"Does he know I exist?" I asked in a small voice, wondering if maybe my mom hadn't actually told him. Maybe she'd known she was a mistress and decided to take matters into her own hands rather than disrupt a court or make him choose. Maybe, if he hadn't known, and learned he had another daughter, he might be remorseful he hadn't known me, would be sick that I'd grown up like I had, wishing he'd known so he could've helped . . .

Hannon looked at Finley.

"He does now," she said smugly. She wiped her hands on a towel and turned around. "Fuck that guy *and* that court." She paused to look at us over her shoulder. "That's between us, obviously."

"Obviously," Arleth murmured.

"Tell them, Hannon," Finley pushed.

Hannon's gaze was compassionate. He felt my emotions where the others couldn't and was the only one who knew I wasn't as unaffected about this as I'd previously claimed. Or even as I'd like to be, really.

"I told him you were out in the world." He tilted his head, sorrow slipping into his eyes. I steeled myself for bad news. "He thought I was trying to bribe him until I mentioned that you are the true mate of Weston, the dragon king's wolf beta."

"Then he perked right up, that dickface," Finley groused. "Didn't care about you when you were just some kid he didn't want. Oh, but a kid with a power level stronger than his? The true mate of the prized wolf of the magical world? He changed his tune, and quick." She leveled a finger at me. "I'm not telling you what to do with your life, and you can have a relationship with him if you want, but I'm going to treat that fucker like the piece of shit he is."

My heart sank as Vemar said, "Hear, hear."

No, then. No silver lining to be had here.

I shouldered the disappointment for a moment and then pushed it away. I told myself this was better, actually. I never had to wonder how things might've been different if he'd known. I didn't have to go back and question the truth of my mother's information. I'd lost what I had with Granny and it had nearly broken me, but I would've died if I learned my mother had lied. No, this was for the best. I had my budding family here, as they'd said. I had all I needed without trying to reshape the past.

"Albeit royally," Arleth told Finley. "With icy disdain and well-placed bursts of rage."

"Yes, yes, fine." Finley waved her away. "Professionally speaking, I'm going to treat him like a piece of shit. No hard feelings."

"Their court now knows that his blood daughter exists," Hannon said, checking in on how I was feeling. It was really very nice having someone who knew what was going on without my having to speak it aloud, especially considering it was something I'd been trained against by many long years with Granny and a village who didn't want to hear my voice. "They know her power and are eager for a connection. They don't know anything about her fairy magic, though. I didn't have details on that information."

"They'd only want her more if they knew how hard the fairies were trying to get her, 'dirty blood' and all," Finley said. "The fairies don't want to share, though. It would be a mess if all this was in their hands." She nodded at me. "You made the right decision. Nyfain won't let them push you around because he would die before he let them push *him* around, and you're in his care. You've got the angriest fucker in this world on your side. You'll come out just fine."

"So he doesn't have any fairy in him?" I asked Hannon.

"No. That must've been your mom."

"Except I know for *sure* both my grandparents on her side were wolves. That's my lot in life, then? A family full of cheaters?"

Finley quirked an eyebrow at Arleth, and I wondered what that was about. Finley then laughed.

"Your dad is gross, yes. Sorry about that, but look, he gave you a healthy dose of power. Take it for what it's worth. Your grandparents, though? Honestly, you have no idea. Maybe your grandma got involved with a fairy, it didn't work out, and your grandfather claimed your mom as his and then helped raise her. That happens all the time. Maybe they both had fairy blood and that was why they found each other, but neither wanted to admit it. That happens, too, in that secular kind of kingdom. No one wants to be different. Without asking them, there really is no way to know what went down. You should give them the benefit of the doubt. All of them. Except your scourge of a father. Fuck that guy, the cheating bastard."

"I got the feeling that he and his mate are together simply to further their bloodlines," Hannon said. "I don't think she is faithful, either."

"But did she send her kid away?" Finley demanded. "He

sent his pregnant mistress to another fucking kingdom, Hannon. Then just pretended his *child* didn't exist. That's a rare level of fucked up. I'm glad it worked out this way—now he gets to meet her at court and see what he tossed away. He'll also get to deal with her *very* powerful mate, who I will make sure has the best gods-damned status of his kind just so he can toss it in that turd's face. We don't need longevity as a kingdom; we just need a shitload of gold. Fuck that guy. Fuck that whole kingdom."

She nodded adamantly, and I wrestled with a smile, my entire being feeling light and content. No, I didn't need a specter from the past. I had these people, who clearly cared about me and would battle on my behalf. I had Weston. It was more than I could've ever asked for.

"Wait until he meets the very mean protector of her asshole," Vemar growled.

"Yeah, or deals with Hadriel's very cutting jabs," Finley added. "Or the host of dragons that will have her back—"

"Okay, okay." I put up my hands, my smile winning. "It's really sweet that you all have my back, but I'm not putting much effort into caring about him one way or the other. Yes, he did my mom wrong, and, by association, me too. But Granny did worse. I need to focus on that first."

"Speaking of that," Hannon said lightly. "The Flamma court wanted to know why it took people so long to find this very strong wolf. I got the feeling they didn't really believe me. I recounted your story, Aurelia, about your being suppressed and Granny telling you that you didn't have magic in an effort to keep you content in her trappings. I might've embellished a little about your setup."

"I doubt that is possible," Vemar murmured.

"I mentioned that Granny knew Aurelia's history as well as I did, and how easy it was for us to put a possible name to her bio-dad. They were already displeased with

Granny because of the types of products crossing their borders, but it had never been personal. Now it is."

Finley furrowed her brow. "You didn't tell me this."

"I wanted Aurelia to be the first to know. I don't know if they are going to take any action against Granny, but they might cite a grievance with the Red Lupine court."

"That won't amount to anything," Arleth said. "Except maybe a strained relationship with the Red Lupine Court and Granny. If anything goes wrong with Granny's business or they start bringing in less gold, they'll exile her or make some other statement and pass her off to Flamma as a show of faith. She'll just be on thin ice if Flamma contacts Red Lupine."

I looked over my workstation, trying to push aside the dread I felt knowing Granny's life was closing down around her. I hated that it was coming to this. I wished she hadn't put me in this position. I didn't want to hurt her; I didn't want to treat her like she had treated me. With the product, though, there was no choice. She had to be shut down, and I was the only one who could do it.

"We're going to be the reason they start bringing in less gold," I murmured, and Hannon's gaze rooted to me. "Speaking of, Finley, here are the mock-ups for the art. Also, what is in that Moonfire Lily brew, and when can I drink it?"

Finley stepped to the desk where I'd put the art. She smiled when she looked at the dragon one. Nyfain's great golden dragon spread its wings in the image, but the coloring of the rest of the packaging matched her dragon.

"His form is just so intense," I muttered. "And he's golden. He was made to be a symbol."

"His dragon will be happy to hear your thoughts." She laughed and passed it off to Arleth. "I love it."

"This is . . ." Arleth puffed out her chest a bit as she showed Delaney the mock-up.

"It looks very fine," Delaney said. "Like a luxury item. Maybe too fine?"

"People like luxury, and it'll still be affordable." I handed off the other.

Finley quirked a brow. "This one is very . . ."

"Loud," Arleth said, looking over her shoulder.

"Bold," Finley said. "Fuchsia? That's what you want to go with for the Moonfire Lily products?"

"Oh." I bit my lip. "I was actually thinking of the stuff I make. I didn't know we were doing a special line for the Moonfire Lily. See the fairy on the symbol?"

"No." Finley shook her head. "Get rid of the fairy on this one. Keep the wolf. Dragons have Everlass. Wolves have Moonfire Lily. If the glowing elixir I made works out, I'm thinking your lily is going to be all the rage, and what's better? The fairies won't have a fucking clue what it is, how we made it, and, most importantly, how we got an elixir to glow. If the fairies play nice, maybe we'll put a fairy on something else. Now. Let's get to work, people. There needs to be a reason I got up this horribly fucking early."

"It's good for you," Vemar told her.

She scowled at him. "Tell me that again and see what happens."

Vemar laughed delightedly. "Maybe I will, Strange Lady." Vemar reserved pet names for people he liked, though I didn't know the origin of Finley's nickname. "I could use a good battle."

37

AURELIA

Vemar didn't end up saying it again, not with all the work we had to do.

Throughout the day, I kept looking at the label I'd done up with Weston's favorite color, trying to picture the symbol without the fairy. It would be too plain. Too . . . simple?

About noon, I realized it wasn't the composition that bothered me, but the single wolf. The image struck me as lonely, like Weston shouldering his duty alone. Solitary, like I had always been before I'd met him. The thought made me sad and a little uncomfortable. I'd need to come up with something else.

"Why the fuck do I always find you fuckers standing over the plants like they might up and run away?" Hadriel pushed into our circle a couple hours later as we stood in the garden, looking down on the Moonfire Lily, snug between the Everlass and happy as could be. Its petals glowed a slow throb, hardly visible in the daylight.

"The glowing is entrancing," Finley said in a hush,

nibbling at her lip. "I really want to showcase that in an elixir. Like, *really* really."

"Fine, think about that later." Hadriel shooed me out of the circle. "You're busy. We're all busy. Come on, it's time for you to go get ready. Finley, my love, get your ass moving. You need to be there."

"What? Where?" I asked as he pushed me away from the others.

"You, my darling, are getting claimed tonight. Time to end all the cumdrop dreams of single ladies and gents everywhere."

My stomach turned over in sudden, dread-laced nervousness. "What? *Tonight?* Weston didn't tell me this."

"That is because Weston has been patiently waiting for the king, who has been patiently waiting for Finley, who has been patiently waiting for Hannon to return. This is kind of a big deal. Given your true mate status and your power, you have the potential to be signing on as a pack leader. As a commander, in other words, of all the land shifters in the kingdom. So far you've only met wolves and dragons. Dragons don't connect through a bond like wolves, but other creatures do, like birds of prey, or jackals, or wily rabbits, or other shit I don't keep track of."

"Birds are fliers."

"Yeah, so?"

"So why don't they group in with the dragons?"

"Dragons are their own brand of clusterfuck. Don't listen so closely."

"But . . . I . . ." I grabbed the door in sudden alarm as we passed through, trying to stop the forward momentum.

I'd been waiting for this, wanting this. I'd thought I was ready. And I was—for Weston. I was ready for the claim, for his mark, for our forever. But coming to terms with the fact it was a super-big deal? Doing it in front of the king and queen and the pack? And what if he finally let me join the pack bond and I mucked it all up? Or what if I couldn't be a commander and it dashed all Weston's hopes? What if I wasn't cut out for all this?

I had the horrible realization that, while I was diligently working on my product, I'd been ignoring the extreme gravity of this situation. Suddenly I was not at all prepared.

"I'm not ready," I bleated, clutching the edges of the door as Hadriel grabbed my legs and tried to pull me through.

Vemar came up behind us and stopped, watching me with a grin.

"Help me, Vemar," I pleaded.

"I really enjoy you, Captive Lady, but I will not stand between you and your panic."

"For such a small fucking thing, she's as strong as a dragon," Hadriel said, wrestling me.

"What in the—"

A whip crack made Vemar flinch and Hadriel jump away from me. He turned to find Leala marching closer, and balled his fists at his sides.

"I hate whips, Leala! How many times do I need to tell you that?" he yelled. "I do *not* get off on pain."

"Oh hush, you big baby, I didn't even touch you." She reached for me, but my mind had frazzled and I was already running.

"Do we chase?" Vemar asked as I put distance between us.

"Yes, we fucking chase! Fuck, she's fast. Hurry, Vemar, you have long legs, get her!"

A thrill came over me. I shed clothes as I went, streaking across the grass and leaving my layers behind me. I stopped long enough to shift, and then my wolf and I were gone, darting between the trees and running like fucking hell.

"What are we doing?" she asked, and I was surprised she was going along with this.

"I don't know. Getting away? Giving ourselves some time? Freaking the fuck out?"

"Why is this scary?"

"I don't know! I'm not prepared. The next chapter of my life is really, actually going to start now, but I don't think my baggage is going anywhere, and he might get tired of it! What if I can't handle a pack? What if I let Weston down, what if he is making a terrible mistake and realizes too late that I'm nobody, what if—"

"Okay, okay. Yeah, that's all valid. Let's hide."

She didn't immediately hide, though, because shifters popped out of the woodwork like insects, trying to tackle us. Or maybe they were playing? My wolf didn't know, but she knew she needed to avoid them. We cut across a village, darted through a square and then out the other side of it, down a lane and through an Everlass field.

"Have you been keeping track of where we are?" I asked.

"I don't know where we are. I've never been over here before."

"Can you get back?"

"You want to go back now? We're still trying to get away!"

She ran through the trees and then into deep brush, thorns scratching along her sides. She went deeper still and found a berm with a hole in it, big enough for her to squeeze down into.

"This isn't a good idea," I said as she wound her way into the earth. *"This isn't a good idea at all. How the fuck are we going to get out of here?"*

"It's okay—this'll work out."

"I really don't see how. Back up! Seriously, stop going

forward and start going back. What if there is something in here?"

"It's a really good idea you're not in charge right now," she said.

"I fail to see how!"

At the end of the animal tunnel was a little den, big enough for her to turn around on her belly and face the way we'd come. She finally stopped.

"What if someone comes down after us?" I asked, our heart pounding.

"Who would be stupid enough to crawl down into this hole?"

I was mute for a long moment. *"I wish I could punch you in the face."*

"Sharing a body with you is like being punched in the face over and over, constantly."

I needed to take some deep breaths, but I wasn't in charge of the body.

"Breathe," I told her, needing to feel our lungs filling with air. *"Just breathe for a second. I need to breathe."*

Thankfully, she didn't push back, humoring me and sucking in air. The den smelled musty and old, like it hadn't been used in a while. That, at least, was positive news. Silence filled the space, and she laid her head down on her paws.

"We need to talk this out," I said, trying to clear my head. *"We're overreacting."*

"You were the one that ran."

"Did you not also run? Are you not hiding out in a random small hole you found after crawling through a bunch of thorns?"

She didn't respond for a while. *"You make some excellent points. We're nobody. We might have power, but our dad didn't want us, our mom had no magic, and you don't even know how to eat soup properly. We don't know how to exist in a real community because we've never been properly welcomed in one, and now suddenly we are supposed to be the head of a kingdom-wide pack."*

She wasn't doing a good job of talking this situation around, nor did she stop there.

"I don't know my ass from my teeth, and training hasn't been going well. I know he said we were waiting for the king's go-ahead, but I think I'm actually the reason he was delaying. I bet Hannon was just an excuse. I can make a bond with Weston, but I take over the bond when I try it with Hadriel. I have no finesse with it. What's going to happen when there's a whole pack to connect to and I fumble it? He's going to have to tell me that I'm not good enough and can't participate. Then what'll become of me? You have a job as a human, but I won't be of any use as a wolf. I'll let them down. What kind of alpha would want a mate that is useless? He could have anyone, literally anyone, and he got stuck with me. Love isn't enough, not for an alpha."

"Breathe," I said, and this time it was for her, not me. *"Why haven't you said any of this before?"*

"If you'd been paying attention, you'd know."

"I thought you were doing well in training. You catch on really fast. There's a learning curve, but you're handling it really well."

"I'm great for a new wolf, sure. I'm not so hot for a twenty-seven-year-old wolf who is about to take over a fucking pack."

She had a point.

"We can't hide here forever," I said, though I had no idea what to do now. What if she couldn't rise to the occasion? What if the wolf part of us *was* useless? Did that mean we would be forced to go to the fairies?

"We're not going to hide here forever," my wolf replied. *"We're going to hide here until you, as the more positive half of this terrible partnership, do your job and talk this situation around."*

So we sat there for a while, me trying to get a handle on things and both of us running from our uncertainties.

"You know," I said at one point, *"if a dragon wanted us out, all he'd have to do was blow fire on the thorns and stuff covering the hole until we ran out of air. That would be an easy way to kill us, actually. Or just blow fire right down the hole. We'd be fucked."*

"What the actual fuck—and I mean this genuinely—is wrong with you?"

We sat in silence for a while longer.

Concern radiated through the bond, and we felt Weston drawing closer. Not panicked or hurried, he made his way to our not-so-hidden location. It was hard to get away when your bond-mate could feel your whereabouts. Hell, everyone could probably smell where we'd gone.

He paused at the surface, way too big to fit down here. There he stayed, patience settling in, waiting at the mouth of our hidey-hole. He could've howled down at us, or yelped, or shifted and shouted for us to come out. He could've even sent a bird or something down to peck at us until we had no choice but to crawl out to flee. Instead, he waited for us to be ready.

"I really do love him." I thought about all the things he probably had to do, a claiming he had to get ready for, and realized maybe he was nervous himself. He'd put all that aside to come for us. *"I really, really love him. I want to be with him."*

"We have a lot of baggage."

"But so does he, right? We've heard about his struggles, and not just personally, but as an alpha. In the first pack he ever ran, he basically stole people for the crown. The next pack essentially brushed him off after he came back from the demons. He's dealing with baggage, too. He's combating it by growing, by ensuring that he is better going forward. He has

trauma he is working through, too. He's just further along in the process."

"Yeah. True, I guess."

"He knows you are new. But this whole kingdom is mostly new. Didn't that guy in the village say that? They were all suppressed until, like, a year and a half ago. It's a kingdom being rebuilt. Even those from elsewhere are new to each other. We're behind, but we work hard, we learn fast, and we don't give up. If we have training—and everyone agrees he's an amazing teacher —we can do what is needed. I can learn to eat soup like a king, and you can learn which end of your body the shit comes out of."

She issued a soft growl at that last bit, obviously annoyed with me, but all I could feel was Weston up there, waiting. Hoping. He wanted this; I knew he did. *I* wanted this. So did my wolf. My past was terrible, and I didn't have very good pedigree, but neither did the queen of the kingdom. She came from a tiny village, she hadn't had a penny, and she'd probably had to learn to eat soup, too. I wasn't alone in this, and more, I had something to bring to the table. While my wolf learned, I could prove our value in other ways.

"We can do this," I said, feeling better. *"This is right. Being with him, starting this new life, finally shrugging off the chains that bound us to Granny . . . We can do this. Crawl out of this hole."*

She didn't budge for a moment. *"But now they'll think we're cowards for running."*

"Get out of this fucking hole!" I shouted at her.

She went slower than she probably could have, but finally my wolf made it to the top. Weston's wolf waited there, lifting his head off his paws when she showed herself. He whined softly and licked her muzzle. Support and encouragement radiated through the bond. His gray gaze met hers, and then he started backing out, the thorns digging into his sides. She followed, smaller and not as troubled by the passage.

Outside of the thick brush no one waited for us; anyone that had followed had been "told" to head out. Weston shifted back into his human form and waited for me to do the same.

"Are you okay?" he asked, his tone hushed and his movements slow. He didn't make a move toward me.

"Yes. Sorry, I had a mild freakout when Hadriel mentioned what we were on the way to get ready for."

He nodded slowly. "I'm sorry. I found out this morning after you'd left. I should've made sure someone sent word to you. What can I do to help?"

"It's fine. I'm good."

"Aurelia." His tone brooked no argument. "What's going on?"

I sighed and then just let it all flow out—my concerns, my wolf's. We walked through the brush, finding a game trail and then following that for a spell. One of the towns, probably the one we'd run through, appeared up ahead, and he veered, intentionally avoiding it.

"I would've had all these worries parceled away if I'd known what the plan was," I said. "I just got a scare, is all."

He took my hand and threaded his fingers through mine. "I didn't know why the king was stalling. He didn't mention it was Hannon, probably because he didn't want to say where Hannon had gone. Did they tell you?"

"Yes. He was in the work shed today."

"Good. You're not alone in your anxiety, Aurelia. I doubt myself as well. It's natural. I worry that I won't be a good mate to you. That I won't be a good father. But then I see your beautiful face, or smell your mouth-watering scent, and I know none of those worries matter. Regardless of what could go wrong, I'd be lost without you. I never really cared about being solitary—it's the nature of the job —until you. Now, if I'm without you too long, it's overwhelming. I have to ask you to brave my inadequacies because, even though you don't know the proper decorum regarding eating soup, I need you. My life is pale without you."

I stopped him and turned, pulling him into a hug. "And mine without you. But who mentioned the soup?"

He laughed and kissed me on the forehead. "Finley. She had a similar experience. I think you two will end up good friends." He kissed me lightly on the lips. "As for your wolf," he said as we started walking again, "there is nothing to worry about. This is just an introduction. I will claim you, and then we will shift so that your wolf can formally enter the pack bond. Only that. If the need takes them, the pack might have a run, but only if it feels right."

"What if she is heavy-handed with the bond? She worries about that."

"I don't think that will happen, but it'll be fine. My wolf can help her back out, and we can try it again another time. Listen, this first time will not be kingdom-wide. We're going to start with the palace army and guard. They all know you're a new, powerful wolf. Dante and the others have done the rounds, making sure everyone is clear on what to expect. We won't have any dragons except the king and queen and Vemar, and the king knows not to challenge. Everyone knows not to challenge, actually. This is only the formality of my mate joining the pack, nothing more."

"What's expected of me?" I asked.

He looked down at me. "You're going to keep your eyes on me as I knot you in front of the pack."

38

AURELIA

Nervousness ran wild through me as a knock sounded at my door.

Leala opened it as I waited behind her, my hair and makeup now done. I was just waiting for the dress.

A red-faced Cecil stood in the doorway, a long black dress shimmering over his arm.

"I have been waiting out there for years and years," he yelled at Leala as soon as he could. "I knock. Hello? Nobody. Again. Hello? Nobody."

"Is this it?" Leala reached for the dress and ignored his comments, as he was only out there for a moment.

"No, no. This is no ordinary dress." He brushed past her, grabbing it by what appeared to be the strapless top. He shook it a little, and the whole thing shimmered. "It is plain. It must be plain, that's what the beta said. Fine. Plain. I get it, I get it. We don't show the boobage, but we show the neck. Fine. Shoulders? Fine. But where is the dicks with wings? I can't do that with plain dress."

I put a hand to my chest. "Did I create this dick obsession? I'm really sorry if I did. Not all clothes have to have dicks on them, Cecil. I'd definitely be happy for one piece of clothing without a dick stitched on it somewhere."

He lowered the dress a little, trying to read my face. "You want a vagine?"

"Or maybe just normal clothes without genitalia. That could be fun."

He narrowed his eyes. "I see." I worried that he probably didn't. "But here is this." He held up a finger, reached behind his back, and pulled a fuchsia sash from his pocket. "The beta likes pink, yes? We have a pink sash. It is plain! Except . . ." He lifted his furry brow, and it seemed to act like strings pulling up the corners of his mouth.

"Except?" I reached out and took the sash. Leala leaned in close to see, and then started laughing. In darker pink, little dicks with wings were stitched into the fabric. Apparently this was now my clothing calling card. "Great," I said with a grimace.

Leala laughed harder.

"Yes. There. Plain dress for the beta? Yes. Pop of pink by your request? Yes. Dicks? Yaaassss." He made a fist of victory. "We did it!"

"Did we?"

"Good." Cecil nodded. "In that dress, you make all the dicks stand at attention." He made the fist again, another symbol of his victory, before handing off the dress to Leala. "Do it proud."

With that, he left. I wasn't really sure what had just happened.

"I think Vemar and Hadriel have driven that poor man mad," Leala said with a huge smile. "I wonder if anyone will notice." She held the sash closer to her face and then started laughing again. "I can't believe he made this for the beta's claiming. The beta only gave him another chance at your clothes because he was so adamant about having the perfect thing."

I shook my head. "I just won't wear the sash."

"You have to wear the sash! He was told you were going in all black. He's going to wear all black to match. He has no idea that you plan to wear his favorite color, and no one else even knows it's his favorite color. It is the cutest idea. Remember how I gushed? I don't usually gush. It'll be a really sweet surprise for him. You *have* to do it. Trust me, he won't be looking close enough to see the dicks."

I sighed, shaking my head as I looked at the *great many* dicks stitched into this damn thing. It must've taken Cecil forever.

Hadriel showed up not long after I'd pulled on the dress and slipped on the sandals. They had no heels or ankle ties, just one little strap across my toes to hold them in place. It was as though I were walking barefoot. I wore no jewelry, only flowers in my hair and pins to keep it put. My shoulders and arms were bare, waiting for a mark that would never fade.

"Oh my . . ." He put his hand to his chest and gave me a weepy sort of look. "My darling, look at you! You are an absolute dream! Look at how pretty she is, Leala. She is perfect for that hot alpha."

"Beta," Leala said.

"Tonight he is an alpha wolf claiming his mate, dearest. We call him alpha. Don't fuck up and embarrass me."

Leala smiled at him. "Suck a lemon."

He returned the smile. "Fuck glass. Okay, Aurelia, my love, let's get ready, shall we? Everyone is waiting. We'll have a big pig roast. Burt has assured us that he is up for the job. I'm guessing he'll be at least *half* as good as you.

We'll just make do. Oh! Listen to this. Finley asked me earlier if it would be rude to invite you to dinner but ask you to cook it. I told her it would, but that she should do it anyway. Be prepared for that. And we're walking. Here we go."

"Did you see what was on the sash?" Leala said as they walked beside me down the hall.

"No. What?" Hadriel looked at my waist and then back to the fabric flared across the ground behind me. "What is it? I don't see anything." He tsked and gave Leala an incredulous look. "That ape fucker didn't put dicks on that sash, did he? Say he didn't. Leala! Say he did not put dicks on an item of clothing that an alpha's mate is wearing to a claiming!"

Leala bent over laughing again.

"That seeping bell-end!" Hadriel gritted his teeth in frustration. "Well, don't tell anyone. All we need is for the alpha to get pissed when he's at his most primal. The man is as cool as they come, but everyone has their limits."

"I shouldn't have worn it," I murmured.

"Nonsense." Hadriel patted my arm. "Well, maybe not, but it's too late now. It'll be fine. Okay, here we go. We're turning the corner now, and— Where is that dragon?"

"Right here." Vemar stepped away from the wall wearing a crisp black suit with a sparkly green and silver tie. His pants were black, but his loafers sported the same sparkly silver as the tie. I belatedly noticed Hadriel wore the same thing.

"Right, okay." Hadriel shooed Leala to fall back. "But you definitely need to attend this thing, Leala." He looked over his shoulder. "You haven't seen them going at it. It is a fucking marvel. Talk about compatible! The passion is so scorching it will practically burn you."

"Fucking hell," I grumbled, wishing I could hide my face.

"It's okay, Captive Lady," Vemar said as we walked toward a side exit of the castle. "Most of the people here have seen a great many people going at it. Remember all those orgy stories? And remember that party last night I told you about? A lot of them were there. This won't be a big deal."

"It's a claiming," Hadriel said. "The wolves definitely won't think of it as a big deal. Except for how long his knot lasts—that'll turn into some sort of myth or legend, just you watch. No one will fucking believe it. Here we go, and Vemar is getting the door for you."

He jogged to get there before us and pushed open the door, standing there with a smile as I passed through before Hadriel.

"You look gorgeous, Aurelia," Vemar said. "Congratulations."

"Thank you," I answered as butterflies swirled within my belly.

"Okay." Hadriel caught up to me again. "Here's how it is going to go: Vemar and I will walk you into the alpha's general vicinity. Once he sees you, we'll fall away to the sides. All you do is walk straight up to him. You don't look at anyone else, you don't say hi to anyone—nothing. You walk right up to him as though he is the only person in the area. As I said, he'll be at his most primal tonight."

"His most possessive?" Vemar asked.

"Yes, exactly. His most possessive. Jealous as a motherfucker. He'll literally kill someone for touching you, but don't worry about that. You love him and you want this, so I doubt you'll stray very far from him. Once you are in his bubble, he'll handle the rest. Just go with it. Worst case, let your wolf guide you."

I let out a shaky breath, excited and aroused at the idea of Weston being at his most primal. He was always so incredibly hot when he let that out. "Okay."

"Ready?" Hadriel asked me.

The panic from earlier crept back in. I was worried about the people now, about doing something wrong. "I don't know."

"Good enough. Here we go."

The glow of several fires illuminated a whole host of people standing and chatting to each other. They'd all dressed up for the occasion, everyone in suits and dresses, their hair done but their feet bare. I noticed that ties were loose and dresses were like mine—easy to shed. They expected to shift.

Another wave of nervousness swarmed my belly, this one prompted by my wolf. She'd be on show here more than me. This was my night for love, but she'd be expected to adhere to duty, to join the pack and, hopefully, correctly hold the bond.

Pigs rotated on spits, someone cranking them to keep them going. Cups clinked as people cheered and laughed.

As I neared, the chatter started to die away. Smiles slipped as they took me in, looking at my dress and then the sash flowing out behind me. Looking at my face and my shoulders.

I breathed evenly, trying to steady my flip-flopping stomach as nervous energy zinged through my body.

"There," Hadriel said in a hush, nudging me. "Beyond the fires. Walk right through the middle. Our alpha is making a statement."

"What's the statement?" I whispered.

"That your presence demands everyone's attention."

I started to shake with nervousness now. This was such an extreme break from anything in my life before. To stay safe, I'd been taught to be a wallflower, a shadow, a ghost. If people had noticed me, they'd sneered and tried to chase me away. It had always been dangerous to draw too much attention, and now here I was, the focal point, all eyes on me.

"We've got you, Aurelia," Vemar murmured, steel in his voice. "We're right here. You tell us when we should let you go."

"No, that's not protocol," Hadriel hissed. "We need to—"

"I don't give two shits about protocol," Vemar growled. "We go when she says we go. Guard the asshole, always."

We walked between the fires, and a hush fell over the crowd. Then I saw him, a little beyond the fires as Hadriel had said, standing with the king and queen in a black suit that was practically molded to his delicious body. He turned his head when the king stopped speaking, finally seeing me walk toward him.

The world fell away when I saw his handsome face. He wore his tie loose like the others, and no belt. He also stood barefoot, his pant legs just that little bit longer to make that seem normal. He turned around fully then, pulling his focus away from the king and queen and giving me his undivided attention.

I nodded at Vemar, and he and Hadriel drifted away to either side as Weston scanned my face and then raked his gaze down my body. When it hit my sash, his eyes widened and his gaze snapped back up. Surprise and warmth rushed through the bond, followed by hard love and unshakable devotion.

He took several steps toward me to close the gap between us and cupped my face in his hands.

"You are my chosen," he said. The way he said it, in a loud, clear voice, seemed like a ritual or ceremony. His gaze was rooted to mine as his thumbs softly stroked down my cheeks. "My true mate. My beloved. I will die to protect you, Aurelia, and work every day to make you happy. I love you more than words can say, and I am honored that you have chosen me as your mate."

He didn't kiss me. Hunger burned in his eyes.

"I see you remembered my favorite color," he said softly, for me alone. He was going to be really surprised at the Moonfire Lily label.

"We can take turns now," I replied. "One of us can be levelheaded and the other bold. One of us rational while the other takes risks. We can balance each other. Tonight, you can be the dirty, dark, devious alpha, and I'll be the submissive good girl, doing as her alpha says."

His breath hitched, and his fingers slipped down to my neck and tightened as he stared at my lips hungrily. I let my arms fall to my sides, fully under his control as my desire burned through me. I didn't care that people were watching, just like I hadn't cared before. When I was with him, it didn't seem to matter. He was all I noticed, all I focused on. With him, I didn't deny myself, because I knew I'd be protected no matter what happened.

"What do you crave, Little Wolf?" he asked, his voice deep and dark. He pushed up my chin with a thumb before kissing down my throat.

"You, Weston," I moaned. "I crave you."

He tsked, shaking his head. "What do you crave, Little Wolf? What do you need from your alpha?"

He dragged his lips first down one side of my neck and then the other, sucking in my flesh. One hand slid down my chest, cupping a breast before sliding down and around to my ass. He gripped a handful.

"Tell me." His voice was riddled with power.

"I need my alpha's thick cock deep inside of me while

he stamps me with his mark, claiming me. Ruin me for every other male, Weston. Make me yours."

"You *are* mine!" He ripped my head to the side while bending, and sank his teeth into my shoulder. His magic tingled as it worked over my skin and then down into my bones. Heat pooled low. I needed his touch, his cock.

39

AURELIA

Without thinking, I worked at his tie, loosening it further before going after his buttons. They came away easily, as they were not buttons, just snaps. His pants were next as he ripped the sash from my waist, his teeth still in my shoulder.

"Yes, Weston," I groaned, shoving at his pants and taking his cock into my hand. "Yes. Take me."

I stroked as he pulled his teeth from my flesh so he could pull the tie over his head and toss it away. He yanked off the shirt and jacket next, then stepped out of his pants, making me lose contact with his shaft, before slowing a little as he reached my dress. He stood naked before me, a dribble of my blood down his chin, a god among men.

Slowly, he hooked his thumbs into the top of my dress. A cough sounded somewhere, and it reminded me of everyone watching. I nearly looked around to see how many as reality started to seep into this strange dream state.

"Eyes on me," he commanded. "I will always protect you." He inched my dress down. "Even in the hard times, I will love you, unconditionally." He pushed the dress over the swell of my hips until it fell the rest of the way. I now stood nude with him in front of all these people. "I will choose you, every day, for the rest of my life."

Before I could reciprocate, he grabbed the back of my neck and pulled me to him. His lips fastened on mine, deep and delving, his tongue sweeping through. He pulled my body to his, moving his hands along my skin and then reaching between my thighs, feeling my readiness.

"That's right, baby," he said in a voice soaked with sin. "Let's see how you taste."

Like the first time we were ever together, before we ever knew each other, he lay down in the dirt, pulling my pussy over his face and sucking me in. I groaned, gyrating against his lips, feeling his hand come up and his fingers delve within me. He curved them expertly; he'd been great the first time, but now he knew exactly what I liked and how firm I wanted it. He stroked me as he sucked in pulses, rolling his tongue around and working his fingers. I groaned louder, then louder still, already taken right to the edge.

He yanked my hips away, leaving me on that edge. I mewed out my displeasure as he positioned me over his cock.

"Rub against that hard dick, baby," he said. "Get it all slick."

I worked my hips while bringing his hand up to my breast. He rolled my nipples in that way I liked, sending pleasure right down to my core. It wasn't enough to get me off, though. His dark chuckle said he knew that.

He sat up slowly, one hand on my back and the other running up my belly to my cheek, making me arch backward so that he held all my weight. So that he was in control. Keeping me there, he sucked a nipple as he slid his hand back down, his fingers landing on either side of my clit so he could rub me just a little bit. He was making me crazy.

"Please, Weston," I begged, suspended, at his mercy. "Please, I need your cock. I need to come."

Still, he rubbed as he teased my nipples. The pressure to climax was unbelievably intense. He ran his lips just under my breasts, from one side to the other, then back to my nipple.

I begged again, trying to gyrate but unable to in this position. And then he sucked hard on my nipple while squeezing my clit and setting me off.

"Ho-ly *fuck*!" I screamed out my release as my whole body shook.

He pulled my upper body against him, positioned me above him, and then slammed me down onto his cock.

I rocked my hips as he bounced me, his cock going in deep, already starting to swell.

"You're going to take my knot like a good girl," he told me, his voice vibrating through my body.

"Yes, Alpha," I purred. I ran my fingers through his hair.

"You're going to come on it, over and over until your legs feel like jelly, and then we're going to shift so my wolf can take his turn."

My wolf shivered within me, suddenly incredibly impatient.

"Isn't that right?" He shook me just a little.

"Yes, Alpha," I replied wantonly.

We worked against each other, his movements getting smaller the bigger his cock got. I twisted and turned, working my clit, still rocking.

"I love you, Weston," I told him, clinging to his shoulders, my lips against his neck. "You are the greatest man I have ever known, and an impeccable alpha. I've struggled with fear and uncertainty all my life, but with you, I don't crave walls or borders. With you I feel safe in a way I didn't know was possible. I will choose you, every day, for the rest of my life and beyond."

He pulled my head back so that he could kiss me as our bodies created the most glorious friction.

"Claim me now, Little Wolf," he told me, love and desire burning brightly in those beautiful gray eyes. "Make me yours. Ruin me for anyone else."

My heart surged, and I did just that, sinking my teeth into him and allowing the magic to come naturally. It wound through us, around us, in us, and then a strange new feeling took over. A delightful, tranquil sort of feeling that carried with it an enormous punch of pleasure.

I cried his name as I shook against him. Weston shuddered as well. We immediately started to build again, and it felt like flower petals descended upon us. Another heartbeat thudded in my chest, pounding once, twice, and then seeming to merge with mine.

I backed off to see his face. His eyes were liquid metal, so open, so soaked with love.

"That's us imprinting, baby," he said with a note of reverence. "Even after all of this, I don't know that I totally believed you loved me. That you could love me. I've done so many things I regret, things I'm not proud of, despicable things that ruined families. And I've done things against my will that . . . I'm such a mess, my head is so fucked up, so dark, I didn't truly believe in my soul that your love could be real. You're too pure, too innocent."

He kissed me in a rush, and I backed him off, laughing.

"I made drugs for a woman who turned them lethal, I've killed a great many people starting when I was twelve, I've helped trap a village, and now I'm pulling a dragon kingdom into the dark side of hallucinogens while they are forced to fight with the fairies because of ill-gotten magic. I don't think I'm as pure and innocent as you've built me up to be. Don't you remember why you were sent to find me? I've ruined plenty, believe me. We've both suffered, Weston. We've both dreamed. And now here we are, fucking in the dirt while people are trying to eat. It's a match made in the heavens."

He laughed, holding me close, brushing back the hair that had escaped Leala's design.

"I'm just glad to have you," he said.

"How many kids do you want?" I whispered, rocking against him. "I never asked."

His arms constricted around me. "As many as you desire, my love. I won't ever get tired of fucking you. You control what comes of it."

"So, like"—I kissed his lips, letting it linger—"a wagonload?"

"The more, the merrier."

I laughed softly and kissed him harder, rolling my hips. Little bites of pain tugged at me from his knot, and he crushed me closer, thrusting and pulling to keep himself embedded deep.

"Fill me up, Alpha," I moaned, my head falling back. "Fill me with your seed. I need it."

"Use me, Little Wolf. Use your alpha to your heart's content. I'm yours."

His body pulsed inside of me then, the delicious vibrations sending blooming pleasure throughout my body. It was even more delicious than usual, more consuming. I mentioned it as we worked toward another orgasm, straining against each other.

"It's the imprinting." He sucked at his claim, making me groan at the exquisite sensations. "It makes everything better."

The pleasure pounded through the bond, sweeping me away. He sucked his claim a little harder, and I shattered, coming on top of him again.

"That's right," he cooed, running his lips up my neck. "Come all over your alpha's cock. Show the pack who you belong to."

We kissed as we kept going, wild and raw, utterly primal. We'd always been good at this, but for the next few orgasms I was lost to him and him alone. Only his touch registered. Only his voice and the heat of his skin.

Our bodies were slick with sweat when I finally laid my head on his shoulder, my lips against his neck. I needed a little break before the next one.

"This can't be comfortable for you," I murmured.

"It's perfectly comfortable. I could move us to a chair, but I like it better here. I like the pack seeing us like this, lost to each other, not giving a shit where we are or how dirty my ass-crack is getting."

"Oh man." I laughed, tracing the muscles on his back with my fingers. "And what are they going to do—"

"Eyes on me," he commanded just as I twisted to look around.

His power forced my eyes to snap to his. Pleasure unfurled within me, and I started rocking against him yet again.

"Yes, Alpha." My tone was smooth as silk. I saw heat bloom in his eyes. "Is looking around against protocol?"

"No, but you're new to all this, and I don't want the moment derailed, not for a second. You asked what they are going to do?"

"Yeah. This is going to take a while. We can't really expect them to stay and wait, can we?"

"The royals? No, though I bet they will, just to see how running with the pack goes. They'll probably remove themselves a little so Finley can sit on Nyfain's lap and have their own fun. The others? Yes, they will stay here until their alpha and his new mate releases them. They'll eat and drink and slip off into the trees in pairs, the males seeing if they can hold their knot as long as the alpha and the females just looking for an orgasm."

"I get the feeling that it'll be more than twos or even threes in this place."

He smiled and kissed my neck gently. "You're probably right. This castle is on another level. You can thank the curse for that."

I rocked as another orgasm bloomed on the horizon. "So we're definitely going to run with the pack?"

"Absolutely. I need to show off my mate—so quick and agile no one can catch her."

Weston

Time started to slow as the orgasms decreased in fervency. I'd prolonged my knot once, having learned that if I just started actively pleasing my mate again, her ardor for me rose high enough that my body responded eagerly. She couldn't seem to get enough of me, nor I of her. It was time to let it wane, though. We had the next phase of the claiming to get to.

She draped around me, her head on my shoulder and chest against mine. Her heartbeat—our heartbeat—pulsed strong and sure within us, something I'd heard happened with imprinting but had never really understood. Feeling it now was comforting. Reassuring, even, with my mate so close—closer than a bond. It was a primal feeling right in my middle, her heart given to me for safekeeping as was mine to her.

Fuck, this was heaven. I didn't want it to end.

The pack lounged around us, having waited for over three hours at this point, which was definitely a record. A few people still lingered in the trees, the whole place having basically fled once we'd joined, ripping off their clothes as they headed for cover and the feel of flesh. Some hadn't even waited to get into the trees before they reached for the first willing partner. Aurelia must've let loose her magic and convinced the whole party to join us in pleasure, not that they'd needed much prompting.

Most people partook in sexual activities during a claiming, watching the lead pair and feeling the heat. Some more than others, of course. A great many alpha pairs were arranged based on power and bloodlines. There often wasn't much passion or desire, which withered most people's interest. It was not so with my mate and me. We would've sparked heat without Aurelia's magic; I'd heard enough rumors about how the pack viewed our compatibility to be assured of that.

The pack's lust was why I hadn't wanted Aurelia to look around. She would've clued in on what she'd done and felt bad about it, or maybe embarrassed. I hadn't wanted that to ruin her experience.

I trailed my fingertips along her back as the king and queen rejoined the group, each wearing a slip like everyone else. It seemed no one cared about getting re-dressed into their finery. They probably figured they'd either shift soon or just end up banging again. Both were probably true.

"We're going to head onto the next phase," I whispered into Aurelia's ear. "Are you ready?"

"No," she grumbled without lifting her head from my shoulder.

I breathed her in, holding her close. The imprinting had mostly settled, though these tranquil effects and my extreme possessiveness and protectiveness over her would continue for days to come. I'd never heard of a shifter who'd disliked it.

"It's time for you to bond with the pack." I kissed my newly laid mark, and she shivered, moving on my cock again. "No, no." I chuckled and held her still, making her groan. She liked when I showed my strength. "No, Little Wolf, stop. We have to stop now, baby."

She pulled back a little, kissing me and letting her lips linger. "I don't want to stop. I want to go back to your room and keep going until I am dripping with your seed."

"Fuck," I groaned, squeezing her close, mashing my lips against my mark. "We will. After all this, we will. But we have to take care of the pack. They've waited long enough."

That made her quiet. She let her hands drift down my back.

"Fine," she grumbled, kissing along my neck. "Let's get this done. My wolf is eager for . . . you know."

"They won't take nearly as long."

"Good." She paused. "Oh, shut up, you can wait a little longer."

Clearly, that was for her wolf.

My cock continued to settle down until she was able to slide off me and stand, her legs stiff. She held on to me as I stood, laughing as we clung to each other to stay upright.

"You must've been miserable," she said as Finley and Nyfain slowly walked closer.

"I wasn't. It was perfection. I wasn't uncomfortable at all." And I hadn't been, not even a little. I'd only been able to focus on her body wrapped around mine, her solid weight, our heartbeat. "I love you."

"Well," Nyfain said as he stopped well away from Aurelia. Finley kept her distance from me. Wolves weren't as volatile as freshly imprinted dragons, but we did have boundaries. "That was fun. I've said it before and I'll say it again, I wish dragons could do that knotting."

"That looked like a good time." Finley's eyes sparkled as she took in Aurelia. "Are you happy?"

Aurelia slipped her arm around my waist. "Yes. Very."

Finley nodded. "Good. Okay, Nyfain and I are going to shift and take to the sky so that Aurelia doesn't get weird and have wolves climbing trees trying to find a way to attack us. You guys can shift and do what you do. If there is a problem, give us a howl and we'll help figure it out. No one is supposed to challenge, though, right?"

"Correct," I replied. "This should just be a bonding experience. There will probably be more intimacy, though the shifters aren't required to stay for that. They usually do, however, many of them joining in. It's one of the few times wolves . . . engage when they aren't in heat. They are usually all eager, even more so than the humans."

Finley grinned, grabbing Nyfain's hand. "In that, we have it better. Okay, we'll get out of here. Good luck, Aurelia. You'll do great!"

Nervousness rippled through the bond. Aurelia's heart beat faster, increasing the speed of mine. What a trip.

"It's going to be fine, love." I pulled her close and kissed the top of her head. "If you don't feel the bond, we'll just run. Only do what feels natural."

Vemar and Calia emerged from the tree line as Finley shifted and lifted off. Nyfain wasn't far behind her, the great golden dragon blotting out the moon for a moment. The shifters discarded their flowing clothes, some folding them and setting them down and some just tossing them where they stood. Calia and Vemar got close, though he reached out to stop her from getting *too* close.

"Well now, Captive Lady, are you more relaxed?" he asked with a smirk.

She turned into me a little more. "Very much so, at least until this moment."

"Oops." He covered his eyes with his hand. "There, better?"

"Aurelia, I am so sad!" Calia told her, giving her a little pout. "I wanted you to come back to my kingdom with me."

"I'm sorry," she said, leaning her head against me. "I should've told you in person. I wasn't thinking. I chose here because . . ." She shrugged, looking up at me. "It'll be the best place for our family, I think. It'll be the best place for me to start over."

I pulled her in tighter, the warmth radiating through me catching my breath.

Calia smiled at Aurelia as Vemar peeked between his fingers at her.

"Just between us—and the royals know this," Calia said, "I can't blame you. Why do you think I have a residence here? I count the people here as friends, or as close as someone in my position can get to friends. But . . ." She affected a stern face. "As a representative of my kingdom, I will say that you are making a huge mistake. Be prepared to sever all ties. We do not take kindly to people who shrug off our offer of aid." She winked at Aurelia. "I'll chat with you later. Apparently soon you will be making food for the dinner you are invited to." She shrugged. "Welcome to a kingdom with a mediocre cook, I guess."

"Shall I just head into the sky, Alpha?" Vemar asked me, taking his hand away now. "Or should I skedaddle?"

"Your choice. You seemed able to shrug off her magic, so I don't think you're a danger."

He arched an eyebrow. "I didn't do much to shrug off her magic earlier."

"Yes, she is very strong." Calia smiled at Aurelia, whose expression had turned quizzical. Then she smiled at me. "You're a lucky man, Alpha. And I just want to tell you . . . You were my rock in the demon dungeons. I don't think I ever said that to you. You were a rock to a lot of us. You kept us steady. I think many of us would've lost our will to live if it hadn't been for you. You kept us going until Finley could get us out. For that, I thank you. Truly. You deserve all the happiness."

I bowed to her. "It was a dark time. I'm glad we were able to help each other through it, and that we are able to keep in touch, too."

Vemar nodded his agreement. He'd been on a different level in those dungeons, but he was no less affected by the experience.

"Okay. Away." Vemar waved us gone. "Go! Let's see what the new wolf can do!"

40

WESTON

A thrill of nervousness rolled through Aurelia before she steeled herself with determination. She nodded at Vemar, said goodbye to Calia, and then stepped away to wait for me. I glanced out over the gathered crowd, feeling their anticipation running high. Many of them had seen Aurelia streak through the forest or earlier through their town, all of them marveling at her speed. Many had also offered or tried to push the bond on her, wanting her to join up, liking the feel of her energy. She'd eluded them all, giving them the thrill of the chase. And now she was ready to show them all what they'd been wondering about, what Hadriel had told everyone was the most amazing bond experience he'd ever felt.

I turned to her. "Ready?" She answered by shifting.

I was right behind her, my wolf taking over and breathing in her wolf's new scent, one that now mingled ours with hers. We weren't done yet, though. True mates didn't just claim once; they had the ability to do it twice, something only afforded to that natural pair. My wolf was eager to lay his mark.

"Later. They're waiting," I prompted.

"You're one to talk," he sniped at me.

He yipped, and the rest of the pack shifted, sinking down onto four legs, most covered in fur, most of them wolves, but not all. For guard duty, a pack of wolves had often been the most effective, as we could use the bond more easily, allowing us to work with each other seamlessly. Lionesses fit right in, as did our lone young elephant. Solitary shifter animals had a hard time working as a unit.

My wolf waited for all the other animals to jog forward a bit, crowding in, trying to make it easier for Aurelia to find and connect with them all.

They needn't have bothered.

Her magic swept over us easily, spreading unity, love, and her longing for a sense of community. That was the fairy magic. Then came the reach for the bond. She accepted it from my wolf first, as we'd practiced, zipped out to Hadriel within the throng, whom she was comfortable with, and then extended out to everyone in the vicinity. Like a rope pulling taut, everyone snapped into tighter focus before the steel clamped down, strengthening the connection. Once that was established, the magic of our true mate pairing filtered in, tranquil and warming and encompassing, turning a means of order and command and communication into a pleasant oasis, merging us all together a little tighter, sharing more of our emotions, deepening the pack bond.

An overwhelming surge of support colored the bond; the pack approved of her connection and applauded her on managing it.

Her wolf rubbed against mine, pleased.

"And now we show her off," my wolf said, nipping her flank as he sprinted forward.

Her wolf's delight unfurled, and then she urged the pack on. *Follow the alpha.*

"She doesn't think of us as a beta to this kingdom, but solidly their alpha," my wolf said. "Her *alpha."*

"She likes when I exercise my dominance."

"Sex is one thing; leadership in a pack is another. What I'm saying is her wolf has joined the pack with power equal to ours, but she is very clearly looking for guidance. She's making it known that she is learning, and that I am her lead. She's not presenting herself as half an alpha pair, but as a member of the pack who needs to earn her place."

I couldn't decipher the complexities and nuances of body language and positioning, but I knew what certain things meant within pack dynamics. She was making it clear to everyone that, despite the position her power and pairing afforded her, she would not assume command unless she had earned it. Unless she was capable of it. Until that time, if or when it ever came, she would follow her alpha. She would be one of them.

She was remarkable, particularly considering any other alpha mate I'd ever heard of had felt like they had earned their place at the top of the hierarchy because of power and blood. Even without an opportunity to lead, as was the case with most alpha mates, they would demand respect and obedience because of their status.

Aurelia was looking to be immersed. She wasn't above anyone—she was one of them. I knew if she ever led, she would be elevated by them.

My heart felt full to bursting.

"That is perfect," I said as she easily caught us and almost seemed to prance at our side.

"Yes, it is," my wolf said with pride. *"It's better than we could've hoped for. It's a solution we never thought of."*

"No alpha or alpha mate would've. It's certainly not some-

thing a potential co-alpha would've considered. It isn't how our people, especially those with power and prestige, are brought up. She wasn't trained with the inherent pride and conceit that we were. It's . . ."

"Humbling," my wolf finished.

"Yes, it is. It is also good for pack unity, and she craves that above all else. Above being a fairy. Her upbringing, as rough as it was, prepared her for this. She'll always know she made the right choice."

"Once she visits those gods-awful arrogant fuck-stains, yes." My wolf showed his teeth. *"Calia is the only one I actually liked."*

"Her sister."

"She's not a fairy."

True enough.

"But yes," my wolf said, *"I liked her sister a great deal. But back to our incredible mate. Shall we play a game of chase?"*

My wolf bent his head back as we ran and bit into Aurelia's leg, hard enough to make her yelp. She darted to the side, so fast when she changed direction it was dizzying. The bond relayed the way she recoiled, as though she'd done something wrong, but it only took her a moment to realize it was a game—a vicious one.

The pain from her bite registered before her darting toward us had, and then she was gone. Through the bond, her message was crystal clear: *Catch me if you can, fuckers.*

As was my wolf's: *She is* mine*!*

He ran after her like he was being chased by the hounds of hell. He was much larger than her and had a longer stride. He gained slowly, nearly on her now, ready to sweep her back legs out from under her and tackle, but just as he was reaching her, she changed direction and put on a burst of speed.

"Damn it," my wolf said, delighted anticipation coiling within him. *"Our Little Wolf is making me work for it."*

He did love a good chase.

He blocked out her ability to feel the bond and then used it to spread out the pack, who'd all started to lag behind us. Some shot out right, intercepting Aurelia when she attempted to turn that way. She flitted between them, nipping and bashing into them with her body, doing just enough to work her way through and out the other side.

Another section of the pack I'd sent right didn't head her off in time. She streaked past them, Dante barking at her as she went.

I changed my course and sent some of my fastest runners to cut into her path. She ran smack into them; they jumped out from the brush and difficult-to-spot hidey-holes. Tanix caught up to her, positioning himself so that she would slam into his side. Given he was larger and stronger, she should bounce off, which would allow the rest of them to easily surround her and keep her put until my wolf came to collect.

Right before impact, though, just as Tanix braced himself, she startled and leapt over him. Slight pain reverberated through the bond—she might have landed a little awkwardly—but then she was off again, moving toward my left. I could hear Tanix's annoyed howl from here.

"If we didn't have a bond with her, we'd be hard-pressed to keep track of her once she sprinted away from the pack," my wolf said, his pride glowing stronger. The challenge heightened his anticipation; his strong desire pumped through us.

"She has spent her entire life running or hiding. She has developed a sixth sense in regard to danger and anything like it. It shows."

"It does, thank the gods. It'll be easier to protect her."

She took off toward that town she'd run through earlier, curving away when she was nearly there, and ran into Nova and her team. Nova spread out, not running *at* her but *with,* closing the distance little by little, slowing Aurelia down. It was a damn fine strategy. Her promotion ceremony was set for a week's time. She'd earned the increase she'd get.

Aurelia was nearly stopped, the circle closing in, her heart not speeding up.

"She's not concerned," my wolf said, running for all he was worth in that direction. *"Why is she not concerned?"*

She proved why in the next moment when she darted toward who I knew was the weakest member of that squad. I felt pain and panic from that wolf, and then Aurelia was through again, running off into the wood.

"Clearly she is learning well during your fight training," I told my wolf.

"Indeed."

The rest of the pack was already moving into position, fanning out around her and then tightening their circle. Once they got close, I'd pull the stronger wolves to the front and block her in, positioning the others behind in case she jumped like a little fawn.

The dragons circled overhead. They watched my strategies from above so they would know how to train the other dragons to work with them.

Aurelia hit the first wall of my defense, and I could tell through our bond that she was calculating a way through. That came up empty, though, as my strategy was tight. She changed position, quickly coming up against another wall of wolves.

Finley roared, swooping down and then back up. She roared again, her rage plain, before a burst of fire shot out above the tree line.

Understanding surged through the bond. A moment later, my wolf's communication with the pack was instantly severed.

"Fucking dragons," my wolf mumbled.

"What just happened?"

"We're playing a game. Finley just coaxed Aurelia into playing dirty."

"Like we are?"

"Exactly like we are." He worked to get the communication back up as he tore off in her direction. He tried to wrestle control away from her wolf, but she wasn't trying to control anything; she was just blocking his attempts to do so. His power smashed into hers, grappling, ripping at it. She allowed him to get hold of it for a moment—she didn't waste the energy needed to hold on—but only allowed him a glimpse of where everyone was before she deadened him again.

"Fucking Little Wolf," my wolf grumbled, frustration mixed with pride. His anticipation grew; her location was not far.

She hadn't trained as extensively as we had. She couldn't run as far, and she'd been chased and corralled. She was losing steam fast.

"Cheat to win," I told him, laughing.

"As long as I fucking win."

He worked at that pack bond, refusing to give up, feeling incredulousness within it. Everyone was surprised Aurelia could be so effective against a wolf of our caliber. Did they not believe a true mate would have the same power level? Or did they simply not think an untrained wolf new to her fur could be so wily?

"She is perfect," I said again.

"She is getting on my last fucking nerve, and my claiming

bite is going to be hard and deep." His adrenaline was running through him, boosting his desire.

The pack had stopped moving when communication deadened; they were awaiting further instructions. They had no backup plans laid out to keep them going. There was no precedent for an alpha chasing his true mate through the woods, though their stopping meant their barriers were still in place.

Aurelia came upon one section, trying to get around, but the pack closed in to keep her put. When my wolf could access a glimpse of the bond, he felt their unease about this. They didn't want to trap her. They didn't want to gang up on her. That was good for the health of the pack, but it meant we needed to cut this short.

"I know," my wolf said, feeling it and beating me to the punch.

He pushed harder, running faster, nearly on her now. She hit another wall, turned back, and then we were there, barreling into her with all our speed and might. Both wolves rolled through the dirt; we knocked the wind out of them. She was still up blindingly fast, but my wolf was ready, pouncing on her, closing his teeth around her neck.

She stilled, her body turning languid as she whimpered in submission. Her desire burned as brightly as his.

He loved a chase, and she loved being caught and dominated.

They both released the effects they'd had on the bond, letting the pack know all was well and safe and there were no hard feelings or animosity. The pack started jogging to our location as the dragons continued to circle overhead.

"Now we make that human highly uncomfortable," my wolf growled.

He licked her fur where he'd bitten, rubbed his head against her side where he'd tackled her, and then waited for her to get to her feet. She rubbed against him before turning, and he wasted no time mounting her. He chomped into her unmarked shoulder, his magic coming from the same place as mine as he claimed her for the second time.

Pleasure spiraled between them, between us. Aurelia didn't shy away from it this time. She reached for me through the bond and basked in it all—pleasure at being claimed, pleasure at feeling the bond still so solid, desire from our chase and the playful struggle.

This time he didn't cut it short. Aurelia vibrated within the bond, her fairy magic once again affecting anyone who'd made it to our location. The king and queen climbed in the sky, and it seemed the dragons were going to partake as well. Vemar continued to circle lazily, the ultimate voyeur.

When the wolves finished, Aurelia's wolf would complete the double claim on him and they'd probably all do it again.

"This is what life is meant to be," my wolf said as he was with his mate. *"That dragon wished he could knot, though I do wish I could purr like they do."*

"Don't tell him. His ego is big enough as it is."

"Didn't need to be said."

41

AURELIA

Two months passed by in a blink. We worked at a frantic pace to get product made, packaged, and sent. Orders were coming in like crazy from our kingdom; people loved the samples and wanted to purchase large quantities. We'd also sent our first shipments abroad, offering products at reduced prices to get people to try them, hoping it would drain away Granny's sales. If it didn't, step two would be to start visiting the possible production spots, looking for increased Everlass elixir sales, and hope one of them panned out.

The fairies and Nyfain still hadn't made any solid progress. Given things were going really well with the pack and my training was going great, Nyfain felt he had plenty of time. He wouldn't settle for less than I deserved.

It didn't feel like I had any time, though. Despite the fact that everything seemed calm and I was the happiest I'd ever been in my life, I couldn't shake the feeling this was all a fleeting moment. Like a deadline was coming up, and all of this was about to be ripped away.

Maybe that was just my uncertainty, my disbelief I could be this blessed in life, because everyone agreed that Weston's defenses were rock solid. The only holes in his defense were by design. Not that it mattered, because Hadriel had chased away anyone that didn't belong in the kingdom, and even some who probably did. I was likely the safest I'd ever been in my life.

For some reason, though, it didn't stop the nagging feeling that I was missing something. That this was not forever.

I took a shaky breath as I braced my hands against the sink in the washroom, feeling a little lightheaded. My face dripped from my having just washed it, and I looked myself over in the mirror. Despite the glowing health of my skin, I looked awfully pale. I was probably doing a bit too much. Training with the pack was great, but it was hard work. I was tired a lot more lately.

I glanced at my body for a moment, lingering on my belly. It looked the same as it ever had.

I straightened up and trailed my fingers across my skin, dragging my lip through my teeth as I donned my work attire—still drab. There was no point in wearing something flashy that was just going to get dirty. This one had a pattern, and hidden within the pattern were dicks with wings. Cecil apparently thought it should be my banner or something. He attributed Weston's sexual prowess and performance at the claiming to the dick sash. He also shook his fist at me whenever he saw me and said, "*Yaaaasssss!*"

The whole situation was very odd. I chose to ignore it.

Back in the bedroom, I leaned over Weston and kissed his forehead. His eyes drifted open and he reached out for me. I took his hand as I kissed his lips.

"Bye," I whispered. "Come and see me if you're passing by."

"Love you," he murmured.

I kissed him again and said it back before I left. The royals were putting the finishing touches on the new apartment we'd be moving into, so Weston and I still had our separate apartments, though I spent most of my time in his room. Vemar waited for me just outside the back door of the castle these days, sitting on a stone bench and sipping his tea. The agreement was that he'd wait for me long enough to drink his morning tea, and then he would head to the work shed. If I didn't show—usually because Weston had been naughty and banged me, thus locking me in bed with him—I'd meet Vemar there later.

"Hey." I sat next to him so he could finish without being rushed.

"Hello, Captive Lady. How do you feel today?"

I dragged my lip through my teeth again, trying not to feel anything. Trying not to get ahead of myself.

"My boobs are sore."

He tilted the cup back to drain the contents and stood. "Well, that's not good. Did the beta get a little too wild this morning?"

I pulled my lips to the side, trying to squish down the joy. I told myself I'd wait a few days longer. That I wouldn't jump to any conclusions yet. I didn't want to be wrong, and I definitely didn't want to say something, be wrong, and then have Weston disappointed.

But then I just blurted it out anyway.

"My period is almost a week late."

A blast of absolute joy gushed through me. I wrestled with the smile.

Confusion leaked through the bond from Weston, who

was surely wondering about the feeling. I tried to calm it all down.

I stood as Vemar set the empty cup on the bench. Someone would come by shortly and collect it. He started walking, looking down at me with his brow furrowed. "Are you insinuating that you are pregnant, Captive Lady?"

"I don't know." There was that joy again. "I didn't tell Weston about my period because I didn't want to get his hopes up. But yesterday my boobs started to feel sensitive, and today they ache when I touch them." I tried to breathe through the threatening excitement. "I think that means something."

"I definitely think that means something. Did you tell Weston about the boob issue?"

"No. You're the first person I've told. I couldn't help it. But I'm trying to stay super chill and not get my hopes up too high. It's only been two months of trying."

He put his hand on his chest. "I am honored you would tell me. In the spirit of the situation, I am also trying to remain chill and not get excited." He stopped. "I think we should go wake the queen and get her to make you that brew that tells you for certain if you are or aren't."

"Gods no." I pulled his arm to get him walking again. "It's the crack of dawn. Very few people like waking up as early as we do. This is not an emergency." I tugged him in the direction of the work shed. "Come on, it can wait."

He grudgingly started moving. "Let's at least poke our heads into the other work sheds and see if anyone knows the recipe."

"No one starts work this early, Vemar, you know that."

He sucked his teeth, looking back toward the castle. "I really don't think the queen would mind . . ."

"Would you come on?" I laughed and pulled him along.

Near the work sheds, though, he pushed me toward the first one. "Come on, let's just check."

As I'd expected, no one was at work yet. He'd have to be content with waiting until the others came in, and I was content to push it out of my mind for now. It was still early. It could mean absolutely nothing. There was no sense in getting worked up when the whole thing was one big unknown.

It was Hannon who walked in first, his hair a mess and his eyes a little puffy. He was going to see if he could impart his magic onto the Moonfire Lily today.

"Late night?" I asked him with a smirk.

"Who cares if it was a late night, man, *where is your sister*?" Vemar yelled at him. He then put up his hands. "That was a little overboard, I admit. I got a little too worked up with that question."

"What's going on?" Hannon studied Vemar for a moment and then looked at me.

"Nothing." I shook my head, going back to my work. "Don't mind him."

"I do not understand the calm rationality of alpha wolves," Vemar muttered. "I really do not."

Hannon was still studying me when Finley walked in. Hope nearly choked me until I worried I actually wasn't pregnant, maybe couldn't be, and then the uncertainty rushed back in. This was why I hadn't wanted to think about it or even tell Weston: I didn't need more pressure to add to my already turbulent emotions.

"Something is going on," Hannon told Finley.

"Yes, *something is going on*," Vemar shouted, and then put up his hands again. "Overboard. That's on me."

"Um . . ." I cleared my throat, thankful to Vemar because I actually did want a woman's opinion. "It's just that I'm six days late and my boobs are sore. But I know it's still early, so I haven't said anything to anyone. Except Vemar just now. Who is making a big deal about it, obviously, so now you both know. But I just want to keep things quiet until I'm sure before I tell Weston."

"I'm confused. Late for what?" Hannon asked.

Finley rolled her eyes at him, then asked me, "Did you even go into your heat?"

I shook my head. "No, not yet."

"Fucking wolves," Finley said with a cockeyed grin. "You sneeze at each other and you get pregnant."

Dawning crossed Hannon's face and he smiled. "Congratulations, Aurelia! That's so great!"

Vemar put up his hand. "We are staying chill, brother. We have not confirmed. We're waiting patiently for Finley to move her fucking ass to see if we should be fucking thrilled. Let's all calm the fuck down!"

Finley laughed. "Dragons view children as precious miracles. They get very excited about pregnancies." She moved around the room. "Let's find out for certain, shall we? Then we can see about telling Daddy Wolf."

"Yes." Vemar inclined his head. "Yes we shall. Does anyone else want to be there when she tells the beta? I really do. That wolf is going to lose his shit."

Uncertainty washed over me again.

"What's the matter?" Hannon asked.

"Nothing." I calmly tucked a strand of hair behind my ear. "Nothing, it's just . . ." I let go a shaky breath. "If I am, and the child doesn't have magic . . . What if the different bloodlines cancel out the magic, like in my mom?"

"Hey, whoa." Finley turned from the pot she was working in front of. "Hey, don't worry about that, okay? First, based on the things you've said, it sounds like your mom *did* have some sort of magic. She was probably an Emoter, like you. She was knocking on the wrong doors and asking the wrong questions about her magic. Second, it doesn't matter if your child doesn't have one drop of magic. They won't be any less welcome here. They will not be treated like you were, Aurelia. They will have a lot of dragon aunties and uncles that will ensure that fact, regardless of what kingdom they go to. Okay? Don't worry. We protect our own. You're one of us now. We'll protect your child, no matter what."

Tears pooled in my eyes as my heart filled with gratitude. To know that my child would never suffer as I had suffered, no matter their magical status, cracked open my heart and warmed my whole body. That a queen would promise me my children would be safe when safety had always been so precious . . .

It was a gift unlike any I had ever received. One I would covet forever.

My tears overflowed. "Thank you," I whispered with a tightened throat.

Arleth and Delaney came in as Finley was finishing the elixir.

"What are you—" Arleth cut herself off and turned, looking at me with wide, delighted eyes. "Is that for you?"

"Congratulations," Delaney said, offering one of her rare work-shed smiles.

"I mean, I'm not sure—"

"We're not fucking sure, man! Stay fucking calm!" Vemar shouted. He threw up his hands. "Overboard." And walked out of the shed.

"I love when that dragon gets his scales ruffled." Finley grinned, setting a bowl of elixir onto the floor. "Okay, we just need a pee sample."

"*What?*" I sputtered. "You mean right here?" I grimaced.

Finley braced a hand on her hip. "Lady, we watched you fuck for, like, three hours. Pee in that motherfucking bowl.

Time to find out if we're going to have a very proud papa on our hands."

"I agree with Vemar—I want to be there when she tells him." Hannon turned his back so I'd have a little privacy to pee into the bowl. I could only hope I wouldn't miss and get it all over the floor. "I want to feel his reactions."

"We're not going to invade their private moment." Finley started cleaning up her supplies. "Though yes, I also wish I could be there."

After I'd finished, we waited. Vemar peeked in every so often. I worked on my product to keep myself calm and tried not to think about it. I didn't dare to hope lest I be wrong, but I was unable to stop the excitement all the same.

It felt like an eternity, but in reality, it wasn't long before the color changed and everyone's faces lit up.

"Congratulations!" They cheered and hugged me, and my world exploded in color. I let my excitement shine through, reaching through the bond to Weston for closeness. My wolf did the same to his. His confusion amplified as he wondered what had happened, and soon I felt him coming my way.

"Now listen to me." Arleth sat me down with a stern expression. "Wolves aren't as hardy with their young as dragons. You can still do most things, though what Weston will *allow* you to do is a totally different situation—"

"Very protective fathers can be suffocating," Finley said. "Wonderful, but a *lot*."

"You will need to listen to your body," Arleth said. "You can't keep these long hours. You're going to need plenty of rest. You can shift until the final stages, and you can train, but you'll need to be mindful when you fight. A dragon can march into battle, but not so much a wolf. Your human form is more fragile as well. As you get further along, you'll need to let your wolf do any running or strenuous activity. You'll need plenty of nutrition. No more refraining from eating to ensure everyone else has enough. I know you still do it. You'll need to eat your fill on every occasion."

"True mate alpha wolves and already a continuation of the bloodline." Finley beamed at me. "Suck on that, fairies!"

Vemar walked back into the work shed with a big smile. He enveloped me in a hug. "Congratulations, Captive Lady. Hadriel is going to be so pissed that I knew first."

I felt Weston coming as Arleth continued to lecture me. When he was near, I turned toward the door. I wanted to share my excitement, my dream come true. A miracle, if you'd asked me just a year ago.

He knocked softly on the frame, drawing Finley's attention. He leaned in a bit to peer around at me but froze, his gaze on the bowl. Shock waves of emotions lit up the bond, and Hannon smiled.

"Congratulations, Daddy," Finley told Weston. "You're going to be a legend around these parts. A three-hour-and-fifteen-minute hold, and now a baby on the way within a few months."

"He's got a magical cock," Vemar said, laughing, clapping him on the back.

Weston stepped in, looking at me, his smile bigger than the whole world. He opened his arms, and I rushed to fill them. He hugged me close, his embrace tight.

"I love you," he said, rocking me. "I love you so much."

He scooped me up into his arms and walked me out of the work shed.

I laughed, arms around his neck. "What are we doing?"

"We're taking the day off."

He walked me across the grass and into the castle. We met Nyfain in the hallway. The king's step was graceful but determined. He slowed as he caught sight of us, his brows drawing together.

"What happened? Is she okay?" he asked Weston.

"She's with child. We just found out." Another explosion of emotion tumbled through the bond: love and devotion and excitement and anticipation.

Nyfain's eyes sparkled, and a grin pulled at his lips. "Fucking wolves," he muttered, winking at me.

Weston turned as the king passed by. "What was that about?"

"Finley said the same thing. They are jealous that we procreate so easily."

"Ah." Smug pride leaked through the bond. "As well they should be."

He took me to his apartment and marched me straight into the bedroom. Leala and Niles looked at us in confusion as we entered, then straightened up as we passed.

"Is everything okay?" she asked, peeking her head into the bedroom as Weston put me down and dropped to his knees in front of me.

He held my sides and gently put his lips to my stomach.

"I'm pregnant," I told her. "We're taking the day off."

She beamed at me. "Oh, that's wonderful! Yes, relax, enjoy the moment. Let me know if you need anything."

She shut the door behind her, and Weston slowly removed my clothes. He kissed me reverently before taking his off and then guiding me into bed. Once there, he gathered me into his arms, caressing my stomach.

"Are you happy?" he asked, his jaw against my forehead.

"You can feel that I am, and I can feel that you are."

"I'm beyond happy. I'm . . ." He shook his head, releasing me so that he could kiss down my body and linger on my stomach. "There are no words." He laid his head on my belly. "No words. I don't have the language to express how grateful I am to have found you. How grateful I am that you forgave me for how we first met, and you are now going to make me the proudest daddy in the world. Gods, I love you, Aurelia. My heart is so full."

He slipped further down, and then I sucked in a breath.

42

AURELIA

I startled awake; something was not right.

I lay in our new apartment within the castle, which was basically just a larger version of his old space but with more rooms, one intended for a nursery. It was the middle of the day, and given I hadn't stopped waking up early and didn't usually go to bed until late, it was now essential that I took naps. I was a little over a month into my pregnancy, and I was so fucking tired all the time during this phase.

Weston was sitting on the edge of the bed beside me, looking down on me fondly.

"Hi," he said, pushing my hair away from my face. "How do you feel?"

I looked around in confusion, dazed from being yanked out of sleep.

"Um . . ." I ran my hand over my still-flat belly. "Good?" I smiled. "Just tired. As usual."

He gave me a slow smile and dipped his hand into my shirt, resting it over mine on my belly.

"You're making Mommy very tired," he said to my stomach, bending over to kiss our joined hands.

I ran the fingers of my other hand through his hair. "Join me?"

He pushed my shirt up a little more so he could kiss my skin before pulling back. "Can't. I need to run to the docks. They found someone trying to smuggle Granny's product onto our shores. I need to check it out."

Apprehension made me jolt. "What? No, you shouldn't go alone. Let me help."

He bent to kiss my forehead. "*Shh.* It's okay. It's a routine inspection, and probably a confiscation of goods. I do them with the larger merchant ships—you know that. Don't worry, we checked things out. This vessel has been here before, and it was stopped for the same things last time. They clearly haven't learned their lesson."

"Still." I licked my lips. Something about this felt wrong. "Just because she hasn't resurfaced in all this time, doesn't mean she won't. It's best to stay away from anything with her name on it."

He braced his elbow on the bed and ran his thumb across my forehead. He looked deeply into my eyes, reading me.

"I have to, baby," he said softly. "It's my job. We know why she hasn't resurfaced, though, right? She found someone else to try to make your product. I'm sure she was handing out punishments when they couldn't make it happen."

It was true; she'd been putting out product these past few months, but word was that it was terrible. She'd gotten someone else to use my recipes, but they couldn't churn out the same results. Weston and the royals had always been right—take out the drugmaker and Granny's reign would end. Without me, she was pushing herself out of the market all on her own.

No one had said, "I told you so." Miraculous.

"It's just . . ." I put my hand on the back of his neck. The fear of her coming for me had never gone away. Maybe it never would; I was terrified I'd have to go back to that life. Terrified I'd be taken from this one.

He hovered close, comforting me, probably giving me the time to work around the fear logically. Only a fool would go after a wolf of Weston's power and position. It was me she'd want to grab, not him. Me she'd tried to lure to the docks.

My wolf had come a long way. Something had clicked within her, and she was on fire as it pertained to learning to co-lead, but she wasn't fully there yet. She had a ways to go before she could be a commander and harness the help of the pack to combat someone like Granny. We were still vulnerable, especially now that we were with child. We didn't have the hardiness of dragons; Arleth went out of her way to remind me of that any time I came back from training tired.

I let my hand slip away.

"You're just too happy," he said with a warm smile. "You're afraid something will happen to crush our perfect life. You don't feel like you deserve this . . ." He shook his head. "This incredible joy. You've finally found true love, true happiness, and you're scared something will happen to make it all go away."

He was speaking for himself, too. We'd had this talk. Everything was going so well. Unbelievably so. Our love strengthened every day. My fondness for him knew no limits. My excitement for our future, both personally and with the kingdom as a whole, was at an all-time high. We were doing something special in this kingdom. We all worked together, came up with new ideas, and the gold we made was always pumped back into the kingdom to foster prosperity and growth of the people. We were expanding, but not so far that we'd become disjointed like the Red Lupine kingdom, with villages falling off the map, isolated and left to the wilds.

We were a pack, all of us. We were strong. Some of us were crazy (dragons). It worked.

My biggest fear was that I'd wake up from this dream.

I nodded slowly.

"Me too," he whispered. "But remember what we said? We can't let fear alter our journey. We need to live in each moment and savor each smile, each touch. We can't let our fear of what might come get in the way of our enjoyment of the here and now. Right?"

I let out a long, slow breath and nodded again.

"Right." He kissed the tip of my nose and then my lips. "I'll have wolves with me. I won't be alone. You stay here, safe and warm, and I'll be back before you know it."

"Are you nuts? I'm not going to stay in bed. Don't you remember the number of orders the queen handed me yesterday? The Flamma kingdom went crazy for the new product, and the merchants are clamoring for more. They especially love the elixirs that glow, even though they are only a mild relaxant. Wolf flower for the win! Take that, dragon weed."

He laughed. "You have more help now, and Vemar is a champ at making the dangerous stuff. Take a break. They'll be okay for a day."

I frowned at him and pushed up to sitting. "They're being very patient with me. I'm not going to slack off."

His gaze turned sharp, but he didn't say what I knew he was thinking: *Take it easy and look after yourself and our baby.*

"I know, I know," I grumbled. "I'll be careful."

He kissed my forehead. "Good girl. I'll see you later." He paused. "I'd planned to make dinner tonight. Don't let Hadriel talk you out of letting me."

I laughed and watched him leave the bedroom before feeling a little naughty and lying back down. I slipped my hand into my pants, finding the right spot and starting to massage. Pleasure immediately rolled through me, and then through the bond.

Desire filtered back through, then frustration. Before I knew it, he was standing in the doorframe, staring at me.

"You're killing me," he growled.

"C'mere, Daddy. Let me suck that cock while I get myself off."

I slipped my other hand up my shirt and tweaked a nipple, moaning with the sensations.

He swore but started forward, working at his belt. He took out his cock and pumped it a couple times before kneeling on the bed, his hand at the back of my head, guiding my face toward him. I sucked him in deep as he fisted my hair and started thrusting, face-fucking me.

I groaned when the sweet taste of precum exploded across my tongue. I worked my fingers faster, building higher. His pleasure coursed through the bond.

"Do you like sucking your alpha's big cock, Little Wolf?" he growled, thrusting.

I moaned out my answer, gyrating as I massaged. My cheeks hollowed with my suction; his smooth skin slid against my lips and his cock plunged deep into my throat. I felt his pleasure build as he worked and released my hand from my nipple to wrap my fingers around his shaft. I slid my hand in time with my mouth.

"Fuck," he ground out, tensing.

I rubbed myself and sucked, working faster, nearly there.

He groaned as he exploded, his delicious flavor flooding my mouth. I sucked it down as an orgasm hit me, making me shake on the bed.

He extracted himself before bending to kiss me, tasting himself on my lips.

"Naughty girl," he whispered, before tucking himself away and heading for the door.

I gave myself a moment with an evil smile before rolling to my feet. A few moments later I heard the exterior door close and felt him moving away.

After a glass of water and a quick bite to eat, I headed for the door myself. As I opened it, I was surprised to find Finley out there, ready to knock. She paused with her hand in the air.

"Hi," I said, blinking out at her.

"Hi. Look at this!" She shoved a piece of paper at me.

I took it, reading down the list of products and then the large numbers next to them. "What is this?"

"This, my dear, is a summary of all the merchant orders for Red Lupine. Word got around that Granny's original drugmaker was working for the dragons now, and they all flocked to our product. No sickness, no deaths, no danger. That's what we advertised, and it was exactly right. But guess what else?"

She stepped to the side so I could exit. We began walking down the hall.

"What else?" I asked.

"People who would never normally touch that kind of stuff were recommended certain things from the medics—since, you know, we insisted some things be treated like medicines. Hitting that market opened up a whole new income stream for your product. You put things out there that didn't exist before, and the need for some of it is high. And you know what else?"

"Not a clue."

"The product design worked like a charm. Like a fucking charm, Aurelia. Sales are up across the board. You nailed that."

"That was Granny's idea. I just applied it to your stuff."

"You created the look of it. People love it." She dug in her pocket and pulled out my Moonfire Lily branding with the two wolves and fuchsia coloring. "They get a kick out of this one in particular."

"Why is that?"

She gave me a flat look. "Don't play coy with me. You pointed out the little heart you worked in there, but you failed to mention the other hidden gem you put in the picture."

I twisted my lips, trying to hide a smile. The negative space between the wolves created a heart, somewhat apparent but not terribly obvious. Weston had really loved that branding. In the corner of the image, though, I couldn't help creating another image in the negative space, one that was small and difficult to notice.

"A flying dick, Aurelia?" Finley said. "Really?"

I busted out laughing. "That branding is Cecil approved."

She looked at it, shaking her head. "I can't believe nobody noticed."

"Vemar noticed. He's good at keeping secrets."

"Fucking Vemar. Of course he noticed. He has that painting you created on his wall, front and center. Hadriel gave it to him as a joke. He gets a good laugh out of it." She shoved the wrapper back into her trousers. "Well, I guess a few other people noticed and absolutely loved it. Now they are looking closely at all the packaging for other little hidden images. I think we should try to incorporate that idea. Maybe have a few different ones released every so often, I don't know."

I kept looking at the sheet. Finley grabbed my arm to stop me abruptly, pushing me toward the wall.

"What's the matter?" I asked in alarm.

"There goes the nanny with Tabitha. She's going for her nap. If she sees me, she won't want to go down."

I longed to peek around the corner to get a glimpse of the little cutie but resisted. Instead, I ran my hand along my belly, hardly able to wait until I had one of my own.

"Okay." Finley jerked her head toward the hall. "Coast is clear." She noticed my hand, and a little smile played across her lips. "Is Weston overbearing yet?"

"No. Whenever he steps in about something, he's right. He's not rough about it, either. Most the time he doesn't bother to say anything. Just gives me a *look*."

She shook her head slowly as we made it to the back door. "You guys are too easy to manage."

"It's too much effort to argue."

"Effort? Fighting about it is half the fun!"

"What's the other half?"

Her eyes sparkled with mischief when she said, "Making up, obviously."

I looked at all the numbers. "This is a lot of product. If Granny had given me this list, I think I would've hyperventilated."

"Granny could've given you a list like that if she hadn't fucked up your product with that coating and started addicting and killing people. Or even if she'd heeded your direction and treated some of it as medicinal, like we're doing. She was greedy and shortsighted, and now we are going to shove her out of the market altogether."

I nodded and knew I should've felt satisfaction over

that; it was what I had been trying to do, after all. The idea of it, though, made me feel hollow. Vengeance had been a great motivator early on, but now that I had a life I loved, a mate of my dreams, and a baby on the way, vengeance just seemed like a poison I didn't want or need.

"This is just the beginning, too," Finley said as we pushed through the door. "The other kingdoms will catch on. The orders will pour in. Nyfain has offered the fairies a cut of the proceeds from the product you drew a fairy on, plus acknowledgment that you have fairy blood, in exchange for that training. Once they see how well it is doing over there, they'll up the percentage of the cut and want to know how you make it. We'll show them some things, but the Moonfire Lily will remain a secret. Given they don't have wolves in their kingdom, they probably have fuck-all growing in their wilds. And even if they do, fairy vision is different than a wolf's night vision. They won't be able to find it. Suck on that, fairies." She glanced at me. "No offense, Aurelia. Anyway, hopefully that'll finally end the negotiations. They really fucking wanted you. Bad. It makes me giddy to see what your magic can really do."

"Do you think they'll teach me all it can do? Won't they be concerned I'll use it against them?"

"We'll bake a sort of ally situation into the contract and have you spend time there and get to know the people. They'll think you wouldn't want to hurt them if you come to think of them as part of your heritage."

"I won't."

"Yeah. And hopefully that won't be a real pity." She laughed as a flash of pain stabbed through me.

I reached out for her and staggered, clutching at my belly, terrified that something might've happened to the baby.

"What's wrong?" she asked, holding me to keep me upright.

A crawling feeling snaked down my spine before melting away, and my breath caught. A feeling I recognized took its place: danger. Specifically, the danger of Alexander turning his sights to me. He meant me harm, and now I was within arm's reach. The punishment would come soon.

"Fuck. Oh no," I said as another stab of pain hit me through the bond. With it came frustrated anger—anger and worry.

"It's Weston," I said, turning in his direction. He was far away, but those stabs throbbed, curdling his anger and increasing his fear.

My own fear rose.

"Fuck. It's Granny. She's come, I know it. I *knew* it." I ripped off my clothes. "He's in trouble."

"Where is he?" Finley shed hers.

"He said he was going to the docks. Hurry!"

"I'll meet you there."

I shifted, and my wolf took off at a sprint. The pack bond was waiting for us, helping my wolf feel everyone's location. Weston wasn't connected, though, and neither was anyone that should've been near his location. They must've been in human form.

My wolf fed a warning through the bond as she ran, communicating Weston's distress and location. She urged the pack to us, her power rising as she cut through the forest.

"Not everyone," I told her as wolves ran to us. *"We need to leave people behind to protect the castle."*

"I know that." She was terse but changed her commands, keeping a force to guard the forest and castle and calling on those not strictly needed.

Weston was uncomfortable, whatever was happening to him. Two points in his body ached. His fear and worry were paramount, but it wasn't for himself. It had turned, and now he worried about *me*. They planned to use him as bait.

Their plan would work.

We cut through the woods on the fastest route possible. Dante, Tanix, and Nova fell in. Sixten would stay behind to help orchestrate the remaining guard.

My wolf felt Dante's question though the bond. *What is it?*

She relayed that she didn't know, slowing a little so that they could continue to keep pace.

"Tell them you think it's Granny. Alexander. They know about our feelings about them," I said.

She did as I said, and I felt the answering rush of anger from the others.

Our fear beat a solid drum in our chest as we drew closer to him. This kingdom was much smaller than that of Red Lupine, so much more condensed. With time, we could build, but I was damn glad of it in this moment.

We cut through one of the smaller towns. People saw us pass, looking up as we did. Dragons flew above us, the great golden dragon beside his mate.

The townspeople shifted quickly and connected to the bond. My wolf directed them based on their power level and experience, and those we needed fell in. Dragons, who couldn't connect with the bond, rose into the sky to join the others.

Eventually the trees started to thin and the ground sloped downward toward the sea. Ships and boats dotted the waters, some tied up, some slowly making their way in or out. Traders had paused in unloading their supplies. Donkeys and horses hitched to carts waited to the side; no one was moving. They were all looking worriedly down the road

As we cut through the market, someone pointed.

"Hurry," the man shouted.

I put on a burst of speed. The dragons soared overhead. Nothing looked out of place except for the people stalling in their activities.

My wolf's feet thumped against the docks as we used the bond to guide us to Weston. He was at the end. As we approached, my stomach got queasy.

On the ship out in the water, Weston stood in a sort of prison, the bars all around him affixed with spikes. If he moved, if his knees buckled, if he shifted, he'd be pierced in too many ways. He'd die.

He'd been posted right beside the railing of the ship so that we could easily see him.

Beside him, wearing her scarlet hooded cloak, waited Granny. She was endangering my mate. Of all the unforgivable actions she'd ever done, that was the absolute worst.

My wolf slowed, baring her teeth.

At the end of the dock, a little boat bobbed, its oars out. Alexander waited at the bow, sitting peacefully, looking at the wolves now crowding the docks.

"Have we got Aurelia in there anywhere?" he called out.

Nyfain roared overhead. Alexander flinched, looking up.

"If those dragons pop off, Weston dies," he shouted. "I'm looking for Aurelia."

"No!" Weston called out across the water. He tried to raise his hands. Pain radiated through his body. "No, Aurelia, don't show yourself. Run, baby! Let them have me. You stay safe!"

Flames danced in my memories.

Run, Aurelia. Save yourself. My mom's voice. *Don't look back.*

Never again.

Never again would I flee and leave a loved one. Either we got out together, or not at all.

Besides, this was my fight, not his. His connection to me had dragged him into this. I would not let him take the fall for my past.

"Shift," I told my wolf.

She wasted no time, and I straightened from my crouch, staring at Alexander. I wasn't helpless anymore. I wasn't alone. I would not let him dominate me. Those days were over.

"Hello again," I said, strangely calm while burning with hatred. "What brings you to my new home?"

His eyes moved over me slowly, taking in my nudity. A sensation like ants skittered across my skin, sickening me. I didn't let it show in my expression; I was practiced at hiding feelings from him.

"I'm really going to enjoy you," he said, his meaning clear.

"I doubt that very much. What do you want?"

"Isn't it obvious? You. Tell those wolves to stand down, tell the dragons to bugger off, and get in this boat."

I looked around incredulously, catching sight of someone suspended in what looked like a harness from one of the dragons flying our way. No, from Vemar; I recognized his dragon's form. I couldn't tell whom he was carrying, though.

"Are you kidding?" I asked, pointing at the sky. "Do you really think the dragons are going to turn and go about their day while you have their shifter commander on that ship?"

"They will if they want to stay airborne. Granny isn't

stupid, Aurelia. She came with magic. Now get in this boat or she pokes another hole in your mate."

They'd done their due diligence. Their people had reported on our milestones. They clearly knew about the kingdom and its rulers. They must know what dragons were capable of. I didn't know what kind of magic they might have, but I did know Granny's confidence was never false. If she was here, it was because she thought she could get away with it, which meant she'd planned the situation carefully.

I looked at Weston, knowing he'd hate this. But there really was no other choice.

"No, Aurelia," he said, his voice filled with pain. "Please, baby, no. Go, please. Let them have me."

"He's delusional," my wolf said. I had to agree.

"Yeah, fine," I told Alexander. I walked forward as the guy with him started rowing toward the dock.

"Aurelia, wait." Nova and Dante had shifted. Nova put out her hand. "Let's not be hasty. The beta does not want you going into that boat."

"I will not run while another person I love is killed," I ground out, watching Alexander draw closer.

"Very touching," he said, bumping against one of the pillars. "Come on. Get in."

I did as he said, sitting several wooden seats back from him, narrowing my eyes at his leer.

"She's not very pleased with you," Alexander said as the man rowed us out toward the ship. "She can understand taking on a powerful mate instead of trying to escape. Why wouldn't you go digging for a little gold, right? You got to see the world for the first time and quickly learned what you need to survive in it. That makes sense. But using your trade to try to push her out of the market? Did you really think she was going to let you get away with that?"

"She intended to take me before that happened," I replied.

"Yes, she did. She always intended to get you back. But now she's pissed—that was my point. And you heal quickly now. I'm going to really enjoy beating you to within an inch of your life."

"And I'm going to enjoy watching my mate kill you violently. I'd do it myself, but I'm going to let it be a present for him."

He snickered. "Your mate is going to spend his lifetime in a cage. Consider him your new encouragement to perform."

A wave of fear swept over me, but I didn't let it show.

"So you think all you have to do is sail away and that'll be it?" I asked, watching the ship as we drew near. "Once we're gone from these shores it's over? No one will come for us?"

"Oh, I'm sure they will. But as they proved during their last trek into our kingdom, they won't have the first clue where to find us. We're not going back to that piece-of-shit, out-of-the-way village. No one will ever hear from you again."

I shook my head and looked at the dragons circling above, my stomach churning. I had those five to seven guesses. I had to pray to the gods that one of them was right. That they could find us.

We got to the side of the ship, and I was made to climb up the rope ladder first, hating the disgusting creature coming behind me. We got to the balcony, and I swung my feet over, seeing people turn Weston so that he would face me. He'd been stripped to the waist. Blood seeped out of two points on his torso and down his skin, soaking into his pants. Those spikes in the cage pushed into his flesh, warning of a terrible fate should anything go wrong.

Granny stood next to him, her face so familiar, the pain of this moment acute.

"My, my, Grandmother," I said as I slowly walked closer, "what big balls you have. You've captured the beta of a dragon kingdom."

"I've captured your true mate, by the looks of things." Her gaze touched on the marks. "You've found yourself quite a prize."

I put my finger in the air, indicating the dragons. "How are you going to get rid of them?"

"As Alexander said, magic. How else? Dragons aren't invincible." She narrowed her eyes at me as Alexander walked around to stand at my side. The bond was thick with Weston's rage. "You've been quite naughty, Aurelia. You get taken captive, and the first thing you do is start making my product to compete against me? I told you I would come for you. Was it the wolf that turned you against me?"

She reached out and shook the cage. Pain came through the bond as the spikes pricked Weston's skin.

I clenched my jaw. "I did not approve of that coating you put on *my* product," I told her in a firm voice. "I did not approve of killing people and addicting them. You need to be stopped."

She quirked her brow. "Do I?" She laughed and motioned for those around us. Deck hands got active, clearly readying to make way. "How about I do the opposite, hmm? You will be going back to your duties, and your mate will help incentivize you to do a good job. Now you will also make that coating. Got that? You will make your improved formulas and you will make the coating. I assume you figured out how to do it better? You were always very good at solving riddles."

I let out a breath, my heart hurting. The sails lifted and the dragons circled.

"Just tell me why," I finally said as Alexander took a step toward me, clearly intending to grab me and force me to wherever they planned to keep me. "Why didn't you tell me I had magic?"

"And have an underling with more power than me? I wouldn't have been able to keep you contained. You should know by now, Aurelia, that you are integral to my operations. Without you, I won't succeed."

Her tone was callous, devoid of even a hint of an apology.

Anger nearly stole my breath. Pain ate at my heart.

"Don't you get it? I trusted you. I looked up to you. I *loved* you!" I shouted. "I wouldn't have tried to leave you. I thought of you as family. But having magic would've meant I could've had friends. People wouldn't have avoided me or spat at me. I would've been included. Instead, I was kept in solitude. How could you do that to me?"

"Aurelia, come now. You can't still be this naïve." She looked at me as though I were an imbecile. "This is business. We had the perfect setup, you and me. You got everything you needed, and you had a job and protection. We had a partnership. Life isn't always fair, but survival isn't pretty, right? It'll be better now. I don't have to keep you in the dark about things anymore. Now maybe we can furnish you with some nicer things. You have your mate, and you'll have everything you need. It'll be great, you'll see."

A tear leaked out of my eye. "Did you ever love me?"

Alexander scoffed, laughing in disbelief. I felt like a fool.

Granny's smile was condescending. "Aurelia, as I said,

this is business. You are too old to hang on to such silly sentimentalities. Time to grow up, dear."

"I'll say," Alexander murmured.

"But it wasn't business when you took me in," I pushed. "Why did you bother? I didn't have an animal yet. I didn't think I had magic. You couldn't have known how it was going to turn out with the business. Why did you shelter me?"

"You absolutely had magic when you came to me. You were emoting heavily, looking for someone to rescue you. For safety. If nothing else, I figured you might have fairy blood. It was worthwhile to put you up for a few years and see what you turned out to be. When I realized the treasure at my disposal, a treasure not because of your blood, but because of your mind . . . Well, the rest is history, as they say." She tilted her head at me. "I can see you're unhappy with this, Aurelia, but trust me, this is better. Once you let go of these sentimentalities, you'll see that business requires a passionless disposition. It requires cool logic. That's how you make gold."

"That's not even remotely how," I spat, the ache in my chest growing. "The dragon queen has nothing but passion in her projects. Those passions make more gold than you can imagine. They make a stronger community. Let my true mate out. It's time I parted ways with you for good."

She laughed and gestured beyond me. "Scatter the dragons and let's get underway. Our reunion is done. Alexander, take them to their room and lock them in. Then come back up here. You can punish her later. Come on, everyone, knock those dragons out of the sky."

43

AURELIA

Fear welled up inside me as people grabbed strange-looking devices—they looked like they were made of silver orbs, but flat on one side. The people walked further out onto the deck, eyes on the sky.

"No!" I said as Alexander grabbed me, yanking me around. Weston yelled, calling my name, but my world reduced down to the fear I felt overwhelming me. The magic devices were turned on, the flat sides aimed at the dragons, the intent to drop them from the sky. Killing them? I had no idea.

My magic rose, and I recognized it now. I knew what it did. This was the fairy magic. The Emoting magic, latching on to my two single needs.

Save the dragons.

Kill Alexander.

I pushed that desire out with the magic, knowing it would reach the people on the deck. Knowing it would encourage them to do as I bade.

"What is—" Alexander jerked, yanking me, half dragging me toward the people with the devices. Granny pushed ahead, clearing out of the way of those on the deck.

The devices clunked down onto the deck, the operators' eyes on him. Almost as one, they rushed him, faces screwed up in anger, hands out like claws. Some shifted, and the fur barreled down on us.

I wrenched my arm, spinning Alexander around though he still held on to me. With my other hand I punched him in the throat.

He gasped, finally loosening his grip on me. I yanked my arm again and broke his hold.

Not a moment too soon.

A body of fur jumped at me, trying to go through me to get to Alexander. I hit the deck and rolled, and claws just barely scraped my shoulder as the wolf passed over me. Another jumped into the fray, ripping and tearing. Alexander screamed, fighting for all he was worth as the entire deck of his people now tried to get to him.

Snapping teeth clamped down on his neck. Another person grabbed his head and twisted. Someone with a knife slashed across Alexander's stomach, letting his insides fall out.

Alexander gargled a scream. A wolf snarled, and then it cut off altogether.

I scurried to my feet, running at Weston before Alexander's body could even hit the deck.

Fire streaked through the sky overhead. Hannon dove toward the deck and then through the throng of fighting people, letting loose an explosion of flame as he did so. He pulled out of the dive and climbed into the sky as wolves bayed and people screamed, their hair and clothes and fur on fire.

A dragon roared above us as I reached Weston's cage.

"How do I open this?" I asked in a panicked voice, running my fingers over the metal, looking for the clasp.

"In the middle, to the side there."

Nyfain swept down over the ship as Granny came running. Her face lit up in alarm and she skidded to a stop, watching the golden dragon bearing down on her. Nyfain's dragon opened his maw, and I turned away, quickly unlatching the clasp and throwing open the door to the cage.

Weston grabbed me and spun me toward the side of the ship.

"You can swim, right?" he asked as heat washed over us from the dragon's fire.

"Mostly."

"*Mostly?*" He swore softly. "We're going to jump. Don't panic. I will grab you, okay? Here we go."

He tossed me over without ceremony.

"Oh shit—"

I windmilled my arms, suddenly weightless before gravity sucked me down. Another dragon swooped over us, followed by the phoenix again, and fire rolled across the ship in a gush. The water rushed up, and I held my breath as cold suddenly enveloped me. I plunged deep, letting myself naturally stop before I—almost calmly—swam my hardest for the surface.

"I can swim. Shift and I'll do it," my wolf said.

"You only learned how to walk a few months ago!"

A hand grabbed my arm and tugged, dragging me to the surface. I crested the water and sucked in a breath as another dragon dove, spraying the burning ship. Calia waited in that sling held by Vemar, off to the side, her hands out and at the ready.

Weston tucked his arm around my chest.

"Just float. I got this." He started swimming us quickly toward the docks.

"I can swim enough to get to the— Well, okay, you're going faster." I watched the orchestrated loop of dragons taking turns blowing fire along the ship, not just across the top but getting near the water and aiming for the sides.

"What is Calia doing?" I asked as people jumped into the water to get away or to stop from burning.

Arrows flew through the air as soon as the people emerged, sticking in the heads or upper bodies or backs of people trying to swim away. The pack had shifted and grabbed weapons. That, or the dock guards were now in action, since Weston had been released. Dragged through the water like I was, I couldn't look behind to see.

"The magic systems Granny was going to use make flight impossible . . ." He was breathing hard as he swam us to shore. "It would've pushed the dragons away or dropped them into the water. Calia's magic can dispel those systems; she's done it for us before. Granny probably thought she'd be gone by now. And she would've if she hadn't stayed longer to finish the negotiations concerning you. Turns out, she wasn't needed."

I could hear pride ringing in his voice, but all I felt was sadness. I closed my eyes so I wouldn't have to see the ship burn or the people jumping. I didn't want to catch sight of a red cloak or graying hair. I didn't want to see the arrows aimed for her.

Weston reached a ladder along the dock, the rungs slippery with sea slime but intact. He pulled me around so that I could grab on and climb up. At the top, Hadriel grabbed me, hurrying me out of the way of the archers.

"Thank the gods' hairy asses that Granny underestimated this kingdom." Hadriel lifted his hand and yelled to the pack, "I need a towel or a blanket or some fucking thing over here." He rubbed my arm. "Everyone who hasn't seen this kingdom in action always underestimates us because we are small and relatively new, with an upstart king. Well, now look. She thought her magic devices were going to be enough?"

"It seems they would've been if not for Calia."

He scoffed. "Hardly. First of all, Calia didn't do a thing—you did. Second, we have a lot of gold coming in, and that buys great shit. This is a new port filled with ships faster than Granny could even comprehend. We would've caught her easily. She's used to those idiots in the Red Lupine kingdom. She had no idea who she was picking a fight with this time."

He stopped me near the shore. Both the pack and the dock guards lined the end of the dock, their bows in hand. They took aim and fired quickly. The ship roared with fire, flames reaching way into the sky. Now the dragons were swooping over the water, blowing fire at those the archers couldn't reach.

Hannon flew over someone that was swimming and paused to aim. The jet of fire that came out of his beak was narrow and almost white. It punched down into the sea, and I could just barely see the form and partially burned gray hair.

I turned away again, bile rising in my throat.

"I got her." Weston's arms came around me. "Let's go. We're not needed here. Come on, you don't need to see this."

But it was too late; I already had.

Deep inside I screamed in misery over what had happened here today. The truths she'd spilled, her resolve to capture me. Despite what Hadriel had said, Granny wasn't prone to underestimating her opponent. No, her shortsightedness here was likely due to her desperation.

Weston's guard and patrol setup was too good to sneak through, so she had to resort to this.

. . . you are integral to my operations. Without you, I won't succeed . . .

I'd proven that, hadn't I? She must've seen her income take an immediate hit and knew what her operation would become. With the dragons' support, I'd not only improved the product, I'd come out with better packaging. I knew the game, and I was just getting started in showing her that I was a competitive player.

This is business.

Business was passionless for her. Emotionless logic. Taking me in, setting up my life: logic. The gifts, bending to my demands when I wouldn't relent: business. Keep the chief producer happy enough to actually produce.

I had been naïve. So naïve.

I didn't regret it, though. I didn't regret loving her and hoping she loved me. I didn't regret my happiness at her gifts and feeling special at being one of the few she would allow into her cottage for a chat. Those things had kept me whole; they'd kept me full of hope. If I'd seen my life for what it really was, a passionless cage where I'd been trapped for business purposes, I would've died inside. I would've been jaded and tarnished, unready or unwilling to love again when Weston beat down my door. I wouldn't have been able to forgive him or to trust him now. I wouldn't trust that the royals here were acting in my best interest. I wouldn't be so eager and excited to expand my family, too worried I'd get hurt again.

Maybe my blindness to reality had been a survival mechanism the whole time. Maybe some part of me had known that I needed to save my heart through those many long years so that I could use it again.

Weston slipped a blanket over my shoulders and then

helped me climb into a carriage. He followed me, draping his blanket over his waist as a driver climbed in.

"Are you okay?" I asked him, trying to get a look at his wounds. They were clean from the water but still seeping a bit of blood.

"I'm fine. I'll heal." I could feel the proof of that through the bond. He stopped me from fussing, hugging me close.

"Ready?" the driver asked as dragons roared their victory.

"Go," Weston replied, looking over his shoulder. In a moment he turned back, resting his palm on my belly. "Are *you* okay?"

I put my hand over his and leaned into him. "Honestly, I know she turned out to be rotten—or had always been rotten and I was just late to the party—but my heart hurts."

"I know, baby. That can't have been easy."

"Not for you, either. What happened?"

He shook his head, and I felt his frustration through the bond. "She staged the thing with her product to get us to check it out. She clearly knew that the size of the shipment would have them calling me in. I came with a few people as backup and boarded the ship. Her trap was well laid out. The people with me were dead and overboard, and I was locked in a cage before I could blink."

I let a breath leak out. "I'm sorry."

"Don't be sorry. You saved me. Now I need to refine our procedures."

"The dragons took down the enemy and saved the day."

He squeezed me. "It was a team effort, and that's the point of a pack. You worked within it marvelously."

Nothing about this felt very marvelous except for one thing:

"At least that horrible prick is fucking dead. Good riddance, Alexander, you fucker." I wanted to spit to commemorate it but didn't want to lean over the edge of the carriage to do it.

"I wanted to have that pleasure," Weston growled, "but this way was probably better. The magic that got you admittance into Granny's village was the magic that was eventually their undoing. The way he went was good enough for me."

I fell into silence. Weston let me be quiet as the horses trotted, taking the carriage back to the castle. Dragons flew overhead and wolves jogged alongside us on our way, watching us pass, seeing Weston safe.

"You didn't pull them all with you," he noticed, stroking my belly.

"My wolf was about to, but I reminded her that she needed to leave some behind to guard the castle."

"Tattletale," she grumbled.

He glanced at those we passed and watched as wolves rushed by, coming from the altercation and heading toward the castle. The battle must be well and truly over, with only a small party staying behind to handle the details.

Weston looked away from them and into the passing trees. "It was a good exercise . . . though I was losing my mind a little being locked in that cage. It felt like it had when I was taken by the demons. But then I felt you coming, and a new fear materialized." His breath ruffled my hair. "I want to tell you never to do that again, never come for me. That you need to protect yourself and the baby. You two are the most important things in my life. I will die happily if you two are safe."

"But . . .?"

Dark humor bled through the link. "I'm not stupid. I know you'll always come for me, like I will always come for you."

"Always."

"And so I will just say that I love you, I don't have words to express how grateful I am that you and the baby are okay, and I'm hopeful we can now finally get some peace."

Nyfain and Finley were at the castle by the time we arrived, with Hannon and Vemar and Calia and everyone else. They had on the slips from the claiming—easy to put on and take off.

The carriage eventually stopped in front of the castle steps, and Leala and Niles stepped forward, handing us a similar sort of garb. We slipped them on as we got out, and Weston led me to stand in front of the king and queen. Our pack spread out behind, all in human form, all looking firm and resolute.

"Weston, good to have you back, brother." Nyfain stepped forward with his hand out.

Weston shook his hand, looked at Finley, then to Vemar and Calia standing off to the side a little, and finally to Micah beyond them. "I had flashbacks of being taken to the dungeons. It was not pleasant."

The others nodded solemnly, clearly knowing all too well what that was like.

"We'll need a rundown of how that was able to happen," Nyfain said. "Come to our apartment later tonight. We'll have a bite and drink too much wine. Well . . ." His golden eyes came to rest on me. "Most of us will."

Calia stepped forward. "You used your fairy magic perfectly, and without training! I see great things for you. I have a formal invite written up, requesting that you and your true mate join me in the fairy kingdom." She made a show of looking sideways at Nyfain. "Just as soon as things are wrapped up in negotiations."

"That isn't my fault," Nyfain mumbled.

"Aurelia." Finley stepped forward. "You were cool under

pressure and made a sticky situation easy to manage. Good work. I know you're not ready yet, but soon you are going to make an incredible co-beta in our kingdom." She put her hand on my arm. "You don't need to bring food tonight. Go back and rest."

"No, I will. I think cooking will help relax me."

She put her hands in the air. "I'm not going to argue. I should—the proper thing to do is definitely argue—but I'm not going to."

"Can I come?" Hadriel and Vemar said together.

"Aurelia, if I may." Hannon stepped up to us, his focus acute. "I made sure it was instantaneous." He paused, and I knew what he was referring to. "She wouldn't have felt any pain. I thought that's what you would've wanted. We don't choose who we love, but I thought maybe you'd want to choose how you said goodbye."

My eyes filled with tears, and I hugged him. "Thank you," I said, pulling back and wiping my eyes. He nodded and stepped back, his hands clasped behind him.

I ended up cooking far more than was necessary. I finished one dish and moved right on to the next, locked in my memories, allowing the pain. This was my goodbye. After today, I would not write Granny into my journal. I would not put in any effort to keep her memory alive. I would not honor her like I did my mom.

After today, I would officially close the chapter on the life I lived in Granny's shadow. It was time to start my new journey.

EPILOGUE - AURELIA

"I am not trying to hurry you, but come the fuck on, will you?" Hadriel motioned me out of the bedroom in our new apartment.

"How is that not hurrying me?" I laughed, attempting to walk forward and mostly just waddling. I was due any day, and Weston wanted to take me on an outing before the baby came.

"That is literally hurrying her," Leala groused. Everyone decided she would stay and be my lady's maid until the baby was born. There was someone in line to take her place, though I hadn't met her yet. It was a fairy—a concession in the negotiations.

"Eat rocks," Hadriel sang.

"Fuck a cactus," Leala sang back.

I hadn't gotten the chance to visit the fairy kingdom yet. By the time the negotiations were signed, I had been too far along to travel. We'd visit after the birth with the baby, and the royals—who had decided a trip was long overdue—would come too. I did get a fairy trainer, though. Three, actually: two of them were Emoters, and one specialized in training fairies to use magic. My training was mostly about moods and focus and things I was picking up on very easily, because I used those sorts of practices in the mundane portions of my job . . .

Which was now on fire.

We had ten work sheds now. We had continual garden expansion. We had a line of Moonfire Lilies growing in between the edges of the Everlass, the two plants co-existing quite happily. We had orders out of our asses. Most of those came from the medicinal stuff we were selling to people who needed a little help and didn't know it had existed in the market.

Granny's operations mostly died with her. Someone tried to put out product a few months after her demise, but it didn't get far. It wasn't good, it was dangerous, and I produced better. We'd killed the threat while keeping me working and our kingdom thriving. Despite how it had come to pass and the bittersweet memories along the way, it had all worked out for the best.

"Grab the . . ." Hadriel shook his finger at the painting he'd *insisted* I give to Finley and Nyfain. "Grab the thing. Leala! *Grab the thing!*"

"Gods help me, Hadriel." Leala shook her head as she finished packing me a picnic, then rounded on him. "If you don't calm down, I'm going to fuck you with the handle of my whip. Remember how much you hate that? Your guardian of your asshole will not protect you from me."

"Why are you so riled up, anyway?" I asked as I waited by the door.

"He thinks you are going to go into labor today," Leala said, handing the basket to him before grabbing the painting. "He claims to have a sixth sense about it."

"I do have a sixth sense. I have predicted four labors."

"Two of those four had already started. How does that count?"

"I didn't know that at the time, though."

Leala rolled her eyes. "Okay, go. Go, go." She shooed him in front of her. "Are you going to go?"

Hadriel put up a finger. "Do not sass me. I am very frazzled right now."

"Clearly."

Weston waited for us at the bottom of the grand staircase, standing with Nyfain and Finley and little Tabitha.

"Hi, baby girl!" I gushed, putting my hands low for her. If I crouched down, I wouldn't get back up.

She ran to me squealing and grabbed my hands. I hoisted her up onto my hip, the position awkward with the size of my belly.

"And how are you?" I asked her as I met the others.

"Let's let Mommy hold you for right now, how's that?" Finley said, eyeing my belly as she took Tabitha. "We don't want to hurt Olly, do we?"

Tabitha hadn't quite gotten my name yet.

"Here, sire." Leala brought forward the painting, as tall as her waist and cumbersome to hand over.

He took it, looking at the image. His eyes found me over the canvas.

"It's . . ." I shrugged. "I painted it when I first met you because you scared the crap out of me, but I didn't know how to mix colors. Annoyed about that, I redid it. I hate unfinished projects. They told me to give it to you instead of throwing it away. Honestly, just throw it away. No hurt feelings. I was going to do it anyway."

Weston leaned in to get a look before leaning away again. "Even with the odd colors, I told her to give it to you."

"Let me see." Finley went around him to look over his arm. He held it out a little for her.

"Da-da." Tabitha pointed. "Dada!"

"Yes, baby, that's right. That's Daddy's dragon." Finley's eyes were wide. "This inspired the product branding image, right?"

"Yeah. Toned down, though," I replied.

"Un-tone it down." Nyfain continued to look at the painting. "Un-tone that branding down. I want it to look like this."

I smiled, preening a little. "It's just a doodle, is all. It's—"

"Do not sell yourself short." Hadriel started trying to bustle us away. "Come on, time to get going. You can hear him gush about the painting later."

"This is fucking amazing," Nyfain murmured.

"Daddy! Language," Finley said, still looking at the painting as well. "Ha! Found it." She reached around Nyfain to point.

He pulled the painting in closer, his head disappearing behind it. "Is that . . .?"

Yeah, it was. A hidden dick with wings.

"May it help you go in heat and bless Tabitha with a sibling." I ducked away, laughing.

"She put a dick in my painting," Nyfain muttered. "How is that right?"

Weston wrapped an arm around me as Hadriel led us outside the front entrance, where horses and a carriage waited. Vemar sat beside the driver in a sparkly jacket that matched Hadriel's.

"No way." Hadriel motioned him out of there. "No! You were there when she found out. You can't be there when she goes into labor. It's my turn. I'll call you when the baby is about to be born."

He gave Hadriel a hostile stare.

"Get out." Hadriel motioned him away. "I'm sitting there. Get the fuck out."

Vemar did, slowly, staring at Hadriel the whole time. If Hadriel was bothered, he didn't show it.

He brushed past Vemar and took the seat next to the driver as Weston helped me inside. "Ready?" he asked me.

"Ready." I didn't bother asking where we were going. I'd done that earlier and only gotten a little smile.

It turned out we were headed to the closest city to the castle, a large, sprawling affair with a dizzying amount of people. He took me to the outskirts where things were slower, down a lane through a lovely area with large homes with gates and hedges and gorgeous gardens. At the end, Hadriel jumped out, opened the gate, and waited for the carriage to go through. He met us at a house made of brick with white pillars in front. Weston helped me down from the carriage and steadied me once I had two feet on the ground. Just that small bit of effort had me breathing heavily.

"Aurelia," Weston said, leading me to the front door. "Welcome to your new home."

I frowned at it, confused. "What do you mean? We live in the castle."

"We have a residence at the castle, and we'll keep it to be close when we need to or want to be. But the castle is owned by the royals. This house . . . is owned by us. I bought it."

I followed him inside and sent awe and rising excitement through the bond. He showed me the polished wood floors and newly painted walls. It had a large kitchen and big pantry, with a big room off the side for parties centered around food.

"This is yours, Aurelia," he told me, showing me the big backyard with ample room for children to play and climb and swing. "It's ours. It is for our family. I know you'd be happy with a smaller house . . ." He smiled at me sheepishly. "I didn't grow up in a tiny place. I like more space."

I put my hands on his chest and looked around in wonder. "You bought us a house?"

"You had an idea of what your fairytale would look like, and I wanted to make sure you achieved it. You wanted a house and a family and safety. This house is very well protected by the elements and the fence, not to mention I will be wherever you are. I will lay my life down to make sure nothing happens to you and our baby. This I swear. As for the fairy contingent, the lady's maid is bringing all the little fairy gadgets and extras that Calia says you'll love. Would you like to see your art room?"

I fell into his deep gray eyes. "You're trying to give me all my criteria for a fairytale life?"

He kissed me. I felt the baby kick and put his hand against my belly to feel it. His eyes were so soft as he stared down at me.

"Our life together didn't start out like most fairytales, and both of us have had dark times, apart and together, but we still deserve a happily-ever-after. I wanted a mate to co-lead. I wanted a family." He paused. "I wanted true love. I found all of that in you. It's only fair I make sure your fairytale comes true too. I want us both to have our happily-ever-afters. Together."

I hugged him tightly, tears filling my eyes.

"Just having you was all I needed for a happily-ever-after. A baby was the icing on the cake. This is . . ." His face swam in my vision. "This is a dream come true."

. . .

My labor didn't start that day, something Hadriel would never live down. It did start the next day, however, and he'd always argue that he was close enough. It lasted longer than I care to remember and hurt more than really should've been possible, given my pain tolerance, but at the end of it I lay in bed with Weston at my side as our new baby boy was placed on my chest.

Weston had tears in his eyes as he snuggled in, his large hand covering the baby's entire back.

"He's precious," he said, kissing my cheek. "Shall we arrange a marriage with the princess now or wait until tomorrow?"

I kissed him. "I want him to find his true mate like we did."

"You never know. Both Finley's parents were wolves. Maybe he'll be the future king."

"Because he'll be a dragon?" I quirked a brow at him as the nurse helped me position the baby at my breast. "I'm going to tell Nyfain you said that."

"Please don't."

"You'll never live it down."

"Seriously, forget it. Pretend I never said it." He kissed my temple.

I beamed up at him. "I love you."

It just went to show, even dark and twisted journeys had happily-ever-afters.

The End

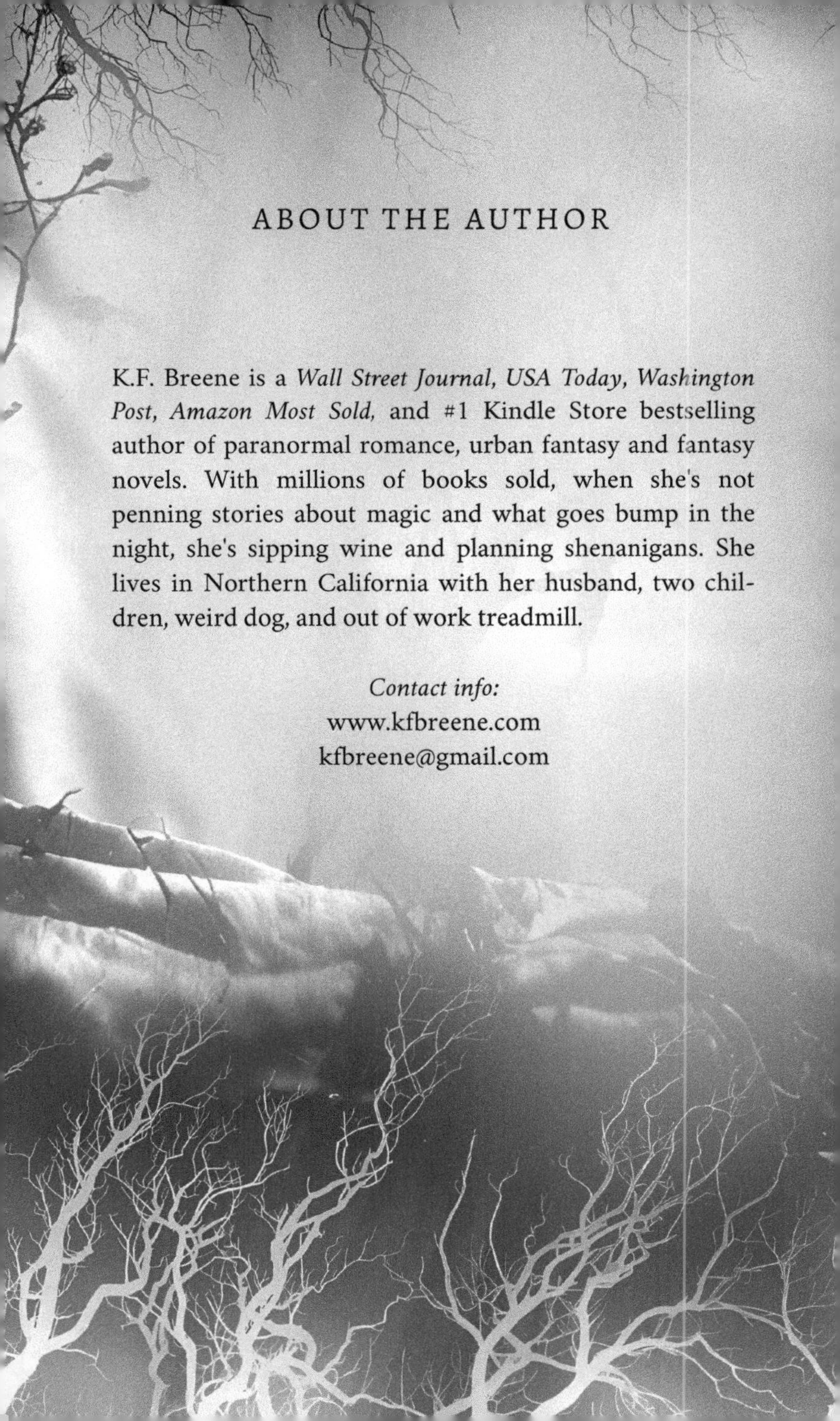

ABOUT THE AUTHOR

K.F. Breene is a *Wall Street Journal, USA Today, Washington Post, Amazon Most Sold,* and #1 Kindle Store bestselling author of paranormal romance, urban fantasy and fantasy novels. With millions of books sold, when she's not penning stories about magic and what goes bump in the night, she's sipping wine and planning shenanigans. She lives in Northern California with her husband, two children, weird dog, and out of work treadmill.

Contact info:

www.kfbreene.com

kfbreene@gmail.com